Dilly Court gr[illegible] in Nor[illegible]h-east London and began her career in [illegible] scripts for commercials. She is married with two [illegible] children and four grandchildren, and now lives in Dorset on the beautiful Jurassic Coast with her husband. She is the bestselling author of twenty-one novels.

Also by Dilly Court

Mermaids Singing
Born into poverty and living under the roof of her violent and abusive brother-in-law, young Kitty Cox dreams of working in a women's dress shop in the West End.

The Dollmaker's Daughters
For Ruby and Rosetta Capretti, life in the slums of the East End holds little promise. Despite their humble background, Rosetta is determined to work under the bright lights of the music hall and Ruby longs to train as a nurse.

Tilly True
Dismissed from her position as housemaid under a cloud of misunderstanding, Tilly True is forced to return home.

The Best of Sisters
Twelve-year-old Eliza Bragg has known little in life but the cold, comfortless banks of the Thames, her only comfort the love and protection of her older brother, Bart.

A Mother's Courage
When Eloise Cribb receives the news that her husband's ship has been lost at sea she wonders how she and her children are ever going to manage.

The Constant Heart
Despite living by the side of the Thames, eighteen-year-old Rosina May has wanted for little in life. Until her father's feud with a fellow bargeman threatens to destroy everything.

A Mother's Promise

When Hetty Huggins made a promise to her dying mother that she would look after her younger sister and brothers, little did she know how difficult this would be.

The Cockney Angel

Eighteen-year-old Irene Angel lives with her parents in a tiny room above the shop where her mother ekes out a living selling pickles and sauces, whilst her father gambles away what little money they do manage to earn.

A Mother's Wish

Since the untimely death of her husband, young mother Effie Grey has been forced to live on a narrowboat owned by her tyrannical father-in-law Jacob.

The Ragged Heiress

On a bitter winter's day, an unnamed girl lies dangerously ill in hospital. When two coarse, rough-speaking individuals come to claim her, she can remember nothing.

A Mother's Secret

When seventeen-year-old Belinda Phillips discovers that she is pregnant, she has no option other than to accept an arranged marriage, and give up her child forever.

Cinderella Sister

With their father dead and their mother a stranger to them, Lily Larkin must stay at home and keep house whilst her brothers and sisters go out to work.

A Mother's Trust

When her feckless mother falls dangerously ill, Phoebe Giamatti is forced to turn to the man she holds responsible for all her family's troubles.

The Lady's Maid
Despite the differences in their circumstances, Kate and Josie have been friends since childhood. But their past binds them together in ways they must never know.

The Best of Daughters
Daisy Lennox is drawn to the suffragette movement, but when her father faces ruin they are forced to move to the country and Daisy's first duty is to her family.

The Workhouse Girl
Young Sarah Scrase's life changes forever when she and her widowed mother are forced to enter the notorious St Giles and St George's Workhouse.

A Loving Family
Eleven-year-old Stella Barry is forced into service when her family find themselves living hand-to-mouth.

The Beggar Maid
Must Charity Crosse give up her dream of running a bookshop and be forced to return to begging on the streets?

A Place Called Home
Despite her difficult childhood, Lucy Pocket is determined to create the family and home she has always longed for.

The Orphan's Dream
Motherless since she was five, Mirabel Cutler was raised by her father to be a lady. But when he dies suddenly, Mirabel finds herself cast out on the street by her ruthless stepmother.

The Cockney Sparrow

Dilly Court

arrow books

1 3 5 7 9 10 8 6 4 2

Arrow Books
20 Vauxhall Bridge Road
London SW1V 2SA

Arrow Books is part of the Penguin Random House group of companies whose addresses can be found at global.penguinrandomhouse.com

First published in Great Britain by Century in 2007
First published by Arrow Books in 2007
This edition published by Arrow Books in 2016

www.penguin.co.uk

A CIP catalogue record for this book is available from the British Library

ISBN 9781784752552

Typeset by SX Composing DTP, Rayleigh, Essex
Printed and bound in Great Britain by Clays Ltd, St Ives Plc

Penguin Random House is committed to a sustainable future for our business, our readers and our planet. This book is made from Forest Stewardship Council® certified paper.

For Clemency South, who also
sings like a nightingale

Chapter One

London, January 1889

The toff was drunk. He could hardly stand straight, let alone find his way from the Strand Theatre to the cab rank outside St Clement's Church. He teetered on the edge of the pavement and then staggered into the road. Judging by the state of him, the masher must have spent most of his time in the theatre bar. Clemency flexed her cold fingers – she needed supple hands and the lightest of light touches to dip into the flash cove's pockets. He might not know what day of the week it was, but he could still turn nasty if he caught her picking his Lucy Locket. A bitter east wind brought with it tiny flakes of snow. Her ragged clothes were no protection against the cold, and her teeth were chattering like a pair of magpies. The wind funnelled between the buildings on either side of Fleet Street, bringing with it the damp chill from the Essex marshes. It snatched at the man's opera cloak, causing it to billow out behind him: this gave Clemency the perfect opportunity to slip her hand into the pocket of his dinner jacket. But just as she did so, he lost his footing on the icy pavement and stumbled against her.

'What the hell?' His voice was slurred, and he glared at her through bloodshot, half-closed eyes. 'Help, police! I'm being attacked.'

'It's all right, mister. I was just trying to save you from falling.' Clemency's fingers curled around the bulging leather wallet. She allowed her shawl to slip to the ground, exposing her thin cotton blouse with the buttons open almost to her slender waist. She might be skinny and underdeveloped for an eighteen-year-old, with a boyish flat chest and just a hint of budding titties, but some blokes liked it that way. Not that she ever let them go too far, but if it distracted their attention for a few seconds, then that was all she ever needed to make a getaway. She smiled up at him. 'Want a hand across the road to the cabstand, guv?'

He gave her a shove that sent her sprawling on the ground. 'Get off me, you little whore.' He staggered crabwise across the Strand, hiccuping and cursing as he went. Clemency scrambled to her feet, snatched her wet shawl from the pavement, and raced off towards Fleet Street with his wallet clutched in her hand. She hardly felt the cold as her bare feet skimmed over the paving stones. She ran until her lungs felt as though they would burst. She had not heard the dreaded shout of 'Stop thief' or the piercing blast from a police whistle, and, as she reached Ludgate Hill, she fell into a dark doorway. She huddled in a corner, sheltering from the snowstorm and gasping for breath. Apart from the muffled sound of horses' hooves on the cobblestones, and the rumble of carriage wheels, there was blessed silence. No one was chasing her. The poor bugger probably hadn't even noticed that his wallet was missing. He would only discover his loss when the cabby delivered him to his door. She chuckled. Serve him right, the dirty dog.

She opened the wallet and stifled a gasp of dismay. It had felt fat and she had imagined that it was stuffed with fivers or even tenners, but the only paper inside was a programme for the comic opera at the Strand Theatre. She frowned as she attempted to read the large print, holding the crumpled sheet of paper so that it caught the dim glow from the street lamp. It wasn't that her eyes were weak; she could spot a gold watch, a full purse or a bobby's uniform a mile off, but she had spent more time wagging school than attending classes. She could read, but it was a struggle, especially if there were big words. She threw the programme out onto the slushy pavement. Either the toff wasn't a music lover, or the production had been so boring that it had driven him to the bar. She tipped the wallet upside down and a small photograph fell out onto her lap. She recognised the simpering face of the voluptuous leading lady, Dorabella Darling, which only confirmed Clemency's opinion that the chap was a masher. Well, tonight hadn't been his night, had it? He'd obviously been turned down by the darling Dorabella and got himself sozzled into the bargain. She shook the wallet again – but there was no money, not even a halfpenny or a farthing. The bloke would have had trouble getting home anyway, silly sod. Her first reaction was to toss the wallet in the gutter, but she thought better of it and tucked it into her skirt pocket. It would fetch a couple of shillings at the pop shop when old Minski opened up in the morning, but that wouldn't buy supper tonight. Wrapping her shawl around her head, she went out into the swirling snow. It was too late to trudge back to the Strand and, anyway, the theatre crowds would have dispersed and gone home by now. She would catch her death of cold if she were to hang round outside the boozers in the hopes of begging a copper or two. She was good at acting the waif, pleading for money for her sick mother and starving brothers and sisters, but that only worked in the summer when the living was easy and there were geezers with their pockets jingling with hard-earned wages, and their bellies filled with beer.

She put her head down and broke into a jogging run, ignoring offers from men loitering in pub doorways who were looking for an uncomplicated tumble in a back alley. Clemency was not going down that path. She had seen her mother go that way and witnessed the effect that it had had on her. She was prepared to steal, cheat and lie, but she was not going to sell herself for money.

By the time she reached Cheapside, she was wet and chilled to the bone. She couldn't feel her feet or her fingertips: she knew if she did not get home soon she would join the rest of the stiffs that regularly froze to death in doorways, and under the bridges that spanned the Thames. She forced her legs to move in stumbling steps; she was getting near now, very close to St Paul's Church and Knightrider Street. She just had to go a hundred yards or so down the street, turn left into Stew Lane, and then feel her way in the dark to the steps leading down to the damp basement room she called home. The snow had funnelled into drifts at the end of the alleyway, and the wooden steps that led to the area were outlined with crisp snow, like the icing on buns in the baker's shop window. Clemency trod carefully, not wanting to end up at the bottom of the steps with a broken ankle, or worse.

As she opened the door and went inside, the stench of unwashed bodies, cheap tallow candles and stale alcohol caught her at the back of the throat, making her retch. Slumped on a pile of sacks, her mother lay sprawled liked a broken doll, her mouth hanging open and her lips vibrating with drunken snoring. On the floor beside her was an empty gin bottle, and cockroaches swarmed over her bare legs and feet. A large Norwegian rat was sitting on the upturned tea chest that served as a table, finishing off a stale crust of bread. It turned its head to look at Clemency with small, ruby eyes, and ambled off with a swish of its tail when she hurled the wallet at it, missing it by inches.

'Hello, Clemmie.' In the flickering light issuing from the stub of a candle, Clemency could just make out the pale face of her elder brother Jack as he sat, propped up against the damp brick wall, his crippled legs sticking out at unnatural angles from his emaciated body. 'Any luck today?' His deep, man's voice was at odds with his child-sized frame, but there was neither self-pity nor resentment in his tone and he was smiling.

His braveness in the face of their dire poverty and his own pitiful state never failed to bring Clemency close to tears. Sometimes she wished he would shout and storm at the cruel illness that had left him unable to walk or even to stand on his withered limbs. She went to retrieve the wallet and placed it in his hand. 'Not much. I got this from a drunken masher outside the theatre: there was nothing in it but a rotten old theatre programme, and a photograph of that singing woman.'

'I bet she don't sing no better than you, Clemmie.'

'Maybe or maybe not – but she's rich and we're poor. Worse than that, we ain't got nothing for supper.' She jerked her head in the direction of their mother. 'Looks like she spent that money I give her this morning on booze. She promised me she'd get food.'

'He come here again,' Jack said, his cheerful smile fading into a scowl. 'Said he had a friend what was eager to make her acquaintance. And we all knows what that means.'

'The bastard! One day I'll get him, Jack. I'll catch him when he ain't looking and I'll stick a knife right through his black heart.'

'Don't talk like that, girl. If anyone was to kill the geezer it ought to be me. If I wasn't just half a man I'd do it meself.'

Clemency went down on her knees in front of him and took Jack's face between her hands. 'You're more of a man than he is, Jack Skinner.'

'Get on with you, silly mare.' Jack's brown eyes filled with tears and his lips trembled. He pulled her hands away from his face and clasped them to his chest. 'You'll have me weeping like a girl if you carry on like that.'

She squeezed his fingers and leant over to kiss him on the forehead. 'You'll do, fellah. One day we'll be rich and we'll eat breakfast, dinner and tea with supper thrown in. We'll live in a proper house, not just one stinking basement room with cess coming up through the floor. We'll get Ma away from the drink and that pimp what's ruined her life.' Patting his hands, Clemency got to her feet. She looked round the dank room and shivered. The grate was filled with ash, but they had not had enough money to buy coal or even firewood for over a week. It was so cold in the basement room that the windows were frosted on the inside. Her mother's bare arms and legs were mottled and purple, although she probably had enough alcohol in her bloodstream to keep her from dying of the cold. Clemency shot a worried glance at Jack: he was alarmingly pale and drowsy-looking. She must get him something to eat, and some fuel for the fire, or he might slip into the permanent sleep that claimed so many of the undernourished poor in midwinter.

'I couldn't get up the steps today, they was too slippery. So I never got to play me tin whistle outside of St Paul's.' Jack's dark eyes burned like lamps against his pallid skin. 'The other buskers will wonder what's become of me – the crippled boy.'

'Don't speak of yourself like that, I won't have it. You're a wonderful player, Jack.'

'It's the only thing I can do.' Jack picked up the

penny whistle that lay at his side, and he stroked it as tenderly as if it had been a kitten or a puppy. 'I can make a hatful of coppers when the worshippers comes out of the cathedral.'

'Well, they're all tucked up in their nice cosy homes tonight, so don't you fret. I'll pop out and get us some supper and you sit tight. I'll be home in a couple of ticks.'

'You can't go out again tonight, Clemmie. Not in this weather.'

'Don't you worry about me, Jack. You keep an eye on Ma.' She bent over her mother and began searching her pockets. Edith made a noise that was halfway between a snort and a groan, but she did not wake up. Her pockets, as Clemency had feared, were empty, but she dared not tell Jack. She knew he would rather starve to death than allow her to go out on the dip again at this time of night. She closed her hand into a fist and held it up for him to see. 'She ain't spent it all. The bastard, Hardiman, must have missed this little threepenny bit. I'll run to the pub get us some supper.'

She left the room, closing her ears to Jack's protests. The snow underfoot was so cold that it burned her feet, but Clemency was impervious to the weather. She was on a mission and no one and nothing was going to stop her. There was a respectable pub in Carter Lane used by reporters from Fleet Street, bank clerks and businessmen.

It was not as rough as the pubs nearer to the docks and wharves, and they sold hot pies and buttered rum punch. She went inside and gasped as the heat hit her in the throat like a punch, and the thick pall of tobacco smoke made her cough. The bar was packed with men, smoking, drinking, eating and chatting. She received a few cursory glances, but none of them seemed interested in a ragged girl who had not the strength to elbow her way through the forest of men in order to make her way to the bar.

Hunger growled in her empty stomach like an angry tiger. She was desperate, and she would not stand for being ignored: Jack was close to death from cold and starvation, and Ma would need something other than gin in her belly when she awakened from her stupor. A burly market porter got up from his seat to make his way to the bar, and, seizing her chance, Clemency jumped up on his chair and began to sing 'Home Sweet Home' in a clear soprano. Gradually, table by table, the men stopped talking and turned their heads to stare at the girl who sang with the sweetness of a nightingale. She brought such pathos to the words that, by the end of the song, many of them were left with tears in their eyes. There was an emotional silence, broken only by sounds of men clearing their throats or blowing their noses, and then someone started clapping. Soon the taproom was echoing to the sound of appreciative cheers. Taking advantage of her success, Clemency leapt down from the chair, snatched a cloth cap from a drayman's head, and went round to each punter in turn until the cap was filled with coppers.

'Well done, little girl,' the young barman said, grinning down at her with an appreciative sparkle in his hazel eyes. Clemency tipped the contents onto the bar and tossed the cap to the drayman. He caught it with a whoop of appreciation and stuck it back on his head. She gave the barman her best smile, ignoring the insult of being referred to as a 'little girl'. There were times when it paid to be thought of as a child, and this was one of them. 'I'll have three of them hot meat pies, mister. And a jug of buttered rum punch, if you please.'

'That'll be twopence deposit on the jug, missy.'

'That's all right. I got enough here. I'll bring it back tomorrow, first thing.'

The barman wrapped three hot pies in a piece of butter muslin and handed them to her. 'You got a fine singing voice.' He poured rum into an earthenware jug, added a dollop of butter, a generous helping of sugar, and some lemonade. He went to the fire, took a poker from its blazing coals and thrust it into the liquid where it sizzled, sending up clouds of fragrant steam. 'You can give us another song tomorrow,' he said, handing the jug to Clemency. 'You brought tears to me eyes, girl.'

'Maybe I will, and maybe I won't.' She flashed him a smile.

'You got the voice of an angel, miss.' An old man with gnarled fingers and skin wrinkled like a prune patted Clemency on the shoulder.

'Ta, Granddad.' His rheumy eyes were either watering from the smoky atmosphere or filled with tears, Clemency did not know which, but she kissed him on the cheek anyway. She carried the precious bundle of food and the pitcher of rum punch carefully so as not to spill a drop, and the men who had previously ignored her stood aside to let her pass. As the pub door closed behind her, Clemency was conscious of a feeling of elation that was not just due to the anticipation of a good meal. She had felt a connection with those men as she sang to them, a sharing of emotion that she could not explain. The snow was falling in earnest now. The streetlights were almost obliterated in the swirling, dancing flakes that floated down so pure and white from the dark night sky. She quickened her pace. She must get home before the food cooled and the heat went from the punch.

She slept well that night with a full stomach and a head that swam pleasantly from the unaccustomed alcohol. She did not feel the cold seeping up through the crude stone slabs that were laid on bare earth, nor the bites of the fleas and lice that inhabited her bed of straw. She dreamed that she was on stage in the Strand Theatre, singing her heart out, and the toffs in the audience were clapping and cheering. She awakened with a start, and she realised that the sound of flesh on flesh was not clapping, but slapping. She sat upright, blinking and shaking off the remnants of sleep.

'Get off me, you sod,' Edith screamed, lashing out with her feet and fists at the man who was standing over her, slapping her about the face and body with the flat of his huge hand.

'Get up then, you idle slut. I got work for you.'

Clemency leapt to her feet, making a grab for his arm in an effort to stop him hitting her mother. 'Leave her be, Hardiman.'

He threw her off so that she staggered and fell back on the pile of straw that served as her bed. She struggled to her feet as Jack dragged his withered limbs across the stone floor. 'Get off her, you bastard.'

'Don't, Jack,' Clemency cried, terrified that one blow from Hardiman could kill him. She threw herself between them. 'Leave Ma be. Can't you see she's sick?'

'The bitch is still drunk.' Hardiman caught Edith by the hair and dragged her to her feet.

She screamed but she did not attempt to fight him off. 'For pity's sake, Todd.'

'Shut your mouth or I'll shut it for you.' Still holding Edith by her fiery red hair, Hardiman turned to Clemency with a threatening scowl. 'You stay back. Your ma has to earn her living like the rest of us. Say another word and I'll give you what for.'

'I ain't frightened of you,' Clemency cried, sticking out her chin. 'You're a pimp and a rotten bully. She's had enough of you making her sell herself to dirty old buggers.'

Edith rolled her eyes, stretching her arms out to Clemency in a pleading gesture. 'Don't get his temper up, Clemmie. I'll be all right.'

'You're coming with me,' Hardiman said, twisting her hair around his hand with a spiteful jerk. 'And you'll walk proper. No calling out for help or making out you're badly done to.'

'You're scum,' Jack roared, trying ineffectually to get past Clemency. 'If I had me legs I'd knock seven bells out of you.'

'But you ain't got no legs, have you, sonny?' Hardiman grinned, displaying a row of blackened stumps that had once been teeth. 'You're a cripple what lives off the immoral earnings of his slut of a mother. And it won't be long afore your sister goes down that road too. I got me eye on you, Clemmie. But first we needs to fatten you up a bit.' He plunged his hand in the pocket of his pea jacket and producing a silver sixpence, he tossed it on the floor at

Clemency's feet. 'There's an advance on your ma's earnings, not that she's worth more than a threepenny bit, but you put on a bit of flesh, chicken, and I reckon I could get a sov a time for you.'

Clemency fisted her hands and went to punch him, but he fended her off with the toe of his boot. 'Sparky little thing, ain't you? Well, the punters like a bit of spirit.'

'Don't touch her, Todd,' Edith screamed. 'I'm warning you.'

'I'll see you in hell,' Jack said, beating the flagstones with his fists.

'Very likely.' Hardiman hoisted Edith over his shoulder and slammed out of the basement.

'I will kill him, Clemmie.' Jack punctuated his words by punching the ground. 'One day I'll get him, if it's the last thing I does.'

'He's a devil, Jack. I hates him.' Clemency stared at the frosted windowpanes, watching helplessly as Hardiman hefted her mother up the area steps. Her body hung slackly over his shoulder like a rag doll and her hair trailed in the snow.

'Why does she let him treat her like that? She could set the rozzers on him for what he's done to her.' Jack ground his knuckles into his eyelids as if he were trying to gouge out the sight of his mother's helplessness. 'Why?'

'I dunno. But for all he's done to her, I think in

a funny sort of way that she still loves him. Don't ask me why, but whenever I've tried to talk to her about Hardiman, on the odd times when she's sober, she says he weren't always like this. She says he can be kind and loving. If that's kind and loving, then I don't want none of it.'

Jack sniffed and wiped his nose on the frayed sleeve of his jacket. 'I hates being so bloody helpless. I hates meself for being a cripple, Clemmie. I'm no use to man nor beast.'

'No, don't you never say that, Jack. You're a better man than any I know. One day you'll walk proper, I'm sure of it.'

Jack took a deep breath and gave her a wobbly smile. 'You know that ain't true, poppet. But I swear to God, I will do for Hardiman. One day, I will.'

'You're not to talk like that.' Clemency bent down to retrieve the sixpence. 'I'd like to ram this up his bum so far that he coughed it up out of his mouth, but seeing as how that's impossible, I'll go out and spend it on candles, coal and something to eat.'

'No!' Jack's deep voice reverberated round the bare walls. 'It's blood money. Help me up the steps, Clemmie. I'll beg in the streets rather than take anything from him.'

'It's freezing outside. You wouldn't last five minutes out there. Be sensible, Jack.' Clemency snatched up her damp shawl and wrapped it around her head and shoulders. 'I got to take the pitcher back to the pub and they'll give me back me deposit. I'll see what I can get with it, but only if you promises to stay here until I gets back.'

Jack bowed his head, saying nothing, but she could see his shoulders heave and she winced, feeling his pain. There was nothing she could say, and she hurried from the dingy basement, and set off for Carter Lane.

The taproom of the Crown and Anchor was empty except for a couple of old men crouched by the fire in the inglenook. The potman was busy collecting tankards that had been left from the previous night's drinking session, and a whey-faced girl of twelve or thirteen was wiping the wooden tables with a damp rag. Clemency marched up to the bar and set the empty pitcher on the polished oak counter. 'Shop!'

The door behind the bar opened and a middle-aged woman wearing a mobcap and a frown gave her an appraising glance. She hesitated, and then bustled up to the bar counter wiping her hands on her apron. 'Yes?'

'I come to claim back me deposit, missis. Twopence it was.'

'I doubt if the jug is worth twopence. Who give it you?'

'Are you calling me a liar?'

'We'll see.' The woman went to the inner door. 'Ned, come here.' She turned back to face

Clemency, folding her arms across her ample bosom. 'Ned was serving last night. He'll sort you out. And what's a child like you doing in a place like this, I ask myself? And you with barely any clothes on your back and bare feet too. In this weather! What is your ma thinking about letting you go out like that?'

Clemency shifted from one foot to the other. She did not want to admit that her mother was always dead drunk, or else flat on her back beneath some punter, or the bastard, Todd Hardiman. She shrugged her shoulders. 'I'm an orphan, ain't I? Not that it's any of your business, lady.'

'Mrs Hawkes to you, girl.'

'What's the problem, Ma?' Ned Hawkes poked his curly head round the door. A smile of recognition lit his face as he looked past his mother and saw Clemency. 'Why, if it ain't the youngster what sang like a lark last night and had hard men weeping into their beer.'

'So you know her then, Ned?' Nell Hawkes's expression softened as she looked at her son. 'Give her what's due to her and then send her round to the kitchen. The poor little scrap looks perished, and I daresay a cup of tea wouldn't do her no harm.'

She disappeared through the door leaving Ned to take two pennies out of the till, which opened with a loud *kerching*. He handed them to

Clemency with a friendly grin. 'There you are young 'un.'

'Ta!' Clemency seized the money and was about to leave when Ned called her back.

'Don't go, nipper. Didn't you hear what me mum said? She don't give out cups of tea to every waif and stray what comes begging.'

'I ain't begging. And she can keep her tea for them what is.'

Ned threw back his head and laughed. 'Hoity toity!' He lifted the flap in the bar counter and stood looking at her with a mixture of admiration and amusement. 'What's your name, nipper?'

Clemency shot him a sideways glance. He was not exactly good-looking, but he had an open, pleasant face with a snub nose and a generous mouth. He was not much above average in height, but he looked as though he could heft a barrel of beer on his broad shoulders without too much difficulty. Last night it had served her purpose to be thought of as a child, but now it was mortifying. 'Me name is Clemency Skinner and I'll have you know I ain't a nipper. I'll be nineteen in September.'

He executed a mock bow, chuckling. 'Sorry, Miss Skinner. But whatever age you happen to be, you sing like an angel. How would you like to come along tonight and give the punters another treat.'

She was not sure if he was serious or simply teasing her. She eyed him suspiciously. 'What sort of treat, mister?'

'It's Ned, Ned Hawkes. And I meant a song or two, of course.'

'Maybe I will and maybe I won't. Tell your Ma I thanks her for the offer of tea, but I got business to do what won't wait.' Clemency met his eyes and relented when she read genuine hurt and disappointment in his frank gaze. She smiled. 'I might just happen along around nine o'clock.' She had the satisfaction of seeing his features relax, and she left the pub with the coins jingling in her pocket. The cold outside hit her like a smack in the face, and she gasped as the icy air seemed to freeze in her lungs. She had secreted the toff's wallet in her skirt pocket and now she headed for Minski's pawnshop in Fish Street.

Minski was huddled behind the counter in his cellar room beneath a tobacconist's shop. He was muffled in an army greatcoat with several scarves wound round his scraggy neck, and his fingers protruded from greasy woollen mittens like bent twigs.

'Hello, young Clemmie. What you got for me today?'

She slapped the wallet down on the counter. She had been dealing with Minski, who was a notorious fence, since she first started pick-pocketing at the age of seven. Hardiman had started her in the business by making sure that Ma was permanently drunk and incapable. He had found Clemency one day, hanging round in Stew Lane, cold and hungry, having returned from the ragged school and finding herself locked out of their lodgings. Jack had been out selling bootlaces in the street, and Hardiman had promised that he would take her to her mother. Instead, he had taken her to St Paul's Churchyard and left her with a group of urchins who worked the area picking pockets. Operating in pairs, they taught her how to lift a handkerchief from a gentleman's pocket so that he was quite unaware that he had been robbed, and how to avoid capture if the victim raised the alarm. Clemency had learned quickly and had soon become more adept and skilful than any of the boys. She had graduated on to scarf pins and pocket books with no trouble at all, and Minski was always waiting to do a deal.

'How much?' Clemency demanded. 'It's good leather and it's nearly new.'

He examined the wallet, peering at it in the glimmer of light from an oil lamp. 'Empty, was it?'

Clemency nodded.

'I'll give you a tanner for it.'

'You old villain. It's worth ten times that.'

'Not to me it ain't. Take it or leave it, young Clemmie.'

She thought quickly. She was used to bargaining with Minski and she knew that he was trying to do her down. She strolled round the dank cellar, rifling through the racks of clothes that hung damply in the foul air. If she were to oblige young Ned Hawkes, and she was considering it, then she would need to dress up a bit. She fingered a pink satin gown, stroking the cool, slippery material with the tips of her fingers. It felt like a baby's skin and it was the most beautiful thing she had ever seen, but much too fine for her to wear, and not at all suitable. The punters would think she was a harlot touting for business. Reluctantly, she passed it by and found a navy-blue serge skirt and a white, if slightly yellowed, cambric blouse with a high neck and full sleeves. 'Throw in these duds and we got a deal.'

'I ain't the bleeding Sally Army, girl. This ain't a charity.'

Clemency snatched the garments off the rail; she knew by the whining tone of his voice that she was going to win. 'And a pair of boots.'

'Over my dead body.'

Clemency chuckled. 'I'm sure Hardiman could arrange it. Tell you what, Minski. I'll give you another twopence for the boots and I won't tell Hardiman of our little deal.'

She left the cellar wearing a pair of rather down-at-heel, but quite serviceable, high-button boots, and with the skirt and blouse wrapped in a tight bundle beneath her arm.

On her way home, she stopped at a shop in Knightrider Street, and purchased a bag of coal, some kindling, a bundle of candles, a poke of tea and one of sugar, a loaf and a pot of beef dripping. She gave the shop boy a halfpenny to carry the coal back to Stew Lane. He managed to heft it to their door but slipped as he attempted to negotiate the snow-covered steps and scraped his shins. His flesh was mottled and so cold that, at first, the wound did not bleed. He seemed almost too weak to cope with the pain and his small face, covered with weeping sores, puckered into a grimace. Tears spilled from his eyes and rolled down his hollow cheeks. Stricken with pity, Clemency gave him her last penny for his trouble. His simian face cracked into a grin, and he scampered up the remaining steps as if the devil were after him.

With her hand on the latch, Clemency was about to go inside when she heard raised voices. One was Jack's and the other she did not recognise. She burst into the room to find a brute of a man with his hands round Jack's throat.

Chapter Two

Clemency dropped her packages on the floor and hurled herself on top of Jack's assailant, punching, kicking and screaming at him. He lurched to his feet tossing her to the ground as if she weighed less than a bag of feathers.

'Jack, are you all right?' Her first concern was for her brother, who lay back against the wall, blue in the face, clutching his hands to his throat and gasping for breath. He nodded dumbly. Clemency jumped up to face the intruder. 'You bugger! What d'you think you was doing to a poor crippled boy?' For a moment, she thought the big brute was going to strike her to the ground, but he seemed to change his mind, and he shuffled towards the open door.

'Ask him,' he growled. 'Ask him.' He barged out of the room, slamming the door behind him so that the sash window rattled.

There was silence except for Jack's rasping cough as he fought to regain control of his breathing. Clemency bent over him, peering anxiously into his face. 'Are you all right?'

Jack nodded.

'Who was he, Jack? And why did he go for you as if he meant to kill you?'

With beads of perspiration standing out on his forehead, Jack attempted a wobbly smile. 'He's one of Hardiman's gang . . .' He broke off, overcome by a fit of coughing.

'Never mind that now.' Clemency straightened up. This was not the time for explanations – they would come later. 'I'm going to get a fire going, and then I'll fetch water from the pump and make you a nice cup of tea. You rest there, ducks.'

It took her some time to drag the sack of coal from the snow-filled area into the room and to get a fire going in the small grate. It took even longer to negotiate the slippery streets to get to the communal pump to fetch water. By the time she had made a pot of tea, cut slices from the loaf and spread them with dripping, making sure that Jack had most of the nourishing brown jelly at the bottom of the pot, he had recovered enough to tell her what had happened.

'He come bursting in,' he said, in between sips of hot, sweet tea, 'without a by your leave, saying that Hardiman had sent him.' He paused, shaking angry tears from his eyes. 'And all I could do was sit here and try to fend the bugger off with me bare hands.'

With anger and hatred for Hardiman raging in her breast, Clemency bit into a chunk of bread, allowing Jack time to compose himself. If only she were a man, she would show Hardiman and his bully boys what was what.

Jack wiped his eyes on his sleeve and took a shuddering breath. 'It were a warning, Clemmie. He never meant to kill me; it were a threat of what was to come if I didn't do what he wanted.'

'But what did he want?'

'Hardiman is dangerous, Clemmie. He sees you taking Ma's place in his dirty dealings, and he wants me to persuade you to go with him. You got to get away from here, girl. You ain't safe and I'm only half a man. I can't protect you.'

'I won't have it.' Clemency jumped to her feet, dropping her bread on the floor and ignoring the rat that popped out of a hole in the wall to scurry across the floor, seize the food and carry it off in the blink of an eye. 'I'd rather die than sell me body to dirty, stinking men like Hardiman. I'm going to get us all out of this hell-hole if it's the last thing I do.' She retrieved the bundle of clothes that she had dropped near the doorway and began stripping off her ragged garments.

'Clemmie, for God's sake, what are you going to do?' Jack's voice rose in alarm.

Used as she was to living in the confines of one cramped room, Clemency was not shy about undressing in front of her brother. Shivering in her thin cotton shift, she reached for the white blouse and put it on, fastening the tiny buttons with trembling fingers. 'I don't know yet, but I'm going to put a stop to Hardiman's game.' She stepped into the skirt and wrapped it around her slim waist. 'How do I look?'

'Fine. Promise me you won't do nothing stupid, Clemmie.'

'I wish I had a mirror,' Clemency said, peering into the glass windowpanes in an attempt to view her reflection. 'I got to do something with my hair.' She went down on her hands and knees, feeling under the thin flock mattress that was Edith's sleeping place. 'I seen her hiding her bits and pieces somewhere.' Her fingers closed around a cotton pouch. 'Found it.' She sat back on her haunches and tipped the contents into her lap. In the dim light of the tallow candle, she went through the items one by one. Her mother's treasured possessions were pathetically few: a string of glass beads, a black velvet ribbon and three tortoiseshell combs. 'I can remember her wearing these. She was so pretty in them days.' There was a lump in Clemency's throat as she remembered her mother before drink and prostitution had left her with a broken spirit and faded beauty.

'Clemmie, please.' Jack's voice cracked with emotion. 'Don't go that way.'

A hoarse laugh ripped from her throat. 'I'll go me own way, not that of bloody Hardiman. I'll see the bugger burn in hell fire afore I do what he wants.' She twisted her long, flame-red tresses into a knot on top of her head, fixing them in place with the combs. Getting to her feet, Clemency turned to Jack. 'How do I look now? Be honest.'

Jack swallowed hard and his lips moved soundlessly. She raised her eyebrows, waiting for him to answer.

'Beautiful, Clemmie. You look so fine. Please don't do nothing rash.'

She hooked up her shawl and did a twirl. 'I'm going out to conquer the world, Jack. And I'll make Hardiman pay for what he's done to you and Ma. You see if I don't.'

The fire was burning brightly in the hearth, and Jack had enough food in his belly to keep him going for the rest of the day. Clemency left him sitting close to the comforting blaze, having extracted a promise from him that he would not attempt to go out into the snow. In return, she gave him her word that she would not do anything foolish. However, once outside in the bitter cold of a January day, with the future looking equally bleak, Clemency knew that this was one pledge to her beloved brother that she might not be able to keep. With little idea or plan in mind, she made her way to Cheapside, where she sauntered along the pavements looking for a likely victim who might have a full purse or a gold watch. But the weather was her worst enemy, and there were few people out of doors braving the slippery pavements and winter chill. Those who did venture abroad were huddled beneath greatcoats, striding along with their hands in their pockets. The ladies travelled in hackney cabs, and were assisted across the treacherous pavements to the door of their destination by burly cabbies, men who could spot a dipper at a hundred yards or more.

Clemency was getting desperate. Her clothes were decent, but without a bonnet or cape she was poorly dressed for such inclement weather, and this made her stand out in the crowd. She stopped for a moment inside the doorway of a jeweller's shop, stamping her feet and wrapping her arms about her chest in an effort to get warm. If she did not pick a pocket soon, there would be no supper tonight and she would go home to a helpless cripple, and a drunken mother who had spent her immoral earnings on jigger gin. She would leave herself open to Hardiman and his evil intentions.

Then she saw him – a well-dressed young man wearing a city suit beneath a topcoat that was left casually undone, as if he was impervious to the cold. On his head he wore a bowler hat, tipped at a rakish angle, and he carried a silver-headed cane. He was studying something that had caught his eye in the jeweller's window. She sidled out of the doorway and stood beside him.

He did not appear to have noticed her and she slid her hand into his jacket pocket. Her fingers caressed a leather pouch, bulging with coins, and her heart began to race. With her gaze fixed on his absorbed profile, she curled her fingers around the pouch and began to lift it slowly from its warm resting place. Suddenly, and without even turning his head, he caught her by the wrist. She tried to break free but he held her in an iron grip.

'Let me go, mister. I was just trying to get me hand warm. A girl could freeze to death out here.'

He looked at her for the first time and his eyes gleamed like blue diamonds. 'Amateur,' he said in a cultured drawl.

Panic clutched Clemency's heart in an icy fist. 'No, honest, guv. I weren't up to no good. I tells you I was cold and you look like a . . .'

'Nice, kind man? Believe me, young woman, I am not.' He dragged her hand from his pocket. 'And you are not an accomplished thief.'

'I am so.' She could not let that remark pass unchallenged. 'Why, I've been on the dip since I were a nipper of seven.' She stopped, clamping her free hand to her lips. She had done it now – condemned herself out of her own mouth.

'Have you now? I suppose you might suit my purpose, with a bit of training.' He looked her up, with a glimmer of interest lighting his eyes.

'Yes, you might be exactly what I'm looking for.'

Clemency raised her chin defiantly, even though she was inwardly quaking. 'I dunno what you mean. If you're going to call for a copper then do it now, and get it over and done with.'

'I shan't call for the police.' He clamped her hand in the crook of his arm and began walking along the pavement, leaving her no alternative but to run to keep up with his long stride. 'I have plans for you.'

'Where are you taking me? I won't go. I'll scream for help.'

'No you won't. You wouldn't be so foolish. One squeak out of you and I'll deliver you to the nearest constabulary. Don't forget, you were caught in the act.'

It was all she could do to keep her footing on the pavements where the pristine white snow had been trampled into blackened slush. They had left Cheapside and were now walking at a slower pace along Bread Street in the direction of the river. Clemency was on home territory, and was determined to break free at the first opportunity. Given the chance, she could disappear into the maze of back alleys and narrow lanes; he would have to be Spring-heeled Jack in order to catch up with her. Then, without warning, he dragged her down a narrow slit between the tall buildings that opened into Hog

Yard. This was not the sort of place that she would ever have ventured into on her own. The soot-blackened buildings towered above them, five and six storeys high, cheap lodging houses, brothels and haunts of cadgers, magsmen, prostitutes, thieves and swindlers. Even Hardiman would think twice before setting foot in Hog Yard.

'I won't go in there,' Clemency cried, digging her heels into the slush and rubbish that had been tossed out of windows, carpeting the cobblestones with a stinking mess.

He took no notice of her protests, and she was towed along in his wake like the tender of a steam engine, up the front steps and into a seedy-looking establishment. The hallway was long, dark and narrow. He opened a door to the right and Clemency gasped as a wave of hot air almost took her breath away. She found herself standing in a large kitchen with a fire blazing in the range. On either side of it there were boilers bubbling and gurgling with hot water, and pans simmering on the hob exuding tempting aromas of boiled mutton and vegetables. A leg of bacon was hung in the chimneybreast, turning golden brown in the smoke, and strings of onions and herbs dangled from the beamed ceiling. Two long deal tables were littered with the remnants of a meal, and seated at them, on wooden forms, were as motley a crowd of people as ever

Clemency had seen grouped together. The steamy atmosphere was fuggy with tobacco smoke, cheap perfume, spicy stew and hot coffee.

'What you got there, then, Jared?' A fat woman, who had been stirring a pan on the hob, waved a wooden spoon at Clemency. 'I ain't running a soup kitchen for waifs and strays.'

Clemency's abductor took off his hat and greatcoat, dropping them down on one of the benches as if he owned the place, which, she thought, he probably did. She glanced up at him and saw that his grim expression had relaxed into a smile.

'Two cups of coffee, Nancy, my dear. If you please.'

'I ain't your nanny now, Jared Stone. And I ain't at your beck and call. This is my establishment, and you ain't my landlord.' Nancy picked up a jug and took two mugs off the dresser, filling them with steaming coffee. She fixed Clemency with a shrewd stare. 'I'd keep away from the likes of him if I was you, nipper.'

Before Clemency could answer, a young woman entered the kitchen. She was smartly dressed in warm outdoor clothes, with a stylish fur hat perched on her head, and a matching muff dangling from silken cords around her neck. In her gloved hand, she carried a small portmanteau. Clemency felt a stab of envy at the sight of such finery, even though it was obvious from the size of the woman's belly that she was in the family way.

The young woman stopped when she saw Jared, and her pretty mouth turned down at the corners. Her large brown eyes filled with tears. 'Jared! You can't mean to treat me so cruel. I've worked hard for you since I was little more than a nipper.'

His expression hardened. 'You knew the score, Meg. It was a straight business deal. There was to be no hanky-panky with the punters.'

'But I love you, Jared. You can't turn me out on the street just because I made a mistake and give meself to a bastard what ruined me.'

Stone took her by the shoulders and lifted her chin with the tip of his forefinger. 'Come now, Meg. Don't make this hard on yourself. You know you and your child will be better off in the country, and you won't want for money. I'll see to that.'

'I want to stay with you,' Meg sobbed, beating her hands on his chest. 'I hate you.'

'Here, drink this, ducks. You look as though you need it.' Nancy thrust the mug of hot coffee into Clemency's hands. 'Don't take no notice of them. No one else does.'

Clemency looked round and saw that what Nancy said was perfectly true. The men and women seated round the tables were intent on their own business, barely giving the tearful Meg a second glance. Clemency sipped the coffee. It was hot and sweet and already the warmth was returning to her chilled limbs, but the heat had made her chilblains start playing up again – itching and burning as if her legs were on fire. However, that was the least of her worries. She edged towards the doorway, intent on escape, just waiting for her chance while Jared's attention was occupied by Meg's hysterical outpourings.

'Stop this, Meg.' Jared caught her flailing hands as she attempted to slap him about the head and face. 'You'll only harm yourself and the child. You've got enough money to set you up nicely in Havering. You'll have prospective husbands queuing for miles to ask for your hand in marriage, if only to get their hands on your dowry. I'm sure they'll overlook one little bastard.'

'Oh, you brute,' Meg screamed, struggling and kicking out with her booted feet. 'You're so cruel. I really do hate you.'

'Then you will be quite happy to be miles away from me and this den of iniquity, won't you?'

'No, no. I don't want to go home in disgrace,' Meg wept. 'I done everything you ever asked of me, Jared. Don't send me away like this.'

Nancy dropped the spoon into the pan and waddled over to Meg, taking her by the shoulders and twisting her from Jared's grasp. 'Now look here, my girl. You got yourself into this mess. You was happy enough while you was going with him to theatres, gaming houses, racetracks and the like, robbing the rich and enjoying the comforts it brought you. Well, now you got your comeuppance. Take his money and run, that's my advice.'

Meg stopped howling and sniffed. 'He's ruined me reputation. I was a good girl until I met with Jared Stone.'

'Nonsense. You was a runaway, starving on the streets when he found you. You could have done a lot worse. Now go home to the farm and bring up that baby of yours proper.'

Clemency moved a little closer to the door; she wanted to get away, but she was fascinated by Meg, so tragic and so beautiful. Jared was standing there saying nothing now but looking cold and aloof as the statue of Lord Nelson on top of his column. Clemency decided that, at this moment, she hated him even more than Hardiman, and that was saying something. She shuffled backwards and knocked over a stool. It fell with a resounding clatter on the flagstones and this time everyone turned their heads to see what had happened.

Meg turned on her like a white-lipped fury. 'It's all her fault,' she cried, pointing a shaking finger at Clemency. 'He's fetched her in to take me place. Look at her, the skinny, green-eyed little monkey; she's only fit to sell matches in the street, or work as a skivvy. She couldn't pass for a lady not in a hundred years.'

'Here, who are you calling a skinny monkey?' Clemency demanded angrily. 'I couldn't take your place because I ain't a whore.'

A gust of laughter rippled around the tables and a dozen or more pairs of eyes turned on them, watching with some amusement. Meg broke free from Nancy's grasp, and she hurled herself at Clemency with her hands clawed. Jared stepped between them and caught her by the wrists. 'That's enough. I'm putting you in a cab and you're going straight to Liverpool Street Station, Meg. You have your ticket.'

'You can't make me go home.'

'I won't be responsible for the consequences if you don't go.'

Meg's face crumpled and fresh tears spurted from her eyes. 'You don't love me no more.'

'I never pretended that I did. You're twisting everything for your own ends.'

Clemency leapt forward. 'You really are a brute and a bastard, aren't you?' She turned to Meg. 'You're better off without a man like him, take my word for it. And he never brought me here for what you think. I'm a pickpocket, one of the best in the East End. That's me trade and nothing else. You don't have to fret about me ending up in his bed, because I'd rather sleep with one of them chimpanzees at the Zoological Gardens than with the likes of him.'

Howls of laughter drowned out whatever Jared had to say, but the look on his face made Clemency think that the name Stone suited him down to the ground. His jaw and cheekbones stuck out in tight angles as if he had been carved out of a block of granite and his startlingly blue eyes blazed beneath his lowered brows. He pushed a lock of dark hair back from his brow with an impatient hand. Clemency had the satisfaction of knowing that she had pierced the steel-plated armour that undoubtedly surrounded his hard heart.

Taking advantage of the general hubbub, she snatched a knife from the table. 'I'm going, and them as tries to stop me gets this stuck in their breadbasket. Good luck to you, lady. And think yourself lucky to be rid of him.' There was silence as all eyes were turned to Jared. Clemency did not wait to see his reaction. She opened the door and fled.

She ran and did not stop until she reached the corner of Stew Lane where she bent double with her hands on her knees. She struggled to catch her breath, not wanting to arrive home in such a sorry state. Heavy, featherbed clouds had gathered, spilling rain that was now turning to sleet, and she was soaked to the skin in seconds, with icy particles clinging to her hair and eyelashes. As she regained control of her erratic breathing, Clemency hesitated, listening for sounds of pursuit, but there was nothing other than the normal day-to-day rumbling of cartwheels, and the clip-clopping of horses' hooves, mingled with the cries of the street vendors and the distant sounds of the working river. She had intended to go home, and change out of her wet clothes into the ragged garments that she had so happily put aside, but if she did that then she would have to tell Jack what had happened, and she knew that he would be upset. He already suffered the twin torments of physical disability and his inability to protect his mother and sister. She could not face the thought of distressing him even further. If she kept walking, she could keep warm. Maybe if she headed in the direction of Fleet Street and the Strand, she might lift a wallet or even a silk handkerchief or two. She began to walk, striding out and praying silently for a break in the weather. If she kept going at this pace then hopefully her clothes would dry out – if only it would stop sleeting.

She had reached Ludgate Hill without any luck, and there was no sign of a let-up in the strings of iced rain that fell from a pewter sky. She decided to try Farringdon Market. People had to venture out to buy necessities, whatever the weather, and they would have money on their persons. She trudged on, mingling with the crowd that thronged amongst the market stalls. Farringdon vegetable market was famous for its watercress, although she doubted whether anyone in their right mind would spend good money on such a peppery vegetable in the middle of winter. She spotted a well-dressed, middle-aged matron with a young maidservant walking a couple of steps behind her. The woman stopped at one stall and then another, examining apples and oranges, poking a fat, pork-sausage finger into the centre of cabbages, and when she wanted to purchase something, she took a bulging purse from her reticule. Clemency followed them at a safe distance, watching and waiting for a moment of carelessness when the woman might set the purse down, or tuck it under her arm while she haggled over the price of a pineapple or a bunch of grapes. At last it seemed that her patience was about to pay off. The maidservant had spotted a young man and was waving frantically as she tried to gain his attention. Her employer was exchanging angry words with a stallholder, and had dropped her purse. Hardly able to believe her luck, Clemency pounced on it, and was about to make off with it when a hand clamped on her shoulder. She spun round, expecting to see a policeman about to arrest her, but the glib explanation froze on her lips as she found herself looking into the smiling face of Ned Hawkes.

'Why, Miss Clemency. I didn't expect to see you here.'

With the purse clutched in her hand, Clemency felt a guilty flush rising from her neck to her cheeks. Any moment now, the old dame would miss it and she would be found out. 'Just a moment. There's something I got to do.' She flashed a smile at Ned and tapped the woman on the shoulder. 'Excuse me, missis. I think you dropped this.'

'Well, so I did.' She snatched the purse and her face puckered into a frown. 'Where's that dratted girl? Ivy, come here. Stop ogling that young man and do what you're paid for.' She turned her back on Clemency and resumed her verbal battle with the stallholder.

'Don't say thank you,' Clemency muttered beneath her breath. If only she'd been a bit quicker, or if Ned Hawkes hadn't chosen that particular moment to turn up, she would not have had any conscience about stealing the purse from such a miserable old cow.

'So what brings you out on such a dreadful day?'

Clemency realised that Ned had been speaking to her and she managed a weary smile. 'Oh, I just needed to get a bit of food in.'

'Me too. We get through a whole vegetable garden in no time at the pub. Ma makes the best soup in London – she's famous for it. You must try it sometime.'

'That would be nice.' Clemency glanced over her shoulder; she had spotted another likely target, but first she must get rid of Ned. 'Anyway, I must get on.'

'Of course. Don't let me stop you. Will you come to the pub and sing for us tonight?'

She had lost sight of her next victim. Clemency shivered as the chill crept into the marrow of her bones. 'Maybe.'

'Look, Miss Clemency. I don't want to be personal, but you're soaked to the skin and your lips are turning blue. Why don't you let me help you with your shopping, and then you could come back with me to the pub and try a bowl of Ma's soup?'

It was not the most flattering offer, but Clemency was rapidly losing all feeling in her lower limbs, and even her chilblains had stopped tingling. She would sell her soul for a hot meal, but Jack and Ma were depending on her for their supper. She hesitated. 'I dunno.'

'What do you need? Bread, vegetables, fruit?'

'I – I lost me purse.'

'And yet you gave that old trout's purse back to her. Now I call that real honest. Some folk would have said finders keepers and pocketed it, especially when they're hard up.'

'I ain't hard up. I told you, I lost me purse.'

'My mistake, but the offer still stands. How about you letting me buy whatever it is you come for, and you can pay me back later.'

She was tempted, but wary. You couldn't trust blokes – their idea of repayment usually entailed lots of slobbery kisses, a grubby hand down the front of your blouse and, if you weren't too fussy, a bit of a fumble, which could easily get out of hand if a girl weren't quick on her feet. Clemency met Ned's candid gaze with a suspicious look. He seemed like a nice chap, decent, kindly and honourable, if there was such a thing east of Temple Bar, but she was still smarting from her experience with Jared Stone. 'No, ta. I got money put by at home.' She could feel his disappointment and she sensed that her curt tone had hurt his feelings. 'But I will take up your offer of a warm by the fire. I'm wet as a drownded rat.'

'Excellent.' Ned hefted the sack containing his purchases over his shoulder, and offered Clemency his arm. 'Let's get home afore you turn into a block of ice.'

Ned's boast about his mother's soup had not been a vain one. Clemency sat in a corner of the inglenook at the Crown and Anchor with her skirt pulled up over her knees, toasting her feet by the roaring log fire. She had just finished her second bowl of soup, and was wiping up the last delicious drop with a hunk of freshly baked bread. Ned was serving behind the bar, and the pub was filled with men enjoying a pint of beer and a pie or a hunk of bread and cheese, but they barely gave her a second glance.

'Well, dear. You look a lot better now with a bit of colour in your cheeks.'

Clemency looked up and saw Nell Hawkes smiling down at her. 'Ta for the soup, Mrs Hawkes. It's the best I've ever tasted.'

'You needs feeding up, my girl. And just look at you, going about half naked in the middle of winter. Ain't you got no one at home to care for you?'

'I got a good home, ta very much.'

'And your mum doesn't mind you going about half dressed in the bitter cold?'

'Me mum is sick. She's got a weak chest and has to stay in bed.'

'You poor little soul. And what about your dad?'

'Dead.'

'Dear me, how sad. Sit there a moment, dear. I'll be back in two shakes of a lamb's tail.' Nell took the empty bowl from Clemency's hands with a sympathetic smile and edged her way back to the bar.

Clemency stared into the orange and blue flames that licked round the coals in the grate. Why she had lied about her mother she did not quite know, except that she could not admit to a stranger that Ma was a common prostitute and a drunkard. Neither had she mentioned Jack or his crippled state. Ma had always said, when she was sober, that Jack's illness was a punishment for her way of life. God had struck him down just to get even with her for breaking almost all of the Ten Commandments. His disability was her shame. Clemency was not certain that she agreed with this, but there did not seem to be any other logical explanation. She could remember when Jack had legs like any other boy. They had played games of chase up and down Stew Lane like normal children. Her memories of life before that were vague, but she knew that they had to leave the pub after Dad walked out. Then Jack had gone down with a fever, suffering aching limbs and terrible spasms. Ma had packed her off to stay with Mrs Trotter who lived in one of the attic rooms at the top of the building. Mrs Trotter had no children of her own, and smelled horribly of snuff and the raw onions that she liked to eat; Clemency would have run home if the old woman had not locked her in. When she was allowed back into their basement, eight-year-old Jack was lying on his straw palliasse, looking deathly pale and unable to move his legs. Their dad was gone, off to join the Navy, so Ma had said, but he had never returned. Todd Hardiman had moved in, and Ma had taken to the drink. Clemency had been just six years old, and it was then that her childhood had ended.

She realised with a start that the acrid smell rising to her nostrils was coming from her skirt, singeing where a spark from the fire had landed. She crushed the material between her fingers and wiped her hand across her eyes. It was just the smoke from the burning serge that was making them water; she was not crying over the past.

'Here we are, ducks.'

Once again, Clemency looked up and saw Nell standing before her. She was smiling, and holding out a black garment that was so heavy it weighed her arms down. 'It's old, but it's serviceable. A piece of good woollen cloth like this won't never wear out, not unless the moths get at it.' With an effort, Nell held it up for Clemency to see.

The cloak with its faded crimson lining and large hood must have been fashionable a good forty years ago, but as Clemency fingered the coarse material she knew that it would be warm and probably waterproof to a degree. She stared up into Nell's lined face. 'For me?'

'I wanted to get rid of it anyway,' Nell said, shrugging. 'It ain't no use to me and you'd be doing me a favour taking it off me hands. It may not be what the toffs are wearing this season, but it'll keep out the cold and damp. If you want it, it's yours. If you don't, then I daresay there's an old nag in some stable or other as would be grateful for a horse blanket.'

'I dunno what to say.'

Nell dropped the cloak onto the settle next to Clemency and her cheeks looked suspiciously pink as she bent over to poke the fire. 'There's no need for thanks. Like I said, you'd be doing me a favour – but if you don't want it . . .'

'I do want it.' Clemency jumped to her feet, wrapping the garment around her shoulders. Its weight made her sag at the knees, and it smelled strongly of mothballs, but it would keep her warm and dry. She could steal a leg of lamb or a sack of apples and no one would be able to guess that she had anything concealed beneath the folds of the voluminous garment. She hugged it to her, afraid that Mrs Hawkes might change her mind. 'Ta, ever so. I'd best be going now.'

Nell smiled and nodded. 'Going home to tend to your poor ailing mum, I expect. You're a good girl, Clemency. You're welcome round here any time.'

As she trudged home, warm and snug beneath the woollen cloak, Clemency felt a pang of guilt. She had led Mrs Hawkes to think that she was a good person, when in truth she was the very reverse. Hardiman had always told her she would end up in Newgate, and she had no doubt that he was right. He had set her feet on the downward path, and now she could see no other way of existing: but if she was going to be a thief, then she was determined to be one of the best.

She quickened her pace. She would go home and make sure that Jack was all right, and in the evening she would go to the Crown and Anchor to entertain the punters. At least she could earn enough to buy a fish supper for Jack and Ma, and if the opportunity arose, then she might dip the pocket of a drunken city clerk or reporter from one of the Fleet Street newspapers.

The sleet had turned to rain, and the winter afternoon had succumbed to an early dusk by the time Clemency reached Stew Lane. As she opened the door, she felt the hackles rise on the back of her neck. The room was in darkness except for a pale circle of light around the fireplace. She could see Jack's face, a pale shape with great hollows for eyes, like cinders in the snow. His mouth was drawn into a tight line and she knew that something was dreadfully wrong. Her mother was huddled by the hearth with her arms around her knees, rocking to and fro. She turned her head as Clemency entered and her mouth opened in a soundless warning.

A man leapt out of the shadows. His hands were round her throat – she could not breathe. Red lights flashed before her eyes and she thought she was going to die.

Chapter Three

'Leave her be, Hardiman.' Jack's voice dimly penetrated Clemency's consciousness. Her attacker released his grip and she collapsed to the ground coughing and choking. Even as she struggled for breath, she was aware of male voices grunting and cursing. She crawled away from the flailing arms and fists as Jack brought Hardiman to the ground.

'Stop, stop.' Edith's voice rose to a scream.

Clemency scrambled to her feet. She would have attempted to intervene but the fight was already over. Jack had great strength in his upper body and arms but he was no match for Hardiman, who had stunned him with a single blow to the jaw.

'You've killed my boy,' Edith cried, burying her face in her hands. 'You're a murderer, Todd Hardiman.'

'Shut your trap, woman.' Hardiman bent over Jack's prostrate body. 'He'll live.' He straightened up, beckoning to Clemency. 'Come here.'

She took a step backwards, shaking her head.

Hardiman grabbed Edith by the hair, tilting her head back at an unnatural angle. 'Come here, I said. Or do you want me to snap Edie's neck like a twig?'

'What d'you want?' Clemency took a step towards him, keeping out of arm's reach.

'You was seen, my girl. I got spies all over the place, and you was seen.'

'I dunno what you mean.'

Hardiman curled his lip. 'You was with Stone. You went to his drum with him. What's going on?'

'Nothing.'

Edith yelped as Hardiman tugged at her hair. 'Tell him what he wants to know, for God's sake, Clemmie.'

'All right,' Clemency moved swiftly to grab Hardiman's hand. 'Let her go and I'll tell you.'

Hardiman threw Edith to the ground, and wiped his hands on his greasy jacket. 'Are you cheating on me, girl? Because if you are, you know what you'll get.'

Clemency was almost deafened by the blood drumming in her ears. She knew him well enough to be terrified of crossing him, but she held her head high and looked Hardiman in the face. 'I tried to lift his wallet and he caught me. Took me to his place whether I wanted to go or not. I run off as soon as I got the chance. Satisfied?'

'If I find out you been lying to me, I'll strangle you with me bare hands.'

'You won't do that, Hardiman. I'm too useful to you and I'm one of the best when it comes to picking pockets.' Her words were bold, but inwardly she was quaking. She had learned long ago that he was a brute and a bully – if she let him see that she was scared, he would treat her all the worse.

'So good that you let Stone catch you in the act. You're slipping, girl.' Hardiman glanced down at Jack who had come to his senses, and was sitting up, rubbing his jaw. He aimed a savage kick at Jack's wizened legs. 'Keep out of me way, cripple.'

'Oh, Todd. Don't treat me boy so cruel,' Edith sobbed, holding out her hands to him as she rose unsteadily to her feet. 'Let's go back to your place. I'll make it right with you.'

'You're a drunken old whore, Edie. When I wants a woman, I got another in mind.' Hardiman leered at Clemency. 'And I likes them young. You're too grown-up now for dipping handkerchief and wallets, Clem. That's kids' stuff. I got an older profession in mind for you.'

A low growl ripped from Jack's throat as he pitched his body towards Hardiman. Clemency leapt between them, catching the full force of Hardiman's fist on her mouth. Staggering backwards, she held her hand to her bleeding lips.

'Stupid little cow, getting in the way.' Hardiman backed towards the door as Jack slithered towards him, using his knuckles to propel himself across the flagstones. Even in the dim light, Clemency could see that Hardiman's face had paled.

'Keep away from me, cripple.' He pointed a shaking finger at Clemency. 'And you, girl. I'll be back for you when your face don't look like a Christmas pudding.' He slammed out of the room.

There was a moment of stillness, with only the sound of the vermin scrabbling behind the brickwork and Jack's heavy breathing, punctuated by a rasping sob. He broke the silence by beating his fists on the floor. 'I'm so bloody useless. I'd kill him if I could.'

Edith sank to the ground, covering her face with her hands and sobbing.

Clemency wiped the blood from her lips, which had already swollen to double their normal size. 'He's not worth it, Jack. They'd hang you for sure.'

'Well, what use am I with no legs? Tell me that, Clemmie? I can't do nothing except busk on street corners and I can't protect you or her.' He pointed to the shivering figure of their mother, huddled in the corner. 'At least if I got rid of Hardiman then you and Ma would be safe.'

'Shut up, Jack. I won't hear you talk so.'

Suddenly weary, Clemency picked up the galvanised bucket from its place by the hearth. Her head and limbs felt as heavy as her heart. Was nothing ever going to go right for them? She started towards the door. 'I'm going to get some water to make a brew.'

Edith raised her head. 'I need a drink. For pity's sake, Clemmie. I'm shaking all over. Please get me a proper drink.'

'I'll try, Ma.' Clemency frowned at Jack, shaking her head as he opened his mouth to protest. 'I'll be back as quick as I can. Keep her here, Jack. Don't let her stray out into the street, not in her state.'

With Nell's cloak wrapped around her, Clemency ventured into the bitter cold of the early evening, heading for the pump in Knightrider Street. Hardiman's punch had split her lips, and she doubted whether she would be able to sing in the pub tonight. Her mouth hurt, but the real pain was inside her: a gnawing, nagging ache in the pit of her stomach that made her feel sick. Hardiman had dominated their lives for too long and he was destroying them slowly, one by one. She must do something to get Ma and Jack away from his clutches. To stay in their lodgings would bring about disaster, even death.

The water gushed from the pump in ragged spurts as she worked the handle. Every jerking movement of her arm caused her lips to throb painfully, and she stopped for a moment to rest. All around her there was the hustle and bustle of people who had finished their day's work, and were heading for the mainline railway station at Ludgate Hill, or the underground railway at Mansion House. The pondering clouds had given way to a deep starlit canopy above her head, and there was a hint of frost in the smoky air. Out here, the crowd absorbed her, and she felt small and insignificant like a tiny insect in a marching army of ants. She began pumping again, and allowed her mind to wander, following the homeward bound travellers as they hurried towards the underground station. She had never had the opportunity to investigate that awesome, and rather frightening, wonder of the modern age. One day, when things were better, she would join the passengers who travelled on mechanical moles burrowing their way beneath the city. One day, when they were safe and free – the water was spilling from the overfilled bucket, soaking her skirt and trickling into her boots. She was standing in a deep puddle. Clemency stopped pumping and listened.

Above the sound of tramping feet and the constant clatter of horse-drawn traffic, she could hear music: the rhythmic beating of a drum, the warbling of a flute, the breathy tune from a concertina, and the clear voice of a woman, singing. The air was filled with a happy sound, as though the birds had awakened early and begun their dawn chorus. As Clemency strained her eyes to peer into the yellow glow of the gas lamps, she saw the set expressions on the faces of the passers-by relax, as if the tensions of the day were being leached from them by the music. Her own mood lightened, and she found that her foot had begun to tap of its own accord in time to the beat. The musicians were coming nearer and the weary workers trudging along the pavements parted ranks, allowing the band to pass.

The pump was in the middle of the street, next to the stone horse trough, and the music makers stopped so close to Clemency that she could have reached out to touch them. The girl had stopped singing, and she rushed to the pump, working it with one hand and cupping the other in an attempt to catch some water, which she drank thirstily. Someone in the small crowd of office workers, clerks, tellers, type-writers and bankers, began to clap their hands, and soon it was taken up in a welter of applause. The girl curtsied and blew kisses, but it was a middle-aged man who strode to the forefront. He doffed his rather battered top hat and bowed, exposing the shining pate of his balding head. As he straightened up, smiling broadly, Clemency noticed that his ill-fitting tailcoat was threadbare and too short in the arms, and the cuffs of his shirt were grey and frayed. A red carnation drooped from his buttonhole and his trousers only just reached the tops of his black boots. He jammed the topper back on his head, and with an expansive wave of his arms he glanced over his shoulder at the musicians. 'Gentlemen, if you please,' he intoned in a deep theatrical voice.

The band struck a chord and the man in the top hat stuck a monocle in his eye and began to sing 'Champagne Charlie is me name . . .'

Clemency clapped her hands enthusiastically when he had finished. He swept off his topper and bowed to the audience. When the applause died down, he signalled to the girl to join him. Shaking the droplets of water from her hands, she held up her skirts just far enough to reveal a pair of shapely ankles beneath a frilled, scarlet-taffeta petticoat. With her hands clasped in front of her, she launched into the plaintive ballad 'Come into the Garden Maud', but a bout of coughing caused her to stop singing. There was a polite silence while the onlookers waited for her to catch her breath; she made another attempt to sing but her voice cracked. Almost without knowing what she did, Clemency stepped forward and carried on where the girl had left off. She forgot all about her cut and swollen lips, ignoring the salty taste of blood as it trickled into her mouth. She had never before sung to an accompaniment other than that of Jack's tin whistle, and the music flowed through her veins like molten lava. She did not feel the water seeping through the cracks in her second-hand boots, nor the shards of sleet that had begun to pelt down from a passing storm cloud, pricking her face with a hundred tiny needles. Her heart soared with the music, and her voice echoed off the surrounding buildings, coming back to her and turning the solo into a round. As she uttered the last note, the applause was tumultuous and Clemency stepped aside, embarrassed by the realisation of what she had done. She glanced nervously at the man in the top hat. 'Sorry, mister. I didn't mean to butt in. I dunno what come over me.'

He hooked his arm around her shoulders, propelling her forward and taking her down with him in a series of deep bows. 'Don't worry, miss. You were splendid.' He straightened up, signalling to the band, which struck up a military march. He grasped her hand and shook it, pumping her arm up and down. 'Augustus Throop, musical director of this splendid troupe of street artistes. And you are?'

'She's got a blooming cheek.' Having recovered from her coughing fit, the girl pushed Clemency aside. 'Pa, you ain't going to let her get away with pinching me song, are you?'

'Now, now, my silver-throated poppet. This young woman saved you from a nasty tickle. We are indebted to you, Miss – er . . .?'

'Clemency Skinner, sir.'

'Well, Miss Skinner, you have a sweet voice and a good ear for music, but,' he added hastily, wrapping his arm around his daughter's shoulders, 'not quite in the league of my little songbird, Lucilla. Daughter of my heart, pride of my soul.'

'Oh, Pa. Give over.' Lucilla pouted and nudged him in the ribs with her elbow.

'Such spirit!' Augustus pinched her cheek, smiling fondly. 'My little plum-pie.'

Clemency picked up the bucket. It was heavy and her feet were wet, her mouth was sore and the audience had begun to disperse, their enthusiasm curbed by the sudden downpour. 'I'd best be going.'

'As we must also,' Augustus said, signalling the band to stop playing. 'We will move our pitch under cover to Ludgate Hill Station. I can't have my little canary catching a cold.'

Lucilla's mouth turned down at the corners. 'I expect I've caught a chill by now. I told you it was too cold and horrible to come out tonight, Pa. But would you listen to me? No, you wouldn't. Just like a man.' She flounced off to join the bandsmen who had formed a huddle, with their instruments tucked beneath their jackets.

'Artistic temperament,' Augustus said in a stage whisper. 'My little Lucilla is a real trouper.'

'Yes, I'm sure.' Clemency started to walk away but Augustus caught her by the hem of her cloak. She stopped. 'What?'

He leaned towards her, lowering his voice. 'My little songbird is rather delicate and easily upset. Have you ever thought of a musical career, Miss Skinner?'

'I sing in the Crown and Anchor most nights.'

'You have an exceptionally good voice. Surprisingly mature for one so young.'

'I ain't so young, mister. I'm eighteen.'

'Really?' Augustus stood back, looking her up and down. 'You could easily pass for twelve or thirteen. With that face and that voice you would tug at the toughest heartstrings.'

'I dunno,' Clemency said, eyeing Lucilla who was cuddling up to the young man who had played the flute.

Augustus put his hand in his pocket and pulled out a coin that shone silver in the lamplight. He pressed the florin into Clemency's cold hand. 'There's money to be made in street entertainment, Miss Skinner. I'm offering you a place in my troupe.'

She shook her head. 'I got a crippled brother to think about and a sick mother too. I can't just up and leave them.'

He delved into his pocket once more and this time he produced a business card. 'This here is our address in Spitalfields. Think about my offer.

You won't do better than to cast your lot in with Augustus Throop and his musical troupe. It has a ring to it, don't you think?' His booming laugh terrified a passing horse so that it reared up in the shafts, almost unseating the carter, who let out a string of expletives.

Clemency nodded. 'I'll think about it.'

Augustus clapped her on the back. 'Splendid. Now we must hie to Ludgate Hill for our next curtain call. Troupe, are we ready?' He strode off, shooing the musicians in front of him like a flock of geese.

As she trudged homewards, carrying the bucket of water, Clemency thought hard about his proposal. The business card was still clutched in her hand, together with the florin that Augustus had given her. On the corner of Knightrider Street she stopped and set the bucket down on the pavement. Before she plunged into the dark gullet of Stew Lane, she needed to know what was written on the card. Peering at it in the light of a street lamp, she wished that she had paid more attention to lessons at the ragged school. She spelt out the address, mouthing the letters, working them into syllables, and finally forming the words: *21 Flower and Dean Street, Spitalfields.* She tucked the card into her skirt pocket, frowning and thinking hard. Spitalfields was a fair way from here, and it was far from Todd Hardiman's usual stamping ground. The florin would pay for a night or two in a respectable lodging house, but if she were to join his troupe, could she rely on Augustus Throop's continued generosity? If they remained in Stew Lane they would be at the mercy of Hardiman. She might be able to add to the money she made picking pockets by singing at the Crown and Anchor, but if Hardiman found out, he would want his cut. His plans for her future filled her with horror. Then there was Jared Stone. He would not have taken her to his drum in Hog Yard if his intentions had been honourable. She knew very little about him, but Stone was a man to be reckoned with, and he had intended to exploit her skill as a pickpocket. Men like Hardiman and Stone thought of women as chattels and objects of pleasure. She had seen what happened to poor Meg, cast off because she was in the family way. That was not going to happen to her. She was not going to be any man's slave. Clemency picked up the bucket and hefted it into the slippery darkness of Stew Lane.

The plaintive sound of Jack's penny whistle filtered through the cracked windowpanes as she clambered down the steps, endeavouring not to spill a drop of the precious water. It was all they would have for drinking and washing until she made another trip to the pump.

Jack looked up as she entered the room. He stopped playing the mournful tune and jerked his head in the direction of Edith, who had curled up in a ball by the fire and was sleeping fitfully. 'She dropped off after a while. I reckon I could get a job as one of them oriental snake charmers.'

His cheerful grin brought a lump to Clemency's throat. There was no hint of reproach in his voice, even though she had been gone for much longer than it would normally have taken to fetch water from the pump. She busied herself by filling the kettle and setting it on the trivet over the glowing embers of the fire. She added the last few lumps of coal. There would be no fire tomorrow, but then they would not be here. She had made up her mind on that score. She went to sit cross-legged on the cold stones next to Jack. 'I got something to tell you. Just hear me out afore you says anything.' In a low voice, she told him of her plan.

Jack listened in silence. His mouth set in a grim line and he stared down at the tin whistle as he twisted it round and round between his slim fingers. He did not look up until she had finished telling him of her plan to join the street entertainers, taking them to the relative safety of Spitalfields.

Looking him in the eye, Clemency felt a cold shudder run down her spine. Never had she seen such a bleak expression in his dark eyes, nor such pain and despair. He turned his head away, saying nothing. Clemency waited, giving him time to control the emotions that were causing his whole body to tremble. At last, he nodded. 'You got to get away from here, girl. I've known that all along. I knew it would come. But you got to leave me and her. There ain't much that Hardiman can do to us that ain't already been done.'

'What are you saying? What nonsense is this, Jack?'

'Save yourself, Clemmie. Go with the theatricals and make a life for yourself.'

She leapt up, resisting the temptation to give him a good shaking. 'What rubbish you do talk, Jack Skinner. I'd as soon cut off me right arm as leave you here. Even Ma don't deserve that fate.'

'Clemmie!' Jack's eyes widened with alarm, and he clutched at the hem of her skirt. 'What are you going to do?'

She yanked the material from his grasp, too fraught with nervous energy to be gentle. 'I'm going to see about getting transport for you and Ma. You make the tea. I'll not be long.'

She snatched up her cloak and hurried from the room, buoyed up with righteous indignation. How could Jack think that she would leave him, or Ma? She ran all the way to the pub in Carter Lane. She burst into the taproom of the Crown and Anchor, dishevelled and breathless, pushing her way through the forest of burly men until she reached the bar.

Ned's face was a picture of surprise and consternation when he saw her. He called to the potman who was collecting up empty tankards, and, leaving him to serve the waiting customers, he lifted the flap in the bar counter. 'What's up, Clemency? Who done that to your face?'

She managed a weak smile, even though it made her lips crack open and bleed. 'I can't talk here. Can we go outside?' She glanced nervously over her shoulder, wondering if there were any of Hardiman's spies amongst the men who crowded round the tables. She went into the street, glancing warily over her shoulder. There were a few stragglers making their way home. A hansom cab went past, sending up a shower of muddy spray, but there were no suspicious characters loitering in shop doorways. Her nerves were throbbing like the plucked strings of a fiddle. She jumped when Ned took her by the shoulders.

'What's happened, Clemency? You can tell me.'

'Oh, Ned! I need help. I was lying when I said we was all right at home. The truth is that me mum is a drinker and me brother is a helpless cripple. There's a man, a bad man, what's got a hold over us and we got to get away from him, double quick. I needs a favour, and I didn't know who to turn to, except you.'

'Who is this bastard?' Ned's jaw hardened and

his eyes narrowed. 'Just say the word and I'll get some of my mates. We'll beat him to a pulp.'

Her fingers curled into a claw as she grasped his bare forearm. 'You don't understand, Ned. Todd Hardiman is dangerous. It would be folly to cross him.'

'Hardiman! I know of him and he's a true villain. Tell me what you want and I'll do it.'

'Jack can't walk. I need a cart or a wheelbarrow, anything with wheels, so that I can get him away from Stew Lane.'

Ned hesitated for a moment, looking down at her as though he would like to argue, then he nodded, and covered her cold fingers with his hand. 'Leave it with me. Just tell me where to find you and what time you wants the cart, and I'll be there.'

It was pitch dark in Stew Lane. Clemency had been waiting at the top of the area steps for what felt like an hour, although it could not have been more than ten minutes, when she heard the approaching rumble of wooden wheels rolling over cobblestones. She had slept very little, and she knew that Jack had spent the night tossing and turning. When Ma had awakened in the early hours, craving a drink and becoming violent, Clemency had given her a cup of cold tea, spiked with the last drops of laudanum left in the brown-glass bottle, which she kept hidden behind a loose brick. Ma had slept then and had remained in a drugged stupor.

In the distance, Clemency counted the strokes of a church clock – one, two, three, four, five – Ned brought the handcart to a halt. He was not alone and Clemency's spine tingled with apprehension, but he grasped her hand and was speaking to her in the soothing tones that he might have used to calm a nervous horse. 'Don't be scared. Connor is a mate. This is his barrow, and he's come to help.'

In the darkness, she could just make out the shape of a short, stocky man. He bowed from the waist, his jerky action putting Clemency in mind of a shadow puppet she had once seen in a booth at a fair, and she had to stifle the sudden urge to giggle. She wiped her sweating palms on her skirt and held out her hand to Connor. 'Pleased to meet you, I'm sure.' To her surprise, he raised her hand to his lips and brushed it with a kiss.

''Tis a pleasure to help a lady in distress.'

'Don't take no notice of him,' Ned said, following Clemency as she felt her way down the steps. 'He can't help flirting with the ladies – he's Irish.'

'I'm grateful to you both. Mind the bottom step, it's a bit rotten.'

Ned jumped the last step but Connor did not seem to have heard and he landed with a dull thud and a muffled curse. Clemency turned to them as she opened the door. 'You might have a bit of difficulty with Ma. She's not quite herself.'

They followed her into the room where Edith lay slumped on her straw palliasse. Clemency felt a moment of embarrassment mingled with shame, but Connor went straight to Edith and hefted her over his shoulder. 'Ah so, isn't this a woman after me own heart? And haven't we all had a drop too much every now and then. I'll make her comfortable on me barrow.'

'Let's hope she don't object to the smell of fish. Connor is on his way to pick up his daily load of haddock and herrings from Billingsgate.' Ned winked at Clemency and then he turned to Jack, holding out his hand. 'How do, Jack. I'm Ned.'

Clemency held her breath, watching Jack's face. She crossed her fingers behind her back, praying that he would not take one of his sudden dislikes to Ned, and refuse all offers of help. Jack was stubborn when it came to his disability: she knew he would rather crawl along on his knuckles than allow himself to be carried like a helpless child. She could have cried with relief when his taut features relaxed into something like a smile and he shook Ned's hand. 'We must leave now, Jack,' she said urgently.

'You'd be surprised how quick I can move when needs be,' Jack said, casting a challenging look at Ned as he hauled his body across the flagstones.

Ned stood back, nodding. 'Just speak out if you needs a hand, old chap.'

Clemency picked up the bundle that contained their few possessions and she smiled at Ned, mutely thanking him for understanding Jack's need to prove his independence. If he was shocked to see Jack walking on his knuckles, relying on the strength he had developed in his shoulders to keep his buttocks from scraping the ground, then he concealed it well. When Jack stopped at the bottom of the steps, Ned stepped forward, hooked his arm over his shoulders, and carried him to the waiting cart. It was done without fuss or pity, and Ned hoisted Jack up beside Edith, who was curled up like a sleeping infant where Connor had laid her on the barrow.

'Where to?' Ned whispered.

'Spitalfields. Flower and Dean Street. I dunno where it is exactly.'

'It's off the Commercial Road, miss,' Connor said. 'I know it well. Didn't I have a pretty young thing that was mad with love for me, living in Frying Pan Alley, not a stone's throw from the street you mention?'

'On we go then, mate.' Ned grabbed one of the handles. 'Let's get away from here while the streets are quiet.'

'I'm so grateful to you,' Clemency said softly, as she walked by his side. 'You done us a big favour and I'll never forget it.'

'Anyone would do the same for a lady in distress.'

A lady! She'd never been called a lady before and it sent a warm glow coursing through Clemency's veins. She quickened her step to keep pace with their long strides; even though it was still a dank predawn, she felt her spirits rise.

It was still dark when they trundled the hand-cart past the Bank of England in Threadneedle Street, but the City was slowly stirring into life. Street sweepers were out in full force, clearing the horse dung from the cobblestones, and a battalion of cleaning women armed with mops and buckets were bustling in and out of the banks and office buildings, scrubbing steps and polishing brass door furniture. Liveried door-men and messengers were arriving at their places of business, and postmen had already begun delivering the early morning mail. Clemency would have been glad to stop for a rest, but Connor and Ned wanted to push on, and she could not argue with that. Putting as much distance as possible between them and Hardiman had been her aim, and they were hardly inconspicuous as they pushed a barrow containing a semi-conscious woman and a young man with withered limbs through the city streets. If Hardiman had put out the word, then his minions would be on the lookout for them.

Soon the streets would be filled with people and clogged with horse-drawn vehicles: they must keep moving.

They were nearing Liverpool Street Station when Edith began to moan and thrash about; Jack had to hold her down or she would have toppled onto the ground. Connor steered the barrow into a side street where a refreshment stall, lit by bright naphtha flares, was selling hot tea and bacon sandwiches. The aroma of frying bacon made Clemency's mouth water and her stomach rumbled.

'I don't know about you good folk,' Connor said, pushing his cap to the back of his head, 'but I'm famished.'

Clemency exchanged worried glances with Jack. She fingered the florin in her pocket, but that was earmarked for their board and lodging. She shook her head. 'You go ahead and get something. We're all right, ain't we, Jack.'

Jack nodded. 'We'll eat later.'

Ned gave them a straight look and then he went up to the counter. 'Five teas, please, mister. And five bacon sandwiches.'

'No, really,' Clemency protested.

'Sure, you look as though you need feeding up, young miss,' Connor said, winking. 'It's Ned's job in life to see that people get fed, so don't you go spoiling his day.'

Before Clemency could answer, Edith raised

herself up on her elbow. 'Where are we? I could murder a drop of gin.'

'A cup of tea will do you more good, Ma,' Jack said, placing his arm around her shoulders. 'And something to eat.'

'Look at me, Jack. I'm shaking all over. Nothing but a drop of tiddley will stop the shakes.'

Ned came over to them carrying two thick china mugs filled with tea. He handed one to Clemency and the other to Jack. 'Is she all right?'

'Young man, for the love of God, get me a drink.' Edith held her hands out to him, her face crumpled like a wet rag.

Clemency tried to give her the mug of tea, but Edith knocked it from her hand with a loud screech that was not quite drowned by the thunder of a steam engine as it roared out of the station. The mug shattered into shards on the pavement, and hot tea trickled into the gutter. She stared at it in horror – now Ned would have to pay for the breakage – and passers-by were staring at the madwoman struggling to get off the handcart.

Connor stepped forward and lifted Edith up as easily as if she had been a toddler. 'Now, missis. Don't take on. Connor will sort you out.' Supporting her with his arm around her waist, he turned to Clemency and Jack. 'It's a drop of the hard stuff she needs. Leave it to me.' Without waiting for an answer, he helped Edith across the street and they disappeared through a pub door.

Clemency glanced anxiously at Ned. 'She's not always like this. It's the move upsetting her.'

Jack pulled a face. 'Don't, Clemmie. He can see she's a hopeless case, and so can Connor.'

'It happens. I see it every day.'

'You're a good fellow, Ned,' Jack said. 'I can't thank you enough for what you're doing for me and Clemmie.'

Ned blushed to the roots of his mouse-brown hair. 'Think nothing of it. I'm glad to help.'

Clemency's heart swelled with gratitude and she threw her arms around his neck, kissing him on the cheek. 'You've saved our lives and I'll never ever forget it.'

She felt a tremor run through him, and there was a startled look in his eyes that was replaced almost instantly with puzzlement; he was staring at her as if he had seen her for the first time. She pulled away, wondering if she had offended him somehow.

'Three teas and five bacon sandwiches.' The vendor's voice boomed out from the stall.

Ned jumped visibly, and he strode off to collect the food.

'What's wrong with him?' Clemency turned to Jack for an explanation. 'What did I do to upset him?'

Chapter Four

When Jack merely shrugged his shoulders, Clemency was even more baffled. She did not pursue the topic as Ned was making his way back to them with the tea and sandwiches. She went to help him, and was relieved when he smiled at her. She decided that she must have been imagining things, and sank her teeth into the twin doorsteps of bread that encased two rashers of crisp bacon. She chewed, savoured and swallowed; this was food heaven. Surely the old queen herself could not have enjoyed a more delicious breakfast? She sat down on the pavement, resting her back against the cold brick wall behind her, and in between mouthfuls of the sandwich, she sipped the hot, sweet tea. Those leaves were freshly brewed, if she was not mistaken. She glanced up at Jack, seated like a king on the cart, and she could tell from his expression that he too was enjoying every mouthful.

When every last crumb was eaten and she had drained the mug of tea, she licked her fingers and wiped them on her skirt. She jumped to her feet as her flagging energy was revived by a full stomach. She could conquer the world after a breakfast like that. Connor and Edith had emerged from the pub and were crossing the street arm in arm. To her surprise, Clemency saw that Ma was laughing at something that he had said and, if she was not actually walking straight, she was not staggering like a drunken crab. Connor lifted her onto the barrow next to Jack. It seemed to Clemency, in that moment, that a miracle had happened. There were spots of colour in Ma's cheeks and her eyes sparkled. She was laughing and the careworn lines on her face seemed to have been erased. She looked ten years younger, and almost pretty.

'That was fine fun,' Connor said, biting a chunk from his sandwich. 'But we must get on or I'll not get me day's stock of fresh fish from the market.'

Dawn was just breaking when they finally arrived in Flower and Dean Street. The sky above Brick Lane had faded from ash-grey to the delicate blue-green of a duck egg, and particles of frost glittered on the paving stones. The street was quiet in contrast to the early morning bustle of the Commercial Road, but Clemency knew they were dangerously close to Hanbury Street, where Jack the Ripper had attacked, killed and mutilated the prostitute, Annie Chapman. That terrible crime had happened just a few months ago, in September, and there had been two more murders in the same month; one in Berner Street and the other in Mitre Square. They were in Ripper territory and Clemency couldn't help looking over her shoulder, half afraid that the shadowy figure was going to leap out from a doorway, or suddenly appear at the top of an area steps.

'This looks like it. Number twenty-one, wasn't it, Clemency?' Ned looked up at a tall, narrow house in the middle of the grim, smoke-blackened terrace. 'This ain't much of a place, if you ask me.'

'It's the address he give me,' Clemency said, trying to sound positive, when all she really wanted to do was run away. She could not help wondering whether she had done the right thing in coming here. Flower and Dean Street, Spitalfields. It had sounded wonderful when she had spelt out the address on Throop's card, and in her mind's eye she had pictured a country field spiked with scarlet poppies and white daisies, but the reality was starkly different. If the financial heart of the City was getting ready to begin a new day's trading, it was just the opposite here, where it was still the depth of night. At intervals along the street there were bodies slumped in doorways, either dead or sleeping, no one seemed to care which. Feral cats were out hunting the rats that scavenged amongst the heaps of rotting rubbish. A little way down the street, women who were probably no better than they should be were staggering up the steps into cheap lodging houses, looking very much the worse for wear. This was indeed a terrible place, but she would not let Ned or Jack see how it depressed her. She managed a smile. 'I'm sure Mr Throop wouldn't have chosen to live here if the house weren't clean and respectable.'

'Sure, I've been in worse places,' Connor said, helping Edith from the handcart.

'I don't like leaving you here.' Ned laid his hand on Clemency's arm, his face puckered with concern. 'If I'd realised it was so close to Hanbury Street, where the Ripper done in that Chapman woman, I'd never have agreed to bring you here.'

Edith gave a low moan. 'What have you brought us to, Clemmie? We'd be better off with Hardiman than the Ripper.'

'The police will catch them both,' Jack said stoutly, working his way to the edge of the cart. 'They ain't got nothing on Hardiman yet, but it's only a matter of time afore the mad bugger beats some poor woman's brains out.'

'Jack's right, Ma,' Clemency said, making an effort to sound cheerful. 'We're here now, so let's make the best of it.' She turned to Ned and Connor. 'I dunno what else to say but ta, ever so.'

Ned shifted from one foot to the other, a dull flush rising from his neck to his cheeks. 'I ain't sure we've done you a favour, bringing you to this place.'

'Don't worry about us. We'll be fine.' Clemency shook his hand, not wanting to embarrass him with a kiss. She held her hand out to Connor. 'I won't forget what you done for us, Mr Connor.'

'Nor I,' Edith said, slanting a look at him beneath her eyelashes.

Connor took off his cap and held it to his chest. 'It's Michael, so it is. Mickey to me friends. I'll be off now, but don't be surprised to see me turn up again one of these days, Edie.'

Jack gave a polite cough. 'Help me down, Ned, there's a good fellow. Before the mad Irishman takes me back to Billingsgate and I end up under a pile of wet herrings.'

'Well, it would give me an excuse to come back, now wouldn't it?' Connor winked at Edith and, as Ned lifted Jack to the pavement, he grabbed the handles and spun the cart round to face the Commercial Road. He rammed his cap on his head. 'Are you coming, Ned?'

'I'm coming.' Ned grasped Clemency's hands. He squeezed her fingers, looking earnestly into her eyes. 'If you need help you know where to come.'

She smiled. 'You're a pal and no mistake.'

'You will take care of yourself, won't you? Whatever you do, don't go out alone at night.'

'I won't.' She pulled her hands free, pointing down the street. 'You'd best run or you'll not catch the Irishman.'

Ned opened his mouth as if to say something, but he closed it again, shaking his head, and hurried off after Connor.

Clemency held up a warning hand as Edith tried to follow her up the steps. 'No, Ma. I dunno if the geezer was serious about taking me on. You two wait here while I go in and have a word.'

'This place is the devil's midden. We'd have been better off staying in Stew Lane.' Reluctantly, Edith went to sit on the bottom step next to Jack. 'Don't take too long, or we'll freeze to death out here.'

Clemency rattled the doorknocker. She could hear brisk footsteps clattering on a tiled floor. The door opened and she was faced with a tall, middle-aged woman who was all points and angles. Her grey hair was caught up in a tight bun on the top of her head, emphasising her pointed chin, and a triangle of a nose that would not have looked out of place on the wooden face of a puppet. She stood, arms akimbo, staring at Clemency over the top of steel-rimmed spectacles. 'What sort of hour do you call this to knock on the door of a respectable lodging house?'

'I – I come to see Mr Augustus Throop.'

Clemency pulled his card from her pocket and held it out for inspection.

'Come inside. Stand on the mat. Don't move from that spot.'

Clemency did as she was told. She stood on the doormat and watched the angular woman march away into the unlit part of the house. The flickering gas mantle gave off a yellowish light and the distinctive odour of coal gas. Clemency shivered. It was as cold inside as it was outside, and just as cheerless. She could just make out a steep flight of stairs rising into blackness, but there were no signs of life, and it seemed that the occupants of the house must still be asleep. After a minute or two the silence was broken by the sound of heavy footsteps. Augustus Throop came steaming towards her with his nightcap askew on his head, and his dressing gown flying open to reveal a long nightshirt.

'Who wakes me at this godforsaken hour?' He stopped in front of her, staring through half-closed eyes as he knotted the tasselled cord of his robe. 'Who are you?'

'I'm the girl what sung for you last evening in Knightrider Street. You give me your card. Remember?'

Augustus scratched his head. 'Can't say that I do. However, at this early hour of the morning, I can barely remember my own name, let alone a face in the crowd.'

'But mister, you said I could join your troupe. I got the voice of a nightingale, you said as much.'

'Nightingale, blackbird, crow – it's all the same to me until I've had my first cup of coffee. Follow me, young lady. We'll prevail on the good Mrs Blunt to let us partake of her excellent brew.' Augustus swept off with a theatrical flourish, beckoning to Clemency as he headed off into the gloom.

She followed him along the passage and down a flight of stairs into the basement kitchen. The aroma of hot coffee and baking bread sent signals to her stomach, whetting her appetite, despite the bacon sandwich that she had enjoyed less than an hour ago.

'My dear Mrs Blunt.' Augustus held out his arms. 'What a perfect sight with which to begin a new day. Behold, Miss – er . . .'

'Clemency Skinner.'

'Miss Skinner, behold this woman, our esteemed landlady – the veritable epitome of womanhood, encompassed in one lissom body.'

Mrs Blunt took off her specs, huffed on them and wiped the lenses on her starched apron. 'Piffle, sir. Twaddle! And I'll thank you not to mention me body, it ain't seemly, especially in front of a young girl.'

'I humbly beg your pardon, ma'am. I was merely praising your housekeeping and wondering if there might be a cup of coffee for a thirsty thespian and his young visitor.'

'You theatricals is all the same. Words, words and more words.' Mrs Blunt sniffed, and the pointed end of her nose quivered. She turned to a girl who was sweeping the floor with a besom. 'Fancy, two cups of coffee.'

Fancy dropped the broom and hurried to the range where she picked up a large earthenware jug, which she set on the scrubbed deal table while she bustled over to the dresser to fetch the cups. Augustus sat on one of the forms set on either side of the table, and motioned to Clemency to take a seat.

'Breakfast ain't until seven o'clock,' Mrs Blunt informed them as she headed towards the staircase. 'And if she's looking for a room, you can tell the young person, Mr Throop, that I don't encourage unattached females to take a room in my establishment. This is a respectable house and I'll thank you to remember that.' She swept up the stairs with a swish of starched petticoats.

As she disappeared through the baize door at the top of the stairs, Clemency uttered a sigh of relief. It seemed as though she had been holding her breath ever since she first clapped eyes on the angular Mrs Blunt. She sat down opposite Augustus. 'I got a good voice, you said so yourself. And I wouldn't want much in the way of pay, just me room and board, until I proved meself, like.'

'My daughter Lucilla is my little canary; she has the face of an angel and the temperament of a prima donna.'

'But you said I got the voice of a nightingale. You did, mister.'

Fancy placed two cups of coffee on the table in front of Augustus. She did not resume her work immediately, but stood with her head angled, staring at Clemency.

'What are you staring at?' Clemency demanded.

'Nightingale, huh!' Fancy tossed her head. 'Blooming cockney sparrow, more like.'

'You take that back.'

'Shan't.'

'Cockney sparrow,' Augustus said, rolling the words round in his mouth as if they were made of chocolate. 'I like it. Maybe I could use you, Miss Skinner.'

Clemency stuck her tongue out at Fancy. She knew it was childish, but she couldn't resist the temptation. Fancy turned away with a disgusted snort. She picked up the broom and went about the floor whisking dust out of sight beneath the dresser.

Augustus rose to his feet and struck a pose. 'It might make a striking contrast – the street urchin, a cockney sparrow – singing a duet with my fragile flower.'

'Fragile flower, my eye,' Fancy muttered beneath her breath.

Clemency couldn't help agreeing with her. From what she had seen of Miss Lucilla, fragile and flower-like were not the words she would have used to describe the spoilt little barrel of lard. But she would work with the devil himself if it gave them a roof over their head. She eyed Augustus cautiously. 'So you'll take me on then?'

'A trial period of one week should be ample time to see if our takings increase.'

'And I gets board and lodging?'

'You may share a room with Lucilla, although you will have to sleep on the floor.'

Fancy sniggered and then turned it into a cough. Clemency ignored her. She stood up, clasping her hands in front of her. 'I needs a room of me own, Mr Throop, sir.'

'Impossible.'

'But – but I snore something terrible, sir.' Clemency shot a warning look at Fancy, who turned away with her shoulders shaking silently. 'I couldn't deprive the young lady of her sleep, now could I?'

Augustus stroked his chin, frowning. 'I can hardly put you in with the men – that wouldn't be seemly, as Mrs Blunt so aptly puts it.' He turned his head to stare thoughtfully at Fancy. 'I don't suppose . . .'

'Don't look at me. I'd sooner share with a pig,' Fancy said, waving the besom at him. 'Anyhow, I'm just a skivvy. I sleeps on a mat by the fire, in case you hadn't noticed, guv.'

'A room of me own, sir,' Clemency repeated. 'Or I shall have to take up the offer of the other lot what offered me a job.' She had no idea if there were any more bands of street entertainers, but it was worth a try.

Augustus stared at her in horror. 'They made you an offer? They were trespassing on my territory?'

Clemency nodded.

'A room you shall have. I'll go and find Mrs Blunt and arrange it right away.'

The room that Mrs Blunt allocated to Clemency was little more than a large cupboard at the rear of the kitchen. A small window set high in the wall, with a pigeon's-eye view of the area steps, allowed in just enough light to reveal the outline of objects stacked against the brick walls, and a half-glassed door led out into the area. The floor space had been used to store mops and brooms, buckets and articles that were disused, but might come in useful later, together with sacks of flour and potatoes. Rats and mice had obviously been nibbling at the hessian, creating gaping holes and leaving telltale paw prints in the dust. Clemency's heart sank as she gazed round the room; it looked like a junkyard. The air was thick with dust and the putrid smell of rotten potatoes, but it was not as damp as the basement room in Stew Lane, and was free from the stench of rising sewage. It would have to do until she could find better accommodation.

Mrs Blunt ordered Fancy to seek alternative cupboard space for the useful articles, and to sweep up the mouse droppings and the dried carapaces of dead cockroaches. Fancy obliged, grumbling all the while beneath her breath, and making it clear whom she blamed for causing her the extra work. Clemency was left to heft the sacks into the kitchen, which Mrs Blunt said would be a better storage place anyway, as it would be more difficult for the rats and mice to get at them.

'You'll have to share with the rats,' Fancy whispered, as Clemency dragged the last sack of potatoes into the kitchen. 'I bet it won't be the first time you've slept with a rat, Miss Sparrow.'

Clemency tossed her head. 'I'd rather sleep with a dozen rats than share with you, ferret-face.'

'Sparrow-legs.'

Clemency did not dignify this with a retort. She was much too worried about Jack and Ma, waiting outside in the freezing cold, wondering whether or not they would have a roof over their heads tonight. Fancy stomped off but returned a few minutes later with her arms full of bedding. She dropped a flock mattress, some patched blankets and a couple of pillows in a heap on the floor. 'I dunno why you should get your own room. I been here ten years, since I was took from the orphanage, and I still has to sleep on the floor by the range.' She flounced into the kitchen and slammed the door, as if to underline her discontent.

Clemency could wait no longer. She went out into the area and ran up the stone steps. She found Jack, seated on the ground playing a tune on his whistle; Ma was huddled on the bottom step with her head tucked between her knees.

'I got us a room, Jack. It ain't much of a place, but until Mr Throop says I definitely got a job, I didn't dare to tell him about you and Ma. Not yet, anyway.'

Jack stopped playing and smiled, pointing to his cap that lay in front of him. 'Twopence, Clemmie. All in farthings, but it'll buy us some bread and maybe some dripping.'

'Let me help you down the steps. Then I'll see to her.' Clemency jerked her head in the direction of Edith, who appeared to have fallen asleep curled up like a robin with its head under its wing.

'I can manage, ta.' Jack tucked his tin whistle into his pocket and reached for his cap. 'You see to Ma.'

She went to wake Edith.

'You should have left me to sleep,' Edith grumbled. 'I would have slipped away peaceful, just like them stiffs they find in shop doorways, frozen to death.'

'Stop it, Ma. Don't talk like that.' Clemency helped her to her feet. 'I got us a room.'

'I can't walk. I can't feel me feet. Oh, Gawd, I got frostbite for sure.'

'No, Ma. Just put one foot in front of the other and I'll help you down the steps.'

'Not another blooming basement.'

'Come on, one little step at a time.'

'I could murder a drink. Me throat is so parched I could spit feathers.'

'I'll get you a cup of tea from the kitchen. Just be quiet, Ma.'

'Tea! I meant gin, or a drop of porter.'

Clemency remembered the florin that lay untouched in her pocket. Since they weren't paying rent for the room, she could spend it on food for Ma and Jack. 'Maybe I can get a drop of Hollands for you, but only if you keep quiet and don't let no one know you're in me room.'

It took some time to get Edith down the steps, but when Clemency finally got her into the room she found that Jack had settled himself on a corner of the mattress. Even in the dim light, she could see that his expression was grim.

'It's just temporary,' she said, lowering Edith

down beside him. 'And at least we're safe from Hardiman. He'll never find us here.'

'It's not right, Clemmie,' Jack said, shaking his head. 'You shouldn't have to bear the burden of the two of us. What happens if we're discovered? You'll lose your job for sure. And the worst of it is, I can't do nothing to help.' He thumped his hand down on the ticking and a spurt of dust flew up in the air.

'Shut up, Jack. This is just the start. When I gets in well with old Throop, I'll introduce you and your tin whistle. You're a better musician than the bloke what plays the flute. Why, I bet if you had a fine instrument like that, you could charm the pigeons down off the lions in Trafalgar Square.'

Edith leaned back against the brick wall and closed her eyes. 'Never mind all the chitchat, fetch us that cup of tea, Clemmie, love. Me head's splitting.'

'All right, Ma. But please keep quiet. Mrs Blunt mustn't find out you're here or we'll all be out on the street.' Without waiting to see what effect her words had, Clemency opened the door and went into the kitchen.

To her surprise, the room was now crammed with people. Some of them were seated on the forms at the table, eating their breakfast, and others were standing about, drinking coffee and chatting. At the far end of the room, two young women were practising their dance steps, doing high kicks and showing their knickers, to the obvious enjoyment of the men seated at the table. Augustus was halfway down the stairs that led to the hall, and behind him came Lucilla with her blonde hair still tied up in rags and a sulky expression on her red lips. The rest of the band were already seated with their heads down, stuffing bread, cheese and cold meat into their mouths as if their lives depended upon it.

'Ah, there you are Miss Clemency.' Augustus stopped on the bottom step, causing Lucilla to bump into him.

'Oh, Daddy!'

'Look where you're going, my little poppet. You trod on Papa's heel and these are my best patent leather shoes.' He advanced towards Clemency, beaming so broadly that his eyes almost disappeared into his florid cheeks. 'As soon as we have broken our fast, Miss Clemency, we will give you a proper audition.' He waved his arms as if embracing everyone in the kitchen. 'You see, my dear. Most of these good people are fellow artistes, and who better to judge whether you have the makings of a real trouper?'

A desultory round of applause followed his speech, which Augustus acknowledged with a smile and a bow. He held his hand out to Lucilla and led her to a space at the table next to the man whom Clemency recognised as the flautist.

Lucilla slumped down on the bench beside him and he slid his arm around her waist.

'Fancy, my little ray of sunshine, be so good as to bring me the coffeepot.' Augustus pulled up a chair and sat at the head of the table. He beckoned to Clemency. 'Have you sampled Mrs Blunt's culinary masterpiece? I speak of bread, soft, chewy, mouth-watering bread hot from the oven, and jam. Plum jam made by the same fair hands, using purple plums picked in the garden of England.'

'Shut up, Daddy,' Lucilla said, cramming a hunk of Cheddar cheese into her mouth. 'You're making a spectacle of yourself.'

'Sorry, my pet. I couldn't hear that remark through the half pound of Cheddar you have just forced into your mouth. Cheese is the enemy of the singer's vocal cords. You should eat honey, my little canary. Honey straight from the comb. Here, Fancy, hurry up with that coffee.'

Clemency stood watching the performance. One of the dancers had her foot on the mantelshelf while she poured tea into a mug. How she got her leg up there was a mystery to Clemency: it didn't look natural to split a body that way. The other girl was bent double, touching her toes with her bum stuck up in the air – folded in two like a hairpin. Whatever would they do next? Fancy hurried over to fill Augustus's cup with coffee and she was smiling. What a difference a smile made, Clemency thought, staring at her. She was really quite nice-looking when her face was not screwed up as if she had been sucking lemons.

Augustus buttered a slice of bread and spread it with jam. He bit into it with relish and washed it down with a mouthful of hot coffee. For a moment, Clemency thought that he had forgotten about her. No one else seemed to be bothered whether she was there or not. Even Fancy was ignoring her, which suited her very well. She went to the range and poured tea into a mug, adding milk and three heaped teaspoonfuls of sugar. She was about to take it in to her mother, when Augustus called her name.

'Miss Clemency. I'm ready to audition you.'

Suddenly nervous, Clemency set the mug down on a shelf.

'Over here, girl. I can't hear you if you hover by the door.' Augustus pointed to an empty space on the bench. 'Jump up there, my dear. And give us your best.'

It felt to Clemency as though she were wading knee deep in the river, as her legs turned to lead and she made her way to the table. The drummer offered his hand to help her up on the form. 'You show 'em, miss,' he said, and his waxed moustache seemed to move of its own accord as he smiled up at her.

'Ta, mister, er . . .'

'Ronnie, miss. Ronnie Briggs. Don't be nervous, you can do it.'

Clemency wished she were as certain about her ability as Ronnie. She stood there, gazing down at the expectant faces turned towards her, and her throat went dry. She licked her lips.

'What's the matter?' Lucilla demanded, her pretty mouth disfigured by a spiteful sneer. 'Cat got your tongue?'

Last night it had been so easy to take up the tune where Lucilla had left off, and when she had jumped on the table in the Crown and Anchor, it had seemed the most natural thing in the world to open her mouth and sing. She cleared her throat again but her voice cracked on the first note. She couldn't remember the words or the tune of 'Come into the Garden Maud' – she tried again, but the sound came out in a hoarse croak. Lucilla was laughing and Clemency could see Fancy leaning against the wall with her arms folded across her chest.

'Call yourself a nightingale,' Lucilla said, curling her lip. 'I've heard sparrows sing better than what you can.'

'Cor blimey,' Fancy said, giggling. 'A cockney sparrow.'

Everyone laughed, although Clemency could see that some of the men looked uncomfortable. She tried again, but she had lost the tune. Then, without warning, she heard the clear silver tones of Jack's tin whistle as he played the introduction. They had often performed this song together. She looked across the room, and her heart missed a beat as she saw him sitting in the doorway. There was a stunned silence and all heads turned to stare at him.

It was too late to stop him – now all the lodgers knew of Jack's existence, even if they did not know who he was. He had appeared, as if by magic, and he played the introduction again.

This time she hit the right note. Clasping her hands in front of her, Clemency threw back her head and sang to Jack's accompaniment. When the song ended, she had the satisfaction of seeing Augustus wipe a tear from the corner of his eyes, and the sneer had left Lucilla's face.

'Encore!' One of the dancers called out, clapping her hands.

Soon everyone was clapping, everyone except Fancy. She was staring down at Jack with a rapt expression on her face. Clemency leapt down from the bench, ignoring the calls for a repeat performance. She ran to Jack's side, ready to take on anyone who dared to laugh at him or call him names. With her hands fisted, she glared at Fancy, daring her to mock him.

But Fancy was staring at Jack with open admiration transforming her features and a smile curving her lips. 'That were lovely,' she said softly. 'But who the hell are you?'

Before Clemency could speak, Jack had shaken Fancy's hand. 'How do, miss. I'm Jack Skinner, and this here is my little sister.'

'You don't say!' Fancy cast a sideways glance at Clemency. 'Who'd have guessed the cockney sparrow was related to a good-looking cove like you.'

For a moment, Clemency thought that she was making fun of him, and she was ready to scratch the bitch's eyes out, but even as she clawed her fingers, she realised that Fancy was in earnest. Her smile was genuine. She had looked at Jack and seen the man, not the cripple. She had heard his music and it had struck a chord in her, touching her deep down inside. Clemency sniffed and dashed her hand across her eyes.

'That was indeed a virtuoso performance, Miss Clemency.' Augustus had left the table and was standing by her side. She looked at him dumbly, too filled with emotion to speak. 'I'd be proud to include you in my musical troupe,' Augustus said, wiping the jam off his lips with a spotted handkerchief. 'As to you young man,' he looked down at Jack, 'you have great talent. It's a pity you have no legs.'

Clemency punched Augustus on the arm. 'Here, you can't talk to me brother like that.'

'No offence meant. I was stating a point. To be a wandering street musician, one must be able to walk. Otherwise I might have considered taking both of you under my professional wing.'

'Daddy!' Lucilla's voice echoed round the kitchen. 'Tom Fall plays the flute in our ensemble. We don't need no one else. And she don't sing as well as I do, does she, Tom?'

Tom looked doubtful for a moment, but, noting the lines deepen between Lucilla's fair eyebrows, he shrugged and patted her bottom. 'You're the nightingale, love.'

Augustus shot an angry glance at Tom, but Clemency tugged at his sleeve. 'Never mind him, mister. Have I got a job or haven't I?'

He glanced down at her. 'I've said so. Augustus Throop doesn't go back on his word.' He made a threatening motion with his fist at Tom. 'Don't let me see you taking liberties with my little girl, Tom.'

'No, guv,' Tom replied, winking at Lucilla. 'I won't let you see me.'

Clemency saw that this could turn into a full-scale battle, and she tugged again at Augustus's sleeve. 'And you won't tell Mrs B about Jack?'

'What are you talking about, girl? What should I not tell Mrs Blunt?'

'What indeed, Mr Throop?' Mrs Blunt stood at the top of the stairs, staring at Jack and quivering from the top of her bun to the pointed toes of her black boots. 'What is going on? Get that creature out of my house at once. I don't take in fairground folk or freaks.'

Chapter Five

'Freak! Who are you calling a freak?' Edith pushed past Jack. She pointed a shaking finger at Mrs Blunt. 'You – woman. I'm speaking to you.'

There was a moment of silence as everyone stopped what they were doing, and all heads turned to stare at Edith. She stood over Jack snarling like a tigress protecting her cub. Her flame-coloured hair hung in snake-like strands around her face, seeming to leach the colour from her pale skin. Her eyes burned with the ferocity of a madwoman and she was trembling from head to foot. Clemency seized her by the arm in an attempt to quieten her, but Edith thrust her away and advanced slowly on Mrs Blunt, who retreated back up the stairs. 'My son ain't no freak,' Edith cried with passion in her voice. 'He was struck with a terrible illness when he was a nipper. It took the strength from his legs but not from his heart. He's worth ten of every man present here.'

Edith swayed on her feet and Clemency had to support her. She cast a fearful glance at Mrs

Blunt, certain that they were all about to be forced out onto the street.

'Shame on you, Mrs Blunt.' A voice from the table broke the silence. The cry was taken up in a chorus of blame. 'Shame! Shame! Shame!' The sound of hands drumming a slow beat on the table made the rafters shake.

Mrs Blunt covered her ears with her hands and the tip of her nose quivered. 'Stop, stop. This is my house and I'll evict you all if you don't stop that noise.'

Augustus stepped forward. He held his hand up for silence, and placed his arm around Edith's shoulders. 'Come now, madam. We must show some respect for our good landlady.'

The drumming and chanting ceased, and Mrs Blunt came slowly down the stairs, but it was obvious to Clemency that her confidence was shaken; she almost felt sorry for her. 'Please, ma'am,' she said. 'Don't throw no one out on our account. I know I should have asked permission to bring me mum and brother into the house, but I was scared that you'd say no. We'll leave directly.'

Mrs Blunt opened her mouth to speak, but her lips moved wordlessly, as if she had lost the power of speech.

'No one is to leave,' Augustus said firmly. 'Mrs Blunt, I will undertake to pay the board and lodging of this family, until they can afford to support themselves. If anyone can recognise talent, then it is I, Augustus Throop. This young girl and her brother are a find, madam. A true find. And they should not be cast out into the cold, cold snow because of the young man's infirmity.' He released his grip on Edith and raised his hands in a theatrical gesture of supplication to Mrs Blunt, which was greeted with another round of applause.

Clemency held her breath as a multitude of emotions crossed Mrs Blunt's face. Was she going to lose the chance of a lifetime? If they were thrown out onto the street they had nowhere to go but the workhouse. Being the best pickpocket in London was not going to save Ma and Jack from destitution. She willed Mrs Blunt to reconsider.

Mrs Blunt nodded slowly. 'Very well, Mr Throop. But on your own head be it. I'll allow them to stay for a week. The woman and the girl can sleep in the attic, but the cripple will have to stay in the back room. I can't say fairer than that.'

Edith lurched forward, but Clemency held her back. 'Leave it, Ma.'

'She can't talk about my boy like that.'

'Hush, Ma. We've got a place to stay. Be thankful for it.'

Augustus hurried to the foot of the stairs. 'You are a just woman, Mrs Blunt. Augustus Throop thanks you for your wisdom and charity.'

'Charity be blowed,' Edith hissed. 'I need a drink.'

Clemency hurried her from the room and made her sit down on the mattress. 'I'll fetch you some tea. Stay there and don't move.'

Edith drew her knees up to her chest, wrapping her arms around her legs. 'I'm so cold, Clemmie.'

'Here, wrap this round you,' Clemency said, handing her Nell's old cloak. 'I'll be back in a couple of ticks.' She went into the kitchen to find Jack sitting in the chair that Augustus had vacated at the head of the table. Fancy was pouring coffee into his cup and he had a plate of cold meat and cheese in front of him. He looked up and smiled at Clemency. 'This is a turn up for the books.'

It was so good to see him looking happy that Clemency had to turn her head away so that he would not see the tears welling up in her eyes. She had thought she was so tough and hard, having grown up on the streets, and here she was, crying like a baby because their luck had changed. She sniffed and poured fresh tea into a cup. She added a generous amount of sugar and took it to Edith. 'Here you are. I'll bring you some food in a bit.'

'I couldn't eat, ducks. Me stomach is burning for a nip of gin. You couldn't pop to the pub on the corner, could you?'

'Later, but first I got to sort things out with Mr Throop. I need to start work as soon as I can if we're to pay our way.' She left Edith with her hands wrapped around the cup, sipping her tea. In the kitchen, Jack was tucking into his meal with Fancy hovering at his side, ready to replenish his plate or refill his cup with coffee. Everyone else had left the room, with the exception of Augustus, Ronnie, Tom and Lucilla, who was tugging the rags from her hair, and dropping them in a heap on the table.

'But, my little jewel, you will still be my star performer,' Augustus said, patting her on the head.

'Give over, Daddy. You'll ruin me curls. I don't want her singing against me. I've always been the main attraction.'

'And you still are, my love. No one can touch my little princess when it comes to warbling a ditty.'

'I don't warble. I'm a soprano like Dorabella Darling. Why, I bet I could out-sing that simpering ninny any day of the week, given a chance. And I don't want her competing with me.' Lucilla shot a darkling look at Clemency.

'Lucy's right, guv,' Tom said. 'She's the star. You can't have two nightingales singing their heads off. It wouldn't look right.'

'It would end up in a cat fight with hair-pulling and all the things girls do.' Ronnie cast an apologetic smile at Clemency. 'No offence meant, miss.'

She glanced anxiously at Jack. He stopped eating and leaned forward, addressing Augustus. 'You may not be able to have two nightingales, Mr Throop. But how about a nightingale and a sparrow?' He winked at Clemency.

Lucilla shook her head. 'It don't matter what you call her, she'll still try to upstage me, Daddy.'

Ronnie cleared his throat. 'Ahem. If it would look wrong to have two young ladies singing against each other, then how would it look if one of them was dressed as a boy?'

'A boy?' Augustus stared thoughtfully at Clemency. 'She is small enough to pass as a young lad.'

'She looks like a boy, you mean, Daddy,' Lucilla said, pulling a face at Clemency. 'Her chest is so flat you could eat your dinner off it.'

'I'd rather be mistaken for a boy than a tub of lard,' Clemency countered.

'Now, now, ladies.' Augustus held up his hands, scowling at Tom and Ronnie, who were openly chuckling at this exchange of cattiness. 'It might work at that. We could give it a try.'

'What if I says no?' Clemency whispered in Jack's ear.

'Think about it, Clemmie. If you go singing on

the streets, sooner or later you're going to bump into Hardiman. He's not going to recognise you so easily if you're togged up like a boy.'

'I'd like to see you dressed as a boy.' Tom pinched Lucilla's bottom. 'I bet you've got a lovely pair of legs under all them skirts.'

Lucilla slapped his face. 'Keep your hands to yourself, Tom Fall.'

'Quiet,' Augustus roared. 'All of you. How can a man think when you're creating such a hubbub?' He turned to Clemency and his expression softened. 'Miss Clemency, I didn't mean to offend you. You're a very pretty young lady, but you would make a charming boy. I'm certain you could put such pathos into cockney songs such as "The Ratcatcher's Daughter" and "The Soldier's Tear" that you would melt the hardest heart.'

'I can do pathos, Daddy,' Lucilla wailed.

'Shut up, daughter.'

Gasping in surprise, Lucilla dwindled into a heap of curls and frills. Quite obviously, Clemency thought, with some satisfaction, the spoilt brat was unused to being scolded. Now was her chance! If she didn't take it they would be back on the streets. She smiled up at Augustus. 'I don't know them songs, guv. But I'll give it a go.'

'Well said.' Augustus slapped her on the back. 'Now we must find you some suitable clothing, and begin rehearsals. That is, if we're to be ready to perform on the streets tonight.'

'Tonight?' Clemency was about to tell him it was impossible, when she saw the triumphant gleam return to Lucilla's eyes. She could do it – she would do it. 'You're on!'

Lucilla's smile drooped into a pout.

Augustus rose to his feet. 'Lucilla, fetch the sheet music from my room. Tom, make yourself useful for once. There's a dollyshop in Petticoat Lane: go there now and get a pair of breeches, a shirt, a jacket and some boots that would fit Miss Clemency.' He drew some coins from his pocket. 'And I want some change.'

Tom took the money. 'I ain't no wardrobe mistress. How am I to know what will fit her?'

'Just say they're for your young brother, and he's a skinny little lad of twelve or thirteen. It don't matter if they fit badly: that will make her all the more appealing. Now get going or do I have to boot you up the arse?'

Tom went off muttering.

'If good flute players weren't as hard to find as hens' teeth, I'd send that young chap packing. Now then, Clemency, or Clem as I shall call you from now on, let us begin. Ronnie will accompany you on his drum and perhaps young Jack would be kind enough to play the melody on his tin whistle.'

Clemency looked to Jack, who gave her an

encouraging smile. She was still not sure that this was going to work. Singing in the pub was one thing, but dressing up as a boy was a shocking idea. No decent girl would expose her legs above the ankle, unless they were like those dancers from the Pavilion Theatre; but they performed on the stage, not wandering half-naked amongst the London crowds. Clemency stood, undecided, watching Augustus supervise Ronnie who was moving tables and benches to the far end of the kitchen, out of Fancy's way. It seemed as though they were being swept along on the tidal wave of Augustus's enthusiasm, helpless and adrift like the flotsam on the Thames. She was beginning to feel that picking pockets was the easy option.

The situation worsened when Lucilla returned with the sheet music and thrust it into Clemency's hands. She pretended to study the words, but the letters danced up and down in front of her eyes, darting about the page like hundreds of tiny tadpoles. She tried to catch Jack's attention with a mute plea for help, but he was intent on learning the tune as he listened to Ronnie beating out the rhythm on his drum and humming the melody. With his quick musical ear, Jack picked up the tune within minutes, but Clemency was still struggling to form the letters into words.

Lucilla snatched the song sheets from her hands with an impatient groan. 'Give it here. I'll show you what a true professional can do.' She threw back her head, took a deep breath and gave a stirring rendition of 'The Ratcatcher's Daughter': a tragic tale of a girl who sold sprats in the street, and her star-crossed love for a vendor of white sand. Resisting the temptation to wipe the condescending smile off Lucilla's plump face with a slap, Clemency knew that she had to listen at least once again in order to remember the words. She sat on her itching hands and forced a smile. 'That were lovely. Can you sing it again?'

Lucilla stared at her suspiciously and then she tossed her curls so that they bounced around her head like tightly coiled watch springs. 'Did you hear that, Daddy? The sparrow admits that I've got the best voice.'

Augustus puffed out his chest. 'No doubt about that, petal. Let her hear you sing the ditty once more.'

By the time Tom returned with the second-hand clothes, Clemency had learned the whole of 'The Ratcatcher's Daughter' and 'The Soldier's Tear'. Jack had no difficulty at all in picking up the tunes, even though he freely admitted that he could not read music. Augustus did not seem to think the worse of him for this. Clemency could see that Fancy was more than impressed, despite the fact that she was in deep trouble with Mrs Blunt, who scolded her volubly for watching the rehearsal when she ought to have been preparing the vegetables for supper. Fancy suffered a clout round the head that would have felled a grown man, let alone a slip of a girl. Clemency could see that this angered Jack, but she thought that Fancy deserved to be taken down a peg or two. Now if Augustus were to give Lucilla a good thumping, it would make her even happier.

The clothes that Tom had bought in the dollyshop smelled horrible, and a shower of fleas spattered onto the flagstone floor when Clemency gave them a good shaking. Mrs Blunt happened to be standing nearby and she cried out in horror. She made Clemency take them outside into the area, instructing her to beat the garments against the wall, and not to bring them back into the house until the last flea had been shaken out. Shivering and inwardly cursing Tom for not examining the clothes, Clemency stood outside in the cold whacking the jacket and breeches against the wall until she was certain that nothing living could have survived. She hurried back indoors and undressed, folding her blouse, skirt and cotton shift neatly, and placing them on the mattress beside Edith, who was lying on her back, snoring. Clemency shrugged on the calico shirt, which did not feel too different from a blouse, but when she pulled on the fustian breeches she shuddered as the coarse material scratched her legs. Having her lower limbs encased in material felt strange, and looked even odder as she stared down at them. She felt a blush rising to her cheeks, even though there was no one to see her in this peculiar garb. She took the peaked cap and tucked her long hair into the crown, wishing that she could examine her appearance in a mirror, and then deciding that perhaps it was better this way. She was pushing her bare feet into the boots, which were two sizes too large, when Edith stirred and opened her eyes. She jerked into a sitting position and screamed. 'Who are you boy? Get out of me room.'

'Ma, it's me. Clemency.'

Edith peered at her. 'It sounds like Clemmie, but it can't be.'

Clemency tugged off the peaked cap, allowing her hair to tumble about her shoulders. 'It is me, Ma. Augustus wants me to dress like a boy so I don't put his lardy-Lucy in the shade.'

'Well, I never. I thought the drink had done for me brains and I was seeing things.'

'No, it's me all right. But I wish the boy what first owned these clothes had washed hisself now and again. They smell something horrible.'

'What have we come to, Clemmie? What dreadful depths has that brute brought us to?'

Clemency went down on her knees and wrapped her arms around her mother. 'We won't let Hardiman beat us, Ma. If you didn't recognise me, then he won't neither. I'm going to make more money singing for me supper than I ever did from dipping for him to line his blooming pockets, not to mention that old crook Minski. We'll be all right, Ma. You'll see.'

That evening, Augustus led his troupe to perform on the main concourse of Liverpool Street Station, in time, he said, to catch the office workers hurrying to catch their trains. At four o'clock it was already dark and very cold. They set up under the clock, and Lucilla began with 'Home Sweet Home', which Clemency thought quite appropriate, but the passengers seemed more intent on actually getting home than listening to someone singing about it. Augustus took the hat round, but came back grim-faced and ordered Ronnie and Tom to play something more cheerful. They began to play 'Sir Roger de Coverley', but the lively music only seemed to make the travellers move faster towards the platforms, and on a bitterly cold January evening, no one wanted to stop and dance, let alone toss their hard-earned coppers into the hat. After almost half an hour of bone-chilling standing about, Augustus pushed Clemency to the front.

'"The Ratcatcher's Daughter", young Clem. Give it all you got.'

Lucilla tugged at his coat sleeve. 'Let me do it, Daddy.'

'Save your voice for later, poppet-pie. Now. gentlemen, one and two and three . . .'

Clemency felt desperately self-conscious dressed as a boy, and she was certain that everyone would be able to see through the disguise, but there was no going back now. With her heart thudding against her ribs, beating out a much faster rhythm than the one that Ronnie was playing on his drum, Clemency launched into the cockney ditty. At first it looked as though they were going to be ignored, but then one person stopped to listen and another, until there was a small crowd grouped around them. Responding to the audience, she threw herself heart and soul into the tragic tale of the ill-fated lovers. The cathedral-like acoustics of the railway station sent her pure soprano voice echoing across the platforms. She had become so emotionally involved in performing the song that she was barely conscious of the tears that trickled down her cheeks. It was only when she sang the last note that her spirit returned to the cold reality of the station, the clouds of steam hissing from the engines and the sooty smell of hot coals. A muffled sob from someone in the crowd broke the momentary silence and then someone began to clap. It rippled round the onlookers like the pattering of rain on the glass roof. Then coins began to jingle in the cap that Augustus was handing round. Ronnie patted her on the back. 'Well sung, nipper.'

'I could have done it just as well,' Lucilla snapped, cuddling up to Tom. When he said nothing in reply, she nudged him in the ribs. 'Couldn't I, Tom? I could have done it just as well.'

'If you say so, ducks.'

'Daddy!' Lucilla gave Tom a shove that sent him staggering back against the wall, and she flounced over to Augustus. 'Daddy, he's being mean to me.'

Augustus shook the cap, staring into its greasy interior. 'Is he, pet? That's nice.' He turned to Clemency with a broad smile. 'If we go on like this, my dear Clem, I will be a happy man.'

Clemency wiped her eyes with the back of her hand. Her nose was running and she could not feel her feet. 'Can we go home now?'

'Home? My dear boy – I mean girl – we're just starting. We'll make our way towards the Strand. Fleet Street is always good for a few bob, and we'll catch the queues waiting outside the theatre. If we do as well all evening, I'll treat everyone to a pie and mash supper. I can't say fairer than that.'

It was almost midnight by the time they returned to Flower and Dean Street. Augustus led them home at a brisk marching pace, twirling his malacca cane, which doubled as a conductor's baton, and stepping out with boundless energy. Lucilla leaned heavily on Tom's arm and Ronnie walked behind them, dragging his feet. It was all that Clemency could do to keep up with them. She plodded along, barely noticing where she was treading, regardless of the piles of horse dung, dog excrement and rotten vegetables that lay mouldering on the thoroughfares and pavements, awaiting the arrival of the early morning street sweepers. The night sky seemed to have compressed the smoke from thousands of chimneys into a thick blanket, which rested on the tops of the flickering streetlamps. Clemency's throat was sore and she was certain that she was losing her voice. She was painfully aware that the ill-fitting boots had rubbed blisters on her heels. Augustus led them up Petticoat Lane, cutting through Wentworth Street where prostitutes solicited from shop doorways. The banks and businesses in the City might be sleeping, but here the narrow alleys teemed with the nightlife of the underworld, but Clemency was too dog-tired to worry about who might be lurking in the shadows. The terrifying phantom of Jack the Ripper meant little to her at this moment. All she wanted was to crawl into whatever sort of sleeping arrangement Mrs Blunt had thought fit to give her. She knew she would fall asleep as soon as she laid her head on the pillow, always supposing that she was to have the luxury of a pillow.

At last, when she thought she was about to collapse, they reached Flower and Dean Street. Augustus unlocked the door and went inside, but he came to a halt at the foot of the stairs so unexpectedly that Tom and Ronnie cannoned into him. He raised his fingers to his lips. 'Hush, we don't want to wake the whole house. But I think we've earned ourselves a drop of hot toddy, just to keep the cold from our bones, of course. What d'you say?'

Tom nodded. 'You're on, guv.'

'Ta, but I'm going to me bed,' Ronnie said wearily. He hobbled off along the passage.

'Me too. I'm fair done in.' Lucilla grabbed the banister rail with one hand and began to haul herself up the stairs.

'Goodnight, my little nightingale,' Augustus called in a stage whisper. 'You were magnificent tonight, as always.'

Clemency said nothing. She followed Lucilla up the staircase, parting company outside her room on the second floor and wearily mounting the final flight that led to the attics at the top of the building. The dancers from the Pavilion Theatre shared one of the tiny rooms beneath the eaves. Doreen and Flossie, the two young chambermaids, slept in the middle room, and Mrs Blunt had grudgingly allowed Edith and Clemency the use of the smallest room at the end of the narrow corridor. Clemency felt her way along the wall, unable to see even the faintest chink of light in the darkness. Her fingers closed round the latch and the door opened with a squeal of rusty hinges. She blinked as her eyes grew accustomed to the silvery stream of moonlight slanting through the skylight. They were beneath the rafters that supported the roof. It was bitterly cold and the wind whistled through holes left by broken or missing tiles. There was head height at one end of the room only, and the floor and ceiling met at a sharp angle just above where Edith lay sleeping.

Clemency stooped to cover Ma with the rough woollen blanket. In this light, her face was smooth and unlined as a marble statue in the graveyard, and, in startling contrast, her hair spilled over the mattress ticking in a fiery halo. Even in her state of complete exhaustion, Clemency could see that Ma must have been beautiful once, a long time ago before poverty and Todd Hardiman entered her life. She shuddered. This was not the time to dwell on the past. Above all she needed to sleep. It was too cold to undress. She tugged off her boots and crawled across the floor to lie down beside her mother. A spider's web tickled her nose and something was scrabbling in the eaves, very close to her head, but she was too tired to care. She closed her eyes.

It seemed as though she had just fallen asleep

when the shrill ringing of an alarm clock awakened Clemency with such a jolt that she sat upright and banged her head on a rafter. It was still dark, but she could hear sounds of life through the thin partition wall. There was whispering and muffled giggling and she realised that it was the chambermaids getting ready to start their daily chores. Clemency rubbed the bump on her head and stretched her stiff limbs. The coarse material of the breeches irritated her skin: she felt sure that some of the fleas must have survived, and had been feasting off her blood. She crawled out of bed and stripped off the offending garments, slipping on her cotton shift, which clung damply to her flesh, and thrusting her arms into her blouse. It was difficult to do up the buttons with numbed fingers but she managed somehow. She stepped into her skirt and fastened it around her waist.

Edith groaned, and in the fading moonlight Clemency could see that her eyes were open and staring. 'What is it, Ma? Are you ill?'

'Me belly aches, Clemmie. I'm hot and cold all over. I need a drop of gin, ducks. It's the only thing that will give me ease.'

'I got no money left, Ma. And the gin will do for you one day. You're best off without it.'

Edith raised herself on to her elbow. 'You had a florin. I know you did.'

'And Mrs Blunt had it off me for the use of the

bedding. The old besom said it was extra on top of the charge for lodgings, and it were up to us to pay it. I couldn't let you or Jack sleep on the floor, now could I?'

'Me guts is being cut with knives. Me stomach is full of cramps. It's worse than when I was giving birth to you and Jack. Can't you find me a drop of something? Anything, I don't care. Laudanum will do if you can't get a drop of tiddley.'

'I'll go down to the kitchen and see what I can find.' Clemency crept out of the room. Doreen and Flossie were already halfway down the staircase. They glanced up at her, but she could not see their faces clearly in the dim light. She followed them downstairs to the kitchen, where Fancy was kneeling in front of the range energetically working a pair of bellows.

'Ain't you got the kettle on yet?' Doreen demanded. 'I can't start work until I've had a cup of tea.'

'Me neither.' Flossie turned to stare at Clemency. 'What d'you want?'

'Mind your own business. I'm a paying guest in this house.'

'Ooh, my. Hoity toity,' Doreen said, mimicking Clemency's voice. 'What are you today then? A girl or a boy? Or don't you know the difference?'

Flossie sniggered. 'I bet she's got a whatsit, just like a fellah.'

'If you had half a brain you'd scare me,' Clemency said, curling her lip. 'I could whop you with one hand tied behind me back, so don't give me no lip.'

Flossie's dishwater-pale eyes widened and she backed away. 'I was just joking.'

'Leave her alone, Floss,' Doreen said over her shoulder as she went to open the door to what had been the broom cupboard. 'You make the tea and I'll fetch the cleaning stuff.'

Fancy stopped pumping the bellows and glanced over her shoulder at Clemency. As their eyes met, Clemency was certain she caught a glimmer of amusement in Fancy's expression. At the same moment, Doreen uttered a loud scream and ran back into the kitchen, clutching her chest.

'He's in there, the man with no legs.' She turned on Fancy. 'You bitch, you might have warned me. And it ain't funny.'

Fancy sat back on her heels and rocked with laughter. 'You should see your face.'

Flossie rushed to comfort Doreen. 'That ain't fair. You never told us the cripple was in there.'

'You never asked,' Fancy said, wiping her eyes on her apron. 'And for your information, you dumb-bell, he ain't a cripple and he has got legs, they just don't work proper. And if I hears either of you say anything nasty about him, or to him, you'll feel the back of my hand round your silly faces.'

Doreen and Flossie went to sit on one of the forms, silent and glowering, waiting for the kettle to boil. They shot dark glances at Clemency, who ignored them. She went over to Fancy and touched her on the shoulder. 'Ta for standing up for me brother.'

Fancy flinched and pulled away from Clemency's touch. 'Just because I think a lot of Jack don't mean that I like you. You got the room what ought to have been mine. I'll not forgive you for that.' She clambered to her feet and went to the table to set about hacking slices off a loaf of bread. Clemency could see that it was useless to argue. She wanted to reason with Fancy and tell her that if Mrs Blunt had intended her to sleep in the filthy attic, then she would have done so, but she could see that nothing she could say or do would make the slightest bit of difference. Fancy was a stubborn mule and had a mouth on her the size of the Blackwall Tunnel, but she was good to Jack and that made her all right in Clemency's book. The kettle on the hob had begun to bubble. Doreen and Flossie seemed unwilling to risk annoying Fancy any further and they sat side by side on the bench, like a pair of starlings on a washing line.

'I'll make the tea then, shall I?' Clemency did not wait for an answer. She warmed the large brown teapot and made the tea. She sniffed the scented steam rising from the pot. These tea leaves had not been used and reused – this would be a lovely fresh brew. Mrs Blunt might be a bit of a harridan, but at least she was not mean when it came to catering for her lodgers.

After the lodgers had breakfasted and gone about their daily business, Clemency and Jack took a seat in the far corner of the kitchen, well away from Mrs Blunt and Fancy who had begun preparing the day's meals. Jack had wanted to hear all the details of last night's street shows, and Clemency had related everything, making light of the gruelling march through the London streets in the biting cold.

'If only I could get about better,' Jack said, staring moodily into the distance. 'I don't like sending you out on the streets, Clemmie. It ain't right. It's a pity I can't have wheels strapped to me bum so that you could pull me along.'

He laughed, but Clemency was quick to hear the bitter note in his voice. She could think of nothing to say that would comfort him, and she bent her head over the song sheets that Augustus had left for her to read and learn. If it had not been for Lucilla's caustic tongue, she would have admitted that she had difficulty in reading, but she did not want to lose face in front of that stuck-up little madam. It had been a relief when, during breakfast, Augustus suggested a shopping trip to Lucilla. He had promised her a new bonnet, and Lucilla said she had seen just the thing in a shop window in Commercial Street. She had practically dragged her father from the table, and he had gone off with a hunk of bread in one hand and a slice of ham in the other. Tom had not come down to breakfast. Ronnie said he had drunk too much hot toddy and was feeling the worse for it. Clemency decided that she liked Ronnie. He was a lot older than Tom, who must be in his early twenties. Ronnie seemed to be closer in age to Augustus and he had a world-weary look, as though life had beaten him soundly and now he accepted each day as it came, without either enthusiasm or fear. He was, Clemency thought, the calmest and quietest person she had ever met.

He had come back into the kitchen and politely asked if he could join them at the table. Jack welcomed him with a wide grin, and Clemency knew that if Jack liked a person, they were likely to be all right. From his permanent sitting position, Jack had had time to study people, and he was a good judge of character. Although, Clemency thought, chewing her finger as she watched Fancy sidle over to stand by his side, even Jack could be wrong sometimes.

'How are you doing, Clem?' Ronnie asked, sitting down beside her.

She met his frank gaze, and was about to say

she was doing well when she saw a flicker of understanding in his grey eyes. 'To tell you the truth, Ronnie, I can't read. Well, I can make out the letters, but it takes me ages to work out the words.'

Ronnie's waxed moustache quivered upwards as he smiled. 'That's not a problem. I'd be pleased to help, if you'd let me.'

'I'd be ever so grateful. But why would you want to help me? I ain't nothing to you.'

'I had a daughter once. She died of the smallpox and it took my wife too. Effie would have been about your age now, had she survived. You've got a lovely voice, young Clem. You could go far, especially if you could read.'

Clemency shot a furtive glance at Fancy, but she was too busy flirting with Jack to have overheard the conversation. She turned to Ronnie and smiled. 'Ta, you're a brick.'

They were out on the streets by midday, performing up West outside the large stores. Augustus had taken them on the underground train, an experience that took Clemency's breath away, and left her gasping for air as they emerged into the winter sunshine in Oxford Street. She had never been any further west than the Strand Theatre, and she had certainly never seen anything like these imposing shop fronts.

The windows were filled with luxury goods that she could never have begun to imagine. The horse-drawn omnibuses, broughams, hackneys and hansom cabs jostled for position in the busy streets, and pedestrians took their lives in their hands as they attempted to weave in and out of the traffic. Uniformed chauffeurs leapt out of motor cars to assist their elegantly dressed passengers to alight. Liveried doormen hurried to open the glassed doors of the department stores, and the intoxicating mixed scents of perfume and expensive toiletries wafted out in a gale of hot air. Clemency could barely sing a note as she stood, open-mouthed on the pavement, completely fascinated by this exotic new world. In her shabby boy's clothes, she felt even more like a cockney sparrow than before. One day, she thought, staring at a particularly beautiful young lady being handed out of a cab, I'll be dressed in silks and satins, with a whole dead bird and a pound of grapes on me hat. Lucilla nudged her in the ribs and hissed at her to stop gawping and sing.

In the afternoon, they moved from Oxford Street to Regent Street, and by teatime they were in Piccadilly Circus, where they had to vie for position with the flower sellers, who took a dim view of their pitch being queered, and other groups of buskers, who were as territorial as fighting cocks. Augustus allowed them brief stops for refreshment at a pub and a teashop, and by late evening they had made their way back to Carter Lane.

Augustus stopped outside the Crown and Anchor. 'This will be our last stop for tonight.'

'Daddy!' Lucilla whined. 'I'm exhausted. I can't sing another note.'

Augustus pushed the door open with his shoulders. 'My old friend Cyril Hawkes was mine host here, that is until he run off with a barmaid from Wapping, which made him a fool, in my opinion, as his wife is the best cook in London. We'll do our turn and then I'll treat you to supper. I can't say fairer than that. Now can I?'

'You could send me home in a cab,' Lucilla muttered, pushing past him into the smoky interior of the pub.

Clemency followed last. She did not want Ned to see her dressed like this, but perhaps he would not recognise her. She pulled her cap down a bit further over her eyes. The bar was packed with customers: Augustus cut a swathe through them with the aid of his cane and his loud voice. He came to a halt by the inglenook, claiming a table that had just been vacated by a group of men. Clemency had to push to get through the crush of male bodies.

'Here, look where you're going, boy.'

The familiar voice sent an icy shiver down her

spine. Todd Hardiman gripped her by the shoulders, shaking her like a terrier with a rat. 'Where's your manners, boy?'

Chapter Six

It was all over. She was convinced that Hardiman had seen through her disguise. He was holding her in a bone-crushing grip, with his fingers clamped on her thin shoulders. She bent her head and stared down at the ground. 'Sorry, mister.'

He shook her again. 'I've a good mind to take you outside and give you a good thrashing. That'll teach you to respect your elders and betters, me lad.'

'I said I'm sorry.' She tried to make her voice sound gruff, more like a boy, but it came out in a squeak. She darted a sideways glance at Hardiman. He was staring down at her, his penetrating gaze hard and cold as hailstones. Just as she thought he was going to rip away her disguise, Ronnie elbowed his way towards them.

'Anything wrong, mate?'

'Is this your nipper?' Hardiman's harsh voice was slurred with drink.

Clemency angled her head to send Ronnie a mute plea for help. Reaching out, he grabbed her by the ear. 'I'll take the young scoundrel, mate.

And I'll give him what for when I gets him home.'

Hardiman's fingers tightened and then relaxed. He shoved Clemency away from him with a disgusted snort. 'See that you do. Teach the little bugger a bit of respect, I say.' He lurched off, pushing people out of the way as he headed towards the street door. Then, just as Clemency thought she was safe, he stopped and turned. Their eyes met and she felt her blood run cold. She didn't wait to see if he recognised her. She bolted, head down, barging through the punters. Dodging behind the bar, she ignored Ned's order to stop and darted into the kitchen, almost knocking down a scullery maid who was carrying a pail filled with potatoes. The girl staggered backwards with a stifled scream, just managing to right herself without spilling the contents of the bucket.

'Lord above, what's going on?' Nell bustled forward, wiping her hands on her apron. 'Annie, never mind snivelling. Put those spuds on to boil. And you, young shaver, what are you doing in my kitchen?'

Before Clemency could speak, someone grabbed her by the scruff of her neck. She lashed out with her feet.

'Hold on, there. I ain't going to hurt you, nipper.'

It was Ned's voice, but panic had gripped her

insides with icy hands and she struggled to get free. Hardiman might have recognised her in that split second, and he wouldn't hesitate to follow her. 'Let me go, you big oaf.'

'What the devil?' Ned spun her round to face him. 'Clemency?'

At any other time, his shocked expression would have made her laugh, but all she wanted now was to escape through the back door. 'He mustn't find me,' she said breathlessly. 'Hardiman's in the bar. He was the one we run away from.'

'Hardiman? Are you sure?'

'Of course I'm sure. How could you let a wicked man like him drink in your pub? Shame on you, Ned Hawkes.'

'Shame on me! I just serve ale. I know of him, but I can't say I've ever seen him. Not knowingly, at any rate.'

'You ought to be more careful. He's a bad lot. He's nothing but trouble.'

'And what sort of trouble have you got yourself into? Why are you dressed like a boy? It ain't seemly.' Ned tugged the cap from her head, freeing her mane of hair.

'Give it here,' Clemency made a grab for the cap. 'Are you stupid or something? What if he were to come through that door? He'd know for sure it were me.'

'You look ridiculous,' Ned said, frowning.

'And it ain't proper for a young lady to go about in breeches. It ain't decent.'

Struggling to get her hair tucked back beneath the cap, Clemency stamped her foot. 'Better to be ridiculous than dead.'

'Stop this bickering, both of you.' Nell hurried to Clemency's side, placing a protective arm around her shoulders. 'Who is this bloke Hardiman? And why are you so frightened of him, ducks?'

'He's a bad, bad man, Mrs Hawkes. You don't want to know nothing about him.'

The door opened. Stifling a cry of alarm, Clemency hid behind Nell's ample body.

'Better come quick, gaffer,' the potman said urgently. 'There's customers demanding ale.'

'Tell them I'll be there in a tick.' Ned shooed him off with an impatient wave of his hand. As the door closed, he turned to Clemency. 'Just tell me why you're going about London dressed like that.'

'I've taken up with a troupe of street musicians. This garb is part of the act.'

Ned did not look impressed. 'You look like a common pickpocket.' His scowl faded into a suspicious frown. 'That's what you was doing in the market with that woman's purse, wasn't it? You was on the dip.'

'I was then, but it ain't like now. We're professionals, we are. Lucilla and me sing the songs.' Clemency puffed out her chest. 'They call me the cockney sparrow.'

'Well I never did.' Nell gave her a hug. 'Don't be hard on her, Ned. At least she's trying to earn an honest living.'

'That's no excuse for exposing her – limbs.'

Clemency felt the blood rush to her cheeks. What right had he to criticise her? And it was embarrassing to have a man staring at her legs. 'I'll thank you to wipe that stupid, shocked expression off your face, Ned Hawkes.'

He opened his mouth to reply but was cut short by a screech from Annie. 'Pan's boiling over, missis.

'Move it to the back then, silly girl,' Nell said, with an impatient wave of her hand.

'Sparrows don't sing,' Annie muttered, shifting the pan off the heat.

'Well, this one does,' Clemency retorted angrily. 'Who asked you, anyway?'

Annie shrugged her shoulders and disappeared into the scullery.

'Now, Clemency, love,' Nell said gently. 'Don't pay no heed to Annie; she's a bit simple. And don't be cross with Ned, he's just worried about you. We both are.'

'I can take care of meself, ta.' Clemency jammed the cap down over her eyes. 'You been good to me, Mrs Hawkes. I don't forget a kindness, but don't let on to no one what you just saw. Hardiman's got spies everywhere. He mustn't find out where we are.'

'Gaffer!' The potman stuck his head round the door. 'There'll be a riot if you don't come quick.'

'I'm coming.' Ned hesitated, frowning. 'There must be some other way you can keep your mum and Jack. I didn't like leaving you there in Spitalfields, not with the Ripper still at large. And now I see you out on the streets late at night, I like it even less.'

'Ta, but it ain't your problem.'

'I got to get back to work, but I'll come and see you at your lodgings, if that's all right with you.'

'It's all right with me. Now, will you take a quick look and tell me if Hardiman is still in the taproom. He's a big, burly bloke with black hair and eyes like chips of coal. He's got a scar on his lip that makes him look like a mad dog.'

'Oh my Lord,' Nell said with feeling. 'He sounds awful.'

'You don't know the half of it.' Clemency waited while Ned opened the door and peered into the crowded taproom.

'Can't see him. I think he must have gone.' Ned went to serve the waiting customers who were rhythmically beating their tankards on the bar counter.

Clemency kissed Nell's lined cheek. 'Ta, for everything.'

'You take care of yourself, dearie. And come back soon.'

Clemency blew her a kiss and followed Ned into the bar. She could hear Augustus's loud voice calling for quiet, as his little nightingale was about to sing. She edged her way through the crowd to where Lucilla was standing on a table, and she sat down on a settle next to Ronnie. He smiled, and handed her a glass of mulled wine. 'Are you all right, Clem?'

She nodded, sipping the warm spiced drink. 'Yes, ta.'

'I thought you was took bad.'

'I'm all right now.'

'Who was that evil-looking cove?'

'Someone best avoided.'

Augustus rapped his cane on the table. 'Tom, Ronnie! Music, gentlemen, please.'

Ronnie got to his feet and began beating out the rhythm while Tom, slightly the worse for wear it seemed to Clemency, swayed from side to side as he put the flute to his lips. Lucilla began to sing 'Believe me if all those endearing young charms . . .' but no one was listening. Augustus's call for silence was received with boos and jeers.

'No one's dead. This ain't a wake.'

'Sing us something cheery, girl.'

Clemency craned her neck to see who had dared to call out, but the taproom was packed with drinkers, and no one was about to own up. Lucilla kept going, and Clemency could only admire her for being such a trouper, but her quavering soprano was lost in the general babble of voices.

'Come, Lucilla,' Augustus boomed, lifting her down from the table. 'Don't waste your voice on these peasants.'

'Here, guv. Who are you calling a peasant?' A drunken man with a bulbous red nose and sandy eyebrows that met over the bridge of his nose lurched towards Augustus with his hands fisted. 'Say that again, if you dares.'

Augustus attempted to bluster his way out of the situation, but a crowd of angry men converged on them, and, with the fire at their back and the angry punters cutting off their escape, Clemency could see that things were about to turn nasty. She leaned over to whisper in Ronnie's ear. 'Play that song you taught me this morning. You know – the one about the workhouse boy what got lost on Christmas Eve and ended up in the stew pot. That ought to get their attention away from the guvner.'

Ronnie's moustache quivered, as it always did when he wanted to laugh, and he whispered to Tom, who grinned foolishly but somehow managed to take up the rhythm.

Clemency climbed onto the table and began stamping her foot in time to the beat of Ronnie's drum. It took a minute or two, but gradually the comic words of 'The Workhouse Boy' and the cheery tune, turned the angry mob into an appreciative audience. Having dealt with Ma when she was swipey, Clemency knew very well that a drunk could turn in a moment from happy to nasty. She ended by dancing a jig on the table-top with everyone clapping in time to the music.

'Well sung, boy.' The man with the red nose attempted to slap her on the shoulder, over-reached himself and fell flat on his back. Much to the amusement of the crowd, he lay there kicking his legs in the air like an upturned beetle, until one of his mates went to his aid and helped him to his feet.

'Well done, indeed, Clem.' Augustus murmured, lifting her down from the table. 'And now I think a hasty retreat is indicated, before the mood of the mob swings back to fisticuffs.'

'Let's have another drink, guv,' Tom said, sliding his arm around Lucilla's waist. 'Just a tot to keep out the cold. And you promised us supper. You said . . .'

'Never mind what I said.' Augustus picked up his battered top hat. 'We'll get some fish and chips on the way back to our lodgings.'

'Daddy! I can't walk all that way,' Lucilla wailed.

'I'll give you a piggyback ride, love,' Tom said, fondling her buttocks.

'I saw that!' Augustus roared, brandishing his cane in Tom's face.

The drunken man with the red nose, having recovered from his tumble, lurched forward, leering at Lucilla. 'I'll give you a ride, ducks.'

Tom made a growling sound deep in his throat, pushed Lucilla into Augustus's arms and lunged at the drunk, flailing his fists.

'Oh my Lord, that's done it!' Augustus hitched Lucilla over his shoulder and seized Clemency by the hand. 'Let's get out of here.'

Ronnie snatched up his drum and just managed to catch Tom's flute, which had catapulted from his hands as his assailant punched him in the stomach. As Clemency was being dragged unceremoniously out of the taproom, she glanced over her shoulder in time to see Ned vault the bar to hurl himself upon Tom and his opponent. They went down in a flurry of punches. Augustus did not stop until they were outside on the pavement. It was raining.

'Daddy, we can't leave Tom in there. They'll do for him,' Lucilla cried, beating her fists on his chest and sobbing.

'Now, now, my little strawberry, don't take on so. You'll damage your vocal cords.'

'Bugger me vocal cords. My fellah is being murdered and all you worry about is whether or not I can sing. I hate you, Daddy. I hate you.'

Augustus released her so suddenly that Lucilla

fell against Clemency, almost knocking her off her feet. Clemency just managed to save herself from falling. She set her cap straight, scowling at Lucilla. 'Here, watch where you're treading, you blooming elephant.'

'I'll scratch your eyes out if you keep making rude remarks about my size,' Lucilla said, dry-eyed and hissing like an angry snake. 'I'm the prima donna, not you – you drab little sparrow.'

'Girls, that's enough.' Augustus stepped in between them. 'This is no way for professionals to behave. Ronnie, go inside and rescue Tom from those ruffians.'

'You're bigger than I am, guv. You go in there.'

Augustus puffed out his cheeks, making spluttering noises.

'Oh, you big sissies!' Clemency exclaimed, throwing up her hands. 'I'll go.' Before anyone could stop her, she opened the taproom door almost colliding with Ned, who was about to frogmarch Tom out of the pub.

'I take it he's one of yours.'

Clemency nodded, speechless. Tom had his hands to his mouth and blood was trickling through his fingers. He had a cut over one eye and the other was swollen and already half closed. 'Tom! What have they done to you?'

Shaking his head, Tom groaned.

Ned set him down against the pub wall and Tom slumped to the ground. Lucilla screamed and ran to kneel on the wet pavement in front of him. 'Tom, Tom! My poor Tom.'

'He took on the wrong one with Swipey Sam,' Ned said, chuckling.

'How can you be so heartless?' Clemency demanded. 'Your bloke has half killed him by the looks of it.'

'And he's one of the best flute players in the East End,' Augustus groaned. 'Go and find a hackney carriage, Ronnie. He can't walk in that state.'

'And he's bleeding all over the place.' Ned pulled a dishrag from his pocket and handed it to Clemency. 'Best mop him up a bit. Blood on the pavement ain't good for business.'

'I'm seeing a new side of you tonight, Ned.' Clemency snatched the rag and tossed it to Lucilla. 'And I don't like it.'

Ned shrugged his broad shoulders. 'And I could say the same for you, miss.' He turned to Augustus. 'See she gets home safe, or you'll have me to answer to, mister.'

He went into the pub and the door swung shut with a bang.

'Do you know that young man?' Augustus asked, peering at Clemency through the pouring rain and in the fractured beams of the gaslight.

'Daddy, does it matter?' Lucilla scrambled to her feet, holding the bloodstained rag. 'Who cares if that tart has slept with all the publicans in

London? My Tom has lost all his front teeth. He'll never play the flute again.'

Even allowing for Lucilla's habit of exaggeration, next morning it was apparent to everyone in the lodging house that Tom's musical career had ended. His features bore a strong resemblance to a joint of topside rather than a human face. He had two black eyes, his head looked more box-shaped than round, and his lips were swollen to twice their normal size. His front teeth were missing, and as he found it almost impossible to speak, no one liked to ask him if he had swallowed them or had spat them onto the taproom floor for the cleaning woman to find in the morning. One of the ballet dancers suggested that Swipey Sam might have had them strung into a necklace. This remark sent Lucilla off into a bout of hysterics and Mrs Blunt thumped the kitchen table with a wooden spoon, calling for order.

'I won't have ruffians lodging in my house. This is a respectable establishment, Mr Throop. If he's going to cause trouble,' she said, pointing the spoon at Tom, 'he'll have to go. And that goes for the lot of you, ladies excepted.'

'I can assure you, madam,' Augustus said, with dignity, 'that the disturbance in the public house was not of our making.'

'Yes, you old cow,' Lucilla said, scrunching her

face into a mean look. 'Tom was defending my honour.'

'Honour! That's a laugh.' Fancy wiggled her hips in a suggestive manner. 'I heard tell as how you lost your honour when you was twelve.'

Lucilla let out a loud screech. 'Daddy! Are you going to let that slut from the foundling hospital talk to me like that?' She flung her arms around her father's neck and began to sob loudly.

Fancy snorted and stood with arms akimbo, as if daring Augustus to take her on. The five O'Malley brothers, burly Irishmen who worked as navigators digging out the tunnels for the underground railways, and three stevedores who had just come off the night shift at the London Dock, all stopped eating and were watching the scene with evident enjoyment, as if anticipating an all-female, hair-pulling, bodice-ripping contest. The two dancers from the Pavilion theatre, and the young lady type-writer who worked in a bank, had ranged themselves behind Fancy. Mrs Blunt stood in the middle, bristling and rolling up her sleeves as though she intended to throw them all out onto the streets.

Clemency went to stand behind Jack, who was sitting on the chair at the head of the table. As she rested her hands on his shoulders, she could feel his muscles tensed and vibrating like a clock spring. She knew she had to say something to calm the situation. She gave Jack's shoulders a gentle squeeze and cleared her throat. 'It's true, Mrs Blunt. Tom was standing up for Lucilla. A randy old sod was making comments that would have made any man want to punch his lights out.'

The O'Malley brothers murmured in agreement, and the stevedores nodded wisely as they munched their bread and cold meat. The girls moved away from Fancy, as if distancing themselves from her and her opinions.

'Well, we must give the young man some credit then,' Mrs Blunt said, nodding. 'But I'll thank you all to remember my rules. No fighting, no spitting and no hanky-panky under my roof.'

'Well said, Mrs Blunt.'

A voice from the top of the stairs caused everyone to turn their heads and stare at the well-dressed man who had entered through the baize door, unseen and unheard in the uproar.

'Mr Stone!' Mrs Blunt gasped, her thin face flushing red and then paling to ashen.

Clemency's hands dropped to her sides. She could not move or speak. She stared in horror as Jared Stone came slowly and purposefully down the staircase. She had put the memory of their first meeting firmly out of her mind, but it came back to her now in a wave of anger and revulsion. She stared at him, taking in the details of his charcoal-grey frock coat with its black-velvet collar and cuffs, his tapered, pinstripe trousers and the starched wing collar of his white shirt. He had removed his top hat and his kid gloves, and his hair gleamed blue-black in the gaslight.

Mrs Blunt rushed to the foot of the stairs, wiping her hands on her apron. 'I wasn't expecting you, sir. Is anything wrong? Has there been a complaint about the way I runs this house?'

Jared paused on the bottom step. 'Not that I know of, Mrs Blunt.'

'I've paid me rent. On the dot.'

'I haven't come about the rent. I leave that to my agent.'

'Then, sir, if I may be so bold as to ask, why have you come?'

'You're probably aware that I own a couple of the properties on this side of the street?' Jared cast a dispassionate glance around the room. His question was met with total silence. Clemency held her breath, praying that he would not recognise her.

'I am, sir,' Mrs Blunt said, plainly agitated.

'Thanks to the machinations of the Ripper, property prices in this area are falling. I've decided to sell up, before values drop even lower. One more murder and I won't be able to give these buildings away.'

'No, sir. No, please don't sell this house. It's me livelihood and me home, sir.' Mrs Blunt sank to her knees in front of him, clutching at his coat-tails.

A ripple of consternation went round the room. Clemency gripped Jack's shoulders so hard that he looked up at her, his face puckered with concern, and he patted her hand. 'Are you all right, Clemmie?'

She managed a wobbly smile and nodded. The last thing she wanted was to draw Stone's attention to them, even though he seemed fully occupied as he attempted to free himself from Mrs Blunt's frantic grasp.

'Please, madam. Control yourself.'

'It's all right for you, mate.' The eldest of the O'Malley brothers got up from the table and shook his fist at Stone. 'But what about the likes of us honest, hard-working men? After a day's digging out the London clay, all we wants is a hot meal and a clean bed for the night.'

'It's right he is.' The youngest, and usually most talkative, O'Malley brother jumped to his feet. 'And that ain't so easy to find round these parts. Ma Blunt might be a stickler for the rules but it's a fine cook she is. Sure, you'd be hard put to find any bugs in the beds here.'

Stone held up his hand for silence as everyone began to speak at once. 'I'm pleased to hear that I have such a good tenant in Mrs Blunt. But I'm sure you will all find alternative accommodation, and that is your problem, not mine.'

'Oh, please, sir.' Mrs Blunt sobbed, shaking her head so that pins shot out of her bun, flying in all directions like small arrows. 'Don't do this to us. Won't you reconsider?'

'It's a business matter, Mrs Blunt. Nothing personal. My inspection is to ascertain the value of each property. In future you will be dealing with my agent. We will not meet again.' Stone flicked his coat free and started back up the staircase. Halfway up, he paused, looking down at the grumbling lodgers. Clemency tried to hide behind Augustus, but it was too late. She saw a gleam of recognition in Stone's eyes. He pointed at her. 'You, girl. Come here.'

'No, Clemmie.' Jack twisted round to clasp her hand. 'Don't do it. He can't make you.'

She was not so sure about that. Clemency lifted her chin and met Stone's gaze with an unflinching stare. He beckoned to her, but she shook her head.

'I said, come here, Miss Skinner.'

Augustus turned to her with a curious glance. 'Do you know this fellow, Clem?'

'Never set eyes on the cove in me life.' Clemency stood firm, determined not to go near Jared Stone ever again. Just as it seemed she had won the battle of wills, the baize door opened and Edith wandered through it, standing at the top of the stairs with a bewildered look on her face. Clemency sucked in her breath; she could tell by Ma's unkempt appearance, and the dark shadows beneath her eyes that she must have got hold of liquor last night, and this morning she was much the worse for wear. Clemency could almost smell the stale gin on her breath, even from this distance.

'What's going on?' Edith leaned over the banister rail, waving her hand at Clemency. 'What's going on? I could hear the din from the top of the house. And me head's aching something awful.' She went to pass Jared on the stairs, but he caught her by the arm.

'Do you know that girl?'

'Know her?' Edith's head wobbled on her neck, as if she could not quite support its weight. Her lips curved in a tipsy smile. 'I should say I know her. Clemmie's me daughter.'

Jared kept his hold on Edith and he beckoned to Clemency. This time, there was no refusing him. She started forward but Jack caught her by the hand.

'Don't,' he said in an undertone.

'Let me go. There's nothing to worry about,' Clemency replied with more confidence than she was feeling. 'I can look after meself.'

'You have to, because I can't.' Jack's tone was bitter. 'I'd give anything to be able to walk across the floor and demand to know what that bastard wants with me sister.'

Fancy pushed one of the ballet dancers out of

her way in her hurry to reach Jack. She laid her hand on his shoulder and nodded to Clemency. A flash of understanding passed between them. Their tacit agreement needed no words to seal the bargain. Clemency knew then that Fancy would stand by Jack, no matter what.

'Let me go.' Edith slapped ineffectually at Jared with her free hand.

'What's to become of me?' Mrs Blunt wailed.

Jared ignored them both. He stood, immobile as his name, waiting for Clemency to make her way through the now silent onlookers. As she mounted the stairs, he released Edith, who staggered and clutched Clemency's arm. 'Don't go near the brute. I seen his type afore, Clemmie. He's a bad 'un.'

'He won't hurt me, Ma. You look after Mrs B. She's in a bit of a state.'

Edith opened her mouth to argue, but a warning look from Clemency silenced her.

Augustus and Ronnie, followed by the O'Malleys with their sleeves rolled up and their hands fisted, advanced across the floor to stand at the foot of the stairs.

'We don't want trouble, mister.' Augustus put his foot on the bottom step, glaring up at Jared. 'But harm one hair of that young person's head and you'll have us to deal with.'

Jared took Clemency by the hand. 'No harm will come to Miss Skinner. I suggest you all get about your business, or you men will be needing to look for new jobs as well as new homes.'

'What do you want with me?' Clemency demanded, as he led her to the top of the stairs.

Jared opened the baize door. 'Come out into the passage where it's quiet and we can talk.'

'I've nothing to say to a scoundrel like you.' Clemency wrenched her hand from his grasp. 'You may look and sound like a gent, but I ain't forgot that you tried to keep me against me will. And you threw that poor girl out onto the street, just because she was in the family way.'

'You should get your facts straight before you come out with such wild accusations.'

'You may talk like a lawyer, but you're just a magsman. A common criminal done up like a toff. You're nothing but a crook.'

Jared threw back his head and laughed. The sound echoed off the high ceilings, bounced off the cornices and dissipated up the stair well. 'It takes one to know one, my dear.'

'I ain't on the dip now. I've given all that up.' She eyed him suspiciously. 'What d'you want with me? And how did you know I was here?'

'I had no idea that you were here. It wasn't until I saw that flaming-red mop of yours that I realised I had found you. Do you realise, Miss Clemency Skinner, that I've been looking for you ever since you ran off as if the devil himself was after you?'

'You might be the devil for all I know.'

'You aren't a bit afraid of me, are you, Clemency?'

'I ain't afraid of no one, least of all a dandified cove with a big mouth.'

He ruffled her hair. 'You're a bold one and that's exactly why I want you to come and work for me. I could train you to dip the pockets at fashionable gatherings, theatres and racecourses. With a few fine feathers and some lessons in manners, I could even pass you off as a lady.'

Clemency angled her head, studying his aquiline features for the first time. He was not exactly handsome, but he had the aristocratic looks of a toff, and the voice to match. When he smiled, he was actually quite passable looking, but she neither liked nor trusted him. 'Why would a toff like you need to steal off other rich folk?'

'Owning property in Spitalfields is more of a burden than a boon. As to the other – I do it for my own enjoyment. I don't think of it as stealing, more the redistribution of wealth. I take from the rich and give to the poor and needy. What do you say, Clemency? Are you with me? I could turn you into a young lady.'

'You,' Clemency said, cocking a snook at him, 'can kiss my arse.' She had the satisfaction of seeing the smile wiped off his face. She turned on her heel and slammed through the baize door.

In the kitchen, she found Edith squatting on the floor by the prostrate figure of Mrs Blunt, while Fancy wafted the burning tail feathers of a boiling fowl beneath Mrs Blunt's nose. There was no sign of the O'Malley brothers or the dockers, who had all apparently escaped through the door that led into the area. The dancers and the lady type-writer, twittering like caged birds, hurried past Clemency and made their way up the stairs. Augustus and Ronnie were seated at one of the tables, in deep conversation with Jack, and Tom sat glumly, peering at them from beneath his swollen eyelids. Unusually silent, Lucilla sat by his side holding his hand.

Fancy looked up and scowled at Clemency as she descended the staircase. 'You keep fine company, I must say.' She dropped the burning feathers on the flagstones and stamped on them. 'But I suppose you'll be all right. When we're all thrown out on the street, you'll be living with your fancy bloke.'

'You're the only fancy one round here,' Clemency shot back at her, 'and he ain't my bloke.'

'So what was you talking about? I bet it weren't the weather.'

'You got a dirty mind, Fancy, if that's your real name. Or didn't they give you one in the orphanage? Was you just a number? Perhaps that accounts for you being such a spiteful bitch.'

Fancy's eyes narrowed to cat-like slits. 'I got a name, and I ain't no bitch. I was left on the steps of the foundling hospital one Good Friday and the nurse said, "Fancy that! A beautiful little girl abandoned on such a day. We'll name her Fancy Friday." And if you dares to laugh, Clemency Skinner, I'll tug your carroty hair out, strand by strand.'

Jack turned his head and smiled at her. 'That's a lovely name.'

Turning her back on Mrs Blunt, who was coughing and retching on the fumes of burnt feathers, Fancy left her side and sashayed over to stand by him. 'Ta, Jack. You're a gent. Not like her.' She jerked her thumb in Clemency's direction. 'She's a cow.'

'Clemmie's all right,' Jack said, taking Fancy's hand in his. 'I wants you two girls to be friends. We all got to stick together, considering that bloke, Stone, is going to sell the house over our heads.'

'It might never happen.' Clemency helped Mrs Blunt to her feet. 'He just said he was considering it, Jack.'

'I'm ruined,' Mrs Blunt wept. 'I'll never find another place at my age. I'll be left to join them crawlers what sit in shop doorways and beg for scraps of food and cups of tea.'

'Shut up moaning, you silly mare.' Edith sat back on her heels, clutching her head. 'I got navvies with picks drilling inside me skull. And your weeping and wailing is making it worse.'

'Ladies, ladies.' Augustus rose to his feet. 'Let's take one problem at a time. Fancy, my dear, be a good girl and make us all a fresh brew of tea. I'm sure that Mrs Blunt and Mrs Skinner would feel all the better for a cup of Rosie Lee. And I believe I have a bottle of Dr Collis Browne's Chlorodyne medicine in my valise. Suitable, so the label says, for curing everything from cholera to hysteria. Lucilla, my precious, if you could tear yourself away from Tom for a moment, would you go to my room and fetch the said medication?'

Lucilla looked as though she might refuse, but Tom mumbled something in her ear and she got up from the table. 'All right, Daddy. But only if Tom can have some too.'

'Of course,' Augustus said, waving his hand. 'Happy to oblige. And a spoonful might help to relieve Edith's sore head as well.'

'A drop of gin would do the trick,' Edith muttered. 'Help me up, Clemmie.'

'Ma,' Clemency whispered in her ear, as she helped her up, 'you got to stop drinking. It's doing you no good, and we got enough problems without you falling down drunk all the time.'

Edith drew herself upright, pushing Clemency away. 'You ungrateful child. Haven't I done dreadful things just to keep a roof over our heads? And all you can do is criticise me for wanting a drop of tiddley now and then to relieve the heartache of a deserted woman, left with a daughter and a crippled child to raise.'

'Be quiet you foolish woman.' Mrs Blunt's hands flew to her hair to push back tendrils that had escaped from her bun. 'Think yourself lucky that you have two children. I and my dear departed was never blessed with issue, and look at me now, working me fingers to the bone to run a respectable lodging house, and about to have it taken away from me. I'll have nothing and no one to call me own.' She clutched her hands to her chest, and fell to the floor in a dead faint.

'Now look what you've done,' Augustus said wearily. 'She's the best cook in Spitalfields, and you've done for her with your silly squabbles. Who's going to cook our dinner now?'

'Well, it ain't me,' Edith said, running her hand through her tangled mop of hair. 'Give me some money, Clemmie. I'm going to the pub.'

'Don't give it her,' Jack shouted.

Clemency backed away. 'No, Ma. I haven't got any money, and even if I had, I wouldn't give it to you. Anyway, the Ripper might be lurking outside, looking for his next victim.'

'I got to have a drink.' Edith lunged towards Clemency. 'Give me some money. I ain't frightened of the Ripper.'

'No, Ma, but you are scared of Hardiman. I saw him in the Crown and Anchor last night. And I'm almost certain that he recognised me. He could be lurking outside the front door this very minute.'

Chapter Seven

Edith's screech was louder than the steam whistle of an express train. She collapsed against Clemency, sobbing hysterically.

'Fancy, give me a hand.' Clemency hitched her mother's arm across her shoulders. 'Jack's right, we got to pull together or we're all in trouble.'

'Help her, Fancy, love,' Jack said softly. 'I'd do it meself if I was able.'

Reluctantly, Fancy crossed the floor, stepping over Mrs Blunt's prostrate figure. 'Well?'

'Take her other arm,' Clemency said, struggling to keep hold of Edith who was fighting to get free, and was, by this time, completely hysterical. 'We're going to stick her head under the pump in the back yard. That'll sober her up good and proper.'

Ronnie got to his feet. 'Can I help?'

Clemency nodded. 'Best get Mrs B upstairs to her bed. She's not going to do much cooking today.'

Fancy let out a yelp of pain as Edith caught her round the ear with the flat of her hand. 'Ouch! It's the pump for you, you old soak! One more slap and I'll hold you under till you drowns.'

'And I'll help you,' Clemency said, through gritted teeth. Edith was a dead weight and a mass of flailing hands and feet. Quite how they got her out through the scullery and into the back yard, she never knew. She was tempted to lock her mother in the privy at the far end of the yard, and leave her there until she sobered up, but after a prolonged struggle they managed to drag her to the pump. Clemency held her while Fancy worked the handle. Water gushed out, soaking all three of them, but they held Edith's head under until she stopped fighting and screaming.

She went down on her knees, gasping for air. 'All right. You can stop now. I'm sober, really I am.'

Fancy gave the pump handle another jerk. 'Just for luck,' she said, grinning. 'Are you sure you're sober, Mrs S?'

'As a judge,' Edith said, scrambling to her feet. She wrapped her arms around her wet body, her teeth chattering so violently that her blue lips could barely frame the words. 'I – I'm qu-quite s-sober.'

'And I'm soaked to the skin.' Clemency followed them into the scullery. 'I got no clothes to change into except me boy's duds.'

'Shut the bloody door,' Fancy said, shaking the water from her hair. 'That was the best fun I've had in years. I'll lend you me second best cotton print, as a favour. But I wants it back, washed and ironed. And don't think this makes us friends, because it don't. I'm just doing it for Jack's sake.'

Augustus was deep in conversation with Ronnie and Jack. They stopped talking and stared in amazement at the sight of three soaking wet women, dripping water all over the flag-stones.

'Blimey!' Jack said, his lips twitching. 'Three drownded rats.'

Edith cuffed him round the ear as she went past. 'Th-that's no way to speak to your mum.'

Jack's face split into a grin and he winked at Clemency. 'The cold water treatment done the trick then.'

She kissed him on the cheek, smiling. It was so good to see him cheerful again. It seemed like years since she had heard Jack laugh. It was worth the soaking, but it did not lessen the discomfort.

'Best change out of them wet things afore you all catches your death,' Ronnie said, shaking his head. 'A lung infection can creep up on a body without warning. I've seen folk go down with a fatal chill from just getting their feet wet on a winter's day.'

Edith had gone to stand by the range and steam was billowing from her clothes. 'All I got is what I stand up in.'

'Well at least it's had a wash,' Fancy said, taking off her mobcap and wringing the water out of her long, dark hair. 'You'll smell a bit better now, Edie.'

'Less of your cheek, young madam.' Edith glared at her and then she chuckled. 'What would Ma Blunt say if she could see us now?'

Clemency stared at her mother in surprise. If anyone else had spoken to her like that, she would have given them what for! What, she wondered, was it about Fancy that had caused Jack to fall in love with her? And now Ma was allowing her to say things that she would never have taken from anyone else. It wasn't fair and it wasn't right. Her own mother had abandoned Fancy when she was just a few hours old. No one had wanted her then, and now she was just a skivvy. She was not even pretty, and yet Jack had fallen under her spell, and now it looked as though Ma was being taken in as well. Snakes of jealousy writhed in Clemency's stomach. She shivered and sneezed.

Fancy opened a drawer in the dresser and pulled out two rough, huckaback towels. She tossed one each to Clemency and Edith. 'Here, dry yourselves as best you can. I'll sort out something to wear.' She crossed the floor leaving wet footprints on the flagstones, and bundling her damp skirts up around her knees she ran up the stairs. She paused at the doorway. 'Old Ma

Blunt is about your size, Edie. I'm sure she can spare you a set of dry clothes.'

Edith wrapped her hair in the towel. 'What are you lot staring at?' She demanded, glaring at Augustus, Ronnie and Tom, even though it was obvious that Tom's vision was obscured by his swollen eyelids. 'Ain't you blokes got nothing better to do than hang about the kitchen?'

Augustus rose to his feet. 'Madam, I apologise for our lack of manners. But we have been discussing what to do about poor Tom.'

'Yes, poor Tom,' Lucilla echoed, holding his hand to her cheek. 'He's the one who's suffering. You brought this on yourself by pouring gin down your throat. Do I feel sorry for you, missis? No, I do not.'

'You shut your mouth, cackling crow,' Clemency said angrily. 'You nearly got us thrown out of the pub last night, so you got no room to talk.'

Jack thumped his hand on the table, sending the cutlery jumping and jingling. 'That's enough of this squabbling. Ma, we come to a decision. I can get a good tune out of Tom's flute. I'm going out on the streets with Augustus and the others.'

Edith opened and closed her mouth, seemingly lost for words as she dried her hair with the towel.

'That's impossible.' Clemency squelched over

to him with water spurting from the holes in her boots. 'I – I mean we have to walk for miles.'

Augustus held up his hand. 'Aha! We've thought of that, Clem. Ronnie has worked it all out in his head. By nailing two broom handles to one of these kitchen chairs, he can turn it into a carrying seat. Tom may not be able to play, but he hasn't lost his strength. Between them, he and Ronnie can carry Jack from pitch to pitch.'

'I don't know about that.' Clemency grasped Jack's hand. 'Are you sure about this? People will stare.'

Jack squeezed her fingers. 'Of course they'll stare. But it will draw the crowds, Clemmie.'

'No!' Fancy shrieked. She came running down the stairs with a bundle of clothes in her arms. 'You'll not turn Jack into a freak show. I won't have it.'

Clemency stared at her in horror. 'Don't you dare call Jack a freak. Take that back.'

'I never said he was a freak.' Fancy thrust the clothes into Clemency's hands and pushed her out of the way. She wrapped her arms around Jack's neck, rubbing her cheek against his dark, curly head. 'He's not a freak but you'll turn him into one if you put him on show.' Tears gushed from her eyes and she sobbed onto Jack's shoulder.

'There, there, Fancy. Don't take on so.' Jack rubbed her back, casting an imploring look at

Clemency. 'She don't understand theatrical folk, Clemmie. You tell her.'

'I say she ought to go down on her knees and thank my Tom for giving Jack the chance to prove himself,' Lucilla said, tucking her hand through Tom's arm. 'Ain't that right, Daddy?'

'I wouldn't quite put it like that, petal,' Augustus said mildly. 'Jack is a trouper and he's going to help us out of a hole.'

Ronnie cleared his throat. 'Jack is a talented musician, miss. When he plays, everyone will listen, and they'll forget all about his – er – condition.'

In spite of everything, Clemency could not help but be touched by Fancy's obvious devotion to Jack. She patted her on the shoulder. 'They're right, you know. You ain't seen Jack when he's been playing on street corners, but I can tell you no one laughs at him, nor even notices that his legs don't work. Even the starlings coming home to roost are quiet when Jack plays his music.'

'Well, it don't shut the blooming cockney sparrow up now, do it?' Lucilla snapped. 'It would serve you right if you lost your voice, Miss Sparrow. Because I can sing circles round you. Last night in the pub they was all drunk, so of course they thought your bawdy song was the best. I appeal to the toffs outside the theatres. They appreciate a good soprano when they hear one.'

Edith banged a wooden spoon against the kettle. 'Shut up the lot of you. Clemmie, bring them clothes here. We'll go and change in Jack's room. The rest of you, get about your business. I wants that table cleared and then I'm going to set about cooking the dinner since Ma Blunt has took to her bed.'

'Someone is talking sense at last,' Augustus said, getting to his feet. 'Lucilla, my angel, you clear the table.'

Lucilla stared at him open-mouthed. 'But, Daddy . . .'

'Do it, now!'

'Yes, Daddy.' Eyeing him warily, Lucilla began to pile up the dirty crockery.

Clemency bent her head over the dry clothing, so that Lucilla wouldn't see her smiling. She helped Fancy to her feet. 'Come on, girl. You're drowning me brother.'

Fancy pulled away from her, wiping her eyes on the back of her hand and sniffing. 'Leave me be.'

Jack caught each of them by the hand. 'Please don't fight. I love you both.'

Fancy gasped. 'You love me, Jack?'

He smiled and raised her hand to his lips. 'I've said so, haven't I? Now, do me a favour, and stop quarrelling with me sister. She's as prickly as a burr when she's crossed, but she can be nice, when she tries.'

Reluctantly, Clemency smiled and ruffled his hair. 'I'll be nice if she will.'

Fancy shrugged her shoulders. 'Likewise.'

'Good. Now get out of them wet duds afore you both catches that fatal chill Ronnie spoke about.'

Augustus barred Edith's way, placing himself in the doorway to Jack's sleeping quarters. 'Don't take this wrong, madam. But can you cook? I don't ask for myself, but for the other lodgers. I mean . . .'

Edith drew herself up to her full height and looked him in the eye. Clemency stifled a giggle at the look on Ma's face. She already knew the answer.

'If I wasn't a lady,' Edith said stiffly. 'I'd smack you in the gob for your cheek. But as I am a lady, I'll tell you, mister. I was serving in the bar of the Pig and Whistle, down Ratcliff Highway, when I met me old man, but mostly I worked in the kitchen doing the cooking. He said he was going to take me away from all that and give me a better life. The lying bastard. But yes, I can cook, and when you've tasted me steak and kidney pudding you can apologise for your bad manners.' She pushed him aside and marched into the old storeroom, leaving Augustus gaping.

Clemency followed her, chuckling. 'Well said, Ma. That put him in his place.'

*

Leaving Ma and Fancy to squabble over territory in the kitchen, Clemency took a cup of tea upstairs to Mrs Blunt's room. She found her prostrate on the bed, still fully dressed, complaining that the light hurt her eyes and that she was suffering from a dreadful headache. The sight of her ashen face and pinched features was enough to convince Clemency that she was not exaggerating her symptoms, and she made her as comfortable as possible, telling her to stay in bed until she felt better. Downstairs in the kitchen, she walked into a scene that caused her to stop and stare in amazement. Ma was wearing one of Mrs Blunt's old dresses with an apron tied around her waist, and her hair tucked into a white mobcap, with just a few wayward strands licking around her temples. It was as though a completely different woman now inhabited her mother's body. Less than an hour ago she had been a hopeless drunk, terrified that Hardiman was going to find her and drag her back to a whore's life on the streets: now she appeared to be full of confidence, and in complete control of the situation.

Clemency closed her eyes and then opened them, half expecting to find that she had been dreaming. But sure enough, there was Fancy standing at the table, grating a lump of suet into a bowl. Ma was wielding a sharp knife and expertly slicing a large beefsteak. Even Lucilla had been put to work. She was sobbing over a pile of onions, but it was difficult to tell whether her tears were of anger and frustration, or caused by the stinging zest from the onion skins. Jack and Tom had been banished to a far corner of the room, and, judging by the sounds emanating from the scullery – hammering, swearing and the occasional yelp of pain – Augustus and Ronnie were attempting to make a carrying seat for Jack.

Edith looked up. 'Is she still sick?'

'Very sick, Ma.'

'No matter,' Edith said, pointing the knife at her. 'Make yourself useful, Clemmie. Fill a pan with water and put it on to boil. This pudding will take at least five hours to cook. I'll give them a meal tonight that they'll never forget. And Fancy, when you've finished with the suet, you can cut up the kidneys. I'll make the pastry crust. I was known for me suet crust in the old days. Light as angels' wings it was.'

By midday, the carrying seat was finished. It looked a bit odd, but Augustus and Ronnie were so proud of their efforts that Clemency had not the heart to say so. The broom handles had not proved to be such a good idea. They had split as soon as a nail was driven through them, and Ronnie had been forced to think again. He had gone out, returning later with two narrow planks and a rusty saw. After another half hour of sawing, and more swearing, the carrying seat was completed. They lifted Jack onto the chair and carried him round the kitchen, but when they attempted to turn, taking the corner too sharply, Jack fell off. Fancy screamed and dropped the sack of potatoes that she had fetched from the scullery.

Clemency rushed forward to help, but he raised himself on his hands and to her intense relief, he was chuckling.

'Are you hurt, Jack?'

'Nothing but me pride.' Jack held his arms up so that Tom and Ronnie could lift him back onto the chair. 'It'll take a bit of practice, boys. Maybe we could slip a couple of tumbles into the act. It would make the punters laugh.'

'Don't you dare,' Clemency said firmly. 'You wouldn't think it so funny if you'd broken a bone.'

Fancy scowled at Tom and Ronnie. 'Take better care of him, you fools. Or you'll have me to deal with.'

'Hush, Fancy.' Jack grasped her by the hand. 'I ain't fragile, pet. I'm made of India rubber, I am. Didn't you just see me bounce off the flagstones?'

The first afternoon out on the streets went well, but progress with the carrying chair was slow. Tom had his face hidden in a muffler and was not feeling very well, but Clemency had to give him credit for not grumbling. He didn't even say anything when Jack hit the occasional wrong note.

They played to the crowds in Petticoat Lane, and went on to Fenchurch Street Station, but by then the sky had turned to ochre and the air was heavy with the sooty smell of a London particular. By five o'clock, the air was thick and green and they were on their way back to Flower and Dean Street battling though a solid pea-souper. Clemency could barely see Jack, even though she had her hand on his shoulder. Tom was just a shadowy shape as he shuffled along at the back of the carrying chair, and she could not see Ronnie, even though she knew he was at the front. Augustus and Lucilla led the way. Clemency could just make out the faint tapping of his cane as he walked like a blind man, using the stick to feel for walls and kerbs. Her ears felt as though they were filled with water, muffling the muted rumble of a train, or the slow, clip-clopping of a horse's hooves as it plodded homeward. There was the occasional waft of warm air, laced with tobacco smoke and alcohol fumes, as an amorphous figure loomed from the fog, and disappeared through an open pub door. It was not a night to be out on the streets. The threat of the Ripper seemed even more menacing as they waded through the fog.

When they finally arrived outside the lodging

house in Flower and Dean Street, Augustus came to an abrupt halt. 'Who left that damned cart outside the house? I could have done myself a real mischief if I hadn't stopped in time.'

'It stinks of fish, Daddy,' Lucilla complained. 'Bad fish.'

'It must be Connor,' Clemency whispered in Jack's ear. 'I'll bet he's come to visit Ma. I thought he liked her when he took her to the pub. Although God knows why, when she wasn't looking or acting her best.'

'I think you're imagining things. Anyway, Ned might have sent him,' Jack replied in a low voice. 'Could be he's got news of Hardiman.'

Clemency felt her heart sink to her boots. What if Hardiman really had recognised her in the Crown and Anchor? She chewed the tip of her finger, waiting until Ronnie had hoisted Jack over his shoulder, and was carrying him slowly down the area steps. Augustus had gone on ahead to open the door, and Tom was attempting to manoeuvre the unwieldy chair on his own. 'Give us a hand, Clem,' he said. 'It ain't heavy, just awkward to get through the gate.'

She picked up the handles and helped him down the steep stone steps, with Lucilla stomping after them, grumbling beneath her breath and coughing.

The steamy atmosphere of the kitchen was fragrant with the aroma of steak and kidney pudding. The O'Malley brothers were just finishing off their meal before going out for the night shift, although Clemency heard Augustus warning them that the pea-souper was as dense a one as he had ever seen. Edith was busy at the range, mashing potatoes in a saucepan, and, seated on a chair close to the fire, Clemency saw Mickey Connor. His cheerful expression changed to one of astonishment as she took off her cap, shaking her long hair so that it tumbled loose about her shoulders.

'Holy Mother of God!' Mickey said, staring at Clemency. 'I'd never have known it was you.'

'Did Ned send you to warn us about Hardiman?'

Mickey shook his head. 'He did not.'

'I saw Hardiman in the Crown and Anchor the other night. I thought he might have recognised me.'

'He never mentioned the fellow, but young Ned is worried about you. He said you had a falling out and he asked me to make sure you was all right.'

'You can tell him, I'm fine. And thank him for asking.'

'And you'll go and see him?'

'Not if he's going to lecture me again about dressing like this. I only does it for the performance, not because I like it.'

Mickey looked her up and down with a nod of approval. ''Tis fine you look. In my humble opinion, more young ladies should wear breeches.'

'You will stay for supper, won't you, Mickey?' Edith cast him a sideways glance beneath her lashes.

'Sure, I was thinking you were never going to ask.' Mickey flashed a disarming smile at her, topping it up with a saucy wink.

Edith giggled and gave the potatoes an extra thump with the wooden spoon. Clemency shot a curious glance at her mother. It was strange to see her smiling and flirting with a man. And she seemed quite sober too. Not a hint of the gin bottle about her. Ma's eyes were clear and bright, her hair was piled up on top of her head in a coronet of copper curls, and there were spots of colour on her thin cheeks.

Edith turned to her, suddenly businesslike. 'Clear the table and set fresh places, Clemmie. I'll make up a tray of supper for Mrs Blunt and then we'll eat.' She raised her voice. 'Fancy! Where is that girl?'

'She's looking after Jack, Ma.'

'That's all very well, but it ain't what she's paid for.' Edith ladled soup into a bowl and took it to the table where she thrust it into Fancy's hands. 'You've work to do, girl. Take this tray up to Mrs Blunt.'

'Your ma is a fine woman,' Mickey said. 'I admire a woman with spirit.'

'She's had a hard time since me dad went away. Sometimes she . . .' Clemency hesitated – she had to make certain that Mickey understood Ma's weaknesses. 'Sometimes she drinks a bit too much, but she's off the booze now. Whatever you do, please don't let her go near a pub.'

'You can trust me on that one. In fact, I'm thinking I might ask her to step out with me on Sunday.'

'That would be good,' Clemency said, with feeling. 'But don't go to any place where you might bump into Hardiman.'

Mickey's eyes followed Edith's slim figure as she bustled about, fetching bread from the crock and cutting it into wafer-thin slices. He frowned. 'What is this man to her?'

'He's a devil, that's what Hardiman is. A devil what took advantage of a widow woman with a crippled son and a young daughter to raise on her own. Make no mistake, Mickey. He's a bad man to cross. Just keep out of his way.'

The O'Malley brothers got up from the table, praising Edith's cooking. Augustus, Ronnie and Tom took their places, passing the dirty crockery and cutlery to Lucilla, who protested that she was not a servant. For the second time that day, Augustus raised his voice and spoke sharply to her, ordering her to clear the table. Clemency almost felt sorry for the spoilt brat, but then if anyone had it coming to her, Lucilla did. Tom looked as though he wanted to say something in her defence, but a frown from Augustus was enough to subdue him.

'You haven't heard a word I was saying.'

Clemency glanced down at Mickey, startled. 'What?'

'I said that Edie told me about the carrying chair they made for Jack. Now it don't take a genius to see that you couldn't get far with a contraption like that.'

'That's true.'

'So it is. I'm lodging not far from here, in Frying Pan Alley, and I'm thinking that you could use me cart in the evenings. That's if the boy don't object to the smell of herrings and haddock.'

'Why would you do that for us?'

He leaned back in the chair, his thumbs hitched in the pockets of his waistcoat. 'Would it not put me in your ma's good books?' He tapped the side of his nose and winked.

Before Clemency could answer, Edith came towards them with her hands full of cutlery. 'I thought I told you to lay the table, miss. Not to stand about gossiping with Mickey.' She thrust the knives and forks into Clemency's hands.

'Don't scold her, Edie. Weren't we just praising your cooking? And didn't I tell her she was lucky to have such a lovely woman for her mammy?'

Clemency held her breath. Ma would surely tell him off for talking a load of tommyrot, but Edie smiled and slapped Mickey's hand in a playful manner. 'Oh, you Irish!'

Every day after that, with the exception of Sundays, Tom and Ronnie took Jack in the carrying chair to the pitches that were close to Flower and Dean Street. In the evenings, Mickey brought his cart round, and in return, Edith gave him supper. The use of the handcart enabled the troupe to go further afield. Now they could perform outside the theatres in the Strand, entertaining the crowds queuing for seats. Jack had soon mastered the flute, and, Clemency thought, he could now play it far better than Tom. Augustus had bought a second-hand concertina from Minski, and Tom could squeeze out a basic tune, although, it had to be said, not very well. He blamed the instrument, insisting that some of the internal reeds were broken, and it did wheeze rather more than it played, but the sound added a lively touch to songs like 'Old Towler' with its chorus of huntsmen's calls and halloos. With Ronnie's help, Clemency soon had the whole repertoire off by heart, from sentimental ballads to comic songs. She had learnt to play the part of a young boy and never, never to try to upstage Lucilla, who trilled away in her frilly frock, with her hair in ringlets and her plump cheeks slightly rouged. Privately, Clemency thought she looked more like an overstuffed, painted doll than a pretty young lady, but she knew when to keep her mouth shut. As long as Lucilla thought she was the star of the show, she behaved like a reasonable human being; but if Clemency received louder applause, Lucilla's bottom lip would stick out so far that a parrot could have used it as a perch.

It was all too easy to offend Lucilla, but Clemency had discovered her weakness for sweets and cakes. If she upset the temperamental nightingale, a bag of brandy balls, almond rock or a stick of barley sugar would be certain to bring a smile back to Lucilla's face. And she would do almost anything for a box of chocolates. Clemency knew for a fact that Tom had found this out long ago. Augustus might think his little petal was untouched and pure as a lily, but Clemency often stayed up late in order to practise her reading skills. When there was no one about to disturb her, she would sit, poring over the reading primer that Ronnie had bought second-hand from a stall in Petticoat Lane. When her eyes were too heavy to keep them open any longer, and the words began to dance about the page, she would creep upstairs to bed. On several occasions, she had seen Tom padding barefoot from the ground floor, where the men shared a large back room, up the stairs towards Lucilla's room. Judging by the noises that began as soon as the door closed on him, Tom had not come upstairs for a chat.

As the cold, foggy days of winter warmed into an early spring, it seemed to Clemency that the house was filled with lovers. Lucilla and Tom might keep their intimate relations a secret from Augustus, but Fancy was openly affectionate towards Jack. On one occasion, late in the evening when most of the household had gone to bed, Clemency had gone outside to the privy in the back yard, and on her return had found Fancy's sleeping place empty. The door to Jack's room had been left ajar and she had not been able to resist the temptation to peep inside. In a shaft of moonlight filtering through the little window high up in the wall, she had seen Fancy, fully clothed, lying down beside Jack with her arms around him as he slept. They had looked so sweet and innocent, like the babes in the wood, that it had brought a lump to her throat. She had tiptoed away, not wanting to break the spell.

After that, Clemency had tried to be extra nice to Fancy, if only for Jack's sake. But it was not easy. Fancy was prickly as a hedgehog, jealous and touchy. Sometimes Clemency wondered if they would ever really be friends; she just had to keep reminding herself that Fancy was genuinely fond of Jack, and that he was happier now than he had ever been, in the bad old days when they had lived in Stew Lane.

Then there was Ma, who had been stepping out with Mickey every Sunday afternoon for two months, and during that time had not touched a drop of strong drink. Mrs Blunt's nerves had never recovered fully from Jared Stone's announcement that he was thinking of selling the property. Sometimes she seemed to be her old self, in charge of everyone, but at other times, she retired to her room and spent days there, locked in and seeing no one. Ma had continued to do the cooking, even when Mrs Blunt was having a good spell. The lodgers were happy, and Clemency had never seen Ma in such high spirits. Released from Hardiman's evil influence she was a different person. The yellowish tinge had left her skin and she had filled out a bit, developing curves that seemed to make it difficult for Mickey Connor to keep his hands off her. It was a fact that Ma stayed with Mickey in Frying Pan Alley most Sunday nights. The first time it had happened, Clemency had been frantic with worry, and had been ready to go to the police station next morning, half expecting to find that the Ripper had claimed yet another victim. Then Ma had breezed into the kitchen, with a big smile on her face. There had been no need to ask where she had spent the night.

Clemency had gone outside to the privy and cried with relief.

With all this springtime billing and cooing, Clemency felt strangely out of place, even though she tried to convince herself that she had no interest in forming a relationship with any man. As far as she could see, they were trouble. Allowing any bloke to get a grip on your emotions would end up one way only – heartbreak and loneliness. Ned had come to call twice, the first time to apologise in person for criticising her costume, and the second time he had brought a fruit cake, baked by Nell, and an invitation to come to the pub for supper. She had accepted the cake and wriggled out of the supper invitation, using working the theatre queues as an excuse. Ned had gone away looking distinctly put out, but Clemency was unrepentant. She liked him well enough, but he was too bossy and if he had any romantic ideas, then he would be sorely disappointed. She hoped that her refusal would not upset Nell, who had shown her nothing but kindness, but she felt that if she allowed herself to be drawn into their tight little family circle, she would be caught like a wasp in honey, unable to escape. And she needed to be free. There was danger lurking in the shadows and it was not just the notorious Ripper. One day Hardiman would almost certainly find them, and Jared Stone was also out there somewhere: a silent menace, hovering in the background. He had not repeated his threat to sell the lodging house, but Clemency had not forgotten the desperate look on the pregnant girl's face when Stone had sent Meg packing. That man worshipped one thing only, and that was money. She knew he would be as ruthless in throwing them all out on the street as he had been with Meg.

It was a chilly evening at the end of March. The wild winds had whipped straw and loose playbills into a spiralling twister that had left a trail of rubbish strewn over the pavements outside the Strand Theatre. The theatregoers had gone inside leaving Augustus and his troupe to pack up their instruments, ready to move on to the Gaiety, the Lyceum and the Adelphi. Clemency stood beneath the poster advertising the latest comic opera, waiting for Tom to fetch the handcart from Surrey Street. It had to be left a fair distance away, so that the stench of rotting fish did not offend the people they hoped to entertain and to relieve of their hard-earned money. The wind had whipped long strands of hair from beneath her cap, and she took it off, shaking out her long tresses. She stared up at the face of Dorabella Darling, smiling down from the poster with gleaming white teeth, and an immodest expanse of bosom exposed above a tightly corseted waist. One day, Clemency decided, she would sing inside the Strand

Theatre instead of out here on the cold pavement. She would be a famous star of the opera bouffe, just like Dorabella.

'Move along there. You're blocking the entrance.' The liveried doorman made wild motions with his hands as a hansom cab drew to a halt at the kerb. He pushed past her to open the cab door and assist a young woman to alight. She laid a gloved hand on his arm and stepped down to the pavement. Clemency had seen many toffs and their ladies, but this girl was an outstanding beauty. Dressed in the height of fashion, with feathers and flowers in her upswept blonde hair, she had the fragile look of a porcelain figurine. She swept past Clemency leaving a trail of perfume in her wake. The doorman ushered her inside, bowing obsequiously. There was something vaguely familiar in the haughty manner of the beautiful young lady.

'I'd recognise that flaming-red flag anywhere.'

She could never forget that voice. With her cap still clutched in her hand and her hair caught by the playful wind, Clemency spun round, coming face to face with the man she had hoped never to see again.

Chapter Eight

Jared Stone was standing so close to her that Clemency could feel the warmth of his body. The tangy scent of sandalwood and Macassar oil brought back unpleasant memories of their first meeting. A sudden gust of wind caught the corner of his opera cloak – it lifted and flapped like the wings of a huge black bird – the blood-red lining caressed her cheek. His voice was deep and seductive. 'Busking outside a theatre! You are wasting your talents, my dear.'

'No one asked for your opinion.'

'And you are content to go about dressed like a street urchin, earning a few coppers a day?' Jared's lip curled in contempt. 'I had you down for an opportunist, Clemency. A girl with ambition.'

'Jared.' The young lady called from the foyer. 'We'll miss the first act if you don't hurry.'

'Go along, Jared,' Clemency mocked. 'Be a good chap and do as she says.'

'I'll be with you in a moment, Izzie.' He waved to his companion, but his eyes held Clemency's in a hypnotic gaze.

She wondered vaguely what the relationship was between Stone and the beautiful young lady. Not that she cared. He could have as many mistresses as he liked – it was no skin off her nose!

'My offer still stands,' Jared said. 'Come and work with me, and there'll be no more of this degrading existence. You're worth more than this.'

'I told you afore; I don't want to go back to being a dipper.'

'I'm not talking about stealing hankies and breast pins. I could open the doors to a different world, if you've got the courage to take a chance.'

'And if I haven't?'

'Then I can close doors just as easily. You need saving from yourself, Clemency. But I'm not a patient man and I always get what I want. Think very carefully before you refuse my offer a second time.'

'And what if I says no?'

'I have a buyer who is very keen to purchase a certain establishment in Flower and Dean Street.'

Augustus came over to them. He stared hard at Jared. 'I know you. You're the fellow that threatened to throw us all out on the street.'

Jared bent his head so that his lips were close to Clemency's ear. 'I'll give you twenty-four hours and then I want an answer.' He turned on his heel and strode into the theatre foyer. The doors closed behind him.

'What did he want, Clem?' Augustus put his arm around her shoulders. 'Don't let him scare you. We theatre folk look after our own. Just say the word and I'll set Tom and Ronnie on him.'

Clemency smiled in spite of herself. The picture of gentle Ronnie and toothless Tom taking on Jared Stone, and the ruffians she had seen in Hog Yard, made her want to laugh and cry at the same time. She shook her head. 'It weren't nothing. Look, here comes Tom with the cart. We'd better move Jack afore he catches a chill in this cold wind.'

As Tom and Ronnie hoisted Jack onto the cart, he leaned over and touched her shoulder. 'What did that bloke want with you, Clemmie?'

'Nothing, Jack. Honest. He was just passing the time of day.'

'Don't lie to me. I may be crippled but I ain't stupid.'

'We'll talk about it later,' Augustus said, taking the cart handles in a firm grasp. 'If we don't move on quickly we'll miss the theatre queues and there'll be no supper for anyone.'

They were about to move on when a man in evening dress rushed out of the foyer. 'Stop, stop. Sir, may I have a moment of your time?'

Augustus hesitated. 'We have to get to our next pitch. Can't it wait?'

'No, I must speak to you now.' He held out his hand. 'Horace Claypole, theatre manager, in a very difficult situation.'

'Augustus Throop, man of business. How may I help you, sir?'

'Please step inside for a moment.' Horace hurried back into the foyer. He held the door open, tapping the floor with the toe of his patent-leather shoe, and drumming his fingers on the glass.

'Best do as he asks,' Augustus said, after a moment's consideration. 'Something tells me it might be to our advantage.'

Lucilla grabbed his arm. 'Daddy! Maybe he's heard me sing and is going to offer me a part in the opera.'

'Only one way to find out, poppet-pie.' Augustus tucked her hand into the crook of his arm. He turned to Clemency. 'Best come in too, Clem. If we lose our little nightingale to the legitimate theatre, we don't want our little sparrow to be taken off by inflammation of the lungs. Follow me.'

They followed Horace through a maze of narrow passages that led eventually to his office behind the stage. Clemency could hardly believe that she was inside a real theatre with a performance in progress. She inhaled the fuggy smell, a mixture of tobacco smoke, expensive perfumes and disinfectant. The full-bodied sound of the orchestra accompanying the singers filtered out through the closed doors to the auditorium. She could only imagine what it was like to be in there, transported by the music, sound and colour to a fairy-tale world where there was no poverty, want or disease: a world of beauty and imagination – the stuff of dreams. She dragged her thoughts back to the present, glancing round to make sure that Ronnie and Tom had brought Jack in out of the cold. Sure enough, they had him suspended between them, with his arms around their shoulders, dangling like a puppet. Jack grinned and winked at her. 'Maybe it's you he wants, Clemmie.'

'All my eye and Betty Martin,' Clemency retorted, chuckling.

They all crowded into the tiny room. Most of its floor space was taken up by a large desk, piled high with papers, and its walls were lined with playbills. Horace seemed even more agitated, and he paced up and down, wringing his hands. The leather soles of his shoes made tip-tapping sounds on the bare boards, and there was silence as everyone waited for him to speak.

'Er, how may we be of service, Mr Claypole?' Augustus asked at length. 'Time is of the essence, if you don't mind my saying so.'

Horace came to a halt. 'Yes, quite. Well, I'll come straight to the point. You've no doubt heard of my leading lady, Dorabella Darling?'

A murmur of assent rippled round the room.

Horace clapped his hand to his bald pate, rolling his eyes towards the ceiling. 'She announced, just before going on stage, that she has accepted a better offer. She leaves tonight on the boat train for Paris, where she will star in the Opéra Garnier. My poor little theatre can't compete with an offer like that. The understudy has laryngitis, and I am desperate for a replacement, at very short notice.'

Augustus puffed out his chest and pushed Lucilla forward. 'I knew that someone would spot my little nightingale sooner or later.'

Horace stared at him as if he had gone mad. 'No, no, sir. You're mistaken. The role requires the actress to play the part of a pageboy who disguises himself as a maid. I need someone who can be convincing in both parts.' He eyed Lucilla's plump form, with a dull red flush rising from above his starched white collar. 'I mean, the replacement for Dorabella needs to be . . .' He coughed delicately and looked past Lucilla to where Clemency was standing. 'You, young lady – I've heard you singing outside my theatre, and I was convinced that you were a young boy. Then tonight, when I saw you without your cap, I realised that you are exactly what I have been looking for. What is your name, my dear?'

'Daddy!' Lucilla shrieked. 'He can't mean it. I'm the one with the golden voice, not her.'

'Hush, petal.' Augustus lifted Lucilla off the ground and thrust her into Tom's arms: a sudden move that would have left Jack hanging helplessly from Ronnie's shoulder if Clemency had not rushed over to support him.

'What is wrong with the young man?' Horace demanded, staring at Jack. 'Is he drunk?'

'No, mister,' Clemency said fiercely. 'Any fool can see that he ain't got the use of his legs. I'll have you know, what's more, that my brother Jack is a fine musician. He's probably better than all of them players in your orchestra put together.'

Horace clasped his hands together, his round eyes made huge by the thick lenses of his spectacles. 'Such fire! Such spirit! What is your name, my dear?'

'Aaarrgh!' screeched Lucilla, beating her fists against Tom's chest.

Augustus turned on her, scowling. 'Be silent, Lucilla.'

With a low moan, she hid her face against Tom's shoulder. He patted her on the head as if he was petting a dog. 'There, there, me love. Your turn will come.'

Lucilla kicked him on the shin.

Augustus thrust Clemency forward. 'This is my protégée, Miss Clemency Skinner. I am her manager. Shall we talk business?'

Horace pulled a large cotton hanky from his

pocket and mopped his brow. 'Certainly, but first I need to know if the young lady thinks she could learn the libretto in a very short space of time – by tomorrow evening to be precise.'

'Absolutely no problem,' Augustus said airily. 'Clemency only has to hear a song once and she has it committed to memory. Isn't that so, petal?'

She nodded, unable to speak. It must be a mistake. This could not be happening to a girl from Stew Lane. She dare not open her mouth for fear that she would wake up suddenly and find that it was all a dream.

'I'll help you, Clem,' Ronnie whispered in her ear.

'We'll all help,' Jack said. 'You can do it, Clemmie. I'm so proud of you.'

'I feel faint,' Lucilla announced, flinging her arms around Tom's neck.

'Take her outside. The night air will bring her round.' Augustus dismissed them with a wave of his hand. He perched on the edge of the desk, leaning towards Horace. 'Shall we talk pounds, shillings and pence, Mr Claypole?'

'Certainly, Mr – er – I'm sorry, but I've forgotten your name. It's all this worry. It's making me quite bilious.'

'Augustus Throop, but you may call me Augustus. I'd give you my card, but I seem to have left them all at home – in my study, on my mahogany desk with the tooled leather top and solid brass handles.'

Lucilla uttered a loud moan and slid to the floor.

Tom rubbed his shin, staring down at her with his eyebrows knotted into a frown. 'What shall I do with her, guv?'

Horace put his hand in his pocket and pulled out some coins. 'Allow me to pay for a cab to take the young lady home.'

'That's uncommon good of you, Horace,' Augustus said, hefting Lucilla in his arms and passing her to Tom. 'Take her home and tell the housekeeper to put her to bed.'

'You should go with them, Jack.' Clemency cast an anxious glance over her shoulder.

Jack smiled cheerfully. 'Don't worry about me, Clemmie. Ronnie and me will stay here with you.'

'I tell you what,' Horace said, beaming. 'I'll have the doorman escort you all to a box at the side of the stage. Miss Clemency, you'll be able to watch the performance. You can listen to the great Dorabella and, if what Mr Throop says is true, it will help you to memorise the libretto.'

'Wait!' Clemency said, as Horace headed towards the door. 'I ain't said I'll do it yet.'

Stunned silence.

Horace made a gobbling sound from somewhere beneath his starched collar. 'But – but . . .'

'As it happens, I will have a go at it, but on one condition.'

Augustus hooked his arm around her shoulders and his fingers dug into her flesh. 'Leave the business side of things to me, Clem.'

'No, Augustus.' She pushed him aside. 'I'll do whatever you want, Mr Claypole, but only if you gives me brother Jack a place in the orchestra.'

Horace peered at her over the top of his specs. 'A place in the orchestra? But my dear young lady . . .'

'Jack's a brilliant musician. It's both of us or neither of us. I ain't budging.'

'It's really up to the musical director and the conductor, but I'll try to arrange for Jack to have an audition. I can't say fairer than that.'

'Done.' Clemency spat on her hand and held it out.

Horace's Adam's apple bobbed up and down above his collar, and then he smiled, and shook her hand.

In the heady excitement of the next twenty-four hours, Clemency forgot all about Jared Stone and his ultimatum. She had sat enthralled during the performance of the opera, committing the music to memory. Once she had a melody in her head, she had always found it easy to learn the words of a song, but whether she could memorise a whole libretto, together with the actions, and in such a short time, was another matter.

When the performance ended and the theatre-goers spilled out onto the street, Clemency's ears were still ringing with the strains of the orchestra and the beautiful singing that had touched a chord deep inside her, making her want to laugh and weep at the same time. She felt as though she was floating on a cloud of make-believe. The cold night air slapped her in the face, bringing her sharply back to earth. Ronnie and Augustus were arguing. Ronnie said they should get a cab back to Flower and Dean Street, but Augustus pointed out that they had to return Mickey's cart, and they set off on foot. Settling down on a pile of old sacks, Jack picked up the flute and began to play snatches of the opera score, and Clemency began to sing. To her surprise, she had already committed some part of the libretto to memory. She barely noticed the chill of the night air, the smell of overflowing drains, stale fish, horse manure and the stench of the river at high tide. Her feet hardly seemed to touch the ground as she walked by the side of the cart, and when they finally arrived back in Flower and Dean Street, she was much too excited to go to bed.

Fancy was roused, groggy with sleep and grumpy, until she heard that Jack might have a place in the orchestra. Suddenly she was wide awake and smiling as she riddled the dying embers of the fire, and put the kettle on the hob. At midnight they were sitting round the table with mugs of hot cocoa laced with sugar. With Ronnie's help, Clemency studied the libretto while Jack played the melodies. In the early hours of the morning, too exhausted to continue any longer, Clemency climbed the stairs to bed. She lay down without bothering to undress and immediately fell into a deep sleep.

When she awakened a few hours later, the memories of last night's events came flooding back: she jerked upright and banged her head on the sloping ceiling. Giggling, she rubbed her head. Ma was still asleep, lying on her back and snoring softly. Clemency crawled out of bed. As she took off the boy's clothing and dressed in her old blouse and skirt, she felt as though she were floating several inches above the floor. Her head was buzzing with words and music and she had a fluttery, excited feeling in her stomach. It was still dark but she just had to tell Ma the good news. She went down on her knees and shook Edith by the shoulder.

'Ma, Ma, wake up.'

Edith opened her eyes, staring blurrily at Clemency. 'What's up?'

'Ma, you'll never guess what happened last night. I'm going to be a proper singer, on the stage.'

Edith raised her head. 'Fetch the po, Clemmie. I'm going to be sick.'

Clemency made a dive for the china chamber

pot and held it while Edith retched. 'What's the matter, Ma? Are you ill?'

Edith lay back on her pillow, pale-faced and with her eyes closed. 'Must've been something I ate last night. I'll be fine in a moment. Tell me all about it.'

By the time breakfast was over, the whole house knew of Clemency's good fortune. She even had a congratulatory hug from Mrs Blunt, who appeared to be having one of her good days. It was then that Clemency remembered Jared Stone's threat to sell the house if she refused his offer. But she had plenty of time, she told herself, and surely he wouldn't really go through with it just because she had turned him down. There must be plenty of other young girls who were prettier and much more adept at dipping pockets than she was. He would find someone else, and forget all about her. Anyway, there were much more important things on her mind at this moment, the main one being to learn the part before she had to be at the theatre for a proper rehearsal later that morning.

Lucilla was still sulking, and refusing to leave her room. Tom had a haunted look about him, but Augustus was so filled with enthusiasm for his new role as Clemency's agent and manager that he did not seem to notice. He sent Tom to the dollyshop to purchase a second-hand evening suit and dress shirt for Jack, declaring that the newest member of the orchestra must not stink of stale fish. Ronnie made Clemency go over and over the libretto, until she felt her head would burst. And finally, just before midday, Augustus sent Fancy out to find a cab to take them to the Strand Theatre.

As Clemency walked onto the stage, wearing Dorabella's costume, which had been pinned and tacked in order to make it fit, she was so nervous that she was certain she had forgotten all the words, and that her voice would come out like the screech of a peacock rather than the mellifluous notes of a nightingale. She was, after all, the cockney sparrow, and the audience would be sure to see through the costume and heavy stage make-up. She blinked, dazzled by the flickering footlights, and her throat felt as though it had closed up. She could not breathe and she wanted to run away.

Then someone in the assembled cast began to clap and soon everyone had joined in. She stared around at the smiling faces, bewildered by the tumultuous applause and the cheers. Horace slipped his arm around her shoulders. 'You see, Clem. There's nothing to fear. Everyone is behind you and they will all help you get through your first performance.'

A girl dressed in the costume of a maidservant came forward. 'I'm Maisie, the understudy,' she said in a hoarse voice, pointing to her throat.

'Lost me voice so I can't sing. Break a leg, ducks.'

'Break a leg?' Clemency turned to Horace, horrified. 'What does she mean?'

He gave her shoulders a squeeze. 'Actors believe that to wish someone good luck brings just the opposite. They're a superstitious bunch, Clem. You'll soon learn their ways.' He smiled. 'Break a leg, my dear.'

The rehearsal was a disaster. Clemency stumbled through her part with much help from the prompter, and whispers of encouragement from other members of the cast, but by the end she was almost in tears, and convinced that she would not be able to perform that evening.

'Don't worry,' Maisie said with an encouraging grin. 'A bad rehearsal is a good sign.'

'Oh, crikey!' Clemency said, sniffing. 'I'll never learn all this stuff.'

'You will, love,' Maisie croaked. 'I got a bottle of Hollands in the dressing room. If you need a drop of Dutch courage, you knows where to find it.' She skipped off stage.

Other members of the cast patted Clemency on the back, offering words of encouragement as they hurried off to their respective dressing rooms. The lead baritone kissed her on both cheeks and the tenor pinched her bottom. She would have run off to her tiny dressing room, but across the footlights she could see Jack sitting in the orchestra pit. He had been following the score, although he could not read a note of music, but his ear was good and this would be a test of his memory. The conductor waited while the rest of the musicians filed out and then he tapped the music stand with his baton, inviting Jack to play solo. Clemency stood alone, centre stage, with her hands gripped tightly together as she willed Jack to do well. The silver notes filled the auditorium with sweet music. She would not have been at all surprised if the gilded birds on the ornate ceiling had flown down to listen to Jack's playing. She was so proud of him that she wanted to cry. To look at him as he sat in the orchestra pit making sweet, sweet music, no one would know that he had such a crippling disability. His thick, dark eyelashes made crescents on his high cheekbones as he closed his eyes, and she knew that he was feeling the music to the core of his being. When the echo of the last note had ceased, there was a moment of complete silence, as if the theatre lay beneath a magic spell, lost in time. The conductor mopped his brow with a spotless white handkerchief and he smiled. 'Well done, Jack. Very well done. I'm proud to have you in my orchestra.'

The afternoon was spent in yet more fittings for the multitude of costume changes that went with the part. Clemency suffered being prodded and pinned, having to stand up, sit down and stand up again to ensure that the hem was the correct length so that she did not trip up and fall on her face. 'If you do,' Florrie, the dresser, explained, 'you must kiss the hem of your frock.'

'Why?'

'Because if you don't it will bring bad luck.'

While she was waiting in the wings for her cue, Clemency was shaking with stage fright. She wanted to run away and hide. She was certain that she would forget every single word and action. And everyone kept pinching her. At first she thought it was pure spite, but the call boy explained in a whisper that it was for good luck. By this time, she was convinced that all theatrical people were quite mad, and that she wanted nothing more to do with them. She was not going to go out there and make a complete fool of herself. She picked up her skirts and was about to turn and run, when someone gave her an almighty shove from behind.

'That's your cue, Clem. You're on.'

She stumbled onto the stage, tripping over the hem of her skirts and blinded by the popping, hissing gas footlights. Her legs had turned to lead; her mind had gone blank. She was doomed to ruin the whole show.

'You can do it, Clem.' She heard Jack's voice in her head. She could not see him across the footlights, but she knew he was down there in the orchestra pit. She felt him willing her on. She picked up the hem of her beautiful gown and kissed it for good luck.

The performance did not go without a hitch. Clemency missed some of her cues and fluffed many of her words. But she soon realised that she was not alone. The whole cast was on her side, covering her mistakes, and helping her through the performance. Off stage they might bicker and quarrel, thoroughly dislike each other and jealously compete for better parts, but all that was put aside when the curtain went up. The audience seemed not to notice the slight pauses when Clemency had forgotten what she was supposed to be doing, or that she improvised when she had forgotten the words. At the final curtain, the applause was deafening, with repeated calls of 'encore'. They took six curtain calls and at the last one, the call boy walked on to present Clemency with a bouquet of yellow roses. She did not know whether to laugh or cry as she followed the rest of the cast off the stage.

Horace came up to her and kissed her on both cheeks. 'The flowers are a small token of my appreciation, Clem. Well done, my dear. We'll make a star of you yet.'

Augustus was waiting in her tiny dressing room. Clemency stifled a giggle as he waddled towards her, looking like an overfed penguin in his second-hand evening suit. His smile was so broad that his eyes almost disappeared behind his puffed-out cheeks. 'Well done, my little sugarplum. I knew you could do it.'

'But I made a terrible mess of some of it, Augustus. I couldn't remember all the words.'

'No matter. That will come, poppet. You touched the hearts of the audience and they loved you. My only talent is that I can spot it in other people. My little Lucilla has a beautiful voice and a pretty face, but she could not have done what you did tonight. With my help, Clem, you will be a shining star in the theatrical firmament.'

Clemency soon discovered that becoming a shining star was not as easy as Augustus had made it sound. Her days were filled with rehearsals, lessons in singing, drama and deportment from a fierce old lady who had apparently once been a star of the Opéra Comique in Paris. Clemency left the lodging house early each morning and caught the green Bow omnibus to the Strand. Augustus and Jack followed later in a hansom cab, leaving Tom, Ronnie and Lucilla to work the streets on their own.

By the end of the first week, Clemency was word perfect. Jack had mastered the music almost from the first, and he was now learning to read the musical score. He seemed so happy and excited with his new career that Clemency was delighted for him. Her own life was so completely occupied with the theatre and her new friends that she had no time to worry about Jared, or even to think about Ned. For the first time in her life she was earning a real wage. She had no need now to beg for a few coppers from Augustus, or to bargain over stolen items in Minski's dingy shop. She felt rich, in spite of having to give fifteen per cent to Augustus, which he said was for managing her business affairs, although as far as she could see there were none to manage. Then she had to pay rent to Mrs Blunt for their board and lodging, which left her a shilling a week to spend on herself, but those twelve pennies meant more to Clemency than if they had been twelve golden guineas. With her first week's wages, she bought some green-glass bead earrings for Ma, which matched her eyes and made her smile. Ma had continued to be poorly in spite of a dose of Dr Collis Browne's Chlorodyne medicine. She had been quieter than usual, although Clemency saw very little of her during the first heady weeks of rehearsals and performances. And now, with the run of the current production coming to an end, the cast had begun rehearsals of *Mother-in-Law, a frivolous comedy,* followed by *Vulcan, or the (h)ammer-ous Blacksmith, a burlesque,* as they were styled on the posters and handbills. Clemency had only a small speaking part in the first play, and the lead in *Vulcan,* but each day she became more confident. She was so happy that she had to keep pinching herself to make certain that she was not dreaming.

On the morning of the last performance, she woke up to find Ma retching into the chamber pot. Clemency wriggled to the end of the mattress and sat up. 'Ma, you ought to see a doctor. You've been sick every morning for weeks. It can't be right.'

Edith raised a haggard face and her mouth twisted into a wry smile. 'I'm not ill, ducks. I was like this both times with Jack and then with you.'

Clemency stared at her, hardly able to believe her ears. 'You mean – no, you can't be, Ma.'

'Why not? I'm only thirty-seven, That ain't too old to fall pregnant, but I never thought it would happen again. Not after all this time.'

'I dunno what to say. Have you told Mickey?'

Edith shook her head. 'He'll run a mile.'

'Maybe not, Ma. He might be pleased.'

'Fat lot you know about men, Clemmie. Blokes like Mickey don't want to be tied down with a family.'

'He might surprise you. You got to tell him, Ma.'

'I'll never see him again if I do.'

'It ain't something you can hide forever. You must tell him. You might be surprised at how he takes the news.'

All morning Clemency worried about Ma. She

had not told Jack. Boys were funny about their mums; she knew that for a fact. Jack would be mad as fire if Mickey didn't do the right thing by Ma. With her mind occupied, Clemency forgot the dance steps and was shouted at by the ballet mistress. With a bit of a struggle, she put Ma's problem out of her mind and concentrated on her work.

At the final curtain, Clemency was presented with a bouquet of flowers. As she danced off the stage, she saw a dark stain spreading down the front of her costume. The flowers were dripping water and their stems were muddy. 'Oy, you. Charlie.'

The call boy came towards her grinning sheepishly. 'What's up, miss?'

'Where did you pinch these flowers? They never come from a shop, now did they?'

Charlie pulled a face. 'Don't you know nothing about the theatre, miss? On the closing night, the leading lady gets a bunch of flowers pinched from a graveyard. I had to risk life and limb to get them for you. It's tradition. So there!' He stalked off with an offended twitch of his narrow shoulders.

'Tradition! They're all blooming barmy,' Clemency muttered, as she went to her dressing room to change out of her costume. She dropped the bouquet into the waste bin with a shudder. 'Who'd want funeral flowers? Not me.'

She wiped off the thick greasepaint and washed her face in a bowl of warm water provided by Nan, the dresser who took care of her. She was fully dressed, and was buttoning her boots, when Charlie stuck his head round the door.

'You're wanted on stage, miss.'

Thinking that it must be Jack who had sent for her, she hurried through the dimly lit corridors to the wings. The auditorium was in darkness with just the ghost light left burning on the stage, yet another old theatrical superstition, to keep the spirits of dead actors from taking up residence after the theatre had emptied. A shiver ran down her spine as a tall shadow emerged from the far side of the stage.

'Who is it?' Her voice shook and her heart had begun to pump wildly; her palms were damp with sweat. 'Who are you?'

'I've been most patient, waiting for your decision.' Jared stepped from the shadows into the flickering candlelight. 'The waiting time is over. I want your answer, and I want it now.'

Chapter Nine

'You must be mad.' The words came tumbling out before Clemency could stop herself. She bit her lip. 'I mean, why would I want to turn back to crime when I'm doing so well in the theatre? I'm a star, in case you hadn't noticed.'

Jared strolled across the apron of the stage. With the light behind him, his shadow crept across the boards to engulf her, and when he stopped just a few steps away from Clemency it was too dark for her to make out the expression on his face. She felt, rather than saw, his anger. 'You're a street singer who had a lucky break, my dear. You have a good voice but you are untrained and undisciplined. You're an amateur.'

'That ain't fair! I've had good reviews in the newspapers.'

'And today those same newspapers will have been wrapped around fish and chips or used to light fires.'

'I don't care what you say. I am a star.'

'And who said so? The idiot Augustus? He's making money out of you, just the same as old Claypole. You may have the leading role this week, but I hear he's going to sign up a star from the Opéra Comique in Paris for the next production. You'll be lucky if they choose you to be her understudy.'

'That's not true. You're lying.'

His laugh echoed round the empty auditorium. 'Ask Claypole if you don't believe me.'

'Go away and leave me alone. I don't want nothing to do with you, Jared Stone.' Clemency stamped her foot, biting back tears of anger and frustration. He was lying, of course he was. Everything he said was aimed at hurting her and to achieve his own selfish ends. 'Go away.'

He took her by the hand. 'Come and work with me. I'm offering you a life of excitement and luxury, the like of which you'll never get in the theatre. Stay here and you'll end up singing on street corners again, or worse.'

'I'd rather sing on street corners than be your creature. I don't envy that poor girl what lives with you now. I suppose you'll throw her out on the street when you've had enough of her, just like you done with Meg.'

'You don't know what you're talking about. And don't you ever mention Izzie's name in the same breath as Meg Jones.' He dropped her hand as if her flesh had burnt him. 'You'll live to regret your decision, but I won't ask you again.'

He walked off, but Clemency could not allow him to have the last word. 'So what will you do then, Mr Stone? Sell the lodging house like you threatened and turn us all out on the street? That ain't what I'd call the action of a gent.'

He paused, turning his head to stare coldly at her. 'I'm not so much of a villain that I would make innocent people homeless. But you won't find my new agent so lenient as the last man. If the rent is overdue then Hardiman will have no alternative but to evict the lot of you, including the landlady.'

'H-Hardiman!' The word almost choked her. 'Did you say Hardiman?'

'I see his reputation goes before him. That is exactly what I wanted. Todd Hardiman won't stand for feeble excuses when it comes to collecting rents. I won't throw you out on the street, Clemency. But I'd advise you not to fall foul of my agent. I gather he's a bad man to cross. Goodbye, my dear. You won't be seeing me again.'

She did not wait for him to leave the stage. Clemency turned and ran back through the corridors to the musicians' dressing room, where she knew Jack would be waiting for her. She found him on his own, smoking a cigarette. He looked up as she burst into the room and he exhaled a plume of smoke. 'Where's the fire?' His smile froze. 'What's up, Clemmie?'

'Jack, we got to leave Flower and Dean Street. We got to get away tonight, or at least first thing in the morning.' She ran to him, throwing her arms around his neck.

'Hey, hey! What's the panic? Who's scared you like this?'

'I just saw Stone. He's hired Hardiman as his agent. I don't think he knows our connection with him, but we got to get away before he finds us.'

Jack stubbed his cigarette in an ashtray with vicious jabs. 'My God, I thought we'd got away from that bastard. Are you sure it's him, Clemmie?'

'There can't be two Todd Hardimans in this part of London, Jack. If he finds Ma now . . .' Clemency shuddered; she couldn't bring herself to tell Jack that Ma was in the family way. Weren't things bad enough already? She paced the floor, wringing her hands. 'We'll leave first thing in the morning. We'll run away.'

Jack looked down at his twisted limbs with a rueful smile. 'I won't be doing much running, ducks.'

'How can you joke at a time like this? I'll think of a way, I will. Even if I have to carry you on me back. We won't tell no one, not even Augustus.'

'Hold on a moment, love. We can't just up and leave without telling him, not unless you means to give up your part in the show.'

'Never.'

'Then listen to sense, Clemmie. We'll talk to

Ma and Augustus when we get back to our lodgings. This ain't something we can decide on our own.'

Reluctantly, Clemency agreed, but all the way home in the hansom cab she could think of nothing but Hardiman and Jared Stone. Somehow their faces seemed to merge into one and she hated them equally.

It was late in the evening when the cab dropped them outside the door in Flower and Dean Street. They usually found the house in darkness with most of the lodgers having retired to bed, but tonight lights blazed from first-floor windows. As soon as she entered the hall, Clemency knew there was something wrong. She paused at the foot of the stairs, the hairs on the back of her neck prickling with some primitive instinct for danger. She was about to go up to investigate when Fancy came running along the passage carrying a steaming jug wrapped in a cloth.

'What's going on, Fancy?'

'It's your ma. She's been took sick.' Fancy hitched up her long skirt, and hurried up the stairs.

Clemency's breath caught in her throat. 'Oh no, she wouldn't have.' She threw off her cape and hurried after Fancy. Ma had been terrified of telling Mickey that she was in the family way, but surely she wouldn't have done anything stupid? But as she followed Fancy into Mrs Blunt's bedroom, her worst fears were realised. Edith was half naked, prostrate on the bed, lying on a pile of blood-soaked towels and rags. Mrs Blunt stood over her attempting to staunch the haemorrhage. She turned to look at them and frowned. 'Take her away, Fancy. She can't do nothing here.'

'Ma!' Clemency ran to the bed and threw herself down on her knees beside Edith. Her eyes were closed and her face was whiter than the cotton pillowcase under her head. Her breathing was rapid and shallow, and Clemency was certain that she was dying. She seized her mother's cold hands and chafed them.

'Mrs B's right,' Fancy said. 'You should leave it to her. She's doing everything she can.'

Clemency barely heard her. All her attention was focused on Ma. She had seen dead bodies before: bloated corpses washed up on the water's edge and stiffs frozen to death in dark alleyways. Ma's face had the all too familiar, corpse-like waxen tinge. 'Oh, my Gawd! What has she done to herself? Is she going to die?'

'Not if I've got anything to do with it, she ain't.' Mrs Blunt dropped a bundle of blood-soaked rags into a bucket. 'Your mum went to one of them old back-street hags what sorts out women's problems. Only she got more than she bargained for.'

'How could you be so blooming stupid?' Clemency clasped Ma's cold hand to her cheek. 'Why did you do such a bloody silly thing?'

Mrs Blunt took the jug from Fancy, and poured hot water into the willow-pattern china wash-bowl. 'Take her downstairs, Fancy, and make her a cup of tea. Put some brandy in it.'

Clemency shook her head. 'No, I won't leave her. Speak to me, Ma. Please don't die. I'll do anything you say, but don't give up.'

Edith's heavy eyelids fluttered open. She stared at Clemency with eyes opaque and frosted, like shards of green glass worn smooth by the river and washed up on a high tide. Her lips had a bluish tinge and they moved soundlessly.

'Let her rest.' Mrs Blunt placed fresh towels beneath her, and covered Edith's lower limbs with a sheet. She turned to Clemency and her harsh features softened into a sympathetic smile. 'Go downstairs, there's a good girl. Your ma won't die because I shan't let her. Now do as I say.'

Fancy took her by the hand. 'She's right. You can't do nothing here. We'd best go downstairs and break it gently to Jack.'

'Can't you think of no one else but Jack?' Clemency struggled to her feet. 'Me mum is close to death, and all you worry about is upsetting me brother.'

'That's better,' Fancy said, smiling. 'You have a go at me, girl. Spit it out.'

Clemency dropped her gaze, ashamed of her outburst when she knew that Fancy had only been trying to help. 'Sorry.'

'Come on.' Fancy led her from the stuffy room with its sickly stench of blood.

'Why did she do it?' Clemency demanded as she followed Fancy down the narrow staircase. 'Ma was upset when I left this morning, but not desperate.'

'Her bloke, Mickey, come round after he finished selling his fish. All slippery and shiny with scales he was, and stinking like Billingsgate Market on a hot day. I dunno how she could let him near her, but there's no accounting for taste.' Fancy stopped as they reached the baize door. 'She took him up to Mrs B's parlour. We heard him shouting and her crying, and then he come thudding down the stairs and the front door slammed. I wanted to go up to her, but Mrs B said not to, she'd be best left alone. I had to go out to market then, and when I come back your mum had been somewhere and got it done. Doubled up in pain she was . . .'

'Don't tell me any more. I got to think what to do next.'

Fancy peered at her in the dim light of the gas mantle. 'What do you mean?'

'Never you mind. I got to speak to Jack right away. In private.'

'No.' Fancy folded her arms across her chest, barring Clemency's way into the kitchen. 'You may be his sister, but I'm Jack's woman. Whatever you got to say to him, you say to me too.'

A wave of exhaustion washed over Clemency, adding to her feeling of desolation. She shrugged her shoulders. 'All right, but you don't know what you're letting yourself in for.'

Fancy opened the door. 'It can't be that bad, but whatever it is, I'm with Jack.'

'So you say now. But you ain't heard the half of it.' Clemency pushed past her and went down the steps into the kitchen.

Jack and Augustus were seated on either side of the range.

'What's going on, Clemmie?' Jack's voice cracked with concern.

Fancy ran to him and gave him a hug. 'Your ma has had a bad time, Jack. But she'll be all right. All she needs now is rest and quiet.'

'But what's wrong with her?' Jack cast an anxious glance at Clemency. 'Has she been took with a fever?'

Clemency shook her head. She sat down suddenly as her legs gave way beneath her. Everything had been going so well, and now it was all going horribly wrong. 'It's worse than that, Jack. Much worse.'

'I'll make a pot of tea.' Fancy made a move towards the kettle, but Augustus stopped her with a wave of his hand.

He rose to his feet, taking a flask from his pocket. 'I think we all need a drop of something stronger than tea. I don't know what it is that ails poor Edith, but Jack has told me about Hardiman. What we need now is a plan of action.'

'Hardiman? What's he got to do with it?' Fancy demanded. 'If someone don't tell me, I swear I'll scream.'

'And what's wrong with Ma?' Jack thumped the arm of his chair with his hand. 'For Gawd's sake, tell me.'

Aided by a large tot of brandy, Clemency told him everything. There was a momentary silence, and then everyone began talking at once: Jack swearing that he would get even with Mickey, and Augustus ranting against Jared Stone for employing a villain like Hardiman to do his dirty work for him. While the men raged, Fancy and Clemency sat quietly, waiting for them to calm down.

'It would be worth meeting up with Hardiman again,' Jack said bitterly, 'if only to set him onto Mickey Connor. Them two bastards deserve each other. I'd pay good money to see them fight it out with bare knuckles.'

'Just as I was making my name in the theatrical

world,' Augustus groaned, taking a swig from his flask. 'As your manager, young Clem, I had my foot on the first rung to success. Why, given a year or two, we could have been in the West End. You could have been as big a star as Dorabella Darling.'

'Self, self, self!' Fancy cast them a scornful glance. 'All you blokes can think about is yourselves. What about us poor women?'

'That's right,' Clemency agreed. 'Never mind worrying about revenge or what might have been – what we got is a problem here and now. How are we going to get Ma and Jack to a place of safety? And where in heaven's name can we go that is safe from Stone and Hardiman?'

'I'd like to kill them both.' Jack fisted his hands, beating them on his withered limbs. 'Useless bloody cripple that I am.'

'Take the boy to his bed, Fancy,' Augustus said, getting to his feet. 'We all need to get some sleep. We'll see things in a different light in the morning.' He lurched across the floor, and made his way slowly up the stairs.

'Things won't look different in the morning,' Clemency said, frowning. 'It will be light in a few hours, and God alone knows what will happen then.'

Jack closed his eyes, resting his head against Fancy's shoulder. 'He's right. We need to get some rest. Help us to bed, Fancy, there's a little love.'

She hooked his arm around her shoulders and hefted him from the chair. Clemency stepped forward to help her, but Fancy shook her head. 'It's all right. I can manage. I'll be back in a tick.'

Clemency waited, pacing the floor, until Fancy tiptoed back into the kitchen. 'He was asleep afore I got his boots off,' she said, smiling. 'Poor boy, he ain't used to strong drink.'

'What's on your mind, Fancy?'

'Strange as it seems, I'm on your side in this, Clem. I seen Jack grow in pride in himself since he's been took on with the orchestra, and I ain't going to let no one put him back to begging on the street. You and me ain't never going to get on like sisters, but I'd do anything for Jack, and I got no quarrel with Edith, except that she's a silly mare for letting a bloke get her in that state.'

The stench of the sickroom and the sight of Edith's waxen face flashed before Clemency's eyes and, for once, she had to agree with Fancy. 'All right,' she said slowly. 'Then you'll agree with me that we got to get Ma and Jack away from here. We got to find a lodging where Hardiman can never find us.'

'Yes, and I'm coming too.'

'I suppose Jack would want that.'

'And Augustus?'

Clemency stared at her. Was it the brandy fumes or just tiredness that was fogging her brain? Nothing seemed to make sense.

'Augustus will want to stay here with Lucilla.'

'No he won't. That's another story. Lucilla and Tom have run off together.'

'But she's his little songbird – he thinks the world of the fat tart. It'll break his heart.'

'She's another silly cow who couldn't keep her legs together, and now she's in the pudding club. She was too scared to tell her dad in case he knocked out the rest of Tom's teeth.'

'Gawd's strewth, what a mess!' Clemency didn't know whether to laugh or cry.

'Don't worry about them. Tom's well in with the O'Malley brothers, and they've promised to find him work. It's a bit different to playing a concertina, but no doubt he'll keep them all entertained in the pub of an evening, afore he goes home to his fat and grumpy songbird.'

'I got to get some sleep,' Clemency said, rubbing her knuckles into her burning eyelids. 'First I'll go and check on Ma, and then I'm going to bed. We'll have to get away early in the morning.'

'But where will we go?'

'I have no idea, but I do know someone who may be able to help. G'night, Fancy.'

Wearily, dragging her feet, Clemency made her way up to Mrs Blunt's room. She peered round the door, holding her breath, terrified of what she might see, but all seemed quiet. In a yellow pool of gaslight, Mrs Blunt was sitting beside the bed. She turned her head to peer at Clemency, putting her finger to her lips. 'She's sleeping peacefully. Don't wake her.'

'Will she be all right?'

'I hope so, dearie.'

Clemency had to be content with that. She crept up the stairs, tiptoed past the maids' door and went to her own room, where she collapsed onto the bed. She fell asleep almost at once, but a succession of nightmares disturbed her rest and she awakened in a cold sweat. It was still dark, with no sign of dawn streaking the night sky, but she now was wide awake. She stripped off her clothes and dressed herself once again in a shirt and breeches.

With no clear plan of action in mind, she crept from her room, and went down the stairs to check on her mother. The gaslight had been turned down low in Mrs Blunt's room, and it made popping sounds as it cast eerie shadows on the walls. Mrs Blunt was asleep in her chair, snoring gently, with her head lolling on her chest. Clemency tiptoed up to the bed, scarcely daring to breathe. Ma was lying so stiff and still beneath the coverlet that, for a moment, Clemency was sure that she was dead. Then, with an almost imperceptible sigh, Edith made the smallest of movements, and Clemency had to bite back tears of relief. She crept out of the room wiping her eyes on her sleeve. Now it was up to her to find a safe haven for them all, and she knew exactly where to go.

She arrived outside the Crown and Anchor just as the first grey streaks of dawn slashed the dark bowl of the eastern sky. She had walked all the way from Whitechapel, unnoticed in the crowds of people making their way to work on the docks, in the markets, manufactories and warehouses that hugged the banks of the Thames. She was just one amongst so many that she had no fear of being seen by Hardiman, who was a creature of the night: come the dawn, he would go underground, like the sewer rats who were his familiars. Just the thought of him made Clemency shudder. She raised her hand to knock on the taproom door, and then changed her mind. She did not want to draw attention to herself. Hardiman had spies everywhere, and it would only take one sharp-eyed sneak to see through her disguise. She shuddered at the thought, and decided that it would be best if she went round to the back of the building. Someone was sure to be at work in the kitchen, even if it was just Annie. She cut through the alley at the side of the pub, and let herself into the back yard, dodging behind a barrel as the scullery door opened casting a shaft of light onto the cobbles. Annie came out carrying a hod and she trudged across the yard to the coalhouse. Waiting until she was safely inside, Clemency emerged from her hiding place. Keeping in the shadows, she crossed the yard and entered the scullery. She could hear sounds of movement in the kitchen and she put her head round the door.

'Gracious heavens!' Nell let out a startled shriek, and then she peered at her. 'Is it you, Clemency?'

'It's me, Mrs Hawkes.' She tugged off her cap. 'I'm in desperate need of help.'

Nell's expression changed from alarm to one of concern, and she waddled across the flagstones to hug her. 'You poor girl. What's happened now?'

'I need to speak to Ned.'

'He's in the parlour having his breakfast. Come and tell us all about it.' She propelled her through a door into a small, wainscoted room where a fire blazed in the grate.

Ned was sitting at the table eating his breakfast of cold meat and pickles. He dropped his knife and fork with a clatter when he saw Clemency, and rose to his feet. 'Well,' he said, with a mock bow. 'This is an honour. The cockney sparrow herself has come to pay us a visit.'

'Now, Ned. None of your sauce.' Nell gave him a warning look. 'Make yourself at home, ducks. I'll fetch you a cup of coffee and a plate of breakfast. Then you can tell us what's brought you here at this hour of the morning.' She hurried back into the kitchen.

Ned held out a chair. 'Take a seat then. That's if the leading lady at the Strand Theatre don't mind sharing the table with a common innkeeper.'

Clemency sat down. 'Don't be like that, Ned. I know I haven't been round to see you, but I've been busy.'

'I know. I seen the posters. I'd recognise you anywhere, even with a stage name and all that stuff on your face that makes you look like a common actress.' Ned sat down heavily, pushing his plate away, leaving his food barely touched. 'So what brings you here in your fancy dress?'

Before she could answer, Nell came back into the room carrying a tray. She set it down in front of Clemency. 'Eat your breakfast and then you can tell us everything. You too, Ned Hawkes, and don't browbeat the girl. She's come to us for help and it's help she'll get, not a lecture on how she earns her living.'

Clemency flashed her a grateful smile. She sipped the hot, sweet coffee and felt the warmth returning to her chilled body. Ned mumbled something unintelligible, but he took his plate and ate silently. Every now and then he shot a piercing glance at Clemency. She could feel his resentment burning into her, making it almost impossible to eat. Nell bobbed in and out of the kitchen, issuing instructions to Annie, then returning to see if they had finished their food. In the end, Clemency pushed her plate away. 'I'm sorry. I can't eat while he's glaring at me like I done something wrong.'

'Ned, you should be ashamed of yourself.' Nell came to sit beside Clemency. 'This poor girl has come to us for help, and all you can do is sit there like some blooming justice of the peace. You tell us all about it, Clemency, love. Don't take no notice of my boy, he's as bad as his father.'

'At least I won't run off and leave you in the lurch like the old man, who couldn't keep his hands off a pretty barmaid.' Ned folded his arms across his chest. 'Go on then. I'm listening.'

'I know I only seem to come here when I'm in trouble.' Clemency stared down at her intertwined fingers. 'But you've both been so good to me in the past, and I – I think of you as part of me family.' She raised her eyes and saw Ned's harsh expression soften. 'I'm sorry, Ned. I don't mean to take advantage of your good nature.'

He smiled reluctantly. 'You're here now, so go on, tell us all about it.'

She explained as best she could, although she stumbled a bit when it came to admitting her mother's falling out with Mickey, who had been Ned's friend. She found it difficult to speak about Ma's near fatal encounter with a backstreet abortionist, but somehow she managed to get through the complicated story. Nell uttered exclamations of horror, interspersed with encouraging remarks. Ned remained impassive. Clemency came to a halt, sipping her coffee, and eyeing him apprehensively.

'Oh, Ned. Haven't you got nothing to say to the poor girl?' Nell got to her feet, wringing her hands. 'After all she's been through. There must be something we can do to help her and her family.'

'So what is this Jared Stone fellow to you?' Ned leaned forward, staring into Clemency's face.

Taken aback, she flinched. 'I dunno what you mean.'

'Why would he go to all that trouble, tracking you down, and making a bit of a fool of hisself, just to get you to pick the pockets of rich folks. It don't make sense, unless . . .'

The air was heavy with insinuation. Clemency jumped to her feet. 'Unless what?'

'Unless he wants you to warm his bed.'

The sound of flesh striking flesh echoed off the panelled walls. Annie stuck her head round the door grinning.

'Ooer,' she giggled, pointing at the red fingerprints staining Ned's cheek. 'I heard that clear out in the scullery.'

'Get back to work, you silly girl.' Nell shooed her out of the room. She paused in the doorway, turning to face Clemency with a worried frown. 'I can't say as how I blame you for that one, ducks. But squabbling won't help the situation. Ned, say you're sorry.'

He clutched his cheek, scowling. 'She hit me.'

'And you deserved it too. Now say you're sorry.'

'I'd best leave,' Clemency said, reaching for her cap. 'I shouldn't have come in the first place.'

'No, wait.' Ned held his hand out to her. 'I shouldn't have said that, even if I think that's what the scoundrel had in mind. As to your need for a place to stay – I got an idea.'

Clemency eyed him doubtfully. 'It would have to be somewhere really safe.'

A slow grin spread across Ned's face. 'Where would your mate Hardiman be least likely to go?'

'Heaven,' Clemency said, unable to suppress a smile.

'Not quite what I had in mind, but close.'

'Lord above! How can you two laugh about it?' Nell threw up her hands, staring at each of them in turn as if they had both lost their minds.

Ned took his jacket from the back of the chair. 'Put your cap on, Miss Cockney Sparrow. And come with me.'

Clemency looked to Nell, who nodded and gave her a reassuring pat on the shoulder. 'Do as he says, ducks. My Ned will look after you.'

A pale, buttermilk sun, hovering just above the smudged outline of rooftops and chimneys, was slowly burning off the early morning mist. An April shower had left the newly swept cobbled streets unusually clean and glistening, but the horse-drawn traffic was gradually building up at the start of another day's trading in the city. Costermongers pushed their barrows between drays, carts and omnibuses. Workers returning home from the night shifts jostled shoulder to shoulder with men and women hurrying to begin their day's work.

'Where are you taking me?' Clemency demanded breathlessly, as Ned strode on ahead of her.

'You'll see soon enough.' He dodged in and out of the traffic on Knightrider Street and led her down a narrow alley into Queen Victoria Street. She could smell the river now, and the stench from the manufactories wafting upstream from Wapping and the Isle of Dogs: boiling bones from the glue factory, roasting coffee beans, burnt sugar, naphthalene, turpentine, linseed oil, horse dung and hot engine oil. Ned walked on at a brisk pace, ignoring the ragged, barefoot street urchins who hung around in packs like hungry animals, and stepping over the legs of drunks sleeping off last night's excesses in dark doorways. He glanced over his shoulder, as if to make sure that Clemency was following him, but he did not stop. She kept as close to him as possible, sensing the unseen dangers lurking within the smoke-blackened walls of the ware-houses and illegal drinking dens that huddled together on the edge of the docks.

The narrow alley opened out into daylight and Upper Thames Street. A forest of masts, funnels and cranes lined the quays and wharves that were dissected by Blackfriars Bridge to the west, and Southwark Bridge to the east. Ned stopped outside a grey stone church that looked strangely out of place amongst the pubs, ship chandlers, warehouses and shipping offices.

'This is it, Clemmie.'

She stared up at the dilapidated building with a garden of green lichen blooming on its weatherworn stones. 'I ain't in the mood for praying, Ned.'

He tried the great iron ring on the studded door, but it would not open. 'Locked.'

'Ned, what are you doing?' Clemency followed him as he edged along the narrow opening between the church wall and a ware-house. The ground was strewn with rubbish and it stank of cats and human excreta. There was a small wooden door at the far end that opened with just a bit of help from the toe of Ned's boot. It was so low that he had to stoop to enter.

'Ned, this ain't right.' Clemency hovered in the doorway. The dank smell of ancient stone, mould and musty prayer books made her shiver. 'We shouldn't be doing this.'

'Come inside and close the door.' Ned's footsteps echoed on the stone-flagged floor. Dust motes danced in the hazy beams of light filtering through stained-glass windows. He came to a halt in the nave at the foot of the steps leading up to the chancel. He turned to her with an encouraging smile. 'Don't worry, ducks. This ain't a working church, so to speak. There ain't been a service here for twenty years or more.'

She stared at him aghast. 'No, you don't mean – you can't think that we could live here?'

He shrugged. 'Why not? No one wants it. I used to come in here with me mates when I was a lad, and we was bunking off school. No one ever thought of looking for us here. We'd smoke baccy and drink beer, and think we was cock of the walk.'

'But living here, Ned. That's a different matter.'

'Why so? Ain't churches supposed to offer sanctuary? And isn't that what you and yours needs right now? A place of safety where Hardiman and that Stone chap won't never think to look for you?'

Clemency glanced up at the altar, bare of its holy trappings, and a superstitious shiver ran down her spine. 'Yes, but it still don't seem right.'

Ned took her by the shoulders, giving her a gentle shake. 'Nothing's perfect, girl. But surely it will do for now. Let's take a proper look round and then you can make a decision, yes or no.'

Chapter Ten

Ned insisted on accompanying Clemency back to Flower and Dean Street. She would have refused his offer, but the news that Hardiman was working for Jared Stone had turned her world upside down. She had hoped that he belonged to the distant past, the grim days of eking out a living in the rat-infested cellar in Stew Lane. She had begun to feel safe in Mrs Blunt's lodging house, and his former hold over them had seemed like a dimly remembered nightmare. Now she was jumping at shadows, and even more scared of Hardiman than of the Ripper. In the first heady excitement of appearing on the stage, it had never occurred to her that he might recognise her face on the posters outside the theatre. The beautiful young woman who smiled down from the hoardings, renamed La Moineau by Mr Claypole, which he informed her was the French for sparrow, was so unfamiliar that she barely recognised herself. She knew that Hardiman could not read, and that his tastes ran to lewd music hall songs and bawdy jokes rather than the opera bouffe. But the thought that he might choose this day to descend upon the lodging house was enough to convince her that moving into the disused church was a good idea. Now all that remained was to persuade Ma and Jack.

They arrived at the lodging house to find Augustus pacing the kitchen floor in a theatrical maelstrom of emotional outpourings against Tom Fall, who had seduced and abducted his precious little nightingale. Ronnie and Jack were sitting at the table, silently watching the performance, while Fancy kneaded bread dough, apparently unmoved. Mrs Blunt was nowhere to be seen and all thoughts of Hardiman were wiped from Clemency's mind as a fresh fear made her stomach contract as though she had been eating unripe fruit.

'Where is Mrs B? Has Ma taken a turn for the worse, Jack?'

He looked up and the worried lines were wiped from his face in a look of sheer relief. 'Clemmie. Thank God, you're back. Where've you been? And why didn't you tell no one you was going out?'

'I had me reasons.' Clemency turned to Fancy. 'You'll tell me the truth. Is Ma—?'

Fancy slapped the dough into a pan and covered it with a damp cloth. 'She's very weak, but Mrs B thinks she'll get over it, providing she don't go down with a fever.'

Ronnie rose to his feet, holding out a chair. 'Come and sit down, Clem.'

'Did you know about my little poppet-pie?' Augustus demanded, coming to a halt in front of her. 'Gone – left without a word. Ruined, besmirched. Taken advantage of by a ruthless bastard.' He stopped, staring at Ned, who had put a protective arm around Clemency's shoulders. 'Do I know you, sir?'

'This is Ned. He's come to help.'

'I remember you now. You're Cyril's boy, from the pub.' Augustus thrust his face close to Ned's. 'We must follow them at once. We must bring her back home, where she belongs.'

Ned stood his ground, squaring his shoulders. 'I'm sorry, guv. But I'm here to help Clemency and Jack. You'll have to call the cops if you want to chase after your girl.'

'Come and sit down, old chap,' Ronnie said, taking Augustus by the arm. 'Getting in a state won't bring her back.'

'Ruined!' Augustus moaned, slumping down in the chair that Ronnie had offered Clemency. 'Her career is ruined by that immoral, womanising bastard. My little songbird, my helpless, innocent child.' He buried his face in his hands.

'Innocent, my eye,' Fancy said with a derisive snort as she dumped the pan on the hob. 'As to helpless! You wouldn't say that if you'd heard the noises coming from her bedroom night after night.'

Augustus raised his head, but Clemency stepped in before the argument could escalate into a full-blown row. 'We're all sorry for what's happened, Augustus. But Lucilla is a grown woman now, and I think Tom really loves her. You've got to let her go.'

'But what shall I do without her? Without my precious songbird, the Augustus Throop musical troupe does not exist.'

'Never mind feeling sorry for yourself,' Jack said firmly. 'We got more important things to discuss. Like where the hell have you been, Clemmie? And what is he doing here?' He shook his finger at Ned. 'Ain't you done enough harm by introducing our mum to that bugger Connor?'

Ned took a step forward, his hands fisted at his sides. 'What d'you mean by that?'

'Shut up, the lot of you.' Clemency leapt between them. 'You want to know where I was, Jack? I went to ask Ned for help, yet again. Because I couldn't think of no one else in London what would get us out of this place before Hardiman finds us. He could be coming up the front steps at this very moment, and then we'd be for it. Ned's found us a safe place to doss down for the time being, until we can find something better. He's offered to help us get Ma there, but we need to make a move now.'

'She's right,' Fancy said, moving swiftly to Jack's side. 'And I'm coming with you.'

Augustus raised his head, staring blurrily at Clemency. 'Not you too. I'm your manager, Clem. You can't mean to desert me as well as my little bird.'

'You mean, you want to come with us?'

'What else is there for me to do? Ronnie and I are all that's left of the troupe. We can't make it on our own, can we, Ron?'

Ronnie's moustache quivered at the waxed tips. 'You mustn't worry about us, Clem. You have to do what's best for you and Jack.'

'You old silly, Ronnie. Of course we need you. Jack can't get about on his own. We rely on you, and Augustus too. After all, if it's true that Mr Claypole is going to hire an opera singer from Paris, then I'll need to find work in another theatre. I need a manager now, more than ever.'

Augustus pulled a hanky from his pocket and trumpeted into it. 'Of course you would. Without me, you would be back to being the cockney sparrow, singing on street corners. And Lucilla will return when she's discovered that her paramour has feet of clay. Then we'll all be together again. Augustus Throop and his musical troupe.'

'Let's hope the baby can wail in key,' Fancy said, grinning.

Jack slipped his arm around her waist. 'Have a heart, ducks. Can't you see he's upset?'

'Sorry.' Fancy murmured, cuddling up to Jack and nuzzling his cheek. 'You won't go without me, will you, love?'

'Never. You and me is a pair, Fancy.'

Ned cleared his throat. 'I don't want to hurry you, Clemency. But I got to get back to work.'

'I know, and I am grateful to you, Ned. I'll go upstairs and get Ma ready to travel.'

At that moment, the baize door opened and Mrs Blunt came slowly down the stairs.

'How is Ma?' Clemency demanded. 'Is she going to be all right?'

'She's very weak and feverish. Only time will tell, Clem.'

'But we got to leave here now. We have to take her with us.'

Mrs Blunt took off her spectacles and polished them with the corner of her apron. 'She shouldn't be moved. She needs looking after.'

Clemency hesitated, thinking of the cold, damp interior of the church. It would be hard enough for the fit amongst them to survive in those conditions, but she could not leave Ma here. She turned to Ned. 'We can't take Ma to that place. It would kill her.'

He looked past her, addressing himself to Mrs Blunt. 'Would Mrs Skinner be fit enough to stand a cab ride?'

Mrs Blunt nodded. 'She'd have to be wrapped up warm and carried all the way. She mustn't put a foot to the ground, not yet, or it could start up the bleeding again.'

Ned turned to Ronnie. 'Looks like you and me got a job, mate. Are you willing?'

'Of course. I'd do anything for Edith.'

'Good man. We'll take Mrs Skinner to the Crown and Anchor. My old lady will look after her. She's as good a nurse as Florence Nightingale ever was. You lot can make your own way to Upper Thames Street.'

'Upper Thames Street – it has a good ring to it.' Augustus got to his feet. 'I'm back in charge of this troupe. Never let it be said that Augustus Throop failed when duty called. Ned, young chap, if you would be so good as to procure a hackney carriage, I will get the idiot housemaids to pack our few belongings in a bag. If the young ladies will make Edith ready for the journey, I will settle up with Mrs Blunt.' He caught Clemency's hand as she was about to mount the stairs. 'I do hope this new lodging will be commensurate with our status, my dear. After all, you are a star and I am your man of business.'

'This is a joke – isn't it?' Augustus stood in the nave staring about him, his eyes wide with horror. 'You can't imagine that we could stay here, Clem?'

Ronnie set Jack down on the front pew. 'I've kipped in worse places than this.'

'It's freezing cold,' Fancy said, shivering. 'We'll catch our death or worse.'

'You didn't have to come. If you don't like it you're free to go back to Mrs Blunt's place.' Clemency hugged her cloak round her. It was cold, bitterly so, but no one, not even Stone would think to look for them in a church.

'You won't get rid of me that easy.' Fancy huddled down on the pew next to Jack.

'It ain't so bad,' Ronnie said, blowing into his cupped hands and rubbing them together. 'It's a bit chilly, but there must be a vestry or a crypt that we could use for sleeping. And the good thing is that it's free.'

'Now that,' Augustus said, smiling, 'is a good point. And it's a lot better than sleeping under Blackfriars Bridge, which I have done during lean times in the past.'

'We'll move on as soon as I'm certain that Stone has given up on me,' Clemency said, hoping she sounded more positive than she was feeling. 'Maybe you could get me a part in one of them big theatres up West, Augustus. With Jack learning to read music and me studying me words, there's no end to what we could do.'

Jack took a packet of Cinderella cigarettes from his pocket and offered one to Ronnie. 'Let's make the best of this. At least it ain't the middle of winter. We'll be fine, so long as we stick together.'

Clemency flashed him a grateful smile, but it froze on her lips as she met Fancy's resentful gaze. 'All right, Fancy. I know you don't like it, but if you're going to stay I suggest you give me a hand to make the place liveable.'

Reluctantly, Fancy got to her feet and followed her into the vestry. She wrinkled her nose. 'It stinks in here.'

'Look here.' Clemency spun round, her patience stretched to snapping point. 'Stop bloody moaning and give me a hand to make this place comfortable.'

'Comfortable?' Fancy looked up at the vaulted ceiling festooned with cobwebs, hanging like veils of black lace. Her gaze travelled down the whitewashed walls where the plaster had fallen off in huge clumps and lay on the floor like lumpy custard. A stack of old hymnals in the corner sprouted hairy blue mould, and the floorboards were coated with mouse and bat droppings.

Their eyes met and Fancy's lips quivered into a grimace that was half laughing, half crying. Clemency felt a gurgle of near hysterical laughter rising in her throat. Before she knew it, they were hanging on each other's shoulders, laughing helplessly.

'I hate you, Clemency Skinner,' Fancy giggled.

'Fains I, Fancy Friday.' Clemency wiped her eyes on her skirt. 'Looks like we're stuck with each other.'

'Fains!' Fancy held her stomach. 'I got belly-ache from laughing so much.'

'They'll think we've gone barking mad,' Clemency said, hiccuping. 'Let's be sensible for once, Fancy. What do we need the most?'

Fancy shuddered. 'A mop and bucket.'

'And?'

'And some bedding, I ain't sleeping on the floor again. Not never.'

'Right. We'll get some money from Augustus and you and me will go out to the nearest popshop and get what we need.'

Augustus knew of a pawnshop in Bleeding Heart Court. He gave them some money, and Ronnie came with them to help carry things. The old man in the pawnshop could have been Minski's brother, although Clemency knew that he was not. Minski had come to England on his own, lived on his own, and was far too mean to spend money on a wife and family. When the pawnbroker in Bleeding Heart Court discovered they had money to spend, his surly attitude melted into one of fawning helpfulness. He even produced a little spirit stove from somewhere in the back of his dingy shop, and threw in a can of paraffin at no extra cost. They purchased blankets, pillows, tin plates and mugs, a kettle that was only slightly dented, and two enamel chamber pots. Ronnie was rapidly disappearing beneath a mountain of items and his knees buckled.

'We'll have to do a couple of trips,' Fancy said, scratching her head. 'And we need candles, matches and tea.'

'Wait.' The pawnbroker disappeared into the back of the shop once again. They heard him scrabbling about, shifting things, swearing a lot in a foreign tongue: it was funny, Clemency thought, her mind oddly detached from their plight – you could always recognise swear words, whatever the language spoken. Then, with a triumphant cry, he reappeared through the tattered curtain, pushing a dilapidated bath chair. 'I knew I had this somewhere amongst me stock. I'll only charge you threepence for the hire, providing you bring it back today.'

A bath chair with a hood – just what they needed! Clemency tried not to look too enthusiastic. 'It's got a wonky wheel,' she said, kicking it with her foot. 'And it's moth-eaten. Look at the hood, it's rotten and the whole thing is dangerous. I don't suppose it'll get us a hundred yards without collapsing.'

Fancy nudged her in the ribs. 'We need this, Clem.'

Ronnie twirled his moustache and he looked thoughtful. 'It is a bit of a mess, guv. Why, that contraption ought to have been chucked on the scrap heap years ago.'

'I'm only asking threepence for its hire. I ain't trying to sell it to you.' Minski's double wrung his mittened hands. 'Be fair.'

'It is a wreck,' Clemency said, taking her cue from Ronnie. 'I doubt it will make the return journey. Seems to me we'd be doing you a favour if we just dumped it in the Thames.'

'No, young shaver. Have a heart.'

'Well, then. What's your best price? Although really you should be paying us to take it away.'

'Half a crown.'

Clemency examined the change in her hand. 'Too dear. I'll give you a shilling and that's me final offer.'

His eyes gleamed. 'One and six.'

Clemency counted out a one-shilling piece and three pennies. 'One and three.'

'You're robbing an honest man, sonny.' He held out his hand. 'But I'll take it.'

That night, Jack rode to the theatre in his bath chair. At first he complained that it made him look like a gout-ridden old man, but Fancy sent him off with a kiss and a promise of long walks by the river in the spring sunshine. By the end of the evening, he seemed to have come to terms with his new mode of transport, and even joked about it with Ronnie as they made their way home after the performance. When they arrived back at the church they found that Fancy had been busy. She had cleaned the vestry so that it sparkled in the candlelight, and the smell of carbolic soap and Lysol had replaced the former musty odour.

Augustus had imbibed several tots of brandy in the theatre bar, and he boasted that Horace had given him a Havana cigar to smoke, which just showed in what high esteem the theatre manager held him. He seemed to have put Lucilla out of his mind, at least for the time being, and, in a haze of goodwill, he sent Ronnie out to the nearest pub to fetch a jug of ale and some hot pies for their supper. They ate their meal seated in the choir stalls. The alcohol had gone straight to Clemency's head, and she was exhausted after a long and emotionally trying day. She barely noticed the cold striking up through the flag-stone floor of the vestry as she lay down on a coarse blanket. They all huddled together for warmth, and with Fancy on one side of her and Augustus on the other, she closed her eyes and drifted off into a deep sleep.

Although it seemed sacrilegious to heat a kettle on the spirit stove in the chancel, Jack said he thought that the Lord would not mind them boiling water for a brew of tea next morning. After all they had eaten pies and drunk ale in the choir stalls in full view of the altar, so it did not seem any worse to fill the old stone font with water from the pump at the corner of Broken Wharf, which they could use for making tea and washing. Ronnie went out first thing and returned with a brown paper bag filled with hot bread rolls for their breakfast. From the capacious pocket in his overcoat, he produced a pot of marmalade and a pat of butter wrapped in a piece of muslin. 'My treat,' he said, beaming. 'There's nothing like a taste of marmalade to start the day off right.'

Clemency ate, but with little appetite. She was worried about Ma and had made up her mind to go to the Crown and Anchor as soon as she could get away. She was telling Jack when Augustus overheard.

'My dear Clem. Do you think it's wise to go about in broad daylight? I mean, you've got two desperate characters looking for you, so wouldn't it be more prudent to visit your dear mama after dark?'

'I need to make sure she's all right now, Augustus. She's not young and she ain't strong like me. I need to be certain that she's not taken a turn for the worse.'

'I'd go if I could,' Jack said, frowning. 'But I'd only draw attention to meself in the bath chair. I can't hardly go in disguise looking like I do.'

'No, but I can.' Clemency patted his shoulder. 'I'm getting used to dressing like a boy, and even though Hardiman might see through it, his mates wouldn't. I'll just go and make sure she's all right and I'll come straight back.'

'Make sure you do,' Fancy said, tossing her head. 'You come back and do your share of the cleaning. I ain't a skivvy now. I'm as good as the rest of you.'

'Don't worry, Clem,' Ronnie said. 'I can handle a broom with the best of 'em. You go and see Edith and give her my best regards. Tell her Ronnie is thinking of her and wishing her well.'

Clemency reached up and kissed his cheek. 'I will, Ronnie. I'll tell her that.'

'And Clem.' Ronnie grasped her hand. 'Tell that young man of yours not to let Edith near the drink. We don't want her falling back into her bad old ways, especially after what she's been through.'

Clemency looked into his earnest brown eyes, realising with a sense of shock that Ronnie cared deeply for her mother. Dear, kind Ronnie, who never had a bad word to say of anyone, was in love with Ma, who had never given him a second glance. She squeezed his stubby fingers. 'I'll give her your message and I'll warn Ned not to let her anywhere near the booze.'

'Just thought I'd mention it. You don't mind, do you?'

'Of course not, Ronnie. You're just like one of the family.'

*

She made it to the pub without attracting any particular attention. No one seemed to take much notice of a skinny boy dressed in shabby clothes. She was just one of the many who roamed the streets, most of them on the dip, and a few on genuine errands for their masters. There was, she decided, a definite advantage to being a male in a predominantly male world. Theirs was a freedom denied to mere females. They could come and go as they pleased; they could toy with women's emotions and then abandon them, just as Mickey Connor had left Ma to take the consequences of their brief affair. She went into the pub kitchen and was met by a surly remark from Annie.

'You can shut up,' Clemency said crossly. 'I ain't in the mood for any of your sauce.' She went into the parlour, looking for Nell, but the room was empty. She went through to the bar, where she found Ned pulling pints of beer. His smile of welcome was sincere enough and it gratified her. She had a warm feeling for Ned, and despite his bossy and proprietorial manner, she knew that he meant well.

He passed the pint tankards over the bar into eager hands. He took the money and handed out the change. 'Edith's not too well. Ma's with her now.' He put the coins in the till. 'She's in the room at the top of the stairs.'

Clemency made her way along the narrow passage that led to a flight of stairs. Her heart was pounding inside her chest, and she had a strong sense of unease as she went up to the bedroom. The door was ajar, and she almost collided with Nell who was on her way out, carrying a pail filled with bloodstained rags.

Clemency could just make out Ma's shape on the bed beneath a white counterpane. 'H-how is she?'

Nell shook her head and her bottom lip quivered. 'Not very well, ducks. She's had a bad night. I called the doctor early this morning but there weren't much he could do. He gave me a bottle of laudanum and she's had a couple of doses, so she's sleeping now.'

'Can I see her?'

'Of course you can, love. But let her rest. The doctor said that's all we can do for her, keep her warm and quiet.'

'But – but she won't die, will she, Nell?'

'I can't say, ducks. I wish I could tell you that she'll pull through, but it's in God's hands now. We done all we can.' Nell bustled out of the room, closing the door behind her.

Clemency went to sit at the bedside. She stared down at Ma's prostrate body, looking so small and frail beneath the spotless white coverlet, which was only a shade lighter than her pale face. Her hair spilled over the pillow in a wild tangle, its vibrant copper colour in stark contrast to her pallid complexion. Her breathing was even but shallow. Clemency laid her hand over Ma's as it rested on the counterpane; it felt cold and bony, like the claw of a dead chicken. She shuddered and bit back tears. Suddenly she was a small child again, sitting beside her mother after a beating from Hardiman had left her unconscious. She was afraid, so afraid. She curled her fingers around Ma's hand, willing some of her own body heat to warm the cold flesh, and desperately hoping to transfer some of her own vitality to Ma's enfeebled body. She did not realise that Nell had returned, and was standing behind her, until she felt a warm hand on her shoulder.

'Don't take on so. You won't help Edie by getting yourself in a state.' Nell gave her a handkerchief. 'She's sleeping peacefully. Best leave her be.'

Clemency mopped her eyes and blew her nose. 'She looks so ill.'

'At least she's alive. We just got to wait and pray. You've got to be strong for her, Clemmie. Come downstairs, ducks. A cup of tea will make you feel better.'

Reluctantly, Clemency left Edith's side. She followed Nell downstairs into the parlour where a tray of tea had been set out on the table. Nell sat down and cut a large slice of currant cake, which she put on a plate and handed to Clemency.

'Sit down and have a nice cup of tea and a slice of cake. I made it myself, though I don't get much time for baking these days. I'd hoped to train that silly girl to cook, but she's as thick as a suet pudding, and next to useless.'

Clemency slid onto a chair, drained of emotion. The room was warm and the hot tea warmed her stomach. She nibbled a slice of cake and smiled. 'Ma used to make cake like this in the old days.'

'When was that, ducks?'

'We lived in a pub down Wapping way. Me dad run off when I was just a nipper and then Ma met Hardiman and we moved to Stew Lane.'

'I thought you told me that your dad was dead.'

'Dead to us, I meant. I don't like to talk about it.'

Nell heaved a deep sigh. 'I know what you mean, dear. When my old man cleared off, I was left to run this place all on me own.'

'But you did it.'

'Oh, yes. I managed somehow. I hired a barman and I took in gentlemen lodgers until Ned was old enough to help out. He's a good boy, Clemmie. And he's very fond of you.'

'I know,' Clemency said, toying with the crumbs on her plate. 'But I'm steering clear of all men. They're nothing but trouble, in my opinion.'

'Some of them are, dear. And some of them aren't. You just got to pick a good 'un, if you can. Although, I have to say it, us women always seems to fall for the bad boys. Me and your mum have got a lot in common. I'll do me very best to look after her, and you must try not to worry. If she takes a turn for the worse, I'll send Ned to fetch you, night or day.'

There was nothing more that Clemency could do, and she left the pub feeling even more despondent than she had when she first arrived. Despite encouraging remarks from Ned, and Nell's steadfast promise to do everything in her power to make Edith better, she could not quite believe that Ma would pull through. She might once have been a strong and healthy woman, but her constitution had been weakened by years of near starvation and terrible living conditions. Hardiman had abused her physically, and her refuge in strong drink had only served to make matters worse.

Clemency couldn't face going back to the church. She couldn't bear to see Jack's face when she told him that Ma was hovering between life and death. She set off to walk to the theatre, where she could escape into the life of another character. She felt safe amongst the theatrical folk who had quickly become her friends. Her heart always lifted as she entered through the stage door. She left Clemency Skinner outside on the street and lost herself in a magical world of colour, light and music. She became La Moineau, which might be French for sparrow, but sounded so much more exotic.

The sky above was a peerless blue and small white clouds floated about like puffy meringues. By the time Clemency arrived at the theatre the hint of spring in the air had lifted her spirits, and she was feeling a little more optimistic. At least they had escaped from Hardiman; he would never find them in Upper Thames Street. If only Ma would make a speedy recovery, then perhaps things weren't so bad after all. She entered the foyer and was met by Horace, who leapt out of the box office, making her jump.

'Ah! Clem, you're early. That's what I like to see in my performers – enthusiasm.'

Clemency smiled and nodded. She was about to walk on when he caught her by the arm.

'You have a visitor, my dear. A young lady who was most insistent that she wait for you, even though I told her you were not expected in the theatre until later.'

'A young lady?'

'A very well-dressed young person. If I didn't know better I would have assumed she was a young lady of quality, but she assured me that she was a friend of yours. She's in your dressing room.'

Mystified, Clemency hurried through to the

theatre. The door to her dressing room was ajar and she went inside, filled with curiosity as well as a feeling of apprehension. A tall, slender young woman stood by the make-up table. Clemency tried not to stare, but she could hardly take her eyes off the confection of feathers and ribbons that formed the smartest little hat she had ever seen. She knew, from watching the wealthy patrons of the theatre, that the lavishly trimmed lilac-silk gown was in the very latest fashion: hoops were definitely out and bustles very much in vogue. She would have given her eye teeth for an outfit like that.

'I am waiting for Miss Skinner, boy.'

She knew that voice; she had heard it once before. It was the young woman who had accompanied Jared Stone to the theatre. Clemency tugged off her cap, shaking her head to allow her hair to fall about her shoulders. 'I am Clemency Skinner. Who are you?'

'Oh!' Her eyes widened in surprise. 'I'm sorry. I mistook you for a boy. I am Isobel Stone.'

So she was his wife. Clemency stared back into the cool blue gaze of the self-assured young woman. 'What do you want with me?'

Isobel's confidence appeared to waver for a moment. She looked away, apparently studying a spider hanging from the ceiling by a silken thread. 'I believe Jared made you an offer.'

Clemency shut the door, leaning against it,

studying Isobel's delicate profile. 'What's it to you?'

'You turned him down. Why?'

'Like I said, what has it got to do with you? I don't want nothing to do with a crook like him, nor his dirty dealings.'

'How dare you speak of Jared like that? If I were a man I'd knock you down.'

Clemency folded her arms across her chest, angling her head. 'If I was a bloke, we wouldn't be having this conversation. Get off your high horse, lady. I ain't impressed, and the answer is still no.'

'You would rather stay here?' Isobel's gesture took in the spiders' webs, the dingy paintwork, the fly-spotted mirror and the dressing table littered with half used sticks of greasepaint. 'You would choose the life of a cheap chanteuse rather than help a noble man to further his charitable cause?'

Now she knew that the woman was completely mad. Clemency blinked hard, wondering if she had heard correctly. But Isobel was obviously working herself up into a state of distress. Her china-doll complexion had paled alarmingly, her breathing was quick and shallow and, to Clemency's amazement, tears sparkled on the tips of her eyelashes. She bit back a caustic comment as to Jared Stone's integrity; the poor girl was obviously besotted with him, and labouring under the illusion that he was a decent man. It would be best to humour her, or she might turn hysterical. 'Look, lady, I mean, Isobel. We got off on the wrong foot. I don't think you quite understand the job that Mr Stone offered me.'

Isobel tugged at the strings of her reticule and pulled out a scrap of lace-trimmed organdie. She dabbed at her eyes. 'I'm sorry. But it makes me so cross when people who know nothing about him criticise Jared, who has devoted himself to raising funds for the foundling hospital, and the mission to seamen, not to mention the home for fallen women.'

'So that's what he does?' Clemency struggled to equate the saintly patron of good causes that Isobel was describing with the hard-nosed businessman who had threatened to throw perfectly good tenants out on the street if he did not get his own way. She could not. The only explanation seemed to be that there were two Jared Stones, or that he was a better actor than the fabled Henry Irving, whose likeness hung over the desk in Horace Claypole's office.

'Of course it is. Jared works so hard fund-raising. He is tireless in his efforts to get rich people to make donations. I can't think why he picked you to help him in his good works, but I trust his judgement implicitly. Won't you reconsider his offer, Miss Skinner? I appeal to your better nature.'

For a second or two, Isobel's obvious sincerity had made Clemency doubt her own judgement, but the memory of Stone's harsh threat to have them all evicted from the lodging house in Flower and Dean Street was still fresh in her mind. No decent man would employ a villain like Hardiman. Clemency shook her head. 'I said no, and I meant it.'

Isobel was silent for a moment, staring down at the floor. Then she raised her eyes to Clemency's face and her lips trembled. 'Won't you think of those poor babies, abandoned by their mothers? The unfortunate young women who have been driven to a dissolute way of life? The seamen who, having served their country, have fallen on hard times, or suffered shipwreck and loss? I don't know why Jared picked you, but I do know when he is troubled and frustrated. We are both determined people, Miss Skinner. And I assure you that I don't give up easily.'

Clemency opened the door and held it open. 'Nor me neither. I'm well suited here and that's me last word.'

Isobel tossed her head and swept past her, leaving a trail of expensive perfume in her wake. 'I shan't give up, Miss Skinner.' She paused, opening her reticule. She tucked the hanky away and took out a small deckle-edged calling card, which she handed to Clemency. 'If you should change your mind, you'll find me at this address.

I won't say goodbye, just au revoir, La Moineau.'

With a swish of silk petticoats and the clickety-clack of high heels on the bare floorboards, Isobel marched off, leaving Clemency standing in the doorway, staring after her. Either the woman was deranged, or she had been seriously mistaken in her opinion of Jared Stone. If his wife thought so highly of him, she was either a complete fool or desperately in love. Clemency went back into her dressing room and sat down at the make-up table. She opened her clenched fist and studied the elegant italic print on the calling card. Her reading was coming along nicely, thanks to Ronnie's patient coaching, and she had no difficulty in deciphering the address:

Isobel Stone,
35 Finsbury Circus,
London, E.C.2

What, she wondered, was Stone playing at? She didn't believe all that nonsense about his good works, but Isobel had obviously been taken in by him. Well, she wasn't such a gullible fool. She went to tear the card in half and then changed her mind, tucking it into the pocket of her jacket. Hell would have to freeze over before she went crawling to Jared Stone.

Chapter Eleven

The performance that evening went well, despite the fact that Clemency could barely keep her mind on her part. With Ma hovering between life and death it seemed wrong to be prancing about on stage, entertaining people who could afford to lash out two guineas for a box, and wouldn't recognise poverty if it came up and bit them on the bum. Every now and then she caught sight of Jack in the orchestra pit, but she was not fooled by his encouraging smile; she knew that he too was desperately worried about Ma. After the final curtain, including several encores, Clemency ran to her dressing room, where Florrie was waiting to help her out of her costume. Complaining bitterly about her bunions and corns, Florrie gathered up the discarded garments, tut-tutted when she saw a greasepaint stain on the bodice, and went off grumbling that she would have to stay late to get it clean. Clemency heaved a sigh of relief when the door closed on her.

Having scrubbed her face with cold cream soap, and washed it off in the warm water provided by Florrie, Clemency dragged the calico shirt over her head and stepped into the coarse fustian breeches. She pushed the vision of Isobel Stone, with her breathtaking gown and pretty little hat, to the back of her mind as she pulled on her thick woollen socks and, finally, the clodhopping boots. She might dress like a woman on the stage, but now she had to revert to her boyish disguise, and she was getting heartily sick of the whole charade. Seeing Isobel looking so elegant in her fine silks and satins, and smelling fragrant as a rose, had touched a chord in Clemency that was now vibrating like the plucked strings of a harp. A small, treacherous voice in the back of her mind was telling her that she could have all those things if she were to comply with Stone's wishes. Hadn't he promised her comfort and security if she worked for him?

'You're a fool, Clemency Skinner.' She glared at her reflection in the mirror as she twisted her hair into a knot on top of her head, and rammed the cloth cap in place. As she tucked the telltale strands of hair out of sight beneath the crown, she saw a pale-faced boy staring back at her. Why, she wondered, would a man like Jared Stone be interested in someone like herself? He had a young and beautiful wife who so obviously adored him. She straightened her cap, shrugged her shoulders and turned off the gaslight. She had more important things to think about than Stone, and the main one was Ma. She hurried through the corridors to find Jack.

The air in the musicians' dressing room was thick with cigarette smoke. It was like walking into a London particular, and breathing in the fumes made her cough. Most of the musicians had already left for home, but Jack was seated in his chair, smoking a cigarette. Standing beside him she saw Ned and her heart gave an uncomfortable jerk inside her chest. It could only be bad news.

Jack looked up and beckoned to her. 'Clemmie. Come here.'

She hurried over to them. 'What is it? Is she worse? Is that why you've come, Ned?'

'She's a bit better. The doctor came this evening and he's more hopeful. He said she's over the worst.'

Clemency swayed on her feet, dizzy with relief. 'Oh, thank God.'

Ned steadied her with his arm around her shoulders. 'He said she's got to rest. She needs warmth and good food, so there's no question of her coming to live with you at present.'

'We can pay for her keep,' Jack said, flicking ash off his cigarette. 'We don't want to impose on you and your mum.'

'There's no need to fret on that score. Ma said Edith can stay with us until she's well again. Tell you the truth, I think she'll enjoy a bit of female company.'

Clemency's knees buckled, and she sank down onto the nearest chair. 'You've both been so kind to her. We can't thank you enough.'

'It was me who introduced her to Connor.' Ned stared down at his boots, and his cheeks reddened. 'I feel to blame in part.'

'You wasn't to know, old chap.' Jack stubbed out his cigarette in an overflowing ashtray. 'I should have sorted the bugger out when I saw what he was up to.'

'Neither of you were to blame,' Clemency said, shaking her head. 'Ma is a grown woman. She made her choice, and she made a mistake picking a chancer like Mickey Connor.'

'I had words with him this afternoon.' Ned flexed his fingers. 'I told him what had happened.'

Clemency gave him a searching look. 'Did he want to see Ma and make things right with her?'

He shook his head. 'Connor didn't want to know, but I give him something he'll remember for a long time to come.'

'I'll shake your hand, mate,' Jack said, with a rueful smile twisting his lips. 'You're a good chap, Ned. If things had been different I'd have done the same.'

Ned grinned and the dull flush spread to the tips of his ears. He took his curly-brimmed bowler hat from the table, and put it on at a rakish angle. 'Let's just say that Connor ain't such a handsome fellow with his two front teeth missing. Maybe he'll think twice before he ruins another good woman's reputation. Anyway, I got to get back to the pub.'

'Tell Ma I'll come and see her in the morning,' Clemency said, walking with him to the door. 'And thanks again, Ned.' She reached up and kissed his cheek.

If she had slapped him, he could not have looked more startled. He stared down at her for a moment, and then he tipped his hat and hurried out of the dressing room. She could hear his booted footsteps echoing along the narrow passageway. She felt suddenly drained. 'Let's get you home, Jack. At least we know that Ma is out of danger now.' She took Nell's old cloak from the peg behind the door and went to wrap it around his shoulders.

'Don't fuss, Clemmie. You're as bad as Fancy.' He snatched the garment from her and laid it across his knees. 'I ain't a gouty old colonel, ducks.'

She clipped him playfully round the ear. 'No, you're a pain in the neck, Jack Skinner.' She leaned over and kissed him on the forehead. 'But I love you, just the same.' She took the handle of the bath chair, and was pushing him towards the door when it opened and Augustus strode in, followed by Ronnie. She could tell by the expressions on their faces that all was not well.

Her heart sank to her boots. 'Augustus? What's wrong?'

'I've just come from Claypole's office. It seems that the rumour was correct, Clem. He's engaged the French opera singer, Louise la Croix, to appear in the next production. He wants Jack to stay on in the orchestra, but I'm afraid there is no part for you, my little sparrow.'

'But he can't do that. We have a contract.'

Augustus struck his forehead with the palm of his hand. 'I thought so too, my bird. But there was small print – I confess I did not see the clause that said he could terminate the contract at short notice, should the need arise.'

'But, Augustus. I'm the star, you said so yourself.'

Ronnie gave her a hug. 'You are a star, Clem. But it seems that someone has put pressure on Claypole to hire the French woman. Who knows what goes on behind the scenes?'

'It's not right.' Jack thumped his hand down on the arm of the bath chair. 'Take me to him, Ronnie. I'll tell him what I think of the bugger. And he knows what he can do with my part in the orchestra. If Clemmie ain't wanted here, then I'm not staying on.'

'This is terrible,' Clemency said, biting back tears. 'But don't be hasty, Jack. We can't both be out of work. I've proved myself here, and I'm sure Augustus can find me a part in another production. There are plenty more theatres, and more trustworthy managers than Claypole. Isn't that right, Augustus?'

He mopped his brow with a grubby cotton hanky. 'Of course there are, poppet. Let's go home to our palace by the river. We'll treat ourselves to jellied eels, washed down with a bottle of port. Nils desperation, that's what I always say.'

Diverted, Clemency stared up into his florid face. 'What does that mean?'

'It's Latin, my dear. It means never give up, or words to that effect. We will triumph over adversity.'

Next morning, Clemency awakened stiff and cold after a disturbed night. Despite the fact that it was late spring, hailstones had pelted the roof and windows of the church, echoing round the vaulted ceilings like a fusillade of grapeshot. Every time she dozed into a fitful sleep, she slipped into nightmares where she was being chased by a shadowy figure. Sometimes it was Hardiman, then it was Stone and lastly it was the man they nicknamed the Leather Apron or the Ripper. She never saw their faces, but she could hear their footsteps coming up behind her, and she could feel hot breath on her neck. She woke up with a start, as the noise of the hailstones grew louder. She realised then that the hot breath on her neck was Fancy's, who had rolled over in her sleep, cuddling up to her to keep warm. It was bitterly cold in the vestry and the hammering sound was growing louder. It was not hailstones, but some unseen person or persons pounding on the iron-studded door of the church. She shook Fancy awake and then crawled over to where Ronnie and Augustus lay sleeping.

'Ronnie, wake up. Augustus, there's someone banging on the door and shouting.'

Slowly, everyone dragged themselves back to consciousness. Ronnie was first to scramble to his feet. Shivering, he reached for his jacket. 'I'll go and see who it is.'

He crept out of the vestry in his stockinged feet and Clemency followed him.

'Open up in the name of the law.'

She clutched his arm. 'What d'you think they want?'

He shrugged, holding his finger to his lips.

'Open up, I say, or we'll break the door down.'

The solid oak timbers shook as if someone had kicked them from outside.

'Here, sergeant. I don't think as how we should do that to the house of God.'

'Mind your own business, constable.'

Another kick on the door was followed by the sound of someone hitting the timbers with a stick.

'Open up.'

She glanced anxiously at Ronnie. 'It's the police. Maybe we should let them in.'

'I think you're right.' He tugged at the heavy iron bolts.

They had to leap for safety as the door flew open and a police sergeant strode into the building with a constable at his heels. 'You people are trespassing on church property.' The sergeant glared at them and began to pace about, brandishing his truncheon and peering beneath pews as if he expected to find an army of squatters lurking beneath them.

Ronnie went after him, at a safe distance. 'We're not doing any harm, officer. We've done no damage.'

The sergeant came to a halt by the spirit stove and the remains of last night's supper. 'I could arrest you for desecrating a holy place.'

Clemency stepped forward. 'Please, sir. We just needed a place to stay. We ain't done no harm, honest.'

The sergeant looked past her, beckoning the constable. 'Search the building, Watkins.'

Augustus and Fancy came hurrying from the crypt. Augustus held up his hands. 'No need, officer. There's just us and a poor crippled boy. We weren't aware that we were breaking the law, sir. We just needed a place to stay.'

The sergeant looked him up and down.

Clemency could see that he was impressed by Augustus's air of authority.

'Yes,' Clemency said, buttoning her blouse. 'You ought to be out chasing villains like Todd Hardiman, not disturbing us innocent folk what was just sheltering from the storm.'

Augustus clamped his hand over her mouth. He cast an ingratiating smile at the sergeant. 'You'll have to excuse my daughter, officer. She's got a mouth on her like the Thames tunnel, but she don't mean no harm.'

Watkins emerged from the vestry. 'Looks like they've been camping here for some time, sergeant. And there's a crippled bloke lying on the floor. Give me a mouthful he did when I trod on him by accident. Shall I arrest him?'

'It ain't worth the bother of taking them down to the station and filling in the paperwork.' The sergeant turned to Augustus, pointing his truncheon at him. 'You seem to be the ringleader, so I'm telling you to clear up your mess and vacate the building by midday. If I come back and find you lot are still here, then I'll have you up before the beak so quick it'll make your head spin. Do you understand?' Without waiting for an answer, he strode out into the street.

The constable followed him, turning to them as he closed the door. 'He's a mean bugger to cross. So I'd scarper if I was you.'

The door grated on rusty hinges and it

sounded to Clemency like a groan of pain. They stood in silence, staring at each other in dismay.

'Don't stand there like a bunch of waxworks.' Jack shuffled out of the vestry, dragging his body across the flagstones. 'Fetch me chair, Fancy, there's a good girl. It looks like we're on the move again, don't it?'

Fancy threw herself down on her knees beside him, flinging her arms around his shoulders and bursting into tears. 'Oh, Jack. What'll we do now?'

Ronnie tugged at his moustache. 'I have to say, things do look bad.'

'Nils desperation, old fellow.' Augustus did not sound convinced. He turned to Clemency. 'I have to admit that I'm at a loss, Clem. We have very little money left, not enough to pay for decent lodgings in a respectable house.'

'I thought we was saving money by living here.' Clemency stared at him, puzzled. She had put her trust in Augustus, but now a worm of suspicion crawled into her mind. 'Jack and me have been earning good money. You was looking after it for us.'

Augustus puffed out his chest and then, meeting her stern gaze, he subsided with a sigh. 'There have been expenses, Clem. And I agreed a wage for you that was shockingly low, but as you were unknown and untried, I thought it reasonably fair. As to Jack, I had to bargain hard to get Claypole and the musical director to take him on at all. His place in the orchestra was on a trial basis.'

'Hold on.' Jack's voice cracked with suppressed emotion. 'D'you mean to tell me that I've been working for nothing?'

'It was a temporary arrangement, Jack. You were gaining experience and expertise, old chap.'

Jack slammed his clenched fists on the wooden arms of the chair. 'No one works for nothing. You're a crooked bastard, Throop. How do I know you haven't spent our hard-earned money on yourself?'

Augustus shook his head. 'I never did that. I'm sorry, old fellow. I know I haven't been the most efficient of managers, but Claypole is a hard man, and I've learnt from the experience. It won't happen again.'

'Too bloody right it won't,' Jack said, thumping the table.

'Fighting amongst ourselves won't help, Jack,' Clemency saw that he was spoiling for a fight. 'There'll be time enough to talk about money later, when we've found ourselves some new digs.'

Augustus held out his hands, palms upwards. 'I am so sorry, Jack. I should have talked it over with you first, but whatever you think of my actions, without me you would still be playing your tin whistle on the pavement outside the theatre.'

'Here, that ain't fair,' Fancy said, raising her tearstained face from Jack's shoulder. 'Jack's a brilliant musician.'

'No one's denying that, Fancy,' Clemency said, getting in quickly before Jack had another chance to vent his anger on Augustus. She understood his outrage, but this was not the time or the place to argue the point. 'We'll be sleeping on the pavement if we don't do something pretty quick.'

For once, Augustus seemed at a loss. He cleared his throat with a nervous cough. 'I can only suggest that we go back to the dear lady in Flower and Dean Street, and beg her to take us back at a reduced rent, until such time as our fortunes change.'

'You know we can't do that,' Jack said angrily. 'Stone will sell the property over Mrs Blunt's head, and Hardiman will be after Ma and Clemmie like a hound chasing after a fox.'

'I've only got until the end of the week at the theatre,' Clemency said, pacing the floor. 'After that we'll have to go back to busking on the streets, unless Augustus can get me into another musical play.'

Fancy wiped her nose on the back of her hand and sniffed. 'You can't make Jack give up his place in the orchestra. He's a proper musician now, even if he don't get paid a proper wage. And whose fault is that, anyway?'

'You got a lot to answer for, Augustus,' Jack said angrily shifting about on the hard stones. 'Will someone fetch me chair? I'm getting a crick in me neck staring up at all of you.'

'I'll go.' Ronnie hurried off to fetch the chair.

Fancy got to her feet. 'I'll get your coat, love. The sooner we get out of here the better.' With an angry toss of her head, she went into the vestry.

Augustus glanced round with a sigh. 'I was just getting used to this place too. It's not exactly the best hotel in town, but I've slept in worse.'

Clemency blew on her cold hands. 'So, we got no money and nowhere to sleep. That's it in a nutshell.'

Augustus slumped down on a pew. 'I'm afraid that's true. And I must take some of the blame.'

Clemency said nothing. There was no point in making things worse than they were now. She looked round as Ronnie trundled the bath chair down the aisle, and she gave him a grateful smile. Dear Ronnie, with his funny little ways, who never made a fuss, and was always willing to give a helping hand. Why, she wondered, was it so easy to overlook someone like him? It was a pity there weren't more men like him in the world. There were plenty of villains, like Hardiman and Stone.

'Here you are, old fellow,' Ronnie said, coming

to a halt by Jack's side. 'Let's get you in your chariot.'

'Never mind humouring me,' Jack said sulkily. 'I ain't a baby.'

Fancy hurried out of the vestry, carrying Jack's coat. She wrapped it around his shoulders. 'Who said you're a baby? I'll scratch their eyes out.'

'No, really, I never said that.' Ronnie backed away, eyeing her warily as if he feared that she might carry out her threat.

'Leave Ronnie alone. He was only trying to help. And for Gawd's sake stop squabbling all of you.' Clemency stamped her foot and the sound echoed up into the vaulted ceiling. 'As far as I can see, the only place for us to go is to the theatre. We're not out of work yet and there's plenty of room under the stage to store our stuff. If we're clever about it, we can dodge the night watchman and sleep in the dressing rooms for a night or two. What d'you say?'

'I say we give it a go,' Jack said. 'Unless anyone has got a better idea.'

'It seems eminently sensible to me.' Augustus plucked his frock coat from the back of a pew. As he put it on, he squared his shoulders and smiled with some of his old bravado. 'And I will pay courtesy calls on theatre managers, putting your name about, my little sparrow. When I've done they will be fighting over who is going to feature La Moineau in their next production.'

Clemency doubted that very much, but for the moment she had other more important concerns. 'As soon as we've moved our stuff, I'm going to the pub to see Ma.'

'I'm coming too,' Jack said. 'I'm sick of hiding from bloody Hardiman.'

Clemency exchanged worried glances with Fancy.

'Now then, love,' Fancy said softly. 'You wouldn't want to risk leading him to your ma, would you? Clem can march into that pub looking like any lad off the street, but we can't disguise you so easily, now can we?'

For a moment it looked as though Jack would argue, then a rueful grimace twisted his lips. 'I suppose you could put me in a long skirt. It would hide me useless limbs, but I'd make one hell of an ugly girl.'

Fancy kissed his cheek, but, when she raised her head, Clemency saw tears sparkling on the tips of her dark eyelashes. A lump seemed to have lodged in her throat but she managed a chuckle. 'I dunno, Jack. If Hardiman saw you in a dress he might fall in love with you, then Ma and me would be safe.'

There was no rehearsal that day. Horace Claypole had taken some time off, and so it was relatively easy for them to smuggle their belongings into the theatre. A couple of cleaning ladies remained, polishing up the brass sconces and scrubbing the floorboards, but they were too intent on their work to take any notice of a few performers carting bundles to the space beneath the stage. Clemency guessed that they were used to eccentric theatrical folk and strange comings and goings, but she heaved a sigh of relief when the last of their things was stowed safely out of sight.

They gathered together in the musicians' dressing room to sort out a plan of action. After some discussion, it was agreed that when the evening performance had ended, one of them would hide beneath the stage until the theatre was cleared and everyone had gone home for the night. That person would then come out of hiding and let the others back into the building. The question remained as to whether to try to dodge the night watchman, or to attempt to buy his silence. It was then that Jack demanded to know exactly how much of their money remained in Augustus's possession. They watched in silence as he emptied his pockets. The result was not encouraging.

'We can't exist on that,' Jack said at last. 'It wouldn't keep us for more than a few days, even if we found the cheapest doss house in the roughest part of Wapping.'

Augustus stared down at the small pile of silver and coppers. 'I know. I was banking on asking for a rise for Clem and a proper wage for you, Jack. Now I am at a loss.'

'You said you would do the rounds of the theatres, Augustus. Maybe now is the time to make a start?' Clemency fingered the coins, doing a rapid count. It didn't look good.

'I'm starving,' Fancy said, rubbing her belly. 'We've had no breakfast and no dinner. We got to eat.'

Augustus scooped the coins up in the palm of his hand and selected a sixpenny piece. 'Then why don't you go out and find a hot potato vendor? That will have to do until suppertime.'

'And it won't be wasted on jellied eels and bottle of port,' Jack said, holding out his hand. 'Give it here, Augustus. I'll take charge of the money from now on.'

'That is an insult, Jack.' Augustus closed his fingers over the coins. 'Are you suggesting that I would deliberately cheat you?'

Clemency leapt to her feet. 'Stop it. I'm fed up with you squabbling like kids. You can all do what you like, but I'm going to visit Ma.'

'Not today you're not, Clemmie.' Ned had entered the room unnoticed. He strode over to them, his face set in a serious expression. 'I thought I might find you all here, and it's lucky that I did.'

'She's not taken a turn for the worse?' Clemency's lips were so numb that she could hardly form the words. 'You're scaring me, Ned.'

'No, it's not your ma. It's Hardiman. He walked into the bar this morning, boasting about his new job and buying drinks all round.'

Clemency licked her dry lips. 'Are you sure it was him?'

'One of my regulars called him by name. He's a nasty piece of work all right. No wonder you're afraid of the bugger.'

'You don't know the half of it,' Jack said, frowning. 'If I had me legs I'd sort him out once and for all.'

Augustus slipped the coins back in his pocket. 'At least he doesn't know where to find you.'

The grim expression in Ned's eyes frightened Clemency more than words. She clutched his arm. 'He doesn't, does he, Ned? Please tell me he hasn't found out where we are.'

Ned shook his head. 'I wish I could, but word gets round. Someone recognised your likeness on the billboard outside the theatre and they told him. That's why I've come now, to warn you. He was settled in the bar drinking whisky when I left, but when he's had enough, it's my opinion that he'll come here looking for you.'

'He won't be able to get past the doorman,' Augustus said, puffing out his chest. 'We'll warn him to be on the lookout.'

'The old codger's drunk. I got in easy enough.' Ned took Clemency's hand in his. 'You ain't safe here, girl. Let me take you back home. He'll never think to look for you there.'

'You've gone white as a sheet, Clem,' Fancy said. 'I think she's going to faint.'

'I am not.' Clemency took a deep breath. The room had swum around her for a moment, but she clung to consciousness like a drowning woman clinging to a spar. She had always known he would find them sooner or later. She must think of a way out of this dreadful situation. She glanced around at their concerned faces, and steadied herself by leaning against Ned. The warmth of his body was comforting: he felt solid, like a splendid oak tree in a forest of saplings. 'I'm all right. And none of you need to worry. Hardiman ain't interested in any of you. It's me he wants, if he can't have Ma. And she's safe as long as no one knows she's living with Ned and his mum.'

'You're not to do anything reckless, Clemmie.' Jack's face had paled to ashen and deep lines were etched on his brow. 'We'll stick together. We won't let him have you.'

'Let me take care of you, Clemmie?' Ned's voice broke with emotion. 'Come home with me. I won't let Hardiman come near you or Edith.'

'Is that wise, old boy?' Augustus rose to his feet. 'I mean, without you, Clem, we won't be able to stay on here. What will happen to Jack if you leave us? Claypole will throw us all out on the street.'

Moving away from the protection of Ned's arm, Clemency shoved her hands in her pockets, trying to look calm, but her mind was a whirl of doubts and fears. It was so unfair that they were putting the onus on her. She had done nothing to deserve this. But she felt completely responsible for all of them. Fancy was glaring at her, as if daring her to run away and desert them. Augustus shifted from one foot to the other, running his finger around the inside of his starched collar, eyeing her warily. She could feel Ned willing her to comply with his wishes. Ronnie was the only one who gave her an encouraging wink and a smile. For once, he was not twirling his wretched moustache, and the waxed ends drooped over the corners of his mouth, giving him a slightly comical appearance. He inclined his head towards her. 'Have courage, little one.'

Resting in the bottom of her pocket, she felt the slippery surface of Isobel's calling card. Suddenly it was all clear to her. One person had put them all in jeopardy. He had employed Hardiman, and he alone could call him off.

She turned to Ned. 'You will keep Ma safe, won't you?'

'Of course I will. But what about you, Clem?'

'Will you see me as far as the bus stop, Ned?'

'Hold on,' Jack shouted. 'You're not going anywhere, Clemmie. I told you we got to stick together.'

'Leave her be, Jack.' Fancy grasped his hand. 'She knows what she's doing.'

'I do,' Clemency said, crossing her fingers behind her back. 'You got to trust me, Jack. I think I know how best to sort this mess out.'

'Don't do nothing foolish, Clemmie.' Jack fumbled in his pocket and drew out a packet of cigarettes. His fingers shook as he opened it, spilling them on the floor. 'Damn! What I'm trying to say is – you're to stay here, safe with us.'

'Let her go,' Ronnie said. 'She knows what she's doing. I think you ought to trust her judgement, Jack. And, Clem, I'll go and see Edith. I won't tell her anything that will distress her, but I can help to keep her mind easy.'

She flashed him a grateful smile. 'Ta, Ronnie. What would we do without you?'

'Ahem.' Augustus cleared his throat. 'This is all very well, Clem. But will you be back in time for tonight's performance?'

'I don't know, but I'll try.'

'And what do we tell Claypole?' Jack's eyes were dark with suspicion. 'I don't like this, Clem. I want to know what you're going to do.'

'If I don't get back before curtain up, tell Claypole that I'm sick and he'll put Maisie on in my place.' Clemency linked her hand through

Ned's arm. 'Let's go quick, afore Hardiman decides to make an appearance.'

He patted her hand. 'All right. I don't pretend to know what you're up to, but let's get out of here.'

Ignoring Jack's continued protests, Clemency left with Ned. The doorman was fast asleep in the booking office. She banged on the glass and he woke up with a start.

'You'd better not let Mr Claypole catch you asleep.'

'I was just resting me eyes.'

'I walked right past you, mate. While you was resting your eyes. You'd best lock the doors after us, if you want to keep your job.' Ned opened the door to let Clemency out into the street. 'Or perhaps you'd like me to report you for drinking on duty?'

The doorman staggered to his feet, cursing loudly and glaring at them as he locked the doors. Clemency gave a sigh of relief. At least it wouldn't be easy for Hardiman to get inside the theatre. He would have to wait until the box office opened that evening, and then he would have to fork out for a ticket. She didn't think he would want to do that, and his meanness would buy them precious time.

Ned walked with her to the bus stop. 'Won't you change your mind, Clemmie? I promise you'd be safe with us.'

She shook her head. 'Ta, Ned. But someone would be sure to snitch on us. That girl Annie don't like me, I can tell. She'd sell her own grandmother for a threepenny bit.'

'Then won't you at least tell me where you're going? Jack's right to be worried about you. I am too.'

The address was etched into her memory: 35 Finsbury Circus. She spotted an approaching chocolate-coloured omnibus that would take her as far as Cheapside. 'Don't worry. I know what I'm doing.' She waved frantically at the driver.

'Be careful, that's all I ask. Get a message to me as soon as you can, just to let me know you're safe.'

'I will, I promise.' The horses pranced and snorted, stopping just long enough for Clemency to leap on board and then they were off again, ploughing into the mainstream of traffic. Holding onto the rail, she leaned out and waved to Ned.

'Where to, sonny?' The conductor came swaying towards her along the narrow aisle.

'Cheapside, please.' She handed him a penny and he gave her a ticket. She went to sit beside a fat woman holding a basket of apples on her knee. The scent of the apples made her mouth water and her head began to spin. She had eaten nothing since last evening and her stomach ached with hunger. She turned her head away and stared ahead. Was she doing the right thing? She sighed and settled back on the hard seat. Whether it was right or wrong, there was no alternative but to go and face Jared Stone, and to offer her services in return for his calling off Hardiman.

Chapter Twelve

Clemency alighted from the omnibus at Cheapside and made her way along Old Jewry to Moorgate. She did not stop until she reached Finsbury Circus, and by this time she was footsore, hungry and extremely thirsty. This was unfamiliar territory, although she had passed this way once, when they had been performing on the concourse of Liverpool Street Station. She felt distinctly shabby and out of place in her ragged boys' clothing. Well-dressed City gentlemen in black frock coats and top hats sauntered along the wide pavements, together with bowler-hatted bankers and clerks. There were nannies pushing babies in perambulators, and matrons out for a stroll with their maids following a couple of steps behind them. Privately owned broughams and landaus jostled for position with hackney carriages and hansom cabs. There was not a cart or a dray to be seen; neither were there any beggars or ragged children. Tradesmen did their business at the back of the terraces, well hidden from public view, and the shoeblacks, hot chestnut vendors, knife grinders and match sellers plied their trade in side streets.

With its elegant curved terraces, built in gleaming Portland stone, Finsbury Circus was a different world from the stews of Hog Yard and Fish Street. There was no stench of cess to pollute the atmosphere and no heavy chemical-laden air from the manufactories. Street sweepers worked constantly to keep the thoroughfares clear of horse dung and dog excrement, and in the centre of all this, like an oasis in the desert, there was a public garden. Fenced off from the traffic by iron railings there were tall trees with the first flush of green leaves sprouting on their branches. Beneath them on blankets of green grass were the nodding golden heads of daffodils. It was as if someone had planted a small patch of countryside in the middle of the bustling city, and the sight of all this magnificence took Clemency's breath away.

She checked the address on the card, just to make sure she was in the right place. She was uncomfortably aware of suspicious glances from both servants and their employers as she searched for number thirty-five. Passers-by gave her a wide berth, as if suspecting that she would beg for money or pick their pockets. Suddenly, her fingers began to itch, and the temptation to revert to the old way of life, on the dip, was almost too much for her. Serve the toffs right if she did relieve them of a full purse or a wallet. What right had they to look down their noses at a poor boy? The wealthy patrons of the theatre had seen fit to clap their hands together at the end of her performances on stage, with their diamond rings flashing like tiny lightning strikes. They had cheered La Moineau and called for encore after encore. They had applauded her then, so why would they despise her now?

She counted the numbers on the grand buildings. Twenty-nine, thirty-one . . . there it was – a six-storey edifice that looked more like a palace than a home for ordinary mortals, or even someone like Jared Stone. She hesitated for a moment, hovering by the railings, and wondering whether to look for the servants' entrance or to walk boldly up to the front door. Then, even as she stared at it, the door opened and a portly gentleman came slowly down the steps. Clemency's first thought was that here was a wealthy cove. His clothes were impeccable and expensive; his black frock coat was unbuttoned, revealing a waistcoat with a heavy gold chain stretched across his fat belly. There would be a gold watch at the end of that chain, and, more than likely, a bulging wallet nestling in his inside breast pocket, just begging to be lifted by nimble fingers. Even at Minski's niggardly rates, something like that would bring in enough money to feed them all for a week, and pay for lodgings well away from Whitechapel and Hardiman. With that much cash, she would have no need to seek help from Stone.

The gentleman stopped just yards from her. Taking a silver cigar case from his pocket, he selected one, and was attempting to strike a vesta when Clemency barged into him.

'Oh, sorry, guv. I didn't see you standing there.' She had not lost her touch. In seconds she had his watch and his wallet, and he had not felt a thing. She wrinkled her nose. His expensive cologne did not quite mask the offensive odour of sweat and bad breath. He had dropped his silver case and the cigar rolled into the gutter.

'Clumsy young idiot.' His florid features crumpled into a scowl.

Clemency bent down to retrieve the slightly dented case. 'You dropped this, guv.' She handed it to him, tipped her cap and backed away. The trick was to scarper before the punter realised that anything was missing. She was about to run when he patted his stomach and let out a bellow like an infuriated bull.

'Stop thief. Stop I say.'

She turned to run and cannoned into a hard, muscular body. A man's hand gripped her by the collar. 'Hold on, young fellow.'

Clemency closed her eyes. She would know that voice anywhere. She waited for Jared to denounce her.

'What did he take, Mr Caruthers?' Jared's voice held the hint of laughter.

Clemency opened her eyes, angling her head in an attempt to read his expression, but he was not looking at her. He held her by the scruff of the neck as if she were a naughty puppy. She was tempted to kick him in the shins – that would wipe the smile of his face.

Caruthers gave a snort. 'My gold watch and my wallet, both gone. Call a constable, Stone.'

Jared gave her a shake. 'Hand it over, Clem. How many times have I told you not to behave in this manner?'

Reluctantly, Clemency produced the watch and wallet and handed them to Caruthers.

'What? Do you know this little villain?' Purple in the face, Caruthers stared at her with his eyes bulging from their sockets.

She stopped struggling and waited to see what Stone had to say to that.

'Unfortunately I do. This boy is my housekeeper's son. I thought he had reformed, but I'm sorry to say that he is a recidivist. It's a good beating for you, my lad. And a diet of bread and water for a week should put a stop to your wicked ways.'

'I don't know, Stone. I think you should turn him over to the law. They know how to deal with his sort.'

'In most circumstances I would agree with

you, sir. But this unfortunate boy grew up without the advantage of a father to teach him discipline.' Jared lowered his voice. 'And his mother, a good woman at heart, was saved from a life of depredation by the home for fallen women, of which you are a most generous benefactor and patron.' He gave Clemency another shake. 'And this is how you repay your poor mother, boy. Shame on you.'

Caruthers tucked his possessions safely back in his pocket. 'Deal with him harshly, Stone. I'll leave his punishment to you, although, in my opinion, it's a crying shame they stopped deportation to the antipodes. We don't want your sort in this country, you young felon.' He hailed a passing cab. 'Goodbye, Stone. I'll see that the funds are transferred to your bank immediately.'

'You are too generous, Mr Caruthers.' Jared waited until Caruthers had climbed into the hansom cab, and then he frogmarched Clemency up the steps and into the entrance hall, where he released her. 'Sorry about the rough handling, but you were a fool to try it on with a man like Caruthers, and in broad daylight.'

Clemency backed away from him. 'I'd have got away if you hadn't interfered.' She stood with her back to the wall. Jared was between her and the door, and she could hear footsteps approaching from the other direction. Turning her head, she thought she recognised the woman who came bustling up to them. She was certain it was Nancy, the woman who had been in charge of the seedy establishment in Hog Yard. She had looked like a slattern then: fat, frowsy and not particularly clean. The starched severity of a housekeeper's attire did nothing to disguise the fact that she waddled like a duck.

Nancy came to a halt, squinting at Clemency with her eyes narrowed. 'I know you, don't I? I never forgets a face.'

Jared reached out and tweaked the cap off Clemency's head so that her hair fell about her shoulders in a fiery cloud. 'You're right, Nancy. This is Miss Skinner, who narrowly missed being carted off to Bow Street for attempting to steal Mr Caruthers' watch and wallet. Badly done, Clemency. You're out of practice, my dear.'

'Oh, shut up!' Clemency could take no more. A wave of dizziness swept over her and she swayed on her feet. 'I – I'd like to sit down.'

Nancy took her arm and hooked it over her ample shoulders. 'What are you thinking of, Mr Stone? Can't you see the poor girl is done in? Come with me, ducks. I'll take you downstairs to the kitchens. A good feed is what you need. Why, you're lighter than a sparrow.'

'I am a sparrow.' A bubble of laughter rose in Clemency's throat. 'La Moineau, that's me. The sparrow.' She felt her knees buckle and Nancy's face became a distant blur. She could hear voices but she could not make out the words. She was floating in the air, weightless and moving through space. When she opened her eyes she found herself lying on a couch with Jared and Nancy bending over her. She tried to sit up but was pushed gently back against satin cushions.

'Don't move, you'll feel better in a minute or two.' Jared felt her brow. 'You don't seem to be feverish. When did you last eat?'

'I dunno. Last night, I think. I can't remember.'

He straightened up, turning to Nancy. 'I think all she needs is a good meal. Will you see to it, please?'

'Certainly, sir. Shall I have the food taken to the dining room?'

'No, a tray here in the drawing room will do, thank you, Nancy.'

'You're all skin and bone, my girl,' Nancy said severely. She left the room with a rustle of stiff petticoats.

Clemency raised herself on her elbow, watching Jared as he strolled over to a wine table and poured something from a decanter into a small glass. He brought it to the couch. 'Do you want to try sitting up now?'

She snapped upright and was immediately sorry as her head began to swim. She leaned against the backrest. 'I – I'm fine.'

He held the glass to her lips. 'Sip this; it will make you feel better.'

'What is it?'

He laughed. 'It's only sherry. I'm not trying to drug or poison you.'

Clemency took the glass and drank the contents in one swallow. She coughed and her eyes watered as the fortified wine hit her stomach with the speed of a bullet.

'I said sip, not gulp. You're obviously not used to strong drink.'

The alcohol had bounced from her belly to her brain; she felt pleasantly muzzy and quite reckless. 'I was raised on gin. It's mother's milk to me, so don't think you can get me drunk, Mr Stone.'

The corners of his eyes crinkled and his lips twitched, but he nodded his head gravely. 'The thought never crossed my mind, Miss Skinner. Now, let's stop playing games and you can tell me exactly why you came to see me.'

Clemency bit her lip; the wine might have emboldened her, but she had not given much thought to what she would say when face to face with him.

He pulled up a chair and sat down beside her. 'It must have been something serious to bring you this far. I know what you think of me.'

She sat upright, eyeing him defiantly. 'I want you to call off your bloodhound.'

'My bloodhound?'

'Don't act all innocent. You know who I mean. That beast, Hardiman.'

'Hardiman works for me, it's true, but he just follows my instructions. He doesn't know of your existence.'

'He's my worst enemy. Do you really expect me to believe you didn't know that?'

There was no hint of amusement in Jared's expression now. 'I had no idea. I hired Hardiman because I'd heard of his reputation as a tough man, someone who would collect rents and, if necessary, evict unsatisfactory tenants.'

'And you set him on us. You was happy to have us turned out of our lodgings with Mrs Blunt, just to get your own way and have me running to you begging for a job. You're as bad as he is – no, worse. He's an ill-bred piece of shit, but you're supposed to be a gent. Well, you don't act like one, that's all I can say.'

Jared rose to his feet and walked away to stand by one of the tall windows, which overlooked the gardens in the centre of the circus. 'You're right, of course. I'm not a gentleman, but I'm not a brute either.' He turned his head to look at her. 'You'd better start from the beginning. Tell me how you know Hardiman and what he is to you.'

Before Clemency could launch into an explanation, the door opened and Nancy came in carrying a tray. 'I brought it meself, sir.' She set it down on a table at the side of the couch. 'Never mind the chat. You eat this while it's hot. I ain't climbing them stairs with another one, so I want to see it all gone by the time I gets back.' She waddled out of the room, closing the door behind her.

'She's right,' Jared said, smiling. 'You'll find that Nancy is nearly always right, or so she told me all those years ago when I was in the nursery. I can wait until you've eaten. Then you can tell me everything.'

Clemency would have liked to push the tray away, and tell him what he could do with his food, but the appetising smell of the soup, and the fragrant steam from the bread rolls, was making her mouth water. Pats of yellow butter were temptingly arranged on a flower-patterned china plate and, on another, there was a slice of chocolate cake.

'I suppose I must,' she said, dipping the silver spoon into the soup. 'I don't want to offend Nancy.' She raised it to her lips, determined to eat daintily. She had been watching the female members of the cast when they snatched their meals in between matinees and evening performances. They didn't cram food in their mouths as though their lives depended upon it; they nibbled, sipped and cocked their little fingers when they held their teacups. They ate with their mouths closed, and they didn't smack their lips. They did not belch appreciatively when their bellies were full, which, apparently, was considered bad manners.

The soup was good, better than good, it was delicious and she forgot all about table manners. She forgot all about Jared and she ate ravenously, wiping the bowl with the last of the bread and licking the spoon until it shone. She could not wait to start on the slice of chocolate cake, which was filled with buttercream and topped with chocolate and crystallised violets. She had only tasted chocolate once before, and that was when she had stolen a cake from the baker's shop. She had gorged the whole thing and been sick afterwards, but it had not put her off, and she had never forgotten the taste and feel of the chocolate as it melted on her tongue.

She was licking the crumbs off the plate when she realised that Jared was laughing at her. 'What?'

'I'm sure there's plenty more in the kitchen. You have only to ask and I'll ring the bell for Nancy.'

She put the plate down on the tray. 'No, ta. I'd throw up if I ate anything else.'

He was laughing openly as he came towards her, pulling a freshly laundered cotton handkerchief from his pocket. Clemency pushed the table away and rose rather shakily to her feet. ''Ere, what d'you think you're doing?'

Jared wiped her face. 'You've got chocolate all round your mouth.'

She snatched the hanky from him and went to look in the mirror above the mantelshelf. He was right; she had a ring of chocolate all round her mouth, as well as a blob on the tip of her nose. She scrubbed it off, scowling at her reflection. Her face was pale and there were dark smudges beneath her eyes. Her hair was a tangled mess, her clothes were dirty and she looked like a guttersnipe. What was worse, she knew she was behaving like one too; no wonder he was laughing at her. She had come to him for help and he had not only saved her from arrest, but had given her a meal such as she had never eaten in her life. Visions of Ma in her sickbed and Jack hiding beneath the stage in the theatre flashed through her mind. She was suddenly ashamed of her behaviour and embarrassed by her lack of social graces. She turned slowly to face Jared, holding out the soiled hanky. 'Ta for the loan.'

He waved it aside. 'Keep it. It's yours.'

'I don't want to be accused of stealing it.'

'Don't be ridiculous. Sit down and tell me why you came here today. And how did you know where to find me?'

Clemency tucked the hanky in her pocket and her fingers closed around the calling card. She handed it to him. 'She come to the theatre and she said you wanted to see me.'

'Izzie came to the theatre?'

'Your lady friend seems to think a lot of you. Or perhaps she's your wife? Did you do the right thing and marry her?' The question was out before Clemency could stop herself.

'Marry her?' Jared stared at her as if she had spoken in a foreign tongue; then he threw back his head and laughed. 'No, you've got it all wrong, Clemency. Izzie is my sister.'

'Your sister? How was I to know?' How dare he laugh at her? She felt the colour rise to her cheeks. 'I don't see what's so funny.'

'You may not, but Izzie will.'

Jared continued to chuckle and Clemency moved towards the door. 'All right, you've had a laugh at my expense. I'll be on me way.'

'No, please sit down. I think I know what it must have cost you to come here, so why don't you start at the beginning, and tell me how you came to know Hardiman.'

She was still smarting with embarrassment, but they were all depending on her. It wouldn't take Claypole long to realise that she had broken her contract and Hardiman might even now be at the theatre, attempting to bully Jack into revealing her whereabouts. At least none of them knew where she had gone, so they would not be caught out in a lie. She began, haltingly at first, but she gained confidence when he proved to be a good listener. She told him everything, from the time when their father had deserted them to the moment when Ned had seen her off on the omnibus. 'So you see, I'm desperate. Not just for meself – I'd stand up to Hardiman, and I'd see him in hell afore I'd become his creature. But I got family to consider, and me friends. They're all relying on me.'

'You need not fear Hardiman. I'll deal with him.' Jared's face might have been sculpted from granite, but his eyes flashed angrily. 'I've no time for men who live off the immoral earnings of women.'

'I ain't sure I believe you. I saw what you done to that poor girl Meg. She was working for you, but you threw her out when she was in trouble.'

'You don't know what you're talking about.'

'For all I knows it was your brat she was carrying. You're as bad as Hardiman.'

'Meg was just a pickpocket and not a very talented one at that. She had a comfortable life under my care, but she allowed herself to be led astray by the first good-looking man who showed her any attention. I don't buy and sell women's bodies.'

'But you hired Hardiman. I can't believe you didn't know nothing about him.'

'If I had known about him and his connection with you, I would never have taken him on. I told you that I'll deal with him, and I will.'

'And that makes everything right, does it?'

Clemency jumped to her feet. 'I dunno why you picked me, mister. But you're as much to blame as he is. Hardiman can't help being a brute, he was born that way, but you – you got all this and yet you wants more. I'd be happy just to have a proper home, even if it was just one room and a privy all to ourselves, not shared between a whole houseful of people.' When he did not answer immediately, she turned her back on him and went to retrieve her cap from the couch. 'I'm going. Ta for the food. I just wish I could have shared it with me friends and family.' She had her hand on the brass doorknob when Jared called her back.

'Wait.' He stood up slowly, holding out his hand to her. 'Hear me out, Clemency. Then if you still wish to leave, I won't stop you.'

She hesitated. Pride made her want to slam out of the room, but common sense was urging her to give him a chance to speak. She turned to face him. 'Five minutes. Then I'm going.'

'Won't you sit down again, please?'

'Ta, but I'd rather stand. Four and a half minutes!'

'All right, just hear me out.' Jared began to pace the floor, his hands clasped tightly behind his back. 'This house doesn't belong to me, I just rent it. I'm not a wealthy man. It was my grandfather who made money, out of slaves and sugar in the West Indies. When he returned to London, he bought a fine house in Islington and he became a benefactor to the poor. He built the foundling hospital and the home for fallen women, as well as the mission for seamen. Perhaps he did all that to assuage his guilty conscience for making a fortune from slavery, I don't know. But what I do know is that my father was brought up to a lifestyle he could not support. He gambled away most of the family fortune, and was cheated out of his home by a man who is my worst enemy, but that is another story. The truth is that I inherited nothing but a few run-down properties in poverty-stricken areas, and the burden of raising funds for charitable institutions that I cannot sell, but of which I own the leasehold. I'm neither a gentleman nor a businessman. I live by my wits.'

'But I heard you talking to that old cove outside. He said he was giving you money, didn't he?'

'That's true, and it's how I manage to live a lifestyle quite beyond my means. Living in this mansion, and keeping up the appearance of having money, attracts wealthy men who want to put back a little into the society that they robbed in order to become rich in the first place. Getting them to donate funds is laughably easy. They want to buy their place in heaven, to be revered as patrons and benefactors, and to see their names etched in stone above the portals.'

'So you get the money off them and spend it on yourself?'

'Not exactly. Well, not entirely. But you've grasped the basic idea. I cream off money for expenses and donate the rest to charity.'

'And you're the charity?'

'No. I do see that they get the major portion of the money I raise, but I have to live, and I have had to look after Izzie since our parents were killed in an accident many years ago.' Jared stopped pacing and turned to face her. 'I do collect rents from my properties in Spitalfields, but they don't pay for all this.' He encompassed the elegantly furnished room with an expansive gesture and a wry smile. 'I supplement my income and that of the charities, by relieving the disgustingly wealthy of trinkets that they would barely miss.'

Clemency put her head on one side, staring at him with renewed interest. 'Let me get this straight. Are you telling me that you're a cheap chancer, and all this is paid for by petty crime?'

'In a nutshell, yes.'

'And that's why you wanted me? You want me to be your trained monkey to dip the pockets of your rich cronies, in spite of the fact that you've already swindled them out of their hard-earned cash?'

'I spotted your talent that day outside the jeweller's shop. I recognised something in you,

Clemency, that hit a chord in me. With a little coaching I could turn you into a woman who could go anywhere, mix with the right people and fleece them into the bargain. Forget singing, forget acting in second-rate theatres. Come and work with me and I promise that you'll never be hungry again. You'll have fine clothes to wear and a carriage to ride in. Together we could make a fortune. What do you say?'

'Where would I live? I ain't going to live in that doss house in Hog Yard.'

'No, of course not. You would live here with Isobel and me. This house is huge. Less than half the rooms are furnished, but it fools the rich merchants into thinking I have money and position.'

'And what about me family and me friends? I can't leave them in the lurch.'

Jared's smile faded. 'I wasn't thinking of taking on the lot of you.'

'It's all or nothing. Take it or leave it.'

For a moment, she thought he was going to refuse, then a reluctant smile lit his eyes and he held out his hand. 'You drive a hard bargain, Miss Skinner.'

Clemency spat on her hand and placed it in his, giving it a determined shake, but when she attempted to pull away he tightened his grip. She tried to break free and failed. 'Let go of me.'

'I will, but there's one thing I want you to promise me, on your honour.'

'How d'you know I got any honour?'

'If we're to get along then we have to trust one another.' Jared released her hand. 'My sister, Isobel, knows nothing about my business dealings, and I intend it to stay that way. She has been brought up to be a lady, well educated and refined. She thinks that our money was inherited and that I am a reputable businessman. I want her to remain ignorant of the truth. Do you understand me, Clemency?'

Rubbing her hand, she stared up into his face, taken aback by the intensity of feeling in his voice. So Jared Stone had a heart after all. She nodded. 'I understand.'

'You can bring your friends and family here, but they must abide by the same rules.'

'Yes, I promise they will.'

'Isobel must think that they have been taken on to work for me. Therefore I'll expect them to earn their keep.'

'That's fair. They ain't a pack of scroungers.'

Jared's tense features relaxed into a smile. 'Then what are you waiting for? Go and fetch them.'

Clemency hesitated, unwilling to ask him for money, but he seemed to understand. He took a handful of silver from his pocket. 'Here, this will pay for a cab fare.'

She took the money. 'Ta.'

'Thank you,' Jared said, as if he were talking to a small child. 'Your education starts here. It's thank you, not ta.'

'Thank you – sir.' Clemency bobbed a mock curtsey, stowing the money safely in her pocket. 'I'll be off then.' She was tucking her hair into her cap when she realised that Jared was staring at her. 'What's up? Have I grown two heads or something?'

He folded his arms across his chest, looking her up and down. 'The first thing we'll do is burn those dreadful clothes. I'm sure Izzie can find something more suitable for you to wear until we've had time to buy you a brand new wardrobe.'

Clemency paused in the doorway. 'Where is she? This innocent young sister of yours?'

'Out, thankfully. On a shopping trip with our maternal grandmother, Lady Skelton.'

'Crikey, you never said you was related to the nobs.'

'And you can stop swearing. Good gracious will do. I can see this is going to be an uphill struggle.'

'Oh, shut up.' Clemency opened the door, determined to have the last word. 'I can learn quick. I'm an actress now – La Moineau. I'm someone, and don't you forget it.'

She left the room before he had a chance to

reply. The coins jingled in her pocket as she crossed the wide landing. She had been semi-conscious when Jared carried her up the sweeping staircase to the drawing room on the first floor, but now she saw the full grandeur of the building with its high ceilings, ornate cornices and richly patterned wall coverings. Her feet sank into the deep pile of the carpet and there was the faint scent of flowers in the air. It was like a palace, she thought, making her way down the staircase. The walls were hung with oil paintings, and there wasn't a trace of dust or mouse droppings on the carpeted stair treads. She could never have imagined that anyone less than Queen Victoria herself could live in such splendour. Whoever said that crime did not pay had obviously never been inside Jared Stone's drum. She grinned, imagining Jack's face when he saw the place where they were going to live. Even Augustus would be stunned into silence.

From somewhere deep in the bowels of the building, she heard the jangle of the doorbell, and then, as she rounded the curve of the stairs, she saw Nancy hurrying along the hallway towards the front door. The bell rang again. Someone was getting impatient. Clemency looked around for a way of escape, but the hall seemed to go on forever, punctuated by doorways leading to goodness knows where. There must be a back entrance, but the quickest way out was definitely through the front door, which Nancy now held open. Two fashionably dressed ladies swept in, followed by a cabby staggering beneath a pile of bandboxes and parcels. Clemency recognised Isobel, and she could only think that the older woman must be Lady Skelton. She pressed herself against the wall, hoping they would not notice her, but it was too late.

'What are you doing above stairs, boy?' Isobel peered at Clemency through the veil on her feathered hat. 'Nancy, send him about his business.'

'I'm sorry, Miss Isobel. It's the cook's boy. I didn't know he was stood there.'

Having paid the cab driver and sent him on his way, Lady Skelton pushed past Isobel, brandishing her furled parasol. 'I don't like the look of him. He looks shifty. Check his pockets, Mrs Spriggs.'

Nancy caught Clemency by the ear. 'Don't say nothing,' she hissed. 'Just act dumb.'

'Ouch!' Clemency wriggled free, kicking out at Nancy with her booted foot. She dodged past Isobel, and ducking a blow from Lady's Skelton's parasol, she fled through the open door, took a flying leap down the steps and kept on running until she reached the safety of London Wall, where she stopped to hail a passing cab.

She had hoped to reach the theatre before the

box office opened, but the hansom cab became stuck in traffic that was not moving in either direction. The driver, when questioned, said he could see a costermonger's barrow had turned over in the street, spilling fruit and vegetables all over the road. What with the horses trying to snatch up apples, and passers-by helping themselves to free fruit and vegetables, he said he couldn't see them moving for a good while. He settled down to exchange good-natured banter with another cabby, while Clemency sat fuming at the delay.

When they eventually reached the Strand Theatre, the doors were open and early theatre-goers were already queuing for tickets. Clemency paid the cabby and hurried round to the stage door. The doorman, apparently having sobered up by now, barely looked up from reading the newspaper. She strolled past him as though she had not a care in the world. The minute she was out of his range of vision, she broke into a run. She had to get them all out of the theatre before the rest of the cast arrived and started asking awkward questions. She burst into the musicians' dressing room, skidding to a halt as she came face to face with Hardiman.

Chapter Thirteen

'Run, Clemmie.' The words were torn from Jack's throat. 'Run.'

But his warning came too late; Hardiman had her in a grip that made her cry out with pain. 'I knowed you lot was lying,' he snarled, twisting Clemency's arm behind her back. 'They said as how you wasn't coming back, but I knowed you wouldn't leave the cripple boy, not never in a million years.'

Clemency stopped struggling; he would break her arm without a second thought. She made an effort to sound calm. Her heart was pumping wildly but she was determined not to let him see she was afraid. 'What d'you want, Hardiman?'

'You know what I want.' His harsh laugh echoed round the room. 'You're coming with me, my girl. I dunno where Edie is, but she was past her best anyway. You and me is going into business.'

'Let her go, sir.' Augustus took a step forward. 'You won't get away with this. I'll have the law on you.'

'That's right.' Ronnie's voice shook, but he

rolled up his sleeves as though he meant business. 'You'll have to fight Augustus and me first, mister.'

Hardiman held a cudgel in his left hand. He raised his arm, brandishing the weapon. 'Take one step nearer and I'll knock your teeth out. She's coming with me and no one's going to stop us.'

'Let her go.' Jack raised his voice to a shout. 'We'll give you money, anything you like, just let her go.'

'Do as he says.' Fancy walked boldly up to Hardiman. 'I ain't afraid of you.'

'Look out, Fancy.' Clemency had felt Hardiman's muscles tense. She knew all too well what was coming next, but Fancy took no notice of her warning. Either she had not heard or she was too angry to care. She rushed at Hardiman and he brought the weapon down with force, catching her on the shoulder and knocking her to her knees.

'I'll kill you, you bastard.' Jack hurled a glass ashtray at Hardiman's head, but it missed and shattered against the wall, sending fag ends and ash flying in all directions. Jack bowed his head, and his shoulders shook.

Blind rage filled Clemency's heart and she kicked out at Hardiman. He gave her arm a vicious twist and she yelped with pain. 'Stone,' she gasped, clinging on to consciousness, 'I'll tell Stone what you just done.'

'What?' Hardiman pushed her away so roughly that she fell to the ground beside Fancy. 'What did you just say?' He raised the cudgel above his head.

She was certain that he meant to kill her, but she was not going to die without a fight. She scrambled to her feet. 'I said I'll tell Stone what you just done. He'll sort you out.'

'Clem.' Fancy raised herself with difficulty. 'Don't make him madder than what he is. He'll kill us all.'

'The trollop's right,' Hardiman said, grabbing Clemency by the scruff of her neck. 'I could finish off the lot of you and walk out of here without anyone being the wiser. And I ain't afraid of Stone. I ain't afraid of no one.' He backed towards the doorway, dragging Clemency with him. 'Don't none of you try to follow me, or I'll wring her neck.' He had to put the cudgel down to open the door, but as Augustus made a move towards him, Hardiman seized the weapon and hurled it. Moving with surprising agility for a large man, Augustus managed to dodge the missile, and it clattered harmlessly to the floor.

'Hello, what's all this?' Horace Claypole appeared in the doorway, and behind him Clemency could see some of the musicians, straining their necks to get a better view. 'What's going on? Who are you, mister?'

'This girl belongs to me,' Hardiman snarled.

'She's my property and I'm taking her with me now.'

His grip on her had slackened just a little, and Clemency twisted free from him. 'It ain't true, Mr Claypole. He's trying to kidnap me.'

'She's me common-law wife.' Hardiman's dark eyebrows met over the bridge of his nose in a ferocious scowl. 'I got me rights.'

'He's lying.' Clemency slipped her hand through Horace's arm. 'Don't believe a word of it, Mr Claypole.'

Horace patted her hand. 'Save your voice, Clem. You'll need it for tonight's performance.' A trickle of sweat ran down his brow, but he squared up to Hardiman. 'You'll sort out your private problems elsewhere, mister. Miss Skinner is under contract to perform in this theatre, and that's just what she's going to do. If you continue to create a disturbance I shall have to send for a constable.'

Clemency held her breath. Would Hardiman back down? She had never seen him back away from a fight. He fisted his hands, glowering at the men as if he would like to take them all on, but he was outnumbered, and he obviously knew it. 'Don't think you're getting away so easy, me girl. I'll be back for you later.' He pushed past Claypole. 'I've got your card marked, guv.'

No one tried to stop him as he barged his way

through the small crowd that had gathered outside the door. Claypole took a spotted silk handkerchief from his pocket and mopped his brow. 'Nice company you keep, Miss Skinner. I'd advise you to steer clear of men like him if you want to continue your singing career.' He turned to leave, clapping his hands. 'All of you get back to your positions. Curtain up in half an hour.'

'Damn that vicious bugger Hardiman. I'd kill him, if I had half a chance.' Jack buried his face in his hands and his shoulders shook with uncontrollable sobs.

Clemency leaned against the door for support, as her legs threatened to give way beneath her. 'He's gone, Jack. Don't take on so.'

He raised a tearstained face, and his dark eyes were filled with anguish. 'I couldn't stop him, Clemmie. I couldn't protect you or me girl. What use is half a man?'

Fancy put her arms around him, cradling his head against her breast as if he were a baby and whispering words of comfort.

Ronnie patted him on the shoulder. 'We was all bloody useless, Jack. I'd like to see the bloke that could stand up to a mad bull of a fellow like him.'

'That was a nasty moment,' Augustus said, straightening his collar. 'Are you all right, girls?'

Clemency nodded. She was shaking from head to foot but she couldn't make out if it was from fear or sheer relief. 'I am. What about you, Fancy?'

'I'm fine.' Fancy grasped Jack's hand, raising it to her cheek. 'But I'd like to do for that brute. He deserves to end up at the bottom of the river with lead weights tied to his plates of meat.'

'What are we going to do?' Ronnie lowered his voice as the musicians filed into the dressing room. 'You heard him, Clem. He said he'll be back, and I believe him.'

'Excuse us, girls,' the leader of the orchestra said, grinning. 'Thanks for the show just now, but hadn't you better get back to your dressing rooms?'

'Are you going to be all right, Clemmie?' Jack's eyes searched her face. 'Will you be able to go on stage after all that?'

She managed a smile. 'I'll have to, won't I?' She went to him, and leaned over so that her lips were close to his ear. 'Tell the others that I've found us a safe place to live. We've just got to dodge Hardiman.' She squeezed his fingers. 'You're the best of brothers, Jack. You're more of a man than the whole bloody lot of them put together.' She turned away quickly, so that he wouldn't see the tears that had sprung to her eyes. 'Fancy, will you come with me? I got something to tell you.'

For once, Fancy did not argue and she followed Clemency to her dressing room. 'Close the door, Fancy. I don't want anyone to hear what I got to say.'

Fancy did as she was asked, staring curiously at Clemency. 'What's going on? And where did you disappear to? Jack was worried out of his mind.'

Clemency sat down to take off her boots. 'Never mind that now.' She put her hand in her pocket and took out Isobel's calling card. 'Don't ask questions, just go to this address and ask to see Mr Stone. Don't speak to no one else but him. Tell him that Hardiman has found us, and there's no way we can leave the theatre tonight if he don't call off his bloodhound. He'll understand.'

'It's more than I do. What's going on?'

Clemency handed her some coins. 'There's your cab fare. If you really care about Jack, you'll do as I say. Just give Stone the message and do whatever he asks.'

Fancy stared at the silver coins in the palm of her hand. 'I thought that Stone was as bad as the other fellow.'

'He could be the devil himself, but he's offered us a safe haven, Fancy. If I work for him, he's promised us a roof over our heads and three square meals a day.'

'He must want you pretty bad to make such an offer.'

Clemency stripped off her shirt and slipped a cotton chemise over her head. She picked up a pair of stays, grimacing. 'He don't see me as a girl. It's me nimble fingers that he wants.' She tossed the stays at Fancy. 'Here, lace me up and then go, quick as you can.'

Somehow, although she never knew quite how she did it, Clemency got through the evening without either fluffing her words or allowing her fears to spoil her performance. Each time she came off stage, she looked for Fancy's return, but there was no sign of her. Nagging doubts began to crowd into her mind. Hardiman might have waylaid her as she left the theatre. Perhaps Stone had decided to go out somewhere, and Fancy had not been able to contact him? By the time the last curtain fell, Clemency's nerves were stretched as taut as violin strings. She sent Florrie away as soon as she had changed out of her costume, and her hands shook as she took off her stage make-up. Why hadn't Fancy returned? Fretting and fuming, she waited in her dressing room until she was fairly certain that the rest of the cast had left the building. She hurried to the musicians' dressing room, where she found Ronnie and Jack looking on while Augustus paced the floor, with his hands clasped behind his back.

'Where's Fancy?' Jack demanded. 'For God's sake tell me what's going on.'

'I sent her to get help, but she ought to have been back long before now.'

Augustus stopped pacing. 'What do we do then? What about our plans to sleep in the theatre? We've nowhere else to go, and I don't relish the thought of sleeping in a shop doorway. Then there's that ruffian, Hardiman. I wouldn't want to meet him in a dark alley.'

Before anyone could answer, the door opened and the call boy looked into the room. 'Mr Claypole says he wants to lock up. He wants everybody out of the theatre, now. We got homes to go to, even if you lot ain't.' He winked at Clemency and sauntered off, whistling.

There was silence and all eyes turned to Clemency. She thought quickly, fingering the coins in her pocket. There was just enough cab fare to get them to Finsbury Circus. They would have to take a chance. She tried to sound confident. 'I've found somewhere for us to stay. We just need to get away without Hardiman seeing us.'

'I won't leave without Fancy.' Jack adopted the stubborn expression that Clemency knew all too well. He met her eyes with a challenge. 'Where is she? You know, don't you?'

'I'm sure she's safe with Stone.'

'With Stone? You sent her to Stone for help?' Jack's voice rose to a shout. 'He's as bad as Hardiman, you said so yourself.'

Ronnie got to his feet. 'What choice have we got, Jack? We have no money and no place to sleep. That hairy oaf is threatening to abduct Clem. If she thinks that this fellow Stone is the lesser of the two evils, then I trust her judgement.'

Augustus reached for his opera cloak and top hat. 'We are but pieces of chaff tossed about on the winds of fate. And I would do almost anything for a soft feather bed, a decent meal and a glass of wine. I say we leave now, and be damned to Hardiman.'

'I'm not leaving.' Jack shook his head emphatically. 'Not without Fancy.'

'We'll find her, old chap.' Ronnie lifted him into his bath chair. 'Don't fret.'

Clemency went to open the door. 'Ronnie's right, Jack. We won't find her by hiding in here. We got to make a dash for it.'

'Come along then, troupe,' Augustus said, placing his top hat on his head and picking up his cane. 'Best foot forward.'

After a brief discussion, they decided that, if Hardiman was waiting anywhere, it would be outside the stage door, and they made their way to the front of house. Horace was in the box office, checking receipts, and he gave them a curt nod as they filed past him. The Strand was still busy with traffic and the theatre crowds drifting to restaurants, bus stops, cab stands and underground stations. Ronnie went out first, looking anxiously up and down the street. He beckoned to them, and Augustus held the door while Clemency pushed the bath chair out onto the pavement.

'No sign of him,' Ronnie said, glancing nervously over his shoulder. 'I don't think he would try anything with all these people milling about.'

'Let's go straight to the cab stand.' Clemency gripped the handle of the bath chair so tightly that her knuckles stood out like white marbles beneath her skin.

Jack looked up at her, frowning ominously. 'We got to wait here for Fancy.'

'I'm sure she's safe, Jack.' The words had barely left her lips when Hardiman leapt out from a doorway. He swept Clemency off her feet, taking her so much by surprise that she let go of the chair and it rolled towards the kerb. Ronnie made a dive for the handle, and caught it just in time to prevent Jack from being crushed beneath the wheels of an approaching hackney carriage. As the cabby drew his horse to a halt, Jared leapt out of the cab, followed by Fancy.

'Put her down, Hardiman.' Jared seized the coach whip from the startled driver. 'Put her down, now.'

Hardiman hesitated and Clemency felt his grasp tighten. 'Keep out of this, guvner. This ain't no concern of yours. This girl belongs to me.'

She could smell the stale drink on his breath and the rancid odour of sweat emanating from his unwashed body. His lips were pulled back in a snarl. She struggled to get free, but he tucked her beneath his arm as if she weighed less than nothing.

She heard the crack of a whip, and Hardiman let out a howl of pain. Clemency sank her teeth into his hand, and he uttered a string of expletives as he dropped her on the pavement. Before he had time to recover his balance, Jared grabbed him by the throat and slammed him against the wall of the theatre. 'I would never have employed you if I had known the true extent of your villainy. You're sacked, Hardiman. Get out of my sight.'

Above Hardiman's head, Clemency's likeness on the billboard smiled down at the gathering crowd. Hardiman's eyes bulged from their sockets and flecks of foam appeared at the corners of his mouth. 'Give over, guv. This is between me and her. She's a whore just like her mum.'

A red mist danced in front of Clemency's eyes. She balled her hand into a fist and smacked it into Hardiman's face. She felt the soft squidge of warm flesh beneath her knuckles and heard the crack of breaking bone. She stared down at her bruised hand, flexing her fingers – the pain was worth it. Hardiman had had that coming to him for a very long time. She watched him slide to the ground, covering his bleeding nose with his hands.

'Remind me not to get into a fight with you, Miss Skinner.' Jared chuckled as he hoisted her unceremoniously into the waiting cab. 'We'd best get away from here before someone calls a constable. Finsbury Circus, cabby.' He climbed in last, and everyone squashed together as the cab lurched forward, overloaded and swaying from side to side.

'Me chair,' Jack said, peering anxiously out of the window. 'We've left it behind, and I can't get about without it.'

'No matter. We'll get you another one.' Jared leaned back against the squabs, and his tone gentled. 'What is it that affects your legs, Jack?'

Clemency caught her breath. She opened her mouth to tell Jared to mind his own business, but Jack astonished her by answering for himself. What was more astounding, he did not even seem to resent the direct question. 'I weren't always like this. I could walk when I was a nipper, but then I got sick with a fever. It left me as you see – a cripple.'

'Leave him alone, mister,' Fancy cried, clutching Jack's hand. 'There ain't no need to rub it in. He can't walk and there's an end to it.'

'It's all right,' Jack said, keeping his gaze fixed on Jared's face. 'Let him have his say.'

'In my profession, I meet quite a few physicians and surgeons. I might be able to get you some proper medical attention.'

Jack frowned. 'I don't want no favours from you, Stone.'

Fancy nudged him in the ribs. 'Hear him out, love.'

'I'm with Jack,' Clemency said, staring suspiciously at Jared. She couldn't make him out at all. One moment he was making threats, and the next minute he was acting like their best friend. 'Why would you put yourself out for us?'

'I'm acquainted with the senior medical officer at the City Orthopaedic Hospital in Hatton Garden. Chance is a good fellow and I think he might be able to do something for Jack.' A hint of a smile flickered across his face as he countered her hostile glance. 'I do occasionally do things out of the goodness of my heart.'

She knew he was teasing her, and she turned her head to stare out of the window. They had escaped from Hardiman for the time being, although she did not think he would give up so easily, but they were now dependent on a man about whom she knew almost nothing. What lay ahead for them was unclear – a puzzle yet to be resolved. The hackney carriage sped on, leaving the bright lights of the Strand behind them. They passed Temple Bar, and entered the bustling activity of Fleet Street where the morning editions of the newspapers were being run off the presses. It had begun to rain, a soft, steady drizzle that turned into a fine mist in the flickering beams of the gaslights. Everyone had fallen silent, lost in their own thoughts in the swaying carriage; hypnotised by the drumming of the horse's hooves and the rhythmic motion of the wheels skimming over cobblestones. The dome of St Paul's Cathedral stood out like a black silhouette against the indigo sky, and the familiar streets of Cheapside gave way to the sleeping financial heart of the City. Clemency closed her eyes, wondering what lay ahead.

The cab drew to a halt and, half asleep, they tumbled out onto the pavement. The rain had ceased and Clemency could smell the scent of damp earth and spring flowers. Augustus and Ronnie stood outside the mansion, staring upwards, their faces a study in amazement. Fancy tugged at Ronnie's sleeve. 'Jack,' she reminded him. 'He's still in the cab.'

Ronnie hastened to lift him out as Jared paid the cabby. Clemency squeezed Jack's hand. 'This is a new beginning for us, Jack.'

He gave her a searching look. 'Yes, Clemmie. But at what price?'

Jared strode up the front steps and unlocked the door. 'Come inside. Mrs Spriggs will show you your rooms.' He disappeared into the house.

After a moment's hesitation, Clemency led the

way up the steps into their new home. The others followed her slowly, seemingly stunned by the grandeur of their surroundings. Ronnie carried Jack into the hall and they huddled together in a small group, staring around them in silence. Jared was nowhere to be seen and Clemency wondered if he was going to leave them stranded here all night, but then she heard footsteps and Nancy came bustling towards them. 'Well,' she said, staring at each of them in turn. 'You're a sorry-looking lot, I must say. Come down to the kitchen and have something to eat. Then we'll sort out sleeping arrangements. I hope you don't expect luxury, because I can assure you, you won't get none of that here.' She headed off without waiting to see if anyone was following her.

'Come on,' Clemency said, making an effort to sound positive. 'It can't be worse than sleeping in the old church.'

Nancy led them through a maze of long passages to the baize door, which opened onto a flight of steps leading down to the basement kitchen. 'He told me you was coming, so I laid out a cold supper. But don't think I'm going to wait on you lot hand and foot. Tomorrow you'll start work and earn your keep.' Nancy paced up and down, eyeing them critically as they took their places at the table. 'You all look half starved. I never seen such a raggedy-arsed collection of people in all me life. I was hoping he'd taken on proper servants to help me, but none of you look up to much.'

'Madam.' Augustus clicked his heels together with a slight inclination of his head. 'I am Augustus Throop, musical director and manager of this young lady, Miss Skinner, who has achieved notable success on the stage of the Strand Theatre. We may have fallen on hard times, but we are professional entertainers, honest folk who are prepared to earn their keep. You won't find us lacking in honesty, morals or willingness to work.' He sat down, mopping his brow with his hanky.

'Fine words butter no parsnips,' Nancy said, sniffing. 'But I daresay we'll all get along, providing you do what I tells you. I'm used to handling all sorts, as Miss Clemency saw when she visited my previous place in Hog Yard. Now get on with your meal because I want to get to me bed.'

Clemency picked up her knife and fork, gazing at the spread laid out on the table. Ronnie had already helped himself to a large slice of pork pie and was heaping pickled onions on his plate. Fancy was carving slices off a baked ham with a glistening sugar crust studded with cloves. Augustus reached for an earthenware pitcher. He gave an exclamation of pleasure as he poured the deep red liquid into his glass. 'The water has turned into wine. Heavens above, it's a miracle.'

'Don't be daft,' Nancy said, easing her ample frame into a chair by the range. 'It's no bleeding miracle. Mr Stone said you was to be treated like gentry with a slap up meal, for tonight at least. Tomorrow you'll be eating tripe and onions or faggots and peas like the rest of us.'

Clemency paused with a slice of ham halfway to her lips. 'How many servants are there, Mrs Spriggs?'

Nancy chuckled. 'There's you lot and me, and a couple of chambermaids – silly little mares what come from the workhouse, but they work for next to nothing and don't eat much. It ain't what you'd call a large staff.' She put her hand in her pocket and pulled out a silver snuffbox, opening it with a delicate flick of her pork-sausage finger. Taking a pinch, she inhaled deeply through one nostril, and then the other.

Chomping on a mouthful of pork pie, Augustus caught Clemency's eye and nodded his head in Nancy's direction. 'I'll wager that's made of silver, not tin. It's the genuine article, if you ask me,' he whispered.

Clemency turned her head just in time to see Nancy put the snuffbox back in her pocket. She nodded her head, saying nothing. It was none of her business how a mere housekeeper could come by such an expensive article. Jared had obviously told her the truth when he had spoken about relieving rich people of their trinkets. Perhaps he had given the snuffbox to Nancy in lieu of her wages. She would worry about that tomorrow, but for now she had her eye on the chocolate cake that she had tasted earlier. Its rich darkness was calling to her and making her mouth water. Maybe going back to a life of crime was worth it after all.

When everyone had eaten and drunk as much as they could, the atmosphere lightened and Clemency sensed a spirit of optimism amongst them that was not entirely due to the wine. No one said much, they all seemed to be too in awe of Nancy, or maybe they were simply tired. Clemency was half asleep, lulled into a comfortable state by good food and a couple of glasses of wine. She was having difficulty in keeping her eyes open, and she could see that Jack was already nodding off.

Nancy heaved herself out of the chair. 'You can clear this lot up in the morning. You'll rise at six and get the fire going in the range. I don't care which one of you does it, that's up to you. Right now it's bedtime, so follow me and pick up a candle each on the way. You with the moustache, you'd best get one for the lame boy.' She lumbered across the room, stopping to pick up a candle from the dresser and lighting it with a vesta.

'Clemmie, wait.' Jack caught her by the hand as she was about to walk past him.

'Yes, Jack?'

'What is it he wants you to do?' His fingers dug into her flesh, making her wince. 'Tell me, Clemmie. Why is he taking us in? What's in it for Stone?'

She couldn't bear to admit that Jared wanted her to return to a life of crime. Jack had suffered enough, in the knowledge that he was unable to protect and provide for her and Ma. She managed a smile. 'He wants me to be a companion to Miss Isobel. He's sorry that he caused us to be thrown out of our lodgings in Flower and Dean Street, and he said he didn't know that Hardiman was a thoroughly bad lot.'

Jack frowned. 'That might explain why he took you on. But why would he bother with all of us?'

'I said I wouldn't come without you. And he expects everyone to do their bit and earn their keep. It ain't a free bus ride, Jack.'

Jack released her hand, but he did not look convinced. 'I'd sooner live in the gutter than have you do anything against your will.'

'You mustn't worry, dear. We'll soon get back on our feet and then we'll find work in another theatre. You've got time to practise your flute. One day you'll be a fine musician, earning lots of money, and keeping us all in style.' She leaned over and kissed his cheek. 'Night night, Jack.'

'Are you coming, miss? Or do you want to sleep in the kitchen?' Nancy called across the room. 'Hurry up. I want to get to me own bed.'

Ronnie had collected his candle and he returned to give Jack a piggyback to the sleeping quarters. They trooped after Nancy as she stomped off along a narrow passageway. She tapped on the closed doors as she marched past them. 'In there's the boot room. That's the flower room, the butler's pantry, the silver store, the linen cupboard, the broom cupboard and the dry goods store. Most of them are empty, so don't get no ideas about pilfering.' She opened a door at the far end of the passage. 'This is the old servants' hall. You fellows can sleep in here. It'll be easier for the crippled boy.' She gave her candle to Clemency to hold while she lit the gas mantle.

The room was large, cold, and felt damp. It smelled of mildew, and fungus grew on the walls, but Clemency could see that it was reasonably clean, and there were three truckle beds laid out with fresh linen, pillows and blankets. It was sparsely furnished with a simple pine washstand, a tallboy and a couple of bentwood chairs on either side of a large fireplace.

'You can light a fire if you got the energy,' Nancy said, taking the candle from Clemency. 'There's a coalhole out in the area and kindling in the scullery. Just make sure you locks up after you. We don't want no vagrants or thieves walking in on us in the middle of the night.'

'What about me?' Fancy asked, as Nancy led them out into the passage, closing the door behind her.

'Are we to share a room?' Clemency had to quicken her pace in order to keep up with Nancy.

'We're probably in the blooming broom cupboard,' Fancy whispered, giggling.

'I'll lock you in there if you give me cheek, young woman.' Nancy hurried on, leading them back into the kitchen and up the stairs, through the baize door and into the hall. She paused at the foot of the main staircase, holding her side and panting. 'These stairs will be the death of me. I'll take you up this once, but you'll have to find your own way round this rabbit warren of a place in future.' She mounted the stairs, breathing heavily and grumbling all the way up to the first floor landing.

Clemency saw a chink of light beneath the double doors that led into the drawing room. She wondered if Isobel was in there with her brother, and what explanation he would give her as to why he had taken a bunch of out-of-work entertainers into his house. But that was his problem. Another flight of stairs rose into eerie darkness, but to Clemency's relief Nancy took them further down the corridor. It felt chilly in this part of the house and their footsteps echoed in spite of the thick carpet. Nancy opened a door at the far end of the passage. 'This is your room.' She ushered them into a large bedroom with two tall windows overlooking the gardens in the centre of the Circus. Pale shards of light from the streetlamps made patterns on the walls, and in the grate a coal fire burned, snapping and crackling, giving the room a friendly feeling of warmth. Clemency looked about in awe. This room was big enough to sleep a dozen people and still leave room for a few more. The four-poster bed could have slept six, without having to lie top to tail. It was too dark to make out the exact colour of the curtains and swags, or the chintz-covered chairs on either side of the fireplace, but they seemed to be pale blue and there was definitely a hint of pink in the flower-patterned carpet.

'It's like something out of one of them ladies' magazines,' Fancy said in awed tones. 'I ain't never seen nothing like it.' She went over to the fireplace, bending down to feel the softness of the hearthrug. 'This is lovely and soft. I'll sleep well here.'

'That you won't.' Nancy lit the gas mantle and the colours of the room bloomed into being, causing Clemency to catch her breath. It was like fairyland – she could not believe that this luxury was meant for her and her alone. But Nancy had already moved on and had opened a door that led into another, smaller room with a single brass bedstead, a washstand, a chair and a bedside table. 'This is your room. What's your name, girl?'

Fancy gulped and swallowed. 'It's Fancy, missis. Fancy Friday.'

'Huh!' Nancy cast her eyes heavenwards. 'Outlandish. Never mind. I suppose you can't help being given a name like that.'

'But this ain't for me, is it?' Fancy laid a tentative hand on the coverlet, as if she expected it to leap up and bite her.

'Of course it is, you stupid girl.' Nancy shook her head. 'Do you think I'd waste my time showing you a room that wasn't yours?'

'We're tired, missis. We've had a hard day.' Clemency could see that Fancy was overwhelmed and close to tears. If it had been anyone else, she would have given her a hug, but Fancy was prickly as a bunch of holly when she was upset. 'We're strangers in this house. We don't know your ways, so I'd be obliged if you'd bear that in mind.'

Nancy shrugged her shoulders. 'Don't you put on airs and graces with me, my girl. I recall the day when Mr Stone dragged you into the house in Hog Yard. You was a common pickpocket then, and that's all you are now, except that he's seen fit to try to turn you into a lady.' She snorted with laughter. 'A lady! He'll have his work cut out.'

'Here, you can't talk to her like that,' Fancy said, bristling. 'You leave Clem be.'

'And you mind your manners. I'm in charge below stairs, and that's where you belong, so don't you forget it.' Nancy's jaw jutted out in a stubborn line above her wobbling chins. She spun Fancy round to face a door on the opposite side of the room. 'That's Miss Isobel's room. You'll be lady's maid to her and to that one over there as well.' She shot a darkling glance at Clemency.

'Don't talk soft,' Clemency said, stifling a yawn. 'What would I want with a lady's maid?'

'Mr Stone thinks you can be turned out smart enough to fool the toffs, and it ain't up to me to argue with the boss. Now get to bed, both of you. And tomorrow morning you can start by filling pans with water and putting them on the range to boil.'

Fancy slumped down on the bed. 'Is it wash day?'

'No, ducks. It's bath day. You'll bring the tin tub in from the scullery and fill it with hot water. Young ladies have regular baths. It's the law.'

'A bath?' Clemency repeated.

'Soap and water.' Nancy sniffed. 'When did you last have a good wash?'

'Mind your own business. I ain't taking off me clothes in front of all and sundry. And no one has a bath at this time of year. It ain't healthy.'

Nancy's steel-grey eyes narrowed. 'You'll have a good scrub down tomorrow morning even if I have to strip you both naked and use the yard broom on you. Sleep tight.'

'And that goes for you too.' Nancy stood, arms akimbo, by the zinc tub filled with hot water. Clemency and Fancy were hovering nervously by the fire, while Augustus, Ronnie and Jack sat at the table, finishing their breakfast of bread and cold meat. 'Men have to be clean as well as the women. I ain't having no fleas and lice in my house.'

Augustus rose to his feet. 'Madam – Mrs Spriggs. Nancy, my dear, I am happy to act as butler or even as a gentleman's gentleman, but I draw the line at public bathing. On the first of May, if it doesn't fall on a Sunday, I visit Nevill's public baths in Aldgate, where, for twopence, I have a hot bath, second class, naturally, and for a penny-halfpenny I wash and dry my undergarments. I go through the same procedure on the first of October, and that sets me up for the winter.'

'And next Tuesday is the first of May,' Ronnie said hastily. 'I think I'll join you in the public baths, Augustus.'

'And me,' Jack pushed his plate away. 'Lift me up and get me out of here, Ronnie. No one's going to get me into that tub.'

'Cowards,' Clemency said, chuckling as she clutched the wrap around her that she had found on a chair in her room. Nancy had informed them that she had taken their clothes, and they were being boiled in the copper, out in the back yard. They had either to wander round naked, or put on the only garment at their disposal.

'All right,' Nancy said grudgingly. 'I'll let you gents off, providing you go to the nearest public baths before the end of the week. To put it mildly, you're all a bit whiffy. I had enough of that in Hog Yard, but we're in Finsbury Circus now, along with the toffs.' Nancy turned her back on them, rolling up her sleeves. 'Right then, ladies. Who's going to be first?'

Augustus hurried from the kitchen, followed by Ronnie, who had hefted Jack over his shoulder. Fancy was cringing by the fire, eyeing the bath as though it was filled with acid that would dissolve her flesh on contact. Nancy had promised them fresh clothes as soon as the bathing ordeal was over, and there seemed to be no way out other than to comply with her wishes. Clemency allowed the wrap to slip to the floor and she stepped into the hot water.

An hour later, scrubbed clean from head to foot and having undergone the humiliation of a fine-tooth comb being dragged painfully through her long hair, she was dressed in some of the loveliest clothes she had ever seen. They had belonged to Isobel, and had apparently been discarded for no better reason than that they were no longer in fashion this season. Clemency could not imagine how anyone could throw out such fine garments; there was not a patch or a darn to be seen, no frayed ends and not a stain in sight. Her skin was still pink and tingling from the hot bath, and the over-enthusiastic scrubbing of her back with a prickly loofah. She was certain that Nancy had enjoyed inflicting pain, but she had to admit, as she perched on the edge of the sofa in the drawing room, that feeling clean was a pleasant sensation. She might smell of carbolic with a hint of Lysol, but the white lawn blouse with lace frills and the French-blue tussore skirt were scented with lavender. She lifted it just far enough to admire the bright moreen petticoats, stiff with starch. Her legs were encased in white silk stockings and on her feet she wore a pair of high button boots that had also belonged to Isobel and were only a couple of sizes too big.

'So my old clothes fit you, then?'

Clemency jumped. She had been so absorbed in admiring her new outfit that she had not heard Isobel enter the room. She looked up into a pair of blue eyes, startlingly similar to Jared's, and a cool gaze. 'They do. Ta – I mean thanks for the loan.'

Isobel tossed her head and the sunlight streaming through the windows caught golden glints in her hair. 'I'd thrown them out anyway. But you're welcome to them. I believe that those of us who have wealth should share it with the less fortunate.'

'Do you now?' Clemency eyed her with interest. She had formed the opinion that Miss Isobel Stone was a spoilt and snooty young woman, used to getting her own way. She had not expected someone with such a lively social conscience.

Isobel moved gracefully, seeming to glide rather than walk. When she sank down onto a chair, her skirts fell into elegant folds, like the petals of a flower. Clemency could not help but be impressed.

'So,' Isobel said, returning her stare. 'What exactly are you doing in our house? What is it that Jared wants with you, Clemency?'

Chapter Fourteen

'Why did Jared have such a desperate need for your company?' Isobel leaned forward, her pretty face alive with curiosity.

Clemency stood up, playing for time while she tried to think of an answer to a question that was still puzzling her. If she did not fully understand Jared's motives, how could she possibly explain them to his sister? Avoiding Isobel's intent stare, she went over to the window, wobbling a little on the unaccustomed high heels. She had grown used to striding along in boys' boots and breeches, or dancing onto the stage in ballet shoes that were lighter than air: she felt uncomfortable in her borrowed garments, and out of place in these unfamiliar surroundings. She realised that Isobel was waiting for an answer. 'I'm blowed if I know exactly. You should ask your brother.'

'And I will,' Isobel replied evenly. 'But you've got a tongue. Tell me about yourself. I'm desperately keen on supporting women's rights, and I don't hold with the exploitation of the female sex by men who ought to know better. He hasn't propositioned you, has he? I mean, Jared hasn't made improper suggestions to you? Not that I'm a prude, but I think we women should have control over our own bodies, and not be subservient to the carnal desires of men.'

'Izzie, that's enough.' Lady Skelton stood in the doorway, frowning at Isobel. 'That sort of talk may go down well with your radical acquaintances, but it's not a fit subject of conversation for unmarried girls.' She swept into the room, followed by Jared.

Isobel rose to her feet, bobbing a curtsey. 'I'm sorry, Grandmama. I didn't know you were there.'

'Go to your room, Isobel,' Lady Skelton said severely. 'I'll speak to you later.'

'Must I, Jared?' Isobel cast an appealing look at him, curving her lips into a winning smile.

'Do as you're told, Izzie.' Jared's tone was severe, but there was a twinkle in his eyes as he pinched her cheek.

Scowling at him, Isobel flounced to the door. She paused, turning to Clemency. 'We'll continue this discussion later.' With a defiant toss of her blonde curls, she left the room.

As the door closed behind her, Lady Skelton collapsed on the sofa clutching her sides and laughing. 'That girl will be the death of me.'

Jared was laughing too, and Clemency looked from one to the other, wondering what it was that had amused them.

'My little sister has a social conscience,' Jared said, chuckling. 'Isobel believes that she can change the world for the better, and the lot of women in particular.'

'I don't see that's no laughing matter,' Clemency said primly.

'No, of course it isn't.' Lady Skelton mopped her eyes with a lace handkerchief. 'Isobel is an innocent, my dear Clemency. She has received the strictest of upbringings, and the best education that money can buy.'

'Look,' Clemency said, edging towards the doorway. 'I dunno what you want with me, but I think you're both loony. Now can I go?'

'Sit down, please, and hear us out.' Jared motioned her to a chair, his expression suddenly serious.

Still suspicious, particularly of the grand old lady who appeared to have taken leave of her senses, Clemency went to sit on the edge of a spindly chair that was near enough to the door to enable a quick escape. She folded her hands on her lap. She would not let them see that she was nervous, and that she suspected Jared had not been completely honest about his reason for employing her. 'Well?' she said. 'Go on then.'

'Really, Jared. You should have told the girl everything from the start.' Lady Skelton began peeling off her white kid gloves.

He nodded. 'I know, Grandmama, but we

haven't really had the opportunity to talk seriously.' He turned to Clemency. 'The first thing you must understand is that Izzie knows nothing of the way in which I supplement our income.'

'You mean she don't know that you're a crook?'

'Precisely so. Izzie is under the impression that our wealth is inherited. We, that is, my grandmother, Lady Skelton, and I, have big plans for Isobel. Our aim is to see her married well, with her future secured.'

Clemency angled her head. 'You mean you're going to sell her off to the highest bidder?'

'You are direct, aren't you?' Lady Skelton exchanged amused glances with Jared. 'She's bright, Jared. I give you that. Maybe she'll do after all.'

'I wouldn't have picked her if I didn't think so, Grandmama.'

'Oy, you two!' Clemency leapt to her feet. 'What's going on? I thought I was working for him.' She pointed at Jared. 'I don't mind a bit of pickpocketing from folks what can afford to lose a quid or two, but if you've got anything else in mind, you'd best forget it.'

'She has spirit too.' Lady Skelton looked Clemency up and down. 'And polished up a bit, with the right clothes and a few lessons in etiquette, we might be able to pass her off as a lady, providing she keeps her mouth shut.'

'Look, lady,' Clemency said, taking a step towards the sofa. 'I'm an actress and a singer. I ain't a high-class whore, so don't you get no ideas about finding me a string of rich geezers who'll pay for me services. If you wasn't a lady, and an old one at that, I'd think you was running a knocking-shop.'

'Clemency! That's no way to speak to my grandmother. I won't have disrespect for her in my house.' Jared's voice was harsh, but Lady Skelton let out a hoot of laughter.

'Leave her alone, boy. She's only speaking her mind and I like that.' She leaned forward to pat Clemency's hand. 'Listen to me, child. I may have a title now, but before I married the late baronet, I was Emily Smith, a haberdasher's daughter from Spitalfields. My face, as they say, was my fortune and I was a quick learner. How I came to marry well is another story, but my husband had a weakness for the horses, and very soon his inherited fortune was gone. Then the selfish man died, leaving me with no money and a young daughter to launch into an unforgiving society, where money counts just as highly as breeding. When Cecily married the wealthy merchant, Oswald Stone, I thought I had done my best by her.' Her voice broke on a muffled sob, and she averted her gaze.

'But, as I told you,' Jared continued, when Lady

Skelton seemed to be unable to go on, 'my father was also profligate with money. They were travelling abroad, escaping their creditors, when their carriage overturned on a mountain pass between France and Italy. They were both killed outright. Izzie was just ten and I was eighteen.' He turned away to stare out of the window. His hands were clasped tightly behind his back, his fingers tightly interlaced. Clemency sensed that just talking of the past distressed him. She was beginning to think he had feelings after all.

'We brought Izzie up together,' Lady Skelton said, dabbing her eyes with her hanky. 'We were both virtually bankrupt. I now live in rented rooms in Half Moon Street, on a small annuity left to me by my late father-in-law, who knew all too well of his son's weaknesses. I, of course, was too old to learn the skills necessary to become a successful thief, but I could train the girls that Jared plucked from a life of destitution on the streets. We fed and clothed them, educated them to a far higher degree than they would ever have reached in their previous lives, and we looked after their morals.'

'So you says. But I saw that girl, Meg Jones, when your grandson threw her out of the place in Hog Yard. Seems to me that you was both a bit careless of her morals, or her needs for that matter, considering that she didn't want to be sent packing.'

'Meg was stupid,' Jared said angrily. 'She allowed her head to be turned by a good-looking rake who had only one thing on his mind, and it certainly wasn't marriage. I warned her not to get involved with him, but she wouldn't listen to me.'

'I've gone straight,' Clemency said, shaking her head. 'I don't want to go back to stealing.'

'It would only be temporary.' Jared moved swiftly to her side. 'There is a certain man who owes me a great deal. He has something of mine that I am determined to retrieve. But once that is done, and I have seen Izzie settled, my business will be done.'

'And we'll all be tossed out on the streets or end up in Newgate. It don't sound good to me.'

'I'll look after you, Clemency. I'll protect you from knaves and scoundrels and you'll be well rewarded. All I ask is that you work with me and keep all of this strictly confidential. Izzie must never know the truth.' His eyes were the colour of roof slates, freshly washed by an April shower and glistening in the sunlight. He held her gaze with an intensity that sent shivers down her spine. 'Will you join us? And will you promise never to tell Izzie what has passed between us today?'

Hypnotised by the sound of his voice, and the obvious sincerity in his words, she found that she could not refuse. 'I promise.'

He took her hand and held it in a firm grasp. 'You won't regret it.'

She felt a tingle, something like pins and needles, running up her arm and shooting down her spine: it was with difficulty that she collected her thoughts. 'What about the others? If I say I'll go along with you, I wants you to promise that you won't suddenly turn round and tell Jack and me friends to leave.'

'They can stay. I give you my word on that.'

'The word of a gentleman?'

He threw back his head and laughed. 'No, the word of one magsman to another.'

'So vulgar,' Lady Skelton said, tut-tutting. 'Tomorrow morning, Clemency, we'll begin your lessons, starting with elocution, grammar and deportment. I'll leave Izzie to help you choose a new wardrobe, and show you how to do your hair.'

'But what do I tell her?' Clemency looked from one to the other. 'How do I explain my presence in this house without making her suspicious?'

Jared shrugged his shoulders. 'Grandmama?'

'Leave that to me, dear boy. I'll think of something that will fit in with her desire to raise women's status in the world. In fact, I'll go and find her now and make my peace with the poor child.' She rose, and turned to Clemency, her smile fading. 'I do adore my granddaughter, and I sincerely desire her happiness. But I also want her to have the security and respect that I have never managed to achieve. Goodbye, Jared. I'll see you both tomorrow.' She left the room with a rustle of silk taffeta petticoats, leaving a faint trace of French perfume lingering in the air.

Jared placed his arm around Clemency's shoulders, but she recoiled from his touch, moving away from him. The simple pressure of his hand had sent the blood fizzing through her veins, as if she had drunk a glass of rum punch too quickly: it was as alarming as it was exciting. Until now, she had never been attracted to any man. Hardiman had put her off the male sex forever, or so she had thought. But strange things were happening to her body, and she was not in complete control of her emotions. Then she remembered Ma, lying on her sickbed at the pub. 'Mother!' She had said it almost without thinking.

Jared stared at her. 'Mother?'

'Me mum is poorly, very poorly. I got to go and see her. I want to go now.'

'I'm not stopping you. You can come and go as you please.'

'Oh!' She stared at him in surprise. 'Ta, then I – I will.'

'And where is your mother, Clemency? Is she in hospital?'

'She's being cared for by friends in the Crown and Anchor pub, Carter Lane.' She hesitated.

'You have called Hardiman off, haven't you? I don't want him to find Ma.'

'He'd be a fool to cross me, but perhaps I'd better accompany you, just in case.'

'I can take care of meself. Haven't I done it for nineteen blooming years?'

'And nearly got yourself murdered into the bargain. Clemency, I'm protecting my interests. I'm coming with you and that is that.'

They entered through the main door of the Crown and Anchor. Jared had insisted on it, although Clemency had wanted to slip in quietly through the rear entrance. She was only too aware that their expensive clothes set them apart from the working men who frequented the pub, and the fear that Hardiman might still be in the neighbourhood was never far from her mind. She hesitated in the doorway, but Jared took her by the arm. 'Don't be afraid. I won't let anyone harm you.'

She shot him a glance beneath her lashes. A few weeks ago she would have laughed if a man had said that to her, but now she found it comforting. She had to remind herself that most men were cheats and liars; most of them wanted one thing, and when they'd got it they vanished like morning mist. Hadn't her father done just that? And she had seen how Hardiman used and abused Ma, not to mention the vile Mickey

Connor. Where once she would have answered back with a smart remark, she merely nodded, and attempted a smile. But her heart was beating erratically, and she couldn't help looking round at the men sitting at the tables, and wondering if it was one of these rough-looking coves who had betrayed her to Hardiman.

Jared steered her towards the bar where Ned had just served a costermonger with a tankard of ale. He was wiping the counter when he looked up and saw them. A multitude of expressions flickered across his open countenance, from pleasure and relief to anger, and then suspicion as he glared at Jared. 'Clemmie! I've been out of me head with worry about you. I went to the theatre this morning, and no one seemed to know where you were. They said there'd been a fight last night, and you and your mates were in the thick of it. The police had been asking questions.'

'I'll explain, but can we go somewhere more private?' Clemency glanced anxiously over her shoulder, but none of the other customers seemed to be particularly interested in anything other than drinking and chatting amongst themselves.

Ned hesitated with his hand on the hatch. He jerked his head in Jared's direction. 'Is he the bloke that had you thrown out on the street? The one you went off to seek his help?'

'This is Mr Jared Stone,' she said, trying not to sound impatient, which was difficult when the two of them were eyeing each other like dogs with hackles raised ready for a fight. 'I'll explain everything. Can we go through to the parlour?'

Reluctantly, Ned lifted the hatch. 'Come through.'

They followed him through to the back room. 'I'd like to see Ma first, and then we'll talk. I'll go upstairs now, if that's all right with you?'

Ned shook his head. 'You won't find her there.'

'What?' A vision of Ma laid out in a coffin flashed through her mind. Clemency swayed on her feet.

'For God's sake, man!' Jared exclaimed, slipping his arm around her waist. 'How bloody tactless can you be?'

'Who asked you to stick your nose into our business?' With an aggressive out-thrust of his jaw, Ned pushed Jared away and he took Clemency by the hand. 'Come with me, girl.'

'Ned, if this is a joke . . .' Clemency allowed him to lead her into the kitchen, where she stopped short in amazement. 'Ma?'

Edith looked up from the table where she was rolling out pastry. She dropped the rolling pin, and hurried across the floor to give Clemency a floury hug. 'Clemmie, love! We was all so worried about you. Where've you been?'

'You were so sick, Ma. I thought you was dying.'

Edith chuckled. 'I'm a tough old bird, ducks. I can't say I'm completely back to me old self, but I'm getting there.'

'We didn't ask her to help – she insisted.' Ned selected a jam tart from a plate and popped it into his mouth. 'She's a wonderful cook,' he added, licking his lips. 'Even better than Mum, and that's saying something.'

Edith's pale face flushed bright pink and she giggled. 'You're just saying that, Ned. You're such a tease.'

Clemency stared at her mother. She looked so different from the sickly creature that she had been less than two days ago; the change seemed almost miraculous. 'Are you sure you're strong enough to be on your feet, Ma?'

Edith went back to cutting out pastry shapes. 'Keeping busy makes me feel better, and stops me brooding on what's happened. And I got to repay Ned and Nell's kindness to me somehow.'

'Where is Nell? I'd like to see her.'

'Mum and Annie have gone to market.' Ned went to take another tart and received a rap across the knuckles from Edith. 'Ouch,' he said, rubbing his hand. 'That hurt.'

'Them's for the customers, me lad. I was famous for me pastry when I worked at the Pig and Whistle in Wapping. That was where I met

Clemmie's dad. The bugger what run off and left us.'

Ned nodded sympathetically. 'Seems like it's a common story in the licensed trade – my dad did exactly the same to us.'

'Have you never heard from your old man since?' Clemency asked, momentarily forgetting her own problems.

'No. Not a word. Good riddance, I say.'

Jared cleared his throat. She looked up to see him leaning against the doorpost with a bored expression on his face. 'We should get going, Clemency. We have things to do.'

'Oh, no! Can't we stay a bit longer?'

'Who are you to tell her what to do?' Ned demanded.

'I'm her employer. She works for me now, and she has a great deal to learn. So, if you'll excuse us, Mrs Skinner, I'll take your daughter away now. But she can come back and visit you whenever she wants.'

Edith clutched the rolling pin as if she would have liked to bop Jared on the head. 'And what sort of work is that, may I ask? What would a toff like you want with a girl like Clemency?'

'Ma, please.' Clemency felt the blood rush to her cheeks. She shot a furtive glance at Jared, but he did not seem to have taken offence. If anything, she thought, he looked a little less severe.

'I understand your concern, Mrs Skinner. But you need not worry yourself about Clemency. She is acting as paid companion to my sister, and they are both in the care of my grandmother, Lady Skelton.'

'Blimey!' Edith's eyes opened wide in surprise, and she sat down heavily on the nearest chair.

'Paid companion?' Ned almost spat the words at him. 'What d'you take us for, mister? Clemmie's a good actress and she's got the voice of an angel, but no one is going to mistake her for a lady.'

Clemency could see by the look on Ned's face that he was going to be difficult. Although it warmed her heart to know that he was looking out for her, his proprietorial attitude was annoying. She might expect Jack to act like a grumpy bulldog guarding a bone, but Ned was just a friend. She laid her hand on his arm. 'It's all right, Ned. I know what I'm doing. And we're all there in Jared's big house, the whole lot of us – Jack, Augustus, Ronnie and Fancy – so there's no real harm can come to me, especially now he's sent old Hardiman packing.'

Edith fanned herself with her apron. 'Thank God for that. Todd Hardiman is a bad lot, Mr Stone. He nearly done for me on more than one occasion. The brute.'

The angry look left Jared's face, and he smiled at Edith. 'He won't harm you again, Mrs Skinner.

I give you my word on that. I would never have taken him on if I'd known his full history. And I promise you that I'll take care of your daughter. You need not fear for her safety.'

'I believe you.' Edith held her arms out. 'Clemmie, love. Give your old mum a hug before you go.'

Hugging her, Clemency bit back tears as she felt how frail her mother had grown. She gave Ned a pleading look. 'You will take care of her, won't you, Ned? You won't let her work too hard? Not until she's fully recovered her strength.'

'Edie will be fine. I wish I was as certain about you.'

'Anyone would think you was me brother,' Clemency said, smiling in spite of her worries. She kissed Edith's hollow cheek. 'Take care of yourself, Ma. I'll be back to see you soon. And if you should want to join us in Finsbury Circus, I'm sure that Nancy would be grateful for a hand with the cooking. Ain't that right, Jared?'

'Yes, of course. Now we really must go.'

She went to Ned, holding out her hand. 'Goodbye for now. And don't worry about me; I can take care of meself.'

He squeezed her fingers. 'Is it all right if I come to call on you one day? I could bring Edie too.'

'I'd love that, ducks,' Edie said enthusiastically. 'Then I could picture you living in a swanky drum just like the nobs.'

'I'd like that too.' Clemency hesitated, looking to Jared for confirmation. 'If that's all right with you?'

'Yes, yes. Of course it is. Good day, Mrs Skinner.'

'See you both soon.' Clemency followed Jared through the bar and out into the May sunshine. He stepped off the pavement to hail a passing hansom cab, but it did not stop. With an exclamation of annoyance, he walked a little way down the street, dodging in and out of the traffic. Clemency waited on the kerb, wondering why men had to be so impatient all the time. It was a lovely day and there did not seem to be any need for such haste. She was so deep in her own thoughts that she did not hear the footsteps coming up behind her until Hardiman was at her side.

'I knew I'd find you here if I hung around long enough.' He tucked her hand into the crook of his arm. 'You're coming with me.'

'Get off me.'

'I got an even bigger score to settle with you now, miss.' Hardiman's lips curled into a ferocious snarl. 'You got me the sack from me job, and I been searching for Edie for days. The old besom at the lodging house said she'd been living there, but had left in a bit of a hurry. So where is she?' He thrust his face so close to Clemency's that she could smell his bad breath.

With a swift movement he twisted her arm behind her back, making her yelp with pain.

'I ain't telling you nothing,' Clemency cried, biting back tears as he bent her arm to snapping point. 'You'd better let go of me. Jared's just up the street.'

'I know. I seen him with you, you little whore. Give yourself to him, did you? Crept into his bed and fed him lies about poor old Todd, did you?'

'Jared.' She screamed his name, although the sound was lost in the traffic noise and the cries of street sellers, costermongers and bootblacks, and the droning music from a hurdy-gurdy man with a chattering monkey on his shoulder. But, as if by telepathy, Jared stopped in his tracks. He turned round, and even at a distance Clemency saw his expression change as he strode towards them.

Hardiman gave her arm a savage twist. 'Say anything and it'll be your neck what gets broken next time we meet.' He let her go, taking a step backwards as Jared bore down on them. 'We was just talking, Mr Stone. Just passing the time of day, so to speak.'

Clemency leapt aside as Jared caught Hardiman by the throat. 'I warned you what would happen if you didn't leave her alone.'

Hardiman's eye bulged from his head, and his face turned purple as he gasped for air. 'I – I never done n- nothing.'

'You nearly broke me arm, you brute.'

Clemency moved to Jared's side, enjoying Hardiman's obvious discomfort. He had hovered over her family like a big black thundercloud for as long as she could remember. He had made Ma give her body to any man that would pay the price; he had kept her fuddled with drink and beaten her into submission. If Clemency had been a man she would have given him what for. She clenched her fists. 'Sock him in the kisser, Jared. Beat him to a pulp.'

He glanced at her over his shoulder, and his features relaxed into an amused smile. 'That's not very ladylike. But I can sympathise with your sentiments.' He released Hardiman with a shove that sent him stumbling into the gutter. 'Go on your way, and don't come back. If you show your face again or come anywhere near this young woman, I'll see that you end up at the bottom of the river. D'you understand me, Hardiman?'

'Aye, guv.' He scrambled to his feet and, with a final malevolent glance in Clemency's direction, Hardiman shuffled off towards Ludgate Hill.

Jared eyed her with some concern. 'Did he hurt you?'

She rubbed her arm. 'A bit.'

'I want you to promise me that you won't venture out on your own. And that you'll keep away from this area in particular. I can arrange for your friends in the pub to come and visit you in Finsbury Circus, and your mother is welcome at any time. Is that understood? Will you give me your word?'

Clemency crossed her fingers behind her back. 'Yes, Jared.'

'Good. Then we'll go to the house in Hog Yard. The owner owes me a few favours, and we can practise the art of picking pockets undisturbed. Some of the most skilful dips and sneaks doss there.'

'So that's why you were in such a hurry.'

He smiled. 'This is our business, my dear. The lessons you learn from my sister and grandmother are the icing on the cake. This is what it is really all about. And not a word to Izzie.'

In the days that followed, Clemency scarcely had time to breathe. There were lessons in elocution every morning with Lady Skelton, who was an exacting teacher and not particularly patient. She made Clemency stand in front of her with a book perched on her head to improve her deportment, while she repeated words over and over again until she had achieved the correct enunciation. Even worse, she was made to read long passages from books that were so boring she could have tossed them out of the window. Although her reading skills were improving, this was largely due to Ronnie, who coached her in the evenings after supper, when they relaxed around the kitchen table.

Augustus had fallen into the ways of a butler as easily as if he had been born to the position, although he still pined for his errant daughter. Ronnie and Jack were not needed in the house, but they had found temporary jobs in the band that played in the Circus gardens at lunchtimes, and all day at the weekends. Clemency knew that Jack still missed being in the large orchestra, but he never grumbled. Jared had arranged an appointment for him to see Mr Chance, the senior medical officer at the City Orthopaedic Hospital, and both Jack and Fancy were convinced that he would soon be able to walk again. Clemency was not so sure, but she did not want to cast a shadow over their optimism. Fancy had proved to be a reluctant and incompetent lady's maid, and had been swiftly relegated to work in the kitchen. She did not seem to mind the demotion, and went about her duties with a cheerful face. Although, Clemency thought, Fancy's change of attitude could have something to do with the ring that Jack had bought for her from a market stall in Petticoat Lane. It might just be made of gilded base metal, with a lump of blue glass for a stone, but Fancy wore it with as much pride as if it had been part of the crown jewels.

Afternoons were spent either with Jared in

Hog Yard, or with Isobel, who took the task of outfitting her very seriously indeed. If the weather was inclement, they pored over fashion magazines, and on fine days they toured the department stores in Oxford Street. Despite her comparatively wealthy lifestyle, Isobel was no spendthrift. She guided Clemency to the stores where they might expect to find bargains in undergarments and silk hose. She was prepared to haggle if she thought the price of anything was too high, and even while they were in the process of selecting silk gowns, fans and evening shoes, she expounded her views on women's rights and the poor housing conditions of those less fortunate than themselves. Clemency did not like to tell her that she knew first-hand about poverty and what life was like in the worst East End slums. She liked Isobel, and admired her social conscience, even if her knowledge had been gained second hand, and was sometimes wildly inaccurate. The only exception to this routine was on Wednesdays, when Isobel went off to her art class, although it did seem rather odd to Clemency that Isobel never brought home any of her work or, for that matter, showed the slightest inclination to pick up a brush or pencil at any other time. The toffs were a strange bunch, she decided, and immediately put the matter out of her head; there were much more interesting things to occupy her mind now.

*

Ned brought Edith to the house in Finsbury Circus one Sunday afternoon. They sat in the kitchen, drinking tea and eating slices of the seed cake that Nell had sent with them. Although they didn't say much, Clemency could tell that both Ma and Ned were impressed with the house. She did not invite them above stairs to meet Isobel and Lady Skelton, who was visiting at the time. It was not that she was ashamed of Ma, who looked very pretty now that she was well again, and had kept her promise to keep off the booze: Clemency sensed that Lady Skelton might make Ma feel uncomfortable, and she was aware that Ned had disliked Jared on sight. It was best for all parties to keep them apart. Nancy seemed to get on well with Edith, and they chatted amicably while Ned talked to Jack and Ronnie. Augustus was having one of his bad days, when he mourned for his lost songbird, and he retired to his room to brood. Apart from that, the visit was a great success, and Ned promised to bring Edith again when they had a quiet afternoon at the pub.

The days slipped into a pleasant routine. Clemency loved her fine new clothes, and she had grown used to having a bath once a week, although it had been a surprise to discover that she was expected to wash her hands and face every evening before going to bed, and to repeat the process first thing in the morning. At first, it seemed like overdoing cleanliness, but it was wonderful to be free of head lice and fleas for the first time in her life. Isobel had given her a pot of cold cream, with instructions to rub it on her face, which would make her skin soft and might eventually remove the dusting of freckles on her nose. She also gave Clemency a bottle of lavender water, informing her that young ladies should smell fragrant. It was unacceptable to leave the rancid odour of sweat in one's wake. Only horses were allowed to sweat – ladies were supposed to glow. Sometimes, Clemency thought her head was going to burst with all this information and instruction.

Although she was reluctant to return to a life of crime, she began to enjoy her secret trips to Hog Yard with Jared. He had managed to convince Isobel that he was taking Clemency to Mr Haines' Riding Stables in Seymour Place, where she could learn to ride safely in the covered school before venturing out on the streets. Isobel had declined an invitation to accompany them, as Jared admitted that he had known she would. He explained that his sister was terrified of horses, and had taken it into her head that their parents' death had been solely due to the vicious temperaments of the animals harnessed to the carriage in question. When Clemency asked him how she would explain to Izzie that she could not ride after so many expensive lessons, he told her they would meet that problem if, and when, it arose. She had to be content with that, although she was not happy about lying to someone as transparently honest and straightforward as Isobel.

'You worry too much,' Jared said one afternoon when she had mentioned her concern about Isobel as they were leaving Hog Yard. 'Izzie is unlikely to discover the deception, since I can't afford to keep riding horses, or even a pony and trap, for that matter. We must start earning money soon, Clemency. The next quarter's rent is due and it costs a small fortune to run the house.'

'There must be places that are a lot cheaper.'

He tucked her hand into the crook of his arm. 'Of course there are, but I have to keep up appearances. The rich benefactors wouldn't trust me with their donations to the charities if they thought I was poor, and might keep some of it for myself.'

'Why don't you sell the hospitals and homes to someone else, and just keep the money?'

'If only I could. My grandfather donated the buildings to the institutions but he kept the leasehold on the land, which is entailed and therefore cannot be sold.' He glanced down at her and smiled. 'You know, you are almost as bad as Izzie. She has a tender conscience too.' He touched her cheek with the tip of his finger, smiling. Clemency felt her heart do a somersault inside her breast. There was a light in his eyes that made her feel as though she were drowning in their blue depths. They were standing outside the dreadful, run-down buildings in Hog Yard with just a little patch of clear sky above their heads. But suddenly it seemed to her as though they were alone in the middle of a beautiful garden. She could smell flowers and hear birds singing in the leafy trees. She gazed up into his face. She was so close to him that she could hear his heart beating – or was it her own? His hands, that minutes ago had been demonstrating how to steal a man's wallet from an inside breast pocket, slid around her waist. The scent of him was as intoxicating as wine. She slid her arms around his neck and closed her eyes.

Chapter Fifteen

His lips brushed her forehead with the lightest of kisses. 'Come,' Jared said briskly, dropping his hands to his sides. 'We should get back to the house before Isobel thinks we've had a dreadful accident.'

Clemency opened her eyes, but he had already moved away, and was striding down the alley towards the main street. She hesitated for a moment, biting back tears of disappointment and frustration. She had offered herself to him. She had made it obvious that she wanted him to kiss her, and he had snubbed her with a token caress as if she had been a child. Humiliation, anger and embarrassment roiled in her stomach. She had been stupid to think that a man like Jared would give a girl from the slums a second glance. She was just a business proposition to him; a partner in crime. She dashed the tears from her eyes with the back of her hand, and, picking up her skirts, she ran after him. 'Here, hold on, guv. I ain't got me breeches on now. I can't keep up with you.'

Jared stopped walking. He turned to her with an apologetic smile. 'Sorry. I forgot.'

She tossed her head. 'I suppose a girl like me is easy to put on one side, not being a lady of quality.'

'You have many qualities, Clemency. Being a lady isn't all it's cracked up to be.'

She sniffed, refusing to return his smile. She was not prepared to forgive him, not yet anyway. 'It's all an act, if you ask me. All this polite business that Lady Skelton is trying to cram into my head. Seems to me that we're all the same underneath, and you're no better than the rest of us.'

'I couldn't agree more.' He offered her his arm. 'And I meant what I said. You've got courage, Clemency. You're brave and you're loyal. You are also a bit of a crook, just like me, and that's why we'll do well together.'

'As partners in crime?'

'That will do for now.' Jared executed a bow from the waist. 'Will you allow me to escort you home, Miss Skinner?'

A reluctant chuckle escaped from her lips and she took his arm. 'It would be a pleasure, sir.'

'You've worked hard, my dear. And I think you've earned a treat. On Sunday, I want you to dress up in some of your fine new clothes and I am going to take you to Hyde Park, where we will promenade with the rich and fashionable.'

Falling into step beside him, Clemency caught her breath. She had heard of the famous park, but had never imagined she might have the chance to actually visit that part of London. Up West was another world. 'Really? You aren't teasing me, are you, Jared?'

'Of course not. It's one of the best places to relieve the unwary of their trinkets. I always take my girls there first. It's easy pickings in such a crowded place.'

She came back to earth with a thud. So it wasn't an outing for two. It was just another training session, or a test to see how much she had learned. 'Oh,' she said dully. 'I see.'

'You don't sound too enthusiastic.'

'I am. I've always wanted to visit Hyde Park. It's just that – maybe I'm not ready yet. I need a bit more practice.'

They had reached the main thoroughfare and Jared hailed a cab. 'You mustn't worry on that score. And you won't be on your own with me. We'll take Izzie and Lady Skelton along too. I don't expect you to do more than lift a couple of wallets and breast pins, but if you can do so without Izzie noticing anything amiss, then I'll say you are ready to begin work in earnest.'

A hansom cab pulled up at the kerbside, saving Clemency the necessity of answering. She climbed in with a cold feeling in the pit of her stomach. She had been correct in assuming that the outing was a test of her skill. Jared had not invited her because he wanted her company. She sat in the corner, staring out of the window as he gave the cabby instructions and leapt in beside her. 'Don't look so glum,' he said, patting her on the arm. 'You need not be nervous. I'll be with you to make sure nothing goes wrong. If you do well, then we'll start doing the rounds of places such as Madame Tussaud's Wax Works exhibition and the Zoological Gardens. Then we'll progress to summer evening parties at Olympia, and maybe even the Crystal Palace. I have confidence in you, Clemency. Together we'll make a superb team.'

Their sortie to Hyde Park on Sunday did not start well. Clemency was more nervous than she had been on her first appearance at the Strand Theatre. She felt self-conscious in her new clothes, and her tightly laced stays left her desperately short of breath. Despite all her lessons in deportment, she was still unsteady on high heels and the fashionable shoes pinched her toes, making each step so painful that she wanted to cry out. She tried not to lean too hard on Jared's arm as they followed Isobel and Lady Skelton at a funereal pace along the north side of the Serpentine. If only they had been here purely for pleasure she would have been deliriously happy, but she could not escape the knowledge that she was here to work. At a given signal from Jared, she was to go into their well-practised routine where she would lift a gentleman's wallet, a breast pin or a gold watch.

The waters of the Serpentine glinted in the late May sunshine and the fresh green leaves on the trees rustled in the light breeze. Birdsong filled the air, competing with the clip-clopping of horses' hooves and the lively chatter of people promenading in their Sunday best. Clemency almost jumped out of her skin when Jared squeezed her hand, nodding his head in the direction of a well-dressed, middle-aged gentleman approaching them. He was paying far more attention to the young woman on his arm than was natural in a husband or a father. Gold rings gleamed on his fat fingers, and a watch chain was stretched to breaking point across his portly belly, suggesting that it might be attached to an expensive half-hunter; but it was the bulge of his inside breast pocket that Jared indicated with a flick of his eyes.

Taking her cue, Clemency pretended to stumble, falling against their victim with a mumbled apology. Her skilled fingers found his wallet and lifted it from his pocket, but her hand was clammy with sweat: it slid from her grasp and fell to the ground. She righted herself, glancing nervously at the wallet. She could neither move nor speak. She looked up and saw a glint of suspicion in the fat man's eyes. His mouth fell open as if he were about to denounce her as a thief. It all happened in the blink of an eye, and before she realised what was happening, Jared had retrieved the wallet and was handing it back to its owner. 'My dear sir, I do apologise for my young friend's clumsiness. This is yours, I believe.'

'Eh? Oh, yes. Thank you kindly.' He stuffed the wallet back into his pocket, but his companion glared at Clemency.

'I say she done it on purpose, Henry. I met her sort afore.'

'N-no,' Clemency said breathlessly. 'It was an accident. I tripped over a stone.' It struck her suddenly that she had made a pun, and she had to bite back a hysterical giggle. She could not look at Jared, but his hand closed tightly on her arm. It was enough of a warning and she struggled to maintain her self-control.

The man, whom the girl had called Henry, began to bluster. 'A likely story. The pavement is as smooth as a billiard table. The girl is lying.'

For a moment, Clemency thought that things were going to turn nasty, but Lady Skelton had heard the altercation, and she was advancing on them like a ship in full sail, followed by a worried-looking Isobel. 'What is the meaning of this vulgar display?'

Henry pointed a shaking finger at Clemency. 'She tried to steal my wallet.'

'How dare you, sir. This young lady is my

ward and has a character above reproach.' Lady Skelton's fur tippet seemed to come alive and bristle with indignation. Clemency would not have been surprised if it had growled.

'I tell you, ma'am, she tried to pick my pocket.'

'I have never heard such impertinence. An apology is called for, sir.'

'Come, come, Grandmama,' Jared said smoothly. 'It was just a misunderstanding arising from a simple accident.'

'Call a copper, Henry.' The girl tugged at his arm. 'I'll swear on oath it was deliberate.'

Lady Skelton shook her furled parasol at him. 'Another word from you, sir, and you'll be hearing from my solicitor. Mr Horatio Porlock of Porlock, Porlock and Stubbins, of Thavie's Inn.'

By this time a small crowd had gathered. Isobel dragged Clemency away along the path. 'Leave it to Grandmama,' she whispered. 'She would make Boadicea look like a Sunday school teacher. I wish I could get her interested in women's rights.'

'You and your women's rights thing,' Clemency murmured as she quickened her pace in order to keep up.

'Every woman should be interested in the movement,' Isobel said earnestly. 'I'll take you to a meeting, Clemmie. Then you'll see.'

'Hmm, yes. All right.'

'But don't you dare mention a word of it to

Jared. He thinks that I spend my Wednesday afternoons at an art class.' Isobel stopped walking and turned her head to look over her shoulder. 'It's all right – they're coming, and the crowd has moved on.'

Clemency breathed a sigh of relief. 'It was just a misunderstanding, Izzie. The stupid man thought I was trying to pinch his blooming wallet.'

Isobel giggled. 'Hush, don't let Grandmama hear you using words like blooming.'

'I don't know how you remember all this ladylike stuff,' Clemency said, shaking her head. 'It's blooming – I mean it's really hard work.'

Isobel patted her hand. 'But you're doing very well, Clemmie. And it's much more fun having you and your family in the house. Life was such a bore before you came to us.' She turned, smiling brightly as Jared and Lady Skelton joined them. 'Did you sort the dreadful man out?'

Lady Skelton chuckled. 'The mere mention of a solicitor always works wonders with tradesmen. Not that I have one, but he didn't know that.'

'Grandmama, do you mean that you told a fib?'

'I improvised, my dear Izzie. Now, after that bit of excitement, I suggest we proceed to the bandstand and listen to the music.' Lady Skelton shot a meaningful glance at Jared, and without waiting for an answer she unfurled her parasol, and marched off in the direction of the bandstand with Isobel obediently following her.

'I'm sorry,' Clemency said, falling into step beside Jared. 'It was clumsy of me.'

'It was just nerves. You'll do better next time.'

'I thought you'd be angry with me for messing it up.'

'I told you, this is just a training session. Now there is your next challenge.' With a nod of his head, Jared indicated a man swaggering towards them, making a great display of a silver-headed ebony cane; waving it before him like a conductor's baton. Following behind him was a soberly dressed woman and two young girls wearing flower-trimmed straw bonnets. 'See that man, Clemency? He owns a blacking factory in Silvertown. He's worth a small fortune, but his employees work in appalling conditions, for pitifully low wages. Let's try again.'

This time she was successful, and she handed Jared a bulging wallet. The factory owner continued on his way, apparently blissfully unaware that he was lighter to the tune of several guineas. She began to relax as they stood listening to the band, and her thoughts turned to Jack, who would now be playing his flute in the Circus gardens. At two o'clock on Tuesday afternoon he was to see Mr Chance, the chief medical officer at the City Orthopaedic Hospital. She needed money to pay for his consultation fee and for any subsequent treatment. She looked round at the people in the crowd, selecting her next victim. Jared and Lady Skelton had primed her well: she was only to take from those who looked as though they could afford the loss. Even if they had not made it a rule, she would have baulked at stealing from hardworking servants on their afternoon off, or clerks and shop workers on a day out with their young families. She spotted a geezer wearing a checked suit and a bowler hat: on his arm was a loud-mouthed woman in a crimson dress trimmed with black braid. Clemency sidled up to them, and while the woman was talking volubly, punctuated with screeches of laughter, she dipped her fingers into the reticule that hung from her wrist. Smiling to herself, she pocketed a haul of rings, brooches and breast pins that were unlikely to have been come by honestly. It amused her to think that she had stolen from a real pro. The man in the checked suit was smoking a cigar, and bellowing with laughter at everything his companion said. Clemency lifted his wallet and relieved him of a gold watch with a weighty fob and chain. She went back to Jared satisfied that she had earned enough to pay for Jack to see the consultant.

After supper that evening, Clemency had just finished regaling Jack and the others with an account of the fashionable promenade in the park, carefully omitting any mention of her nefarious activities, when the bell connected to the drawing room began to jingle on its spring. Augustus rose from the table with a sigh. 'Oh, really! Anyone would think that I was being paid to wait hand and foot on them above stairs.'

'Well, you are in a way, old chap,' Ronnie said, dabbing his mouth with a linen napkin. 'Paid in kind with food and lodging, as we all are.'

'That's called slavery.' Fancy refilled her glass with small ale from a pitcher. 'Yes, I'm grateful for a roof over me head and three square meals a day, but we're stuck here and totally dependent on Mr Jared Stone. If he takes it into his head to throw us out on the street, we can't do nothing about it.'

'It's true,' Jack said moodily, lighting a Woodbine, and inhaling deeply.

The bell jangled impatiently. 'All right. Keep your hair on, I'm coming.' Augustus strode across the floor to the stairs. 'Sometimes I think I prefer the life of a street entertainer. If only my little nightingale would return to her loving papa.' He barged through the baize door, allowing it to swing shut behind him with an emphatic bang.

'You see, Clem,' Fancy said, passing the pitcher to Jack, 'you got it easy, mixing with the toffs upstairs, and leading the life of a lady.'

'That's not fair. You don't know half of what I have to put up with.'

'Oh, pardon me. I was forgetting how hard it must be to be forced to wear expensive duds, and be taken for strolls in the parks up West, pretending to be something you ain't.'

Clemency opened her mouth to put Fancy in her place, but Jack held up his hand. 'Fancy, that's not fair. Clemmie's the one who got us off the streets, and if Stone has taken a liking to her, and wants her for a companion to his sister, then we should count ourselves lucky. We could still be dossing in that abandoned church or camping under the stage in the theatre.'

Fancy swallowed a mouthful of beer. 'I know that, Jack. All I'm saying is that she's got the best of it. Some of us has to work hard for our bread.'

Ronnie gave Clemency a shrewd look. 'I think Clemmie works hard too. She's brushed up on her reading a treat, and she's learning to speak the Queen's English just like them above stairs.'

'Yes, and where will it lead?' Fancy stuck her chin out with a belligerent gleam in her eyes. 'I'm working me fingers to the bone. Augustus is at the beck and call of them above stairs, and you and Jack are out in all weathers playing in the band for pennies. It ain't fair.'

'Shut up!' Clemency's patience snapped, and she leapt to her feet. 'I've had enough of your whining, Fancy Friday. At least you've got a decent room to sleep in now with a proper bed and clean sheets. Anyway, you chose to work in the kitchen rather than act as maid to Miss Isobel and me, like Jared said you should.'

'Huh! Wait on you? That'll be the day.' Fancy stood up, waving her hand in front of Clemency's face so that the stone flashed in the gaslight. 'You'll have to be more respectful when Jack and me get hitched. I'll be your sister-in-law all legal and proper, and he's the head of the family, so you'll have to mind what I say. At least I got a fellow, which is more than you can say for yourself, Miss High and Mighty.'

Clemency stared at her in shock. She knew, of course, that Fancy still resented her, and that their truce was only superficial: she had seen the ring on Fancy's fourth finger, but it had never occurred to her that Jack had proposed marriage. She turned to him, frowning. 'Is this true? Have you asked her to marry you?'

Avoiding her eyes, he tossed his cigarette butt into the fire. 'I ain't in a position to take a wife and Fancy knows it.'

'But we have an understanding,' Fancy said, standing behind him and laying her hands on his shoulders. 'Tell her, Jack. Tell your snooty sister that we'll get married one day, whether she likes it or not.'

Jack covered Fancy's hand with his, and he raised his eyes to cast an appealing glance at

Clemency. 'I loves her, Clemmie. And for some strange reason, she loves me. Although how a girl like Fancy could fall for a useless cripple is beyond my understanding.'

The muscles in Clemency's throat constricted; she felt a rush of pity, mixed with impatience for Jack's self-deprecating attitude. 'You mustn't talk like that. Tomorrow you're going to see Mr Chance at the hospital. He may be able to help you, Jack. You mustn't give up.'

'I won't let him.' Fancy slid her arms around Jack's neck in a protective gesture. 'He'll walk again. You'll see.'

'We're all behind you, Jack,' Ronnie said, clearing his throat.

'I know you are.' Jack's bottom lip trembled. 'But it don't pay to get our hopes up too much. And there's the cost of it all. I know that Stone said he'd pay for the first visit, but I can't expect him to stump up the rest.'

'No? Well he shouldn't make promises that he can't keep. I'll have a few words with Mr Stone.' Clemency left them before anyone had time to question her. She was halfway up the main staircase when she met Augustus on his way down.

He stopped, holding out his hand, palm upwards. 'I take it all back,' he said, staring down at two golden sovereigns. 'Stone gave this to me saying that it was part payment of our wages. Said he didn't expect us to work for nothing, and that he was sorry he hadn't coughed up before, but business had been a bit unreliable. He is a gent, Clem. A real gent.' With a dazed look on his face, he continued on his way.

Clemency watched him until he was out of sight. She must have done better than she had thought on her first attempt at picking pockets in Hyde Park. Jared was obviously in a good mood. She hurried on to the drawing room, and entered without bothering to knock. She had expected to find Isobel sitting in her usual chair, pretending to be absorbed in her embroidery, or reading a book, but Jared was alone. He rose from his seat and his smile seemed genuine. 'Clemency, this is a pleasure. You don't usually seek my company. Or were you looking for Izzie? I'm afraid she retired to bed early with a headache.'

It was still light outside, the long summer evenings having begun. A shadow of suspicion crossed Clemency's mind. It was unlike Isobel to suffer even the slightest of headaches; she was an unusually robust young lady, even if she did have the delicate appearance of a china doll. If it had been anyone else, Clemency would have suspected that she had made the excuse of a headache in order to slip out and meet a young man. But, of course, that was impossible. Isobel would have told her if she was seeing anyone. Wouldn't she? She gathered her scattered thoughts with difficulty. 'Actually, I wanted to speak to you, Jared. In private.'

His eyebrows rose in twin arcs of surprise. 'Really? You'd better sit down and tell me what's troubling you. Is it your mother?'

She remained standing, clasping her hands behind her back. 'No, it's not Ma. It's about Jack's appointment at the hospital.'

'Which is tomorrow afternoon. You see, I hadn't forgotten.'

'I know, and I'm very grateful to you for arranging it. But I want to know if I've earned enough to pay for whatever treatment the doctor thinks is necessary? You never mentioned paying me for me – I mean – for my services.'

He eyed her speculatively. 'No, I didn't.'

'I just seen – I mean, I just saw Augustus on the stairs, and he showed me the money you'd given him for our wages.' She hesitated, twisting her hands together, and finding it difficult to continue. 'Does that include me? What I'm trying to say is, I don't want Jack's hopes raised. Fair enough, if the doctor says he can't do nothing – anything – to help him. But what if he says that he can do something to make Jack walk again, and we can't afford to pay the bill?'

Jared took a step towards her. 'Have you such a low opinion of me, Clemency? Do you really think that I would have suggested the consultation without intending to see that the treatment was followed through?'

She stared down at the Chinese carpet, concentrating on the pink and blue flower pattern. 'I dunno.'

'Look at me, Clemency. Give me your hands.'

She raised her eyes: his steel-blue gaze was hypnotic. Seemingly powerless to refuse, she unclasped her hands and allowed him to hold them. She felt the now familiar shiver of excitement at his touch. He drew her nearer, and she did not pull away. She was locked in his spell, unable to speak or move. The nearness of him was making her feel breathless and light-headed. She closed her eyes, and this time she was not disappointed. His lips touched hers as tenderly as a summer breeze or the soft brush of a butterfly's wings. His arms slid round her waist, and he held her so tightly that she could scarcely breathe, or perhaps it was the pumping of her heart that was robbing her lungs of air, and weakening her will. Beneath his soft caresses, her lips opened, and she wrapped her arms around his neck. As his kisses grew more demanding, she felt herself responding with a passion that she could never have imagined. She was lost in time and space, and she never wanted the sweet sensations flowing through her veins to stop. But suddenly, and without warning, he released her, and she stood alone, cold and bereft.

'I'm sorry, Clemency,' he said, moving swiftly to stand by the window with his back to her. 'I shouldn't have taken advantage of you like that.'

'No. I mean, you didn't. I wanted you to kiss me, just as I wanted you to the other day in Hog Yard. Don't say it meant nothing to you. I won't believe it if you do.'

He half turned, giving her a rueful smile. 'You know so little about men, despite your appalling upbringing. I am truly sorry, my dear. It won't happen again. And, before you ask me a second time, yes, I promise that I will pay for Jack's treatment. We will have him walking again, if it's humanly possible. On my honour, I swear it.'

'Your honour? What do you know of honour?' A moment ago her lips had tingled with his kisses, but now they burned as the scathing words tumbled from them. 'You're as black-hearted as Hardiman. You think you can play with a girl's feelings – pick her up and drop her down again, like a toy. Well, I got news for you, Mr Stone. I ain't a toy. I might be a common girl from Stew Lane, but I can be hurt just as much as a young lady from Finsbury Circus. If you ever touch me again, I – I'll stab you with . . .' She looked round for a suitable weapon, and spotting Isobel's embroidery scissors on a side table she snatched them up. 'I'll do for you.' A sob rose in her throat, threatening to choke her, and tears poured down her cheeks.

Jared opened his mouth to speak, but Clemency threw the scissors into the empty grate and fled. She raced along the landing to her room and went inside, slamming the door behind her. She turned the key in the lock and threw herself down on the bed. Her whole body shook with a storm of sobbing. All her pent-up anger and emotions were raging beyond her control. She pummelled the pillows with her fists, cursing herself for being a fool. She had broken her own rule, and done the one thing that she had so far managed to avoid: she had ignored all the little warning signs and allowed herself to fall in love. How could she have been so blind to her own feelings? Well, he wasn't worth it – no man, apart from Jack, was worthy of a second thought. She raised herself up on her elbow, hiccuping and sniffing. Ned was all right too, if he was kept in order. And Ronnie was a good sort, but then he was too old to try to take advantage of a girl; he must be at least forty-five, she thought, past the first flush of youth and heading for old age. Augustus was not all bad, and he was more of a father figure. She wiped her eyes on her sleeve, slid off the bed, and went over to the washstand to dash cold water on her face. She walked slowly to the window to gaze down on the Circus, wiping her face on a towel. The trees in the gardens were turning sepia in the gathering dusk, and starlings were swooping in black clouds to roost noisily beneath the eaves of the tall buildings. The lamplighter was making his rounds on the pavement below, using his long pole to send the gaslights squirming inside the glass globes like captive fireflies.

Clemency leaned her hot forehead against the cool glass windowpane. She felt calmer now, and oddly relieved of all the conflicting emotions that had crowded inside her breast. After all, things weren't really so bad. Ma was on the mend, Jack would be seeing the bone doctor tomorrow, and Fancy was a pain in the neck, but she was good for him. As to Jared – she would keep him firmly in his place. Their relationship from now on would be purely a business one. She would keep him locked out of her heart, and she would make sure that he never had the opportunity to make a fool of her again.

She was gazing absently at the street below, barely noticing the people who were out for an evening stroll or hurrying homeward after working late in the City, when she spotted a familiar figure. Forgetting everything else, she craned her neck as she saw Isobel walking arm in arm with a tall man. Clemency held her breath. She had been so wrapped up in her own troubles that she had not thought to wonder whether the sound of her sobbing had disturbed Isobel, who slept in the adjacent room, and was supposed to have retired early with a headache. She was certainly not suffering now. On the contrary, Isobel's face was illuminated in a shaft of lamplight as she gazed up at her companion, and Clemency could see that she was smiling. They seemed to be deep in conversation, and then the man took off his bowler hat, leaning over a little to kiss Isobel, who slid her arms around his neck. Clemency could only hope that Jared was not looking out of the window at this particular moment. She willed Isobel to be careful, although she could see by the way they clung together that the two of them were very much in love. A shaft of something like jealousy pierced her heart, and, for a moment, she found herself envying Isobel. Then common sense told her that there must be a good reason for the clandestine meeting, and she felt a rush of sympathy for the young lovers. 'Say goodbye to him, Izzie,' she whispered. 'If you tarry beneath the gaslight someone will see you, and you'd better pray that it isn't Jared.' She watched until Isobel managed to tear herself away from the young man. Blowing him a kiss, she ran up the steps to the house, and out of Clemency's range of vision. He waited by the streetlight for a long time, and she could see that he was quite young, dark-haired and wearing steel-rimmed spectacles that gave him a serious and studious air. He wore a dark suit, but did not look particularly prosperous. Clemency wondered if he was a bank clerk, or perhaps a reporter from one of the newspaper offices in Fleet Street. She heard Isobel's bedroom door open and then close. The young man looked up and waved. Clemency moved back behind the curtain, realising that Isobel must have rushed to her bedroom window to wave a final farewell. She took another peek, just in time to see him walk away. She drew the curtains, shutting out the night. She waited for a few moments, half expecting Isobel to come knocking on her door, eager to share a confidence, but there was silence from her room. Clemency undressed and slipped on her cambric nightgown. Completely exhausted and drained of emotion, she went to bed, closed her eyes, and fell into a deep sleep.

At two o'clock next day, a hospital porter wheeled Jack into Mr Chance's consulting room, with Fancy following close behind them. There had been a brief battle of wills when Clemency had insisted that as his sister she ought to accompany him, but Fancy had fought back, saying that she was his fiancée and that gave her the right to be with him during the consultation. Clemency had been on the verge of slapping her, when Jared had put an end to the argument by siding with Fancy. Reluctantly, Clemency had obeyed his instruction to take a seat next to Isobel. She was still furious with him for kissing her when it meant nothing to him, and even more angry with herself for caring. She had been dismayed when he said he would accompany them to the hospital as he was acquainted with Mr Chance. She was not quite sure why Isobel had wanted to come too, until the door to the waiting room opened and a young doctor entered the room. Even though he was now wearing a starched white coat, she recognised the young man who had kissed Isobel so tenderly last evening. She turned to look at Isobel and saw that she was blushing and smiling.

'Good afternoon. I am Dr Nicholas Wilson, Mr Chance's houseman.'

Jared held out his hand. 'How do you do, Doctor? I am Mr Skinner's employer, and I wish to be kept fully informed of his treatment and progress.'

'Of course, sir.' Nicholas shook Jared's hand. 'I will be supervising Mr Skinner's treatment, under instruction from Mr Chance himself. If you have any questions after the initial consultation, I will be pleased to answer them.' He smiled and nodded to Isobel and then Clemency. She couldn't help noticing that his eyes rested for a moment longer on Isobel than would have been considered polite on a first meeting. He went into the consulting room, closing the door behind him. Isobel was blushing furiously, and Clemency could only hope that Jared had not noticed.

'He seems a reasonable sort of chap,' he said, taking a seat next to her. 'You needn't look so worried, I'm sure that Jack is in very good hands.'

It was the first time he had addressed her directly that day, and still she couldn't meet his eyes. She stared down at her hands clasped tightly in her lap. 'Yes, I'm sure he is, but I would have liked to go in with him.'

He laid his hand lightly on hers. 'I know, but you have to let him go some time, Clemency. Jack is a grown man and even I can see that Fancy cares for him, obtuse thought I may normally be in such matters.'

'I'm glad it was you who said that, Jared,' Isobel said with a stifled giggle. 'I wouldn't have dared. Grandmama is the only person who has the courage to put you in your place. Aren't I right, Clemency?'

She could not answer. Jared's hand was resting on her fingers with a warm grasp that would have been comforting, if it had not been so deeply disturbing. Her instinct was to push him away, but to do so would look petty and childish. He was so close to her in the confines of the small waiting area that she could feel his breath on her cheek and the warmth of his body. The close proximity of him sent dizzying messages to her brain, bringing back the achingly sweet memory of his kiss. She had thought last night that she had steeled herself to resist this strange, terrifying, and yet wonderful attraction he held for her, but now she felt as though it was suffocating her.

'Are you feeling all right?'

The concern in his voice pierced her muddled thoughts, and, for a moment, she imagined that he really did care for her.

'She looks terribly pale, Jared,' Isobel said anxiously. 'Are you unwell, dear?'

'You mustn't fall ill now,' Jared said, removing his hand. 'I have a special treat for you both tonight. I've got tickets for a musical play at the Gaiety Theatre. It's a chance to wear your new evening gown, Clemency.'

So it was business as usual. The thought acted liked a dip in the icy waters of the Thames. Clemency lifted her head to look him in the eyes. 'Don't worry about me. I'll be on good form by tonight.' She thought she saw him wince, but the door to the consulting room opened and Dr Wilson stood there, clutching a notebook.

'Mr Stone, Miss Skinner. Mr Chance would like a word, if you please.'

Chapter Sixteen

Clemency rose slowly from her seat. She had heard people say that their blood ran cold on hearing shocking news, but she had never believed it possible – until now. Icicles of fear stabbed at her heart, and she was not sure whether her feet would carry her as far as the consulting room. In her mind's eye she could imagine Jack's bleak expression if he had been told that he was a hopeless case, and would never walk again. Suddenly, and irrationally, she was furious with Jared. They had never imagined that Jack's condition would improve. He had been resigned to the fact that he would spend his life as a cripple. Then Jared had come up with the notion of consulting a specialist, and a miracle seemed to be within their grasp.

'Come along, Clemency.' Jared had his hand beneath her elbow, and he was propelling her towards the consulting room. She moved like a sleepwalker, bracing herself to receive the awful news.

'I'm coming too,' Isobel said, jumping to her feet.

Dr Wilson barred her way. 'Perhaps it would be more tactful if you remained in the waiting room, Miss Stone.'

Clemency was too concerned with Jack's fate to care whether or not Isobel and her gentleman friend had been granted the opportunity of a few moments on their own. She gripped Jared's arm, pushing all thoughts from her mind, and concentrating on Jack, who was seated on the examination couch with Fancy standing at his side. 'Jack? Are you all right, love?' He did not reply and his face was ashen as though he was in shock. Fearing the worst, she turned to the consultant. 'Tell me, doctor. Is it bad news?'

Mr Chance's set features gave nothing away. He opened his mouth to speak, but Fancy butted in. 'He's going to send Jack away. You mustn't let him, Clem.'

'S-send Jack away?' Clemency's mouth was so dry that she could hardly form the words. Visions of Jack locked away in a prison-like sanatorium flashed through her mind. She shot an agonised glance at Jared, but he seemed maddeningly calm, and he was shaking Mr Chance's hand.

'It was good of you to see Jack so soon, old boy,' Jared said, smiling. 'I appreciate the favour.'

'Not at all, Stone. It's the least I could do, considering the amount of funds you have raised for the foundling hospital.'

Clemency stared from one to the other in horror. Jack's entire future hung in the balance, and they were chatting like a pair of old washerwomen. 'Oy!' she said sharply. 'Cut the cackle and tell us what's wrong with Jack's legs.'

Mr Chance stared at her as though she had just crawled out from a hole in the skirting board. She glared back at him: it was obvious that no one spoke to him like that. She stuck out her chin, prepared to take him on, just as she had taken on the street urchins who had tried to bully Jack when they were both nippers.

'Ahem.' Jared cleared his throat. 'Miss Skinner is naturally very concerned about her brother. We would be most grateful to have your professional opinion, Mr Chance.'

'Will he walk again, or not?' Clemency demanded. 'It's a simple enough question.'

'Yes,' Fancy added. 'And why are you going to send him away?'

'Hush, love.' Jack reached out to take her hand. 'Let the doctor speak. I can take it, mister. Just tell me straight.'

Mr Chance folded his arms across his chest. 'You will never be able to walk unaided, Mr Skinner. You appear to have suffered an attack of infantile paralysis when you were a child, and that has left your leg muscles atrophied and too weak to support your weight.'

Fancy stifled a sob and Clemency moved to

Jared's side, leaning against him for comfort. Nothing mattered now, except Jack.

Jared slipped his arm around her shoulders. 'Is there nothing you can do, Chance?'

'I have a private nursing home in Epping, where we have successfully rehabilitated many victims of this disease. There is no cure, but with daily treatments of physiotherapy, and exercises designed to strengthen the muscles that remain unaffected, we have achieved most satisfactory results. In a matter of months, I am certain that we could have Jack walking with the aid of callipers and crutches.'

'What are callipers?' Clemency cast an anxious glance at Jack, but his expression was unreadable.

'Leg irons. Jack will always need some form of support, but at least he will be mobile. He will be able to get about on his own, and lead a much more normal life.' Mr Chance allowed his stern features to relax in a smile. 'And that would be a great improvement, wouldn't it, Jack?'

Jack's mouth worked silently, as though he were struggling to find words to express his feelings. He nodded, and Fancy flung her arms round him.

Clemency struggled with a jumble of emotions. It was good news and bad news. It would be wonderful for Jack to be able to walk by himself, even if he had to rely on leg irons and crutches, but a private nursing home would cost money. 'H-how much would it cost, doctor?'

Mr Chance raised his eyebrows. 'I can't say exactly, Miss Skinner. It depends how well your brother responds to treatment.'

'That's it then,' Jack said, disentangling himself from Fancy's grasp. 'Sorry to have wasted your time, doctor.'

'The cost is irrelevant, Jack.' Jared turned to Mr Chance. 'How soon could the treatment begin?'

'Providing that there is a bed available, the course of treatment can begin immediately.'

'The sooner the better,' Jared said, holding out his hand.

Mr Chance shook it solemnly. 'I'll ask Dr Wilson to make the necessary arrangements. You must dine with me at my club, Stone, and we can discuss future fund raising for the foundling hospital. It's a charity very close to my heart.'

'And mine,' Fancy muttered, frowning. She waited until Mr Chance had left the room with Jared, then she turned to Clemency. 'Don't I get no say in all this? I don't want Jack sent away to some institution out in Essex where I can't see him for weeks on end.'

'It's for the best, love,' Jack said, stroking her hair. 'Think how good it will be when I can step out with you on me own two feet, even if I do clank along like a knight in rusty armour.'

'You are me knight in armour already, Jack. I just don't want us to be parted.'

'You're just thinking about yourself, as usual.' Her patience at snapping point, Clemency fisted her hands at her sides. She saw the hurt look in Jack's eyes, and she forced her lips into a smile. 'I'm sorry, Fancy. I didn't mean to be sharp with you. I understand how you feel, really I do. But we got to put Jack first. Just imagine how you'll feel when he can walk down the aisle with you, instead of having to be carried by Ronnie, or pushed along in a bath chair.' Jack sent her a grateful look and she responded with a wink and a genuine smile. It was not easy to relinquish her responsibility for him, especially to someone like Fancy, but she knew that the time had come to let him go. She must step aside and allow someone else to look after him. She went to the door, willing herself not to look back. In the waiting room, she found Jared talking earnestly to Dr Wilson. Isobel's cheeks were flushed, and she was sitting on the edge of a chair, fidgeting with the strings of her reticule. Clemency could hardly wait to question her about the young doctor, but she knew that it would have to wait until Jared was out of earshot.

Jared, on the other hand, seemed sublimely oblivious to his sister's agitated state. 'So that's settled then, Dr Wilson,' he said, taking a calling card from his wallet. 'Perhaps you will be kind enough to let us know when the final arrangements are made? If I am not at home, then you should ask for Miss Skinner.' Jared turned to her. 'Clemency, may I introduce Dr Wilson?'

Clemency bobbed a curtsey.

'And you've already met my sister, Isobel.'

'Yes, sir. We've had a most interesting conversation.'

Jared turned to Isobel with a frown. 'I hope you haven't been boring Dr Wilson with talk about women's rights, Izzie?'

She responded by pulling a face.

'We were discussing art. I believe that Miss Stone attends watercolour classes.' Dr Wilson smiled at Isobel, and she looked away with a flutter of her eyelashes.

Clemency glanced at Jared: it was so blatantly obvious that there was something going on between Izzie and her doctor that she found it difficult to believe he had not noticed, but he was holding the door open, and he was not even looking at Isobel. Clemency saw with a jolt of surprise that he was looking at her with a question in his eyes. 'What?' she demanded. 'What's up?'

He lowered his voice. 'I know you are worried, Clemency. But you mustn't even think about the cost of Jack's treatment. I'll take care of everything.'

'And I suppose I'm to start earning it at the theatre tonight?'

'You're still angry with me. I can understand that, but I thought we would just enjoy the show. It's my way of saying I'm sorry for behaving as I did last night. I can assure you that it won't happen again, Clemency.'

'I know. You never mix business with pleasure.' Clemency marched past him, into the hospital corridor that smelt of carbolic soap and disinfectant.

They travelled home in silence. Fancy sat close to Jack, holding his hand as if she would never let him go. This display of ownership might have annoyed Clemency before today, but now she was just relieved that there was a chance that Jack would be able to walk, even if it was not the miracle cure she had secretly hoped for. Isobel sat next to her, staring out of the window, and Jared was disturbingly close to her, seated on her right. She folded her hands in her lap, and hunched her shoulders, making herself as small as possible so that the swaying movement of the carriage did not throw her against him. It was a blessed relief when the hackney pulled up outside the house in Finsbury Circus. Jared lifted Jack down to the pavement, but he then refused further assistance, and hauled himself up the steps on his buttocks. 'Just wait,' he said, as he rested on the top step. 'In a few months' time, I'll be skipping up these steps on me own two feet.'

Jared opened the door. 'We'll lay out the red carpet then, old chap.' He waited while Jack negotiated the door sill and scuttled crabwise across the entrance hall with Fancy hurrying after him. As Clemency stepped over the threshold, he laid his hand on her arm. 'Jack is a brave fellow. Courage runs in your family.'

'Yes, and brains too. I know my place, Jared. So you need not worry that I'll forget myself and show you up.' With her pride intact, and her heart breaking, Clemency marched past him. She went straight to her room and was dragging the hatpins from her feathered hat when someone knocked on her door. She almost stabbed herself with one of the long pins, thinking that Jared had followed her, and then common sense reasserted itself. 'Come in.'

Isobel burst into the room. 'What was that all about?'

'I don't know what you're talking about.'

'Oh, yes, you do.' Isobel perched on the edge of the bed. 'You've fallen out with Jared, haven't you? You could hardly bear to look at him in the hospital.'

'Never mind me. What do you think you're doing? I saw you last night, kissing that young doctor. If you want to keep things secret, you shouldn't stand under a streetlight when you're kissing your fellow goodnight.'

Isobel's hands flew to her mouth, and her eyes widened in dismay. 'Oh, goodness. I didn't think anyone could see us from the house.'

'A few minutes earlier and Jared would have seen you from the drawing room. He obviously doesn't know about your Dr Wilson.'

'Nick,' Isobel said dreamily. 'His name is Nick. You met him today, Clemency. Don't you think he's gorgeous?'

Gorgeous wasn't a word that Clemency would have used for the serious-looking, bespectacled young man. Nice, maybe, but there was nothing particularly remarkable about him. She went to sit beside Isobel. 'You obviously like him, Izzie. But what would Jared say if he knew you were seeing him on the sly?'

'You won't tell him, will you? Swear on your honour that you won't breathe a word of this to Jared, or to Grandmama.' Isobel clutched Clemency's hands, staring earnestly into her face.

'I promise not to tell him, but how long do you think you can keep a thing like that secret? And to what end? You know that they want you to marry some rich bloke who will keep you in luxury for the rest of your life.'

Tears sparkled on Isobel's long eyelashes. 'I know. But I love Nick, and I want to marry him. He's a good man, Clemency. And he's a wonderful doctor. He gives all his spare time to the foundling hospital and the hospital for fallen women.'

'Not all his spare time,' Clemency said, smiling.

Isobel chuckled and wiped her eyes on the back of her hand. 'No. I suppose you've guessed our secret. We meet every Wednesday afternoon, when I'm supposed to be at my art class.'

'It wouldn't take Inspector Abberline to work that one out, Izzie.' Clemency gave her hand a squeeze as she saw fresh tears gather in Isobel's blue eyes. 'How did you meet him in the first place? You're better protected than the queen.'

'At one of Jared's fundraising functions. Mr Chance was there, and Nick and some of the other junior housemen were acting as ushers and handing out leaflets. I took one from him, and our eyes met – I think it was love at first sight for both of us. I know it was for me. Then we started talking about the charities and I said I was interested in the women's movement, and Nick said that he was too. We have so much in common, Clemency.'

'You haven't met many blokes, have you, Izzie?'

'No, but I know he's the one for me. I love him so much.'

'I believe you.'

'And you really do promise not to tell Jared or Grandmama?'

'Of course not, but it's not something you can keep from them forever.'

'I know that. Nick is going to speak to Jared at the first opportunity. Can't you see, Clemmie? Jack having treatment at Mr Chance's clinic is a heaven-sent opportunity for Nick to put himself forward and to get to know Jared. I think it's wonderful, and I'm certain that everything is going to work out so well, for all of us.'

Clemency put her arm around Isobel's shoulders and gave her a hug. She wished that she could be so certain of the outcome. 'I do hope so.'

The trip to the theatre passed off uneventfully. Jared seemed not to notice the slight chill in Clemency's attitude towards him. They had seats in the front row of the dress circle, and during the intermission he escorted them to the bar. They drank champagne from glasses the shape of which, so Isobel informed them, had been inspired by Marie Antoinette's breasts. This comment drew a stern rebuke from Lady Skelton, and Clemency had to cover her mouth with her gloved hand to suppress a giggle. As she met Jared's eyes, she saw that he was laughing too, and this time she did not look away. She could feel the tension leaching from her body, and she began to relax.

'Don't encourage her,' Lady Skelton said,

rapping Jared's knuckles with her fan. 'Young ladies shouldn't know about such things.'

'I read it in a history book,' Isobel protested.

'At least you learned something at that extremely expensive school, Izzie.' Jared rose to his feet. 'I think it's time we returned to our seats.' He proffered his arm to Lady Skelton, but she was looking over his shoulder.

'Jared, isn't that young Darcy Fairbrother standing by the bar? My eyes aren't as good as they were. Ask him over, there's a good fellow.'

Clemency saw that Jared hesitated, but he strolled off with a casual shrug of his shoulders. She wondered if he ever went against Lady Skelton's wishes.

Isobel clutched her arm. 'Don't look now, but he's one of them – the awful eligibles. Whatever you do, don't leave me alone with him.'

Of course, she had to turn her head. Who could resist the temptation to take a peek at an awful eligible? Darcy Fairbrother was coming towards them, chatting amicably to Jared. Clemency eyed him curiously, despite the warning issued by Lady Skelton that she was not to stare. He was of average height, neither fat nor thin, his hair was mousy and his eyes were either grey or blue. But his whole demeanour spoke of wealth and privilege. He bowed and smiled, when addressed by Lady Skelton, and he greeted Isobel with a fulsome compliment. He barely glanced at Clemency when Jared introduced them, and her instant dislike of him was confirmed. He was, she decided, the worst kind of toff: arrogant, conceited and spoiled. She had no first hand knowledge of his type, but she had seen them hee-hawing at each other as they left the theatre, when she had been a humble street entertainer. As far as his sort was concerned, the lower classes simply did not exist, except to wait on them hand and foot or to work in mills and manufactories for criminally low wages. He was shamelessly flattering Isobel, who had a haunted look about her. Then the bell rang to summon the audience back to the auditorium.

Isobel leapt to her feet, and seized Clemency by the hand. 'We must return to our seats. Goodbye, Mr Fairbrother.'

'May I call on you tomorrow, Miss Stone?' Darcy's smile faded into a frown.

'No!' Isobel backed away. 'I mean, I'm otherwise engaged tomorrow, Mr Fairbrother.' She headed for the dress circle, dragging Clemency along behind her. 'Is he following us? Has he taken the hint?'

Clemency glanced over her shoulder. Jared and Lady Skelton appeared to be attempting to placate Darcy, who looked as though he was about to throw a tantrum. 'No. You're safe, but I think your granny might have a few words to say to you.'

Isobel collapsed into her seat, giggling. 'Don't let Grandmama hear you calling her granny. She'll never forgive you.'

Clemency sat down, carefully arranging her satin skirts. 'Let's enjoy the rest of the play. That leading lady is rubbish, if you ask me. She sings like a cat with bellyache and she's got flat feet. I could do heaps better.'

Isobel was still laughing when Jared returned to his seat. He shot her an angry look. 'You were extremely rude to young Fairbrother. His father is the head of a merchant bank in the City, and his mother is an earl's daughter.'

Clemency felt Isobel subside into her seat. 'Leave her alone,' she hissed in Jared's ear. 'You're nothing but a big bully.' The orchestra struck up, and the house lights dimmed before he could retaliate. Clemency shifted her position so that she was almost leaning on Isobel, and as far away from Jared as she could manage in the confines of the theatre seat. He was just another domineering male; always trying to assert his power over women. He had been allowed to get away with it for too long, in her opinion. Maybe there was something in this women's rights business, she thought, staring straight ahead of her as the curtain was raised.

When Darcy Fairbrother called at the house next day, Isobel declined to see him, pleading a headache. That afternoon a bouquet of hothouse flowers was delivered to the door, with a card addressed to Miss Isobel Stone. Clemency took them up to the bedroom where Isobel was sitting in a chair by the window, reading a penny novelette. She tore up the card without bothering to read it, and would have tossed the flowers out of the open window, if Clemency had not rescued them and taken them downstairs to decorate the kitchen. After that, flowers arrived every day, and the bouquets were received with the same lack of enthusiasm. The kitchen was beginning to resemble a florist's shop. Clemency had to use all her powers of persuasion to prevent Nancy from complaining to Jared that the heavy scent of roses, carnations and lilies was affecting her sinuses and making her sneeze.

On the fourth day, Darcy arrived on the doorstep bringing his offering in person, but fortunately, or unfortunately, Clemency could not quite work out which, when she opened the door she found Dr Wilson had chosen this moment to call, and the two young men were standing on the step, eyeing each other like a pair of fighting cocks. Clemency showed Dr Wilson into the morning room and she took Darcy upstairs to the drawing room, where Lady Skelton had been giving Isobel a piece of her mind, which was obvious from the mutinous look on Isobel's face, and the two spots of high colour on her grandmother's cheeks. Isobel leapt to her feet when she saw Darcy, but Lady Skelton caught her by the hand, and pulled her back onto the sofa.

Clemency hesitated in the doorway as Lady Skelton made Darcy welcome. 'If you please, ma'am,' she said, bobbing a curtsey, 'Miss Isobel is needed in the morning room, urgently.'

'What nonsense is this? Of course she isn't needed urgently. Who could possibly want to see Isobel urgently?' Lady Skelton's fingers whitened as they pinned Isobel's hand to the sofa.

Clemency thought quickly. She could hardly say that Dr Wilson had called. Anyway, he had come to see Jared with a message from Mr Chance, but she knew that Isobel would never forgive her if she let him go without seeing her. 'It's the milliner, ma'am. She's brought Miss Isobel's new hat, but she would like her to try it on to make sure it fits.'

'Of course it will fit, you silly girl.' Lady Skelton dismissed her with a wave of her hand.

Clemency stared hard at Isobel, willing her to understand, but there was nothing more she could do. She left the room hoping that Isobel had somehow grasped the unspoken message. She went to the small room at the back of the house that Jared used as a study and she knocked on the door.

'Come.'

She entered, feeling suddenly quite shy. They had barely exchanged more than a few words for days. Her resentment at the way he treated Isobel had faded, but the memory of his kiss could not be so easily forgotten. There was still the fizz of excitement that made her pulses race whenever he was near, and the mere sound of his voice had the power to make her go weak at the knees. The only way to keep herself sane was to avoid him, but that was virtually impossible when they occupied the same dwelling. If Jack's treatment had not depended on Jared's charity, she would have walked out of the house, and out of his life.

'Yes? What is it, Clemency?'

She came back to earth with a jolt. Jared was sitting in a button-back leather chair at his desk, which was littered with papers. He was staring at her with a guarded expression on his face.

'Dr Wilson is here to see you. He's waiting in the morning room.' She turned on her heel, and was about to leave when Jared called her back.

'Clemency, wait.'

She paused in the doorway, but she could not look at him. 'Yes?'

'I can see that you are still cross with me, even though I've apologised for my behaviour.' He twisted the chair round so that he was facing her. 'I treated you like a common serving girl and I'm sorry for it.'

She stared down at her feet. So that was it. There really had been nothing behind that passionate embrace – he had just given in to a moment of lust. He had just said as much. 'It's forgotten,' she lied.

'Good. Now perhaps we can get on with the business in hand. I'll go down and see the young doctor. And tonight, I want you to dress in your best gown. You and I are going to the pleasure gardens at Olympia. Tomorrow we will go to the Crystal Palace. I need hardly tell you that we need extra money to fund Jack's treatment.'

So it was all forgotten was it? Clemency searched his face for a clue as to his true feelings, but it was like staring at a mask. He had put it all behind him, thinking that another apology would clear the air, and now it was business as usual. She took a deep breath. 'I'm truly grateful for what you're doing for Jack. But I'd almost rather he didn't have the treatment than to have to get the money by stealing.'

'It seems a bit late to develop a conscience. I seem to remember that you were trying to pick my pocket when we first met.'

'I stole because we was hungry. I didn't pinch things just for the fun of it.'

Jared sat back in his chair, steepling his fingers. 'The people I target are not so lilywhite, Clemency. I have an instinct for selecting men who have made their money by inflicting misery on others. And I do give some of the fundraising money to the charities in question. I'm not greedy.'

She saw the corners of his eyes crinkle with the beginnings of a smile, and this annoyed her even further. 'It ain't a laughing matter. You talk like you're some blooming Robin Hood, stealing from the rich and giving to the poor.'

'Nothing so splendid, I'm afraid.' His amused expression darkened into something much more sombre. 'But I have a debt to collect from the man who encouraged my father's obsession with gambling. Both he and my mother might be alive today if it had not been for the wealthy man who preyed upon his weakness, and ultimately forced him to flee the country.'

There was a passionate note in his voice that Clemency had not heard before. She felt her resolve weakening, and the desire to throw her arms around him was almost unbearable. She had managed to find a chink in his armour, but it was a pyrrhic victory, and she resorted to the only safe emotion – anger. 'Don't expect me to feel sorry for you, Mr Stone. If you ask me, I think you're just making excuses for your criminal activities. You're too idle to go out and get a proper job, and you enjoy pretending to be one of the nobs.'

His eyes were the cold blue of the sky in winter. 'I wouldn't expect a girl like you to understand.'

'A girl like me? You think that I'm worth less than you just because I'm poor.'

'Poor, but honest?'

There was a glint in his eyes that seemed to mock her, or perhaps it was self-mockery. She could not tell which, but she chose to think that it was aimed at her. 'I don't claim to be honest. I done lots of things that I'm not proud of, but at least I don't pretend to be above me station in life.'

'And I do?'

'You live in a big house that you can't afford and you have to steal to pay for it. You're trying to force your sister into an arranged marriage with a man she don't love, just so that she'll be rich. I tell you, Jared, I don't understand any of it. You're not a bad man. In fact, deep down you're a good 'un. You've been wonderful to Jack, and you've given us all a roof over our heads. So why can't you forget the past and be a bit more ordinary? There are thousands of people who live quite happily in smaller houses earning an honest living, so why can't you?'

For a moment she thought she had gone too far, and then he threw back his head and laughed. 'But think how dull it would be. Don't you find it just a little bit exciting when you're on the dip? Isn't there a thrill to pit your wits against the whole of the London constabulary?'

'There might have been once. But now I'm sick

of it. I was doing so well, singing in the Strand Theatre. Until Hardiman put a stop to it, and you came along with your fancy offers. I wish I'd turned you down then, but now there's no way out.' She saw that he was about to speak and she held up her hand. 'Oh, don't worry. I won't let you down. You're helping Jack, and I'll keep my part of the bargain. But that doesn't mean to say that I like it.' She was about to leave the room when she remembered why she had come in the first place. 'And Dr Wilson is still waiting for you in the morning room.' She turned on her heel and walked away, without giving him the chance to reply.

She was passing the drawing room when Lady Skelton emerged, closing the door behind her with a satisfied smile on her lips. 'Clemency, just the person I wanted to see. Will you send Nancy up with some refreshments for Mr Fairbrother? Some sherry or Madeira wine, whichever comes to hand. That is if the wretched woman hasn't drunk it all.'

'Yes, Lady Skelton.' Clemency bobbed a curtsey and was about to continue towards the staircase when there was a loud scream from the drawing room, followed by a resounding slap. The door opened and Darcy Fairbrother strode out clutching his cheek.

'That girl is a wildcat, Lady Skelton. She attacked me.'

'Isobel would never do such a thing.' Lady Skelton eyed him suspiciously. 'What did you do to upset her?'

'Nothing! On my honour.' Darcy lifted his hand from his cheek, revealing red weals. 'I tell you, ma'am. She attacked me for nothing.'

Isobel appeared in the doorway, flushed and furious. 'You're a liar Darcy Fairbrother. He tried to kiss me, Grandmama. You'd only just left the room and he – he put his hand on my – my bosom – and he tried to kiss me.'

'You pig,' Clemency hissed in his ear. 'You men are all the same.'

'Is this true?' Lady Skelton bristled.

Darcy backed away towards the stairs. 'I may have been a little over-enthusiastic, but I meant no harm. After all, we were about to become engaged. But that is definitely off now. I wouldn't think of allying myself with this family.'

Isobel flew at him, but Clemency caught her around the waist and held her back. 'Don't, Izzie. He's not worth it.'

Jared came striding along the corridor that led to his study. 'What the hell is going on?'

'He mauled me,' Isobel sobbed. 'He touched me where he shouldn't have, and he tried to kiss me.'

'Get out of my house,' Jared stormed. 'No one insults my sister. Now get out before I throw you down the stairs.'

Lady Skelton pushed past him brandishing her parasol. She whacked Darcy round the head with it, and he backed away in alarm. 'I'd only just left the room, you little squit. And to think I trusted you with my granddaughter's honour.'

'Honour?' Darcy's eyes bulged from their sockets as he stumbled in his attempts to flee the hail of blows. 'This is a madhouse. My mother said you were no lady and that Stone's father was a gambler and a cheat… Aarrgh!' he screeched, as Lady Skelton gave him a hefty shove that sent him toppling backwards down the stairs.

The sound of his body bumping from step to step echoed off the high ceilings, his bellowing sounded like a cow in need of milking – then there was silence.

'My God, Grandmama,' Jared said. 'I think you've killed the blighter.'

Chapter Seventeen

Jared was first to hurry after Darcy with Clemency close behind him. As she rounded the curve in the staircase, she saw Darcy lying in a heap on the floor. For a moment she thought that he really was dead, but, as Jared reached him, he groaned and moved. Augustus had appeared from the direction of the kitchen, carrying a tray of coffee. He came to a halt and a flicker of surprise crossed his well-schooled features as he stared at the writhing body. At that moment, Dr Wilson came hurrying from the morning room. He shot a questioning look at Jared.

'He fell,' Jared said, prodding Darcy with the toe of his shoe. 'Tumbled down the stairs before anyone could save him.'

Dr Wilson knelt beside Darcy. 'Don't move, sir. I'm a doctor. You'd better let me make sure that nothing is broken.'

Darcy groaned even more loudly. 'I was pushed.' He turned his head to glare at Lady Skelton, who was standing behind Clemency on the stairs. 'She pushed me.'

'And I'd do it again, you disgusting little man.'

Lady Skelton shook her fist at him, but almost lost her balance as Isobel hurried past her.

'Nick. Oh, Nick. I'm so glad to see you.' She hurled herself off the last step and he leapt up to catch her.

'Darling, what happened?' He held Isobel in his arms, stroking her hair as she sobbed against his shoulder.

'He m-molested me, Nick.'

'What?' Nick glared at Darcy who by this time had scrambled to his feet, clutching his head.

'I'll sue you all for grievous bodily harm. You'll be hearing from my solicitor, Stone. And as for you, doctor – I'll have you struck off.' He staggered across the entrance hall, and Augustus, having deposited the tray on a side table, opened the front door. Darcy stopped on the threshold, turning to Jared with a snarl. 'I'll see that you are barred from every gentlemen's club in London. And no decent man will come anywhere near that lying little trollop.' He pointed a shaking finger at Isobel. 'You led me on, whore.'

'That's it.' Jared exchanged glances with Nick, who handed Isobel into Clemency's care. They advanced on Darcy together, shrugging off their jackets. Darcy took one look at their faces, and attempted to run, but in his haste he tripped over the doorsill and tumbled headlong down the steps, landing on the pavement with a thud.

Everyone crowded in the doorway to view his discomfort. Clemency stifled a giggle at the sight of Darcy sprawled on the pavement, with the passers-by looking on in amusement.

'You haven't heard the last of this, Stone.' Darcy struggled to his feet, brushing the dust off his expensive suit.

'Oh, I think we have, Fairbrother,' Jared said in a voice that dripped acid. 'I don't think you'd want it put about that you mauled and insulted an innocent young girl in her own home.'

'It's her word against mine.'

'There are plenty of witnesses here who will swear in court that you are a cad, sir.'

'Bah!' Darcy turned away to hail a passing cab.

Augustus closed the door as Jared and Nick stepped back into the hall. They faced each other for a moment, and Clemency held her breath. She could feel Isobel's heart pounding as she supported her.

'Jared, please.' Isobel's voice broke as she held her hand out to him. 'Don't be angry with Nick. It's all my fault.'

'No, sir.' Nick squared his shoulders, meeting Jared's stern gaze. 'I take full responsibility. I should have asked your permission to pay court to Isobel.'

'So, you've been seeing each other behind my back?'

Jared's cold tone made Clemency shudder. She

longed to speak up for Isobel, but she knew that she would only make matters worse. Surprisingly, it was Lady Skelton who stepped in between them. 'Now, Jared. Be reasonable. Thankfully there is no real harm done. Isobel has had an unpleasant experience, and we were mistaken in thinking that young Fairbrother was a worthy suitor. However, it seems that we've discovered this romance before things got out of hand. I suggest that you and Dr Wilson have a civilised and frank discussion over coffee in the morning room.'

'Yes,' Clemency said. 'And don't forget Jack. That's why you came here this morning, Dr Wilson.'

'Yes. The reason I came was to tell you that the arrangements are all in hand. If you can have Jack ready within the hour, I've been instructed to take him to the clinic in Epping to begin his treatment.'

'Excellent. Come with me, doctor. There are matters that we need to discuss.' Jared held up his hand as Isobel tried to follow them. 'In private, Izzie.'

Lady Skelton took Isobel by the arm. 'Put on your hat and gloves, Izzie. You and I are going shopping.'

'But, Grandmama, I need to speak to Jared.' Isobel's mouth turned down at the corners as she watched Jared usher Nick into the morning room, followed by Augustus bearing the tray of coffee. She turned to Clemency with a mute plea.

'I'm sure that your doctor can stand up for himself,' Clemency said, smiling. 'At least Jared didn't pitch him down the front steps after Darcy.'

Lady Skelton gave Isobel a gentle push towards the staircase. 'Clemency is right, dear. I'll send Augustus out to find us a cab.'

Isobel looked as though she was going to argue, but Clemency left them to sort out their differences. Her main concern now was for Jack. She hurried to the kitchen, and found that the news had gone before her, as Augustus had already given them an account of the happenings above stairs. Fancy had gone to pack a bag for Jack, and he was sitting in his usual chair, smoking a cigarette. He smiled at Clemency, but she sensed his nervousness.

'You'll be in good hands, Jack.'

'I know,' he said, exhaling a cloud of smoke with a sigh. 'You will see that Fancy is all right while I'm away, won't you. Clemmie?'

'Of course.'

'And you'll let Ma know about me treatment?'

'I will. Miss Isobel is going shopping with Lady Skelton so I'll be free to go round and see her this afternoon.'

Ronnie looked up from peeling potatoes over a bucket of water. 'I'm not playing in the band until this evening. I'd like to go with you, if I may, Clem?'

'Ma would like that, Ronnie.' Clemency went to Jack and kissed him on the forehead. 'I'll be thinking of you, love. You be a good boy and do everything they say.'

He smiled ruefully, but she could see that his eyes were reddened, as if he was fighting back tears. 'Give Ma my love. Tell her that the next time she sees me, I'll be walking on me own two feet.'

Clemency wrapped her arms around him and buried her face in his dark hair: it smelt faintly of tobacco smoke, and Calvert's carbolic soap. She knew that she would miss him terribly: this would be the first time in her life that she had been parted from her brother. She could only hope and pray that the staff in the nursing home would be kind and considerate to his wants and needs.

Ronnie cleared his throat. 'We'll all miss you, Jack.'

'Well, I won't, because I'm going with him.' Fancy marched into the kitchen carrying a bulging carpet bag, which Clemency recognised as belonging to Ronnie. 'Don't look at me like that, Clem. I've made up me mind. I'll sleep in the stables if they won't let me stay in the hospital.'

There was nothing that anyone could say that

would deflect Fancy from her course. She stuck by Jack's side like a burr on a dog's coat until Nick agreed, somewhat reluctantly, to take her with them. The person who protested the loudest was Nancy. She objected to losing Fancy's services as kitchen maid. She threatened to take the matter to Jared, and was only mollified by Clemency and Ronnie's offer to take on the menial tasks themselves, and to help with the cooking. An hour later, Jack and Fancy left in the hired carriage with Nick. Clemency stood on the top step, waving until they were out of sight. 'He will be all right, won't he, Ronnie?'

Ronnie patted her on the shoulder. 'Anything is worth a try. Put it this way, he won't be no worse off, and there's a chance that they might be able to get him walking. You've got to stop worrying about him.'

Clemency wiped her eyes on her sleeve. 'I know, but I've looked out for him ever since I can remember.'

'He's a grown man, and he's got Fancy to care for him now.' Ronnie slipped his arm around her shoulder. 'Let's go and see Edie, and tell her what's happening. You still got your ma to look after, and there's always me and Augustus. We're like family now, ain't we?'

'Of course you are.'

'Then get your bonnet, ducks. We'll slip out

without anyone seeing us and we'll get a bus to Carter Lane. I can't wait to see Edie again.'

Edith was in the pub kitchen preparing a large piece of steak for the pot. She looked up with a delighted smile as they entered through the scullery. Clemency was still wary of walking through the bar, just in case Hardiman had grown bold enough to frequent his old haunts. Edith rushed over to give her a hug. 'This is a lovely surprise.' She glanced at Ronnie beneath her lashes. 'And you too, Ronnie. This is an honour, I'm sure.'

'It's good to see you again, Edie.' Ronnie grasped her hands, despite the fact that they were covered in blood.

Clemency eyed them in surprise. Ma was actually flirting with Ronnie, and he was responding as if he liked it. She had grown used to seeing Ma as she had been in the old days, a poor victim of drink and vice. Now she seemed changed almost beyond recognition; she was plumper and prettier, quite stunningly so considering all that she had suffered. Ronnie seemed to think so too. He was smiling down at Edith with an almost boyish look on his lined face – a mixture of shyness and admiration.

Clemency turned with a start as Nell came bustling in from the parlour. 'Well, this is a nice surprise,' she said, unconsciously echoing

Edith's words. 'You're looking so fine these days, Clemmie. Quite the young lady.'

'And you're looking well too,' Clemency said, smiling. 'As to Ma, well, I've never seen her looking better.'

'She's certainly bloomed since she come here.' Nell's smile faded and she pursed her lips. 'She attracts the punters like flies round jam. Ned says it's good for business, but I like to keep her out of the bar. We don't want that sort of thing going on in a respectable pub.'

Edith turned away from Ronnie and hurried over to the table. 'Don't talk soft, Nell. I don't encourage them silly old sods.'

'That fellow Hardiman hasn't been back, has he?' Ronnie's voice was sharp with concern.

'No. My Ned would throw him out if he dared to show his face.' Nell's expression lightened as she mentioned her son. 'He'll be pleased you've come to visit, Clemmie. Why don't you go through to the bar and give him a surprise?'

Clemency decided that her news could wait until they were all together, and she went through to the bar, where she found Ned serving a customer. He looked over his shoulder as she came up behind him, and his face split into a pleased smile.

'Clemmie.'

'Hello, Ned.' She reached up and brushed his cheek with her lips. It seemed so natural to greet him as she would Jack, but she realised immediately that it had been a mistake. He thrust the tankard into the customer's hands and snatched the money without taking his eyes off her. She had seen that hot look in other men's eyes, and she lowered her gaze as she felt a blush rising to her cheeks. 'Can you spare a moment, Ned? I've got something to tell you all.'

'What is it?'

There was an anxious note in his voice, but she could not look him in the eye. 'Come into the kitchen and I'll tell you.'

He followed her, demanding to know what was so urgent, but Clemency did not answer. She was more concerned about how Ma would take the news, and she made her sit down on a stool next to Ronnie before she told them about Jack's consultation with Mr Chance, and his admission to the private clinic in Epping. Edith's eyes widened and she fanned herself with her apron. 'Well, I never did.'

'Is that all you can say, Ma?'

'I'm flabbergasted! I dunno what to say.' Halfway between tears and laughter, Edith clutched Ronnie for support. 'I never thought he'd be able to walk again. My poor little Jack. My crippled boy.'

Ronnie pulled a crumpled hanky from his pocket and gave it to her. 'There, there, don't take on, Edie. It's good news.'

'It's the best news I could have. When my Cyril left me, I thought nothing would ever come right again, and then I fell in with that bugger Hardiman. Life can be so cruel at times and then something like this happens.' She mopped her streaming eyes with the hanky.

'Cyril! You never mentioned his name before.' Nell said with a sharp edge to her voice. 'My old man was called Cyril.'

Ned hooked his arm around her shoulders. 'It's just a coincidence, Mum.'

'And he was a publican too.' Nell glared at Edith.

'There must be hundreds of pub landlords called Cyril,' Ronnie said stoutly.

'Yes,' Clemency added. 'And my dad was called Cyril Skinner. Your old man was Cyril Hawkes.'

'And my Cyril was the landlord of the Pig and Whistle pub in Wapping.' Edith crumpled Ronnie's hanky into a ball, staring nervously at Nell.

'I heard tell he'd taken another pub, but I never knew which one.' Nell's bosom heaved and all her chins wobbled. 'Cyril left me for another woman. He never told me her name, but suddenly I'm thinking it might have been you Edith.'

'Mum, that's just a wild guess.' Ned gave her a hug. 'Like Ronnie says, it's just a coincidence.'

'She had red hair,' Nell insisted. 'I know, because someone saw him with the whore shortly after he abandoned us. You was only two at the time, Ned. So you don't know what went on.'

'This is madness,' Edith protested. 'I never took your old man, Nellie. I met Cyril when he come into the pub where I worked. It must be twenty years ago, or more. He was so handsome and he fair turned me head with his charming ways.'

'He was tall and dark with a dimple in his chin,' Nell said angrily. 'And he had a tattoo on his chest.'

Edith's mouth worked silently for a moment. She stared at Nell, wide-eyed. 'It – it were a red rose.'

'That it was – and you stole him from me, you bitch.'

Nell broke away from Ned and lunged at Edith, but Clemency leapt between them. 'Stop it, both of you. This is silly. Why, it would make Ned and me . . .' She stared at him in horror. 'It would make us half brother and sister.'

His eyes opened wide with shock and the colour drained from his cheeks. 'It can't be true.'

'There's one way to prove it.' Nell barged past him and disappeared into the parlour. Sounds of drawers opening and closing echoed round the silent kitchen. Annie put her head round the scullery door and drew back again, like a startled tortoise retreating into its shell. Seconds later, Nell erupted into the kitchen holding a framed daguerreotype, which she thrust under Edith's nose. 'There. That's my Cyril. Now tell me that ain't your man. Deny it if you can.'

Edith collapsed against Ronnie's chest in a dead faint.

Clemency turned to Ned and was startled by the look of fury and disgust in his dark eyes. 'Ned, it's not our fault. None of us knew.'

He went into the bar and the door slammed behind him.

Nell threw herself onto a chair with tears flooding down her cheeks. Clemency went to her and laid a tentative hand on her shoulder. 'Nell, I'm so sorry. But it wasn't Ma's fault. She couldn't have known.'

'She must have guessed that he was some woman's husband, but that didn't stop her. I've tried to overlook the fact that your mum was a drunken slut, but now I can't abide the sight of her.'

'Here,' Edith shrieked. 'Who are you calling a drunken slut? I ain't touched a drop since I come here, even though it's there for the taking. I worked hard to repay you, you fat old cow. It weren't my fault that Cyril preferred me to you.'

Ronnie placed a restraining arm around Edith's waist as she threatened to scratch Nell's eyes out. 'Come now, Edie, love. This won't solve nothing.'

'You heard what she called me, Ronnie. What sort of man are you to let her call me names?' She struggled in his arms, but unable to break his grasp, she tore off her mobcap and tossed it at Nell. 'No wonder Cyril left you.'

Nell half rose from her seat and then collapsed back onto it, choking on a sob. 'Get her out of me home. I don't never want to see any of you again.'

Clemency could see that it was useless to argue. She wanted to go through to the bar to make things right with Ned, but instinct told her that this was not the right time. She patted Nell's heaving shoulder. 'We're leaving. I'm so sorry.'

'Just go.' Nell buried her face in her apron.

'Is it all right if I go upstairs to collect Ma's things?'

Edith broke free from Ronnie's grasp. 'I wouldn't stoop so low as to take anything what she give me. I'd sooner run naked through the streets of London than wear her old cast-offs.'

'And I doubt if it would be the first time you'd done so.' Nell uncovered one eye and glared at Edith.

Clemency and Ronnie made a grab for Edith's hand just in time to prevent her from attacking Nell. Together they managed to get her out through the scullery, past Annie who was cowering in the corner and whimpering. When they reached the back yard, the fight seemed to leave Edith and she collapsed against Ronnie's chest, weeping. 'It weren't my fault, Ronnie. I never knew he was married.'

He stroked her tumbled auburn locks back from her forehead. 'Of course you didn't, love. He was the one in the wrong, the wicked sod.' He rocked her in his arms until her sobs subsided. 'Clem,' he said softly. 'See if you can find a cab. I got just enough money to get us home.'

By the time they reached the house in Finsbury Circus, Edith had regained much of her composure, although Ronnie's handkerchief was sodden. Clemency felt numbed with shock at the realisation that Ned was her half brother, and even more disturbed by the fact that he had harboured feelings for her that were not at all brotherly. Once, a long time ago, she might even have returned them, but that was all in the past. She was just thankful that Jack had left for Epping. By the time he returned she would be able to face him with the startling news. At least she would be spared that particular ordeal for a few weeks.

They entered the house through the servants' entrance, and found Augustus and Nancy in the kitchen, drinking tea and talking earnestly.

Nancy looked up, barely registering surprise when Edith followed Clemency into the room.

'Oh, hello, Edie. Nice to see you, ducks. Have a cup of tea.'

Edith sank onto a chair and Clemency was alarmed to see the colour drain from her face. 'Are you all right, Ma?'

Edith nodded. 'It's just hit me, Clemmie. I got nowhere to live. I suppose I could go back to Flower and Dean Street. I always got on well with old Ma Blunt.'

'What's this?' Augustus peered at her over the rim of his teacup. 'I thought you was happy at the pub.'

'Not now,' Ronnie said hastily, taking a seat next to Edith. 'It's a long story. Best leave explanations until later.'

'Fetch more cups, Clem,' Nancy said. 'Maybe this will all work out for the best. We're short of help now that Fancy has gone off to the country with Jack. I'm sure Mr Stone wouldn't object to you staying here at least for a while, Edie. That is, if you don't mind rolling up your sleeves and doing a day's work?'

'You're very kind,' Edith said tiredly. 'To tell the truth, I weren't too keen on going back to Mrs Blunt's lodging house, just in case he's still hanging around.'

Nancy shot a curious look at Clemency, but she was not in the mood for long explanations. 'I'll go upstairs and make sure it's all right with Jared,' she murmured, and hurried from the kitchen. She was about to mount the stairs when the front door opened and Isobel marched into the hall, slamming the door behind her so that the crystal chandelier tinkled a merry tune. But the look on her face was anything but happy, and Clemency could see that she was bristling with indignation. 'What's up?'

'I thought it would all work out nicely,' Isobel stormed, tossing her parasol into the umbrella stand. 'With that idiot Darcy Fairbrother discredited, I thought that Grandmama and Jared would have changed their minds about forcing me into a convenient marriage. I thought that now they've met Nick, they would see what a truly wonderful man he is.'

'And they didn't?'

'Well, yes. Grandmama acknowledged that Nick is a worthy person, but she still insists that he isn't a suitable match for me. What do they think I am, Clemency? A bloody princess?'

Clemency stared at her aghast. She was used to hearing men and women using much worse language than that, but it was quite shocking coming from Isobel who was normally so proper and ladylike.

Isobel glared at her and stamped her foot. 'Bloody, bloody, bloody!'

'Calm down, Izzie. It can't be as bad as all that.'

'Oh, can't it? Well, Grandmama has forbidden me to see him again. She explained so nicely that she didn't want to see me struggle for the rest of my life, but she just wouldn't listen to my side of things. It's so unfair.'

'I'm sure she was just thinking of you, and maybe they'll come round.'

'I thought you would be on my side,' Isobel cried passionately. 'Of all people, I thought you would understand. Well, I won't listen to you or them. I'm not giving Nick up, and I'm going to continue going to the meetings of the women's movement. So there!' Isobel raced up the stairs, sobbing with rage.

Clemency sank down on the bottom step. Poor Izzie, she was such a child. She had led a sheltered existence, and had no idea of the hardships and tribulations that were suffered by other people. She huddled up, wrapping her arms around her knees, and resting her chin on them, as thoughts tumbled through her mind. The father she had never known was a cheat and a liar who had left Nell and taken up with Ma, only to repeat his callous behaviour, abandoning his children and leaving them to fend for themselves. She could never forget the poverty they had suffered in Stew Lane, which had forced her onto the streets as a common thief, and the dark menace of Hardiman that had loomed over them for so long. Had he really gone for good? Or was he still somewhere in the background? Was he lurking in the shadows like the Ripper, who still roamed free? She was so deep in her thoughts that she had not heard Jared's footsteps on the stairs and she jumped as he laid his hand on her shoulder.

'Is there something wrong, Clemency?'

She scrambled to her feet. 'No. I was just thinking.'

'By the look of you, they weren't happy thoughts.' His tone softened. 'Would it help if you were to tell me what is making you look so sad?'

She hesitated: she was tempted to trust him. She longed to be able to confide in him – but she could not go that far. She shook her head. 'It's nothing much. I was just a bit concerned about Izzie. She's very upset because you won't let her see Dr Wilson.'

'I know,' Jared said with a wry smile. 'She shouted at me as she stormed past, and then she slammed her bedroom door in my face.'

'Well, you are being hard on her. She loves him.'

'She's very young, Clemency. She will probably fall in love a dozen times, but not necessarily with the right man.'

'And you know best, I suppose.'

'Whatever you think of me, I love my sister. I don't imagine that allowing her to marry the first young man she fancies is necessarily going to bring her happiness or security.'

'If you forbid her to see him again, you'll only make her more determined to flout you.'

'I haven't said any such thing.'

'That's what Lady Skelton told her.'

Jared sighed. 'My grandmother is a splendid woman, but given to exaggeration. I'm not the ogre that you seem to think I am. Izzie can see her young doctor, providing she does it openly and in the company of a chaperone. My one and only condition is that she allows me to introduce her to other young men, who might be much worthier suitors.'

'That sounds fair. I think.'

'Good. I'm glad we've got that settled. Now, there's something else, I can tell.'

'My mother needs a place to stay for a while. She's willing to earn her keep.'

'I've no objection to her staying here. Heaven knows, we've got plenty of room.'

Jared's eyes seemed to bore into her soul. It would be wonderful to unload her problems onto his broad shoulders, but he would surely take that as a sign of weakness. She made a move towards the staircase. 'Thank you.'

'Don't thank me. I'm sure Nancy will make her work hard. By the way, Clemency, I'm taking you to a reception in the City tonight. There is a certain foreign gentleman who is to be our quarry. I have a special score to settle with him. Be ready by seven thirty.' He strolled off without waiting for an answer.

*

The reception was in the Guildhall under the watchful eyes of Gog and Magog. The Lord Mayor of London himself was present, as were members of the illustrious Gresham Club, who were merchants, bankers and businessmen, all accompanied by their wives. Jared pointed out particularly important people, while Clemency gazed in awe at the women's elegant apparel, set off with glittering jewels. She felt quite drab by comparison, although her own gown of peacock-blue silk was the very latest fashion, but she had not even the simplest necklace or earrings to complement her dress. However, she had little time to brood on such matters as Jared steered her through the assembly. The air was thick with the scent of expensive perfume and pomade. The babble of voices grew in intensity as people competed to make themselves heard above the strains of the chamber orchestra. Clemency was aware that heads were turning in their direction. She thought that it must be Jared who was attracting their attention: he looked splendid in his evening dress, and most distinguished. She felt quite proud to be leaning on his arm, like a real lady. Then, just when she was least expecting it, he drew her aside. 'Look over there,' he whispered, pointing at a group of men just a few yards away from them. 'Do you see the man who is talking to the Lord Mayor? That is Gaston Marceau, the fellow who was the chief architect in my father's downfall. He is wearing a pair of ruby cufflinks that once belonged to my father. They were a wedding present to him from my mother, and Marceau won them by cheating at cards. I want them back.'

Chapter Eighteen

Clemency craned her neck to get a better view. As Marceau raised the wineglass to his lips she caught a flash of fire from one of the rubies. 'Who is he?'

'He is an incredibly wealthy man. Gaston Marceau and his brother own several vineyards in Bordeaux. Gaston runs the export side of things. He also owns a small fleet of ships and a large warehouse in Wapping. When in London, he resides in the house that should, by rights, be mine. He won it by unfair means, and when my father attempted to win it back, Marceau bankrupted him.'

'No wonder you hate him.' Clemency shuddered. 'He's a nasty piece of work all right, but what is he doing here?'

'He is an inveterate gambler, and he belongs to most of the gentlemen's clubs in London. Perhaps he doesn't want his family in France to find out how he spends his time.'

'And is it just the ruby cufflinks that you want from him? It doesn't seem much, considering what he did to your father.'

'That is all for now, although, when the opportunity arises, I'll beat him at his own game and get my property back. This evening, I want to you observe him, as I taught you. Watch his movements and wait for a suitable moment. Don't take unnecessary risks, but I want those cufflinks.'

Clemency swallowed hard; this was not going to be easy. 'I'm not sure I can do it.'

'Of course you can. You're the best dip in London.'

'It would be easier to lift a couple of diamond bracelets or a few wallets.'

Jared tucked her hand in the crook of his arm. 'Come. I'll introduce you to Monsieur Marceau. Keep smiling and say as little as possible.' He led her towards the group of men, who stopped talking to stare openly at Clemency. She felt a blush rising to her cheeks, and she kept her eyes modestly downcast.

'Good evening, gentlemen.' Jared acknowledged them in turn, but Clemency felt his body tense as he greeted the Frenchman. 'Monsieur Marceau.'

'Good evening, Stone. Are you not going to introduce us to your so charming companion?'

Clemency raised her head and found herself looking into the button-bright eyes of Gaston Marceau. There was a calculating look in them that made her feel as if he were mentally stripping her naked. She lifted her chin and returned his stare, but inwardly she was quaking. Despite his charming smile, she sensed that this man was dangerous. He was much older than Jared, possibly in his late fifties, and his hair was a grizzled grey, contrasting with his wrinkled skin that had the texture of a pickled walnut.

'Gentlemen, may I present my ward, Miss Clemency Skinner.' Jared squeezed her arm and Clemency bobbed a curtsey.

'Mademoiselle.' Gaston took her hand and kissed it. He turned to Jared with a smile that did not reach his eyes. 'She is quite enchanting. Why have you kept this little jewel hidden from us, Stone?'

'Clemency is only recently up from the country where she has been attending a convent school. This is her first big social occasion in London.'

'Well, we all have to start somewhere.' A rubicund gentleman, sporting mutton-chop whiskers, smiled benevolently at Clemency. 'I trust you will enjoy your evening, my dear.'

Clemency nodded and smiled, remembering Jared's warning not to speak unless absolutely necessary. She had kept her mouth shut with difficulty when the Frenchman had leered at her, but her acting experience had stood her in good stead. She stood by Jared's side while he and the gentlemen conversed briefly about business matters: fundraising was mentioned, although she was not really paying much attention. She was concentrating on a plan to relieve Monsieur Marceau of his jewelled cufflinks. Dinner was announced, and she would have liked to refuse his offer to escort her to the table, but Jared indicated that she should accept. She had no alternative but to comply. Her heart sank when she found that she had been placed next to Marceau, and, although he also spoke to the lady seated on his left, he gave most of his attention to Clemency. His command of English was excellent and he was openly flirting with her. Apart from the fact that he was old enough to be her father, maybe even her grandfather, she found him quite repulsive, and the thought of attempting to outwit him was daunting to say the least. As he raised his fork to his lips, the ruby caught the light from the chandeliers and dazzled her eyes. She was almost hypnotised by the flashing jewel. She picked at her food, although it was the most sumptuous spread she had ever seen in her life. It seemed criminal that so much had been prepared for so few people, especially when the ladies feigned bird-like appetites and left large portions untouched on their plates. Why, Clemency thought, shutting her ears to the flattering Frenchman, this banquet would have fed a dozen poor families for a month. She dragged herself back to the present as she realised that Marceau was leaning towards her.

'I do not believe you have been listening to a word I have said, mademoiselle.'

'I am sorry.' Clemency fanned herself vigorously. 'It's a bit hot in here.'

'Perhaps you would allow me to escort you to the anteroom, where it would be cooler?'

She shot an agonised look at Jared who was seated on the opposite side of the table, but he was engaged in conversation with the lady seated on his right. The main course had been cleared and the desserts were being placed on the table. There were amazing concoctions of jellied fruit, meringues, ices and towers of small pastries, the like of which Clemency had never seen. Her mouth watered at the sight of such sweet delights, and she was tempted to remain where she was, but Marceau was already on his feet. Reluctantly, she laid her hand on his arm and allowed him to lead her from the table. He took her to a sofa in a secluded part of the deserted anteroom.

'Would you like a glass of water, Mademoiselle Clemency?'

She shook her head and fluttered her fan. 'No, thank you. I'm feeling better already.'

To her dismay, he sat down beside her, taking her free hand in his, and holding it. 'You are a very beautiful young woman, Clemency.'

'Th-thank you, sir.' She gazed at him over the top of her fan and lowered her eyelashes. She could feel his hot breath on her neck as he leaned towards her. She had to suppress the urge to push him away, but she must keep focused. She did not protest when he slipped one hand around her waist, drawing her to him. His breath smelled of wine, garlic and stale tobacco, but she allowed him to kiss her cheek. His hand slid upwards to cup her breast, and she had to quell the desire to slap his ugly face, but she had managed to curl her fingers around one of his cufflinks. His mouth was hot and wet as he searched for her lips. The ruby came away with a twist of her fingers, and she had it in the palm of her hand, but now she needed to secure its twin. She moved her position and parted her lips. His kiss was as nauseating as it was demanding. She tried to concentrate on the task in hand, even though she loathed the way his tongue had invaded her mouth. She closed her nostrils to the smell of his breath, and the expensive cologne that did not quite eradicate the odour of sweat. After enduring his fumbling for what felt like an eternity, she managed to secure the second cufflink. She tucked the pair under the tasselled cushion on the sofa. At the same moment, she felt his hand thrust down the front of her dress.

With a cry of outrage, she gave him a mighty shove that sent him sprawling to the floor, and she leapt to her feet. Her sobs were genuine enough, and Marceau rose hastily, placing his hand over her mouth. 'Be quiet, you little fool.' He did not appear to have heard Jared coming up behind him, and he gave a start at the sound of his angry voice.

'What in hell's name is going on?'

Marceau spun round to face him, and while he had his back to her Clemency seized the opportunity to retrieve the cufflinks. With trembling fingers she tucked them into the top of her stays.

'It was a misunderstanding,' Marceau said, straightening his white bow tie. 'Mademoiselle Clemency felt a little faint. I was attempting to revive her.'

Jared's brows drew together in a scowl. 'It seems to me that you were being a little too attentive, monsieur.' He held his hand out. 'Clemency, I think it is best we leave now.'

She took her cue and laid her hand in his. 'Yes, please take me home, Jared.'

'As a gentleman, I accept your word that nothing untoward happened, monsieur. We'll say no more about it. Come, my dear.' Jared steered her towards the door.

Clemency held her head high; she felt sick and humiliated, but also triumphant. She had tricked Gaston Marceau. It looked as though they had got away with it, although she would not relax until they were on their way home, safely ensconced in a hansom cab. Jared sent a liveried footman out to hail a cab. He turned to her, his face alive with concern. 'Are you all right, Clemency?'

'Yes,' she murmured, although now the danger was over she found she was shaking from head to foot, but she did not want to tell him that. 'It's hot in here. Can we wait outside?'

'Of course.' He opened the door. 'It's a fine evening.'

She hurried out onto the pavement and took a deep breath of the cool air. It might be tainted with the stuffy smell of the City and the pervasive odour of the Thames at high tide, but at least it was an honest smell, unlike the stench of greed and corruption that clung to Marceau. Out of the corner of her eye, she thought she saw a movement in the shadows, but when she turned her head there was no one there. She told herself she was just tired and overwrought. The Ripper had not claimed a victim for months now, and he would hardly venture into this part of the City. The Mansion House was bristling with footmen and guarded by two burly doormen. She could see a police constable patrolling on the far side of the street, and the footman had hailed a hansom cab, which was drawing to a halt at the kerb.

When they were settled into their seats, Jared

turned to her with a questioning glance. 'Did you get them?'

She turned away from him while she thrust her fingers into the top of her stays. The cufflinks were still safely lodged between her breasts. She placed them, still warm from her body, into his outstretched hand.

'Well done, Clemency. I knew you could do it.' He stared at the jewels in the palm of his hand and then he closed his fingers over them. 'That is the first round to us.'

She wiped her mouth on the back of her hand. 'Don't never ask me to do nothing like that again.'

'He didn't hurt you, did he?'

Slightly mollified by the note of alarm in his voice, she shook her head. 'He stuck his bloody tongue in my mouth – the dirty old man.'

'I am sorry for that, but I won't put you in such a position again. Tonight was the exception.'

'I blooming well hope so.'

'Perhaps a shopping expedition tomorrow with Izzie would help to make up for the behaviour of the dirty old man?' Jared's eyes crinkled at the corners and his lips curved into a smile.

Clemency looked away, biting her lip. So he thought a new hat or a pair of kid gloves would make up for being treated like a common whore. How little he knew about her. Suddenly she felt very tired and drained of all emotion. 'Thank you,' she said dully. 'That would be nice.'

Isobel was not in a good mood. She made no secret of the fact that she was furious with her grandmother, who had forbidden her to see Nick again. She was just as angry with Jared, who had agreed that she could see him, but only with a chaperone in attendance, and on the condition that she agreed to meet other suitors of his choosing. She was sulky at first, but she cheered up a little when she spotted a hat she liked in a milliner's window in Bond Street. It was a confection of feathers, flowers and ribbons and extremely expensive. Clemency felt quite faint when the shop assistant told them the price, but Isobel said she would take it, and it would serve Jared right for being so mean to her. She urged Clemency to choose something for herself, regardless of cost, to pay him back for exposing her to a man like Monsieur Marceau. Isobel had listened wide-eyed to a watered-down version of last night's events. Clemency had not mentioned the ruby cufflinks, and she had glossed over the humiliating scene in the anteroom after dinner. She would not have mentioned it at all if Isobel had not been curious as to why Jared had suddenly become so generous. Clemency had told her that Marceau had tried to kiss her, and when that did not satisfy Isobel, she had said that he had touched her in an inappropriate manner. That had the desired effect, and Isobel had been most solicitous all morning, in between ranting at the unfairness of her family and life in general.

They arrived home with their costly purchases nestling in hat boxes. Isobel insisted on seeking out Jared to show him just how extravagant she could be when thwarted. Clemency could not help feeling slightly ashamed of spending a working man's weekly wage on a hat. She would not entirely have blamed Jared if he had been cross, but he merely glanced at their new headwear and murmured something appropriate.

'It was hugely expensive,' Isobel said with a rebellious toss of her head.

'If you like it, Izzie, that's all that matters.'

Isobel blinked as if taken by surprise. 'Well, you wouldn't want me to look like a pauper. And I shall wear it to the next meeting of the Socialist League.'

'Yes, of course.' Jared turned to Clemency. 'I need a word with you.'

Isobel stamped her foot. 'I hope one day to meet Mrs Pankhurst of the Women's Franchise League. And I've read Annie Besant's newspaper, The Link.'

'Yes, Izzie. Not now. I need to speak to Clemency.'

'And I will see Nick whenever I want to.' Isobel stalked off in a huff.

Clemency sensed trouble; she met Jared's eyes with a questioning look. 'What is it?'

'Marceau called on me this morning. He accused you of stealing his cufflinks. Of course, I told him that it was unthinkable, but he knew I was lying.'

'Will he go to the police?'

'No. He wouldn't want it to be known that he had attempted to seduce a young girl at a Mansion House reception. But he's a dangerous man, Clemency. We will have to be careful this evening.'

Clemency stared at him aghast. 'This evening? What do you mean?'

'We are going to a private dinner party at the home of a senior member of the Vintners' Company, and Marceau is certain to be there. If I refuse it will offend my host, who donates generous sums to my charities, and I want to engage Monsieur Marceau in a card game after dinner.'

'But I don't have to go, do I?'

'You must, or it will look like an admission of guilt. One whiff of scandal and we're finished.'

'Why do you take all these risks?'

His eyes flashed, cold as steel. 'I want what is rightfully mine. Marceau obtained my house by cheating, and I intend to get it back, one way or another.'

'But how can you be certain that he cheated?'

'My father knew what Marceau had done but he had no proof. In those days to call a man a cheat would be to challenge him to a duel, which was illegal even then.' His grim expression lightened just a little. 'I can't force you to accompany me, Clemency. If you would rather stay at home, I'll understand.'

She stared at him in surprise. She thought she had seen him in all his moods – arrogant, autocratic, on occasions teasing and even passionate – but she had never known him to be so considerate. She did not want to see Marceau ever again, but, quite suddenly, she was on Jared's side. She met his eyes with a steady gaze. 'I'll come with you. We'll get the bugger, you see if we don't.'

He took a step towards her. For a moment, she thought that he was going to take her in his arms, but he seemed to think better of his impulse and he hesitated. 'I won't give him the opportunity to be alone with you, be sure of that.'

Clemency watched him as he strode off in the direction of his study. A strange mixture of emotions confused her heart and her brain. One moment she hated him, and the next she – she was not quite sure how she felt. She had never been in love before. How could she possibly tell if the churning in her stomach, the fluttering of her heart, and the racing of her pulses every time he was near was a symptom of the ailment that sent perfectly sane people completely daffy? If this was the path to madness, then she was already halfway there. She hurried downstairs to the kitchen and comparative sanity.

But things seemed to be just as fraught below stairs. Augustus was pacing the floor, resembling a demented penguin in his starched white shirt and black tailcoat. Nancy and Edith were eyeing him warily as they prepared vegetables for the evening meal, and Ronnie was making an attempt to calm him down.

'I'm sure that Tom will look after Lucilla,' Ronnie said, matching his step to keep up with Augustus. 'He's not a bad chap at heart.'

'I can't stand it any longer. Anything could have happened to her. She might have died in childbirth. That rogue might have abandoned her, and she could be starving in a gutter.'

'No, no, old chap. You mustn't think like that.'

Nancy threw a half-peeled potato at Augustus, catching him on the head. 'Shut up, Augustus. I'm sick of hearing you going on and on about your silly cow of a daughter. She should have kept her legs crossed and she wouldn't have ended up in trouble.'

He came to a halt, rubbing his head. 'You attacked me, woman. Anyway, you have no children of your own, so how could you know what a parent feels?'

Nancy waved the paring knife at him. 'If I had

a daughter, I'd have looked after her a bloody sight better than you did, old man.'

'Now, now, Nancy,' Edith said, patting her on the arm. 'Don't be hard on him. Can't you see he's upset?'

'What's going on?' Clemency stood at the top of the stairs, staring down at them. 'What's happened?'

Augustus looked up at her with his arms outstretched. 'I'm tortured, Clem. No one understands how I feel. I've done everything I can to find my little nightingale. In desperation, I put an advertisement in *The Times* asking for information as to her whereabouts, but I have not received one single reply.'

'Well it was a blooming silly place to put it, if you ask me,' Nancy said, curling her lip. 'Only toffs read that newspaper. You might as well have thrown your money down the drain.'

'Don't be unkind, Nancy.' Edith went to put her arm around Augustus. 'She don't mean it, love.'

'Perhaps you should go and look for her,' Clemency said reasonably. 'If you find the O'Malley brothers, they might know where Tom and Lucilla are lodging. After all, he did follow them hoping to find work as a navvy.'

Augustus took out a pocket hanky and blew his nose. 'What you say is true. I believe that the O'Malleys were seeking work on the new extension to the District line from Putney Bridge to Surbiton.'

'Well then, old chap,' Ronnie said. 'It would make sense to travel on the underground train to Putney Bridge and make enquiries in that area.'

'Good man.' Augustus grabbed him by the hand and shook it. 'That's the best idea yet. I'll set off right away.'

Ronnie caught him by the shoulders, and pushed him gently onto a chair. 'Best wait until tomorrow, old fellow. Start early in the morning, and it will give you the whole day to find them.'

'Listen to Ronnie,' Edith said earnestly. 'He's making good sense. And he could go with you.'

'Would you do that for me, Ronnie?' Augustus looked up at him with flicker of hope in his eyes.

Ronnie nodded. 'Of course I would.'

'I don't know what to say.' Augustus trumpeted into his handkerchief.

'That's settled then,' Edith said with a satisfied smile. 'And, if Nancy don't mind, I think I'll take the opportunity to visit Hannah Blunt in Flower and Dean Street. She was good to me when I was took ill, and I ain't had the chance to thank her.'

Ronnie frowned. 'Make sure you gets home before dark then, ducks. They haven't caught the Ripper yet.'

'Yes, Ma,' Clemency said, nodding in agreement. 'You should get a cab there and back. I'm sure Jared would gladly give you the fare.'

'Oh! Jared is it now? I hope you're not forgetting your place, girl.'

Clemency felt the blood rush to her cheeks. 'Don't talk soft, Ma.'

'Just remember what happened to Lucilla,' Edith said, shaking her head.

Augustus gave a groan and buried his face in his hands. 'My baby. My little nightingale.'

'Edie!' Ronnie shot her a reproachful glance. 'That wasn't very tactful.'

'No, Ma. And it's not the same thing at all,' Clemency said angrily. 'I just work for Jared – Mr Stone. There's no funny business going on between us.'

'Your ma is right.' Nancy jabbed the knife into a potato. 'Men is beasts, the lot of them. Present company being the exception to the rule. Just remember, young lady, that men can't control their lust when there's a pretty girl involved. Let what happened to Meg Jones be a warning to you.'

Clemency tossed her head. 'There's no need to worry about me. I wouldn't have anything to do with Mr Jared Stone even if he was the last man on earth.' The expression on Ma's face, and the way Nancy's mouth gaped open, together with an indrawn breath from Ronnie, made Clemency spin round. She saw Jared standing at the top of the steps. She knew by the set look on his face that he had overheard her last remark.

'I'll need a cab at seven o'clock, Augustus. Be ready by six thirty, Clemency. I want to go over our plan for the evening.'

There was a moment of stunned silence as the baize door swung back on its hinges.

'He doesn't usually come into this part of the house,' Clemency murmured, as everyone stared at her. 'He should have rung for Augustus.'

'And servants should know their place,' Edith said, wagging her finger. 'You remember that, my girl. Nancy's right – servant girls who forget what they are end up on the street.'

'I'm not a servant,' Clemency cried passionately. 'I'm as good as any of them above stairs. And don't you lecture me on how to behave, Ma. I never stole another woman's husband, nor ended up being used by men like Hardiman and Connor.' She broke off on a sob, and raced up the stairs.

When she reached the sanctity of her own room, she threw herself down on the bed, pummelling the pillows with her fists. She was trapped, like one of the wild animals in the Zoological Gardens, but the bars on her cage were invisible. She was bound by ties of loyalty to see Jack through the course of treatment that might give him the chance to walk again. She must make certain that Ma was fully recovered and safe from Hardiman before she could even think of leaving. Then there was Jared – she owed him much – but she was desperately afraid. She sat up, staring at the little squares of rooftops and blue sky divided up like a puzzle by the windowpanes. Her fear was not of Jared himself, but the tumult of emotion that he had created inside her. Did she hate him – or did she love him? Her head reeled and her heart ached. Her thoughts and feelings were as divided as the individual panes of the window frame. She did not know the answer.

'Clemency.'

She jerked into an upright position as she heard Isobel calling her name, and tapping on the door.

'Can I come in?'

Clemency wiped her eyes on her sleeve. 'Yes. Come in, Izzie.'

With a flurry of silken skirts, Isobel rushed into the room and threw herself down on the bed beside Clemency. 'I thought I heard you crying. What's wrong, dear?'

Sympathy was worse than scorn or anger, and Clemency had to fight to contain her tears. 'N-nothing.'

'It's that brother of mine, isn't it? He's upset you now, as well as me. What has he done? You can tell me.'

'No, it isn't Jared. I lost my temper with Ma and said things I shouldn't have.'

'Oh, is that all.' Isobel gave her a hug. 'I'm

always doing that with Grandmama and Jared. Family mean well, but they will interfere. Look at me, for instance. They're determined to push me into an arranged marriage, and I intend to have Nick as my husband, no matter what.'

Clemency gave an involuntary chuckle. 'I'm sure you will.'

'That's better.' Isobel took a scrap of lawn and lace from her pocket and handed it to Clemency. 'Wipe your eyes. And you can tell me what's really going on between you and Jared. And don't give me that innocent look. I'm not stupid.'

Startled by this sudden and unexpected interrogation, Clemency turned away to mop her eyes. 'I – I don't know what you mean.'

'Yes, you do. I thought you were hired to be my companion and to chaperone me, and yet Jared takes you out almost every evening. What's going on between you?'

Clemency slid off the bed and went to stand by the window. 'There's nothing between us. It's strictly business.'

'What sort of business? Come on, you must tell me. I want to know.'

'You should ask Jared. It's not for me to say.'

'Is he your lover? Is that it, Clemency? Are you sleeping with my brother?'

Clemency spun round to face her. 'No! How could you think that, Izzie?'

'But you love him, don't you? I can tell by the way you look at him. I understand, because I feel like that whenever I see Nick.'

She was caught, like a fly in a spider's web. 'Perhaps I do, but you must promise me you won't say a word to Jared. I can't tell you why he takes me with him on these excursions, but it isn't for my pleasure or his. You must ask him, or simply trust him to do what he thinks is best for you, Izzie.'

'You really do love him.' Isobel rose from the bed. 'I hate to think what he expects of you, my dear. But I admire your loyalty to him. I just hope he doesn't break your heart.'

Clemency shrugged her shoulders. 'He doesn't even know that I have one, Izzie. Your brother has a mission, I can't tell you more than that, but I'm just the cat's paw in his plans. When it's done, I'll leave. It's as simple as that.'

Isobel clasped her hands over her heart. 'Oh, you poor dear. I could kill Jared at this moment. But I won't ask any more questions.'

'Thank you. I'm sure he'll tell you everything when the time is right.'

'And in the meantime, we're going out. I'm going to take you to a meeting of the Social Democratic Federation. Annie Besant is giving a talk this afternoon. She's going to speak about Mrs Pankhurst and the Women's Franchise League. It's really inspiring, and the best part is that I know Jared would hate it. Wash your face, put your new hat on, and we'll go.'

Clemency listened to the speakers at the meeting. She could not help but be impressed by their fervour, and she admired their aims and ambitions for improving the lot of women. But she couldn't help feeling that the well-dressed, well-heeled middle-class women who crowded the assembly hall had little knowledge of what it was really like to live in the slums of the East End. A lot of what was said went over her head and she found herself dozing off at one point, only to be dug in the ribs by Isobel, who was drinking in everything with an ecstatic look on her face.

'Weren't they splendid?' Isobel demanded as they filed out of the meeting hall. 'Aren't you inspired to join the movement, Clemmie?'

'I think they have an uphill fight on their hands,' Clemency replied.

'Absolutely.' Isobel's eyes shone with excitement and she linked her hand through Clemency's arm. 'One day we'll have the vote and be able to make a real difference in the world.'

'I'm sure we will.' Clemency walked on in silence while Isobel enthused about the cause. All she could think about was that tonight she was going to have to face Marceau and feign innocence. She would have to stand by and watch Jared attempting to win back his family home, staking everything on the turn of a card. What, she wondered, would idealistic Isobel think if she knew that their comparatively extravagant lifestyle was paid for by petty crime and embezzlement? Would Isobel be so fond of her, if she knew that Jared employed her as a common thief?

Chapter Nineteen

The evening started badly. The dinner party was held in the grandest house that Clemency could ever have imagined: liveried footmen opened the double doors beneath a temple-front portico. The entrance hall had an echoing, cathedral-like quality, and the air was redolent with the scent of white lilies arranged in huge urns. She was still gazing at her opulent surroundings when she saw Marceau heading towards them, with a scowl deepening the furrows on his brow. He did not bother with the social pleasantries. 'You stole something from me, mademoiselle. You are playing a dangerous game when you cross me.'

Jared stepped in between them. 'Leave her alone, Marceau. This matter is strictly between you and me.'

Although the words were spoken in an undertone, Clemency could see that they were attracting the attention of the other dinner guests, and she tugged at Jared's sleeve. 'Please, not now.'

He glanced down at her and she was shocked by the harsh look that had turned his eyes to chips of granite, and etched his mouth into a hard line. He shook her hand off, and turned to Marceau. 'You and I have some unfinished business, monsieur.'

Marceau's eyes flicked from Clemency to Jared. 'Give me one good reason why I should not call a constable, and have this girl arrested for theft.'

'I challenge you to a card game. Tonight, after dinner.'

'For what stakes? As I understand it, you are a poor man, Stone.'

'I want the house in Islington that should rightfully belong to me.'

Marceau threw back his head and roared with laughter, causing heads to turn. 'You English have a good sense of humour.' His expression hardened. 'But I see that you are not joking. I will play you, but you will not win.'

'I will, if you play fair.'

Clemency held her breath: for a moment she thought that Marceau was going to strike Jared, but his gaze wandered to her, and the undisguised lust in his eyes made her blood run cold.

'Very well,' he said, curling his lips into a smile. 'My house – against your ward.'

'What?' Jared slipped his arm around Clemency's waist, drawing her to him. 'Never.'

'My spies tell me that the little bird sings. Her talents are wasted on you, Stone.'

'What spies? What are you talking about?' Jared's arm tightened around Clemency's waist.

Marceau's lip curved in a wolfish smile, and he tapped the side of his nose. 'What is it you English say? Ask no questions, and you'll be told no lies. There is a man who has a grudge against you both, and that makes him most useful to me.' His smile faded and he turned to Clemency. 'Every move you make is being watched.'

'Hardiman!' Clemency whispered. 'It's Hardiman, isn't it?'

'You are a coward, monsieur.' Jared faced Marceau with a cold stare. 'You prey on young girls, but you are afraid to take me on at a card game. Name any stake you like, but leave Clemency out of this.'

Marceau turned away with Gallic shrug. 'You know my terms, monsieur.'

'It's all right,' Clemency whispered in Jared's ear. 'I trust you. You can beat him.'

He shook his head. 'No. The stakes are too high.'

'Then you will never win back the pile of bricks that is so important to you. But I will have the girl, one way or another, Stone.'

'Come anywhere near her and you'll be sorry. You can pass that message on to Hardiman as well.' Jared took Clemency by the hand, and headed towards the main entrance. 'We're leaving. I won't sit at the same table as that villain.'

'But, Jared, we've only just arrived. We can't just walk out like this.'

'Can we not?' He signalled to the footman, who opened the door and stepped aside. 'I should never have brought you to this place. I'm taking you home.'

'But your charity funds ...'

'Bugger the charity.' He dragged her down the steps to the pavement. Guests were still arriving, and Jared claimed a hansom cab that had just deposited its fare. He handed Clemency into it and leapt in after her. 'Finsbury Circus, cabby.'

He said little on the way home, and she maintained a tactful silence. It was still early evening when they arrived back at the house.

'I need a drink,' Jared said, heading for the stairs. Clemency was about to make for the servants' quarters when he stopped, looking over his shoulder. 'Where are you going?'

'Down where I belong. With my friends and family.'

'I would appreciate your company in the drawing room.'

'I'm sure that Isobel would be happy to join you.'

'Isobel has gone to the theatre with Grand-mama, and she will be staying the night in her lodgings in Half Moon Street.' He held out his hand. 'Please.'

The air between them was charged with

tension. She knew that she ought to refuse, but she was powerless to resist. Moving like a sleepwalker, she laid her hand in his and allowed him to lead her up the staircase to the drawing room. She perched on the edge of the sofa, folding her hands in her lap. The sky was still light, although the sun had gone down, and the shadows were lengthening, giving the room a dreamlike and unreal quality. Jared went to a side table and picked up a decanter. He poured a generous measure of brandy into two glasses. 'I'm sorry about what happened this evening. I never intended to put you in such a dangerous situation.' He handed her a drink, and moved away to stand by the fireplace. 'I had no idea that Marceau would vent his spleen on you.'

'I'm not afraid of him.' She took a sip and felt the strong liquor burn her throat. It hit her empty stomach like a fireball. She had not eaten since midday and she realised now that she was extremely hungry. 'I'm sorry if I spoiled things for you. I know you were desperate to win back your old home.'

'I am, but not at any price. You do know what Marceau wanted of you?'

She gulped down the rest of the brandy in one swallow. 'I'm not stupid. Of course I know. He's a dirty old man. I told you that from the start.'

'So worldly wise – and yet so innocent.'

'Innocent? Me?' For a moment she thought that

he was teasing her, but one look at his face convinced her that he was serious, and she felt the blood rush to her cheeks. She placed the empty glass on a drum table at the side of the sofa, and rose rather unsteadily to her feet. 'I think I'd better go downstairs and get some supper. I'm starving.'

'Of course, you must be. I could ring for Augustus and have supper brought up on a tray.'

There was something in his voice, and a look in his eyes, that made her nerves tingle with excitement as well as apprehension. She wanted desperately to stay, but a small voice in her head told her to run. She made a move towards the door. 'It's all right. I'll go.'

Jared tossed his glass into the fireplace, where it smashed in the empty grate. With a swift movement he was at her side. 'Are you so very hungry?' He drew her towards him, slowly, inexorably. His eyes held hers and she found that she could not look away. She had been here before, and she knew what would happen if she didn't break free, but her arms slid around his neck and she closed her eyes. His mouth plundered hers with a fervour that brought an instant response. She parted her lips, drinking in the taste of him, inhaling the scent of him: intoxicated by a sudden and overwhelming desire to abandon all caution. She ran her hands through his hair, murmuring his name as he kissed the hollow at the base of her throat. His hands caressed the swell of her breasts above the décolletage of her evening gown: she was trembling uncontrollably, and her knees gave way beneath her. She was floating on a cloud of sensation, barely conscious of anything but the urgent need for him. Then, to her utter confusion, the kissing stopped. Jared lifted his head to gaze into her eyes. His arms still held her, but she could sense a sudden change in him.

'This is wrong.' His voice was choked with emotion. 'I can't do this to you, my love.'

'My love.' Clemency whispered. 'You love me, Jared?'

He was holding her so tightly that she was not sure if it was his heart or her own that was pounding so erratically. 'I didn't realise it fully until tonight. But I do love you, Clemency.'

'And I love you too.' The truth came upon her in a blinding flash. She had loved him from the start: perhaps even from that first moment outside the jeweller's shop window. She had never wanted a man before, but now she was ready to give herself to him, heart, body and soul. 'I think I was in love with you from the very beginning, Jared.'

A wry smile curved his lips. 'And I thought you had a soft spot for that boy in the pub.'

'I have, but only in the same way I feel about

Jack. I only recently found out, but Ned is my half brother.'

'Thank God for that.' He traced the outline of her cheek with the tip of his finger. 'I love you, my darling.'

She slid her hands under the lapels of his evening jacket, closed her eyes and parted her lips, awaiting another earth-shattering kiss. But he merely brushed her forehead with the whisper of a caress. She opened her eyes. 'What's the matter? Why have you suddenly gone cold?'

'I've done many things in my life that I'm ashamed of, but I won't add to them by taking advantage of you.'

'But I want you to make love to me, Jared. I really do.'

'And I will, but not here and now. Not like this.'

'I don't understand.' She pulled away from him. 'You say you love me.'

He made no attempt to touch her. 'And I do. I care about you too much to have a casual affair with you, Clemency.'

She stared down at the floor, unable to look him in the eye. 'You're not making sense.'

He laid his hands on her shoulders. 'How do you think I would feel if a man took advantage of my sister's youth and innocence?'

'That's different.'

'No, it's not. Put it another way, how do you

think Jack, or even Ned, would feel if they found out that you and I had become lovers?'

She looked up and met his eyes; there was no doubting the sincerity in them. 'They wouldn't like it.'

'There you have your answer.' He dropped his hands to his sides. 'I can't make you any promises at this moment, my love. But when I've settled my business with Marceau, things will be different.'

'Then we'll do it together. I'll help you in any way I can.'

'No. I should never have introduced you to him in the first place. I allowed my desire for revenge to cloud my better judgement.' He moved away towards the window, running his hands through his hair. 'My God, I must have been mad, or wicked, or both, to have exposed you to such a man. You are never to go near him again, do you hear me? Never.'

'All right, I won't. But you'll have to be so careful, Jared. He's got Hardiman working for him now, and he's a bad man to cross.'

'I'll deal with Hardiman in good time, but until then I want you to stay close to the house. You're never to go out alone. Do you understand me?'

Clemency drew herself up to her full height; the harsh tone in his voice had spoiled everything. The past, in the form of Marceau and

Hardiman, had come between them. 'I was raised in the streets. I can look after myself.' She left the room without giving him a chance to redeem himself. He had stirred up feelings and emotions within her that were both exciting and disturbing. He had made her feel like a desirable woman, and then he had treated her like a wayward child. She went to her room, half hoping that he would follow her, but he did not. She closed the door and locked it. She undid the buttons of the elegant gown and let it slide to the floor. She stepped out of it, leaving it where it had fallen like the skin sloughed off a snake. She was now herself again. She had taken off the costume that made her into a lady – she had been playing a part, just as she had done in the theatre. Take away the satin and lace and she was still Clemency Skinner, the girl from Stew Lane. She had been more than ready to give herself to Jared, and, whatever his reasons, he had rejected the only gift that was hers to give him. She lay on her bed staring up at the ceiling where the pattern of the window frame was etched in long shadows. Jared had sworn that he loved her too much to make her his mistress, and yet he could not bring himself to offer her marriage. He obviously did not care enough for her to bridge the gap in their social standing. Jared Stone had been born a gentleman, and she was the illegitimate daughter of a prostitute and a philandering innkeeper. She closed her eyes to shut out the harsh reality of the cruel world.

She awakened next morning to a room filled with sunshine and the chatter of sparrows outside on the window ledge. She felt a surge of optimism as she swung her legs over the side of the bed. Perhaps she had been too hasty in condemning him. She had allowed the intensity of her own feelings to blot out common sense and reason. Jared had only been trying to protect her, and she had run off like a spoilt child who had not had her own way. She would make it right with him at the first opportunity.

Clemency went downstairs filled with good intentions. In the kitchen, Augustus and Ronnie had finished their breakfast, and were getting ready to leave on their mission to find Lucilla. Nancy was sitting at the table drinking tea, and Edith was busy wrapping sandwiches in a piece of butter muslin. She looked up as Clemency entered through the baize door. 'Hello, love. Did you have a good time last night?'

Clemency felt the blood rush to her cheeks, and then she realised that Ma had meant the dinner at the vintner's house in Russell Square. 'Yes, it was fine,' she said, hoping that no one had noticed her moment of confusion.

But Edith was busy persuading Ronnie to take the sandwiches, even though he said they would probably treat themselves to a pie or some fish and chips. 'You take care then, Ronnie,' Edith said, wiping her hands on her apron. 'And you, Augustus. I hope you find your girl.'

Augustus nodded. 'I do too, Edie. Come on, Ronnie. Let's go.'

Ronnie kissed Edith on the cheek. 'We won't be too late back, ducks.'

'You'd better not be,' Nancy said, scraping butter onto a piece of toast. 'Edie and I will have enough to do with you both taking the day off.'

Augustus headed out through the door to Jack's old room, and Ronnie hurried after him.

'There weren't no need for that, Nancy,' Edith said, pulling her mouth down at the corners. 'You know very well that they did all their chores first thing, and we got a quiet day today with Mr Stone out all day, and Miss Isobel still at her granny's.'

Clemency went to sit at the table. 'So he's out all day is he?' She looked away as Ma shot her a curious glance.

'What's it to you, miss?'

'Nothing.' Clemency reached for the teapot and proceeded to fill a cup with the rapidly cooling and stewed brew. 'Nothing at all.'

Edith frowned. 'Have you done something to upset him?'

'No, Ma. Of course not.'

'Well, I hope you haven't for all our sakes.'

Edith took off her apron. 'We've got a good home here, Clemmie. We got three square meals a day and a comfy bed to sleep in. I hope you appreciate it, and aren't hankering after that silly business of singing in the theatre.'

'No, I never gave it a thought.'

'You've got a chance to be a young lady now. You've come up in the world since Miss Isobel saw fit to make you her companion. Ain't that so, Nancy?'

Nancy made a non-committal noise and shot a warning glance at Clemency, but Clemency was not about to tell Ma that she was still earning her living by dipping pockets, even if it was from toffs who could afford to lose a few bob. So far, it was only Nancy who knew about the way in which she helped Jared supplement his income: they had managed to keep the secret from the others, and Clemency wanted to keep it that way. She stirred a spoonful of sugar into her tea. 'Are you going out then, Ma?'

'I'm going to visit Hannah, like I said last night.' Edith hung her apron on a hook by the range. 'I'll be back in time to cook the evening meal, so don't worry about that, Nancy.'

Clemency spent the morning keeping out of Nancy's way. She had volunteered to sort out the linen cupboard, and when that was done she made an excuse to go upstairs, telling Nancy that she was going to mend a torn flounce on one of

Miss Isobel's petticoats. She desperately needed to speak to Jared. He must have been very angry with her to go off for the day without telling her. She paced the floor in the drawing room, wringing her hands. Where was he when she needed him? He had told her he loved her, hadn't he? If that were true, then why hadn't he followed her to her room last night? Or at the very least he could have tried to make his peace with her before he left the house that morning. She had been ready to apologise for her behaviour, and to beg his forgiveness, if necessary. Now she was torn between anxiety and resentment.

When he had not returned by mid-afternoon, Clemency was beginning to imagine all kinds of accidents that could have befallen him. He might have been killed by a runaway horse, or been crushed beneath the wheels of a brewer's dray. He might have sought out Marceau and challenged him to a duel, or he might have gone looking for Hardiman – Jared could be lying somewhere in a pool of his own blood. She could stand it no longer. Nancy was in a bad mood, and Isobel had not returned from Half Moon Street. Not for the first time, she wished that Jack were here to share her concerns; to give her that funny, crooked smile of his and tell her that everything would come right. But he wasn't here, and there was no one in whom she could confide. Clemency put on her best hat and her new kid gloves. She checked her purse to see if she had enough money for the cab fare to Carter Street. She had to get out of the house, and it seemed natural to go to the only other family she had ever known. She would go to the Crown and Anchor and make things right with Ned, her half brother.

She went in through the back door of the pub. There was just the chance that Hardiman might be in the bar, or that Ned had not yet come to terms with their new relationship and might not want to see her. She preferred to risk a rebuff from Nell, than an outright snub from Ned. Annie was in the scullery washing pans in the stone sink. She looked up and her eyes widened, then she grinned. 'Ooer! You got a nerve, I must say.'

'Mind your own business,' Clemency snapped. Her nerves were already as taut as the strings on a fiddle and she was in no mood to put up with a daft scullery maid. She brushed past Annie, ignoring her protests, and went into the kitchen. Nell was at the range, stirring a pan that smelled temptingly of mutton stew. She did not look round.

'If you've finished the washing up, Annie, get them spuds peeled.'

'It's not Annie. It's me.'

Nell dropped the spoon into the pan and spun round. 'Clemency!'

'Are you still angry? I wouldn't blame you if you was, only none of this was my fault, and I'm truly sorry about your old man.'

Nell stared at her for a moment and then her sour expression evolved into a reluctant smile. She hurried over to give Clemency a hug. 'I weren't never cross with you, love. You wasn't even born when all of that happened.'

Clemency returned the hug. 'I thought you hated me, and I couldn't bear it.'

'I hated her, for a while anyway. Then when I calmed down a bit, I realised that it was Cyril who was to blame. Your mum was taken in, just the same as me. I expect he's peppered the whole of the East End with his little bastards by now.' Nell held her at arm's length. 'You look so fine these days. Quite a lady.'

Clemency couldn't meet her eyes and she looked away, biting her lip. If she knew the truth, she would think she was an abandoned hussy – no better than she should be. She changed the subject. 'And Ned?'

The question hung in the air and Nell's silence was an answer in itself. She hurried back to the pan on the range and began stirring its contents. 'Give him time. He'll come round.'

'Can I see him?'

She nodded. 'Go through, but don't be surprised if he don't want to know you.'

Clemency went into the bar. A quick glance

told her that Hardiman was not present, but the look on Ned's face when he saw her was not welcoming.

'Ned.' She held out her hand. 'Can't we be friends?'

He stared at her upturned palm, frowning. When he looked up at her, his eyes were bleak. 'It don't work like that, Clemency.'

'You're my brother just as much as Jack is. We're family whether you like it or not.'

'Go away, Clem. Go back to your fancy man and leave me and Ma to get on with our lives.' Ned turned away to serve a man who had walked up to the bar demanding a pint of porter.

Clemency opened her mouth to argue that Jared was nothing to her, but the words stuck in her throat. She knew that Ned would not believe her. He seemed to have known by some sixth sense that she had deep feelings for Jared. She felt her throat constrict with unshed tears, but she was determined not to cry. 'I'm going. But I want you to know that I still care for you, Ned. Maybe one day you'll find it in your heart to forgive me for being your sister.' She did not wait to see if he was going to answer, and she pushed past him to open the flap in the bar counter. She made her escape through the taproom, half hoping that he would call her back – but he did not. By the time she reached the street outside the Crown and Anchor, her tears were flowing freely. Everything had gone horribly wrong. She walked blindly on, ignoring the curious glances of passers-by. When she had her emotions sufficiently under control, she went in search of a cab to take her home to Finsbury Circus.

She paid off the cabby and ran up the steps to hammer on the door knocker. Perhaps she should have used the servants' entrance, but she did not stop to think. She was certain that Jared must be home by now and she desperately wanted to see him. She knocked again and yanked the bell pull. She heard heavy footsteps approaching and Nancy opened the door scowling. 'Oh, it's you. What's wrong with the servants' entrance, or are you too grand for it now?'

Clemency dodged past her. 'No, of course not.'

'Don't think you can fool me, my girl.' Nancy glared at her with narrowed eyes.

'I – I don't know what you mean.'

'Don't put on that innocent face with me. I could see it coming a mile off. I thought you was up to something when you didn't come down for supper last night.'

'I wasn't hungry.' Clemency started to back away but Nancy caught her by the sleeve.

'You leave Jared alone. I've looked after him since he was a little boy, and I don't want to see him get hurt by the likes of you.'

'How could I hurt a man like him?'

'He was born a gentleman, and you was born in the gutter. You're encouraging him in his bad ways. If he keeps on after that bloody foreigner, he'll end up dead like his poor father. For some reason he's soft on you, girl, and you've got to talk him out of his obsession with that man. It ain't healthy.'

Clemency bit her lip. Nancy knew Jared better than anyone and she loved him too. Perhaps she was right. 'Is he upstairs?'

Nancy shook her head. 'There's no one in except you and me. Miss Isobel sent a message saying that she's staying in Half Moon Street for another night. Ronnie and Augustus are bound to be late, and your mum ain't showed up yet. I knew exactly how it would be, and I'd have to do supper all on me own. You can forget your airs and graces and give us a hand in the kitchen.'

Reluctantly, Clemency followed her downstairs to the basement. She donned an apron and began peeling potatoes while Nancy cut up some rancid-smelling mutton and tossed it into a pot on the hob. 'When he comes in, I wants you to promise me that you'll try to talk him out of his madness.'

'I will. Of course I will, but where is he?'

'How should I know? He could be floating in the Thames, bloated and swollen with the fishes eating his eyeballs for all I know.'

'Don't say things like that.'

'You've been encouraging him, so it'll be your fault.' Nancy stabbed a piece of gristle with the point of her knife.

'I don't have to listen to this,' Clemency cried, tearing off her apron.

'And where d'you think you're going?'

'Away from you and your nagging. It's getting late and I'm going to meet Ma. I don't like her roaming the streets with the Ripper still at large.'

'That's silly. What could a skinny little thing like you do to protect either of you from a madman?'

A vision of Todd Hardiman flashed through her head, and Clemency rammed her hat on her head, securing it with a hatpin. 'He's never attacked two women at a time. If I go now I'll be safe enough. There'll still be folks heading home from work and I'll run all the way.'

'Jared won't like it,' Nancy said. 'He'll be mad as fire with me for letting you go out on your own in the evening.'

'According to you, I'm a bad influence on him anyway. So you should be glad if I'm out of the way.'

'He cares for you, you stupid girl. What do I tell him when he comes home?'

Clemency snatched up her reticule. 'Tell him what you like, but I'm going anyway.'

She left by the servants' entrance and ran until

a stitch in her side made her stop to draw breath. The streets were much quieter now and the sun had plummeted in the west, leaving the sky streaked with crimson and purple. She continued at a slower pace, casting nervous glances into the openings of the dark alleyways, and looking over her shoulder to make sure that she was not being followed. Clouds of steam hung in a pall over Liverpool Street Station, but the sound of chugging engines, whistles and the general hubbub of a busy terminal were oddly comforting. She crossed Bishopsgate, and entered a different and more sinister network of streets that were little more than dark canyons between tall buildings. She jumped at every small sound, and eyed the men who were slouched in doorways with suspicion. She did not know if she was more afraid of the Ripper or Hardiman. As she neared Flower and Dean Street, the denizens of the night were appearing as if from nowhere. Prostitutes hung about on street corners. Sailors of all nationalities strolled along with their rolling gait as if the deck of the ship was still pitching and tossing beneath their feet. Dockers, navvies and clerks with leather patches on their elbows disappeared through open pub doors that exuded the smell of stale beer, sweating bodies and tobacco smoke.

Clemency hurried on until she reached Flower and Dean Street. Dusk had swallowed up the last glimmers of daylight, and the lamplighter was doing his rounds. She could have cried with relief when she reached the lodging house. She opened the gate that led down to the area. She would go in through Jack's old room and give Ma and Mrs Blunt a pleasant surprise. She ran down the steps into almost complete darkness. She felt her way to the door, and was groping for the handle when a pair of calloused hands closed around her throat. She kicked out with her feet but the vice-like grip tightened. She could not breathe. She knew that she was about to die.

Chapter Twenty

Clemency opened her eyes, but she could see nothing. Her throat felt bruised and sore, and her mouth was so dry that her tongue seemed to be stuck to her palate. Her head ached, and she couldn't move her hands or her feet. Noise filled her ears: a deafening rumble of wheels and the thundering of horses' hooves – she was being tossed from side to side against the leather squabs of a moving carriage. The fog of fear and pain cleared slowly from her brain, and she realised that she was bound hand and foot. As her eyes became accustomed to the darkness, she could just make out the figure of a man seated opposite her. She opened her mouth to scream, but all she could utter was a feeble croak.

'Make a sound, and I'll finish you off this time.'

She closed her eyes again, praying that this was a nightmare, but when she opened them she could see that it was Todd Hardiman who had abducted her. She licked her dry lips, forming the word with difficulty. 'Why?' He leaned towards her, and she retched as she caught the overpowering odour of his unclean body.

'Got a sore throat, ducks?' He took a hip flask from his pocket and unscrewed the cap, holding it to her lips. 'Drink.'

She gulped thirstily. The liquid had a strange taste. Dimly she wondered if he had poisoned her, but her head was swimming, and the interior of the carriage was spinning round and round. The sound of his laughter grew fainter until it became a distant echo.

When she opened her eyes again, she was almost blinded by the bright light of day. As she came slowly to her senses, she realised that she was no longer in a carriage. She was lying on a bunk in a room that moved up and down. She squinted into the source of the light. Through the porthole she could see water, grey-green waves flecked with white foam. She tried to sit up, but fell back against the pillows, overcome by a wave of nausea. Was this part of the same nightmare? Or was she really on a ship at sea? The cabin door opened, and Hardiman squeezed into the small space. His mouth curved in a contemptuous grin. 'Not feeling too well?' He jerked her roughly to a sitting position, and thrust a mug into her hands. 'Here, drink this. I don't want you puking all over me boots when we land.'

'Wh-what is it?' Clemency sniffed the brown liquid. It smelt like tea, but she vaguely remembered drinking something in the coach that had made her sleep.

'It's tea. Drink it, or do I have to pour it down your throat? Don't think I won't do it, neither.'

She sipped the tea. It was strong and sweet, and it soothed her sore throat. Surprisingly it also settled the queasiness in her stomach. She peered at him over the rim of the mug. 'Where are you taking me?'

'Wouldn't you like to know?' Hardiman made a noise in his throat, halfway between a growl and a chuckle. 'If it was just for meself, I'd have pitched you into the river. But I got orders from the Frenchman.'

Clemency's heart seemed to leap into her throat, choking her. She could barely breathe. 'M-Marceau?'

He produced a length of cord from his pocket, and, taking the mug from her hand, he lashed her wrists together. 'He's paying me well to bring you to Paris in one piece. But if you gives me any trouble, I'll enjoy giving you what for, and bugger the Frenchie.' He left the cabin and she heard the key turn in the lock.

She lay back on the bunk and closed her eyes. Her head ached miserably and she had a terrible taste in her mouth. She was too numb with shock to feel frightened. All she could think about was Jared. He wouldn't know where to look for her. She might never see him again. Ma would be frantic with worry. She felt herself slipping into unconsciousness.

Every time she opened her eyes, she was in a different place. The cabin gave way to a white-walled room that smelt strongly of tobacco, only not the kind that Jack smoked at home. There were people chattering in a foreign language. A woman wearing a huge white headdress that flapped like a seagull's wings was feeling her forehead. Clemency thought dimly that she must be a nun. She tried to beg for help but no one around her seemed to understand. The nun made sympathetic noises, and held a glass to her lips. She did not want to drink, but her throat was parched and she sipped the bitter-tasting brew. The kindly face and the white wings spun into a vortex and disappeared.

When she struggled back to semi-consciousness she was once again in a horse-drawn carriage. She could not keep her eyes open: her lids were heavy and all she wanted to do was to sleep. Wheels rumbling over cobblestones – pounding hooves – Clemency had the sensation of hurtling through space.

Then all was silent and the movement had ceased. She opened her eyes, blinked, closed them and slowly opened them again, one at a time. She was lying on bed looking up at a painted ceiling. Fat little cherubs cavorted with brightly coloured birds amongst gilded flowers. She raised herself on her elbow and gazed in amazement at walls covered in silk and hung with oil paintings. The furnishings would have graced a palace, and the air was filled with the scent of flowers. The door opened and a maid-servant entered the room. She approached the bed, smiling shyly.

'Mademoiselle.' She plucked a diaphanous garment from the chair beside the bed, and held it up so that the material shimmered in the candlelight.

Clemency sat up slowly. She felt light-headed, and the gilded cherubs seemed to be laughing at her. She realised, with a shock, that beneath the satin sheets she was stark naked. The maid seemed to want her to get up, and she did not want to spend another moment in this grand, canopied bed. She attempted to stand, but her legs felt weak and she sat down again, shaking her head. Eventually, with the aid of sign language and a helping hand from the maid, she managed to walk into the marbled-tiled bath-room. Hot water gushed out of taps shaped like exotic fish into a huge cast-iron bath, filling the air with scented steam as the maidservant poured coloured crystals into the water. She helped Clemency to bathe, as though she were quite incapable of doing anything for herself, which in her present state was very near to the truth. Even in her weakened condition, she could not fail to be impressed by the unimaginable luxury of her new surroundings. There was nothing like this even in the house in Finsbury Circus. The thought of home made her throat constrict, and she ducked her head beneath the water to wash away the tears that flowed freely from her eyes. She might never see home again. She was a prisoner, trapped like a canary in a golden cage. She allowed the maid to help her from the tub, and to dry her with soft fluffy towels. At any other time she would have refused, and tried to force her way out of this place, but the effect of the drugs had not completely worn off; she felt listless and malleable like an obedient child.

She put on the negligee without a murmur, and she managed to walk into the bedroom unaided. A fire burned brightly in the grate, and Clemency sat on a chair by the ornate fireplace, watching the flames lick up the chimney while the maid combed her damp hair so that it fell about her shoulders in a mass of shining curls.

She was half asleep when Marceau strode into the chamber. The maid bobbed a curtsey, and left hurriedly. He stood a little way from Clemency, eyeing her critically, as though she were a prize cow up for sale in the marketplace. 'Stand up.'

Moving like an automaton, Clemency did as she was told. The feeling of unreality persisted: she could not believe that this was really happening. In a moment she would wake up and find that it was all a terrible dream. He walked round her, silently and without touching her, but she could feel the heat of his body and smell that all too familiar aroma that clung to him. 'Better than I anticipated,' he said at last. He took her by the shoulders and spun her round to face him. 'You do know why you are here, don't you?'

She nodded dully. 'You want to get your own back on Jared.'

'That too. But I think I am going to enjoy my revenge.' He tugged at the sash of her robe, and it fell to the floor so that she stood before him naked.

Somehow nothing seemed to matter. She suffered in silence as his eyes raked her body with a hot look of desire. She expected the worst. There was nothing she could do to stop him. Then, to her surprise, he bent down and retrieved the filmy garment. He wrapped it around her shoulders. 'You have courage, mademoiselle. Most young women in your position would be on their knees crying and begging for mercy. But not you.'

She tied the sash around her waist, eyeing him coldly. 'It would do no good.'

He laughed. 'Quite right. However, we will dine first. I am a civilised man, but I am ruthless when crossed. Remember that, and we will do well together.'

'I'm not dressed for dinner.'

'Oh, but you are. I shall feast my eyes on you while I introduce you to French cuisine. You

English eat like pigs. When I am done with you, Mademoiselle Clemency, you will be a Frenchwoman, through and through.'

She did not argue. She held her head high, and, moving in the unreal world that she now seemed to inhabit, she allowed him to lead her down the grand staircase, past Grecian statues holding lighted lamps, and across the entrance hall to a dining room that could have seated fifty people at dinner, and still had room for more. The vast mahogany table was groaning with silverware, and epergnes filled with flowers and fruit, but a smaller table had been laid for two in front of a blazing log fire. She knew what was to follow their meal; there was no escaping it, not tonight anyway. Marceau summoned the servants with one tug on a bell pull, and they appeared almost instantly, bringing one course after another. Clemency ate with a surprisingly good appetite; she could not remember the last time she had eaten and she was ravenous. Tomorrow she would find a way to freedom.

Marceau ate very little. He watched her eat with an appreciative gleam in his eyes, and he kept her glass filled with wine. She drank until he reached out and took the glass from her. 'No more. I think you have had enough.' He rose from the table. 'Come. Tonight you start repaying your debt to me and that of your lover, Jared Stone.'

'He is not . . .'

'No? Then that is his loss. He is more of a fool than I took him for.'

Throughout the long night, she attempted to detach her mind from her body. There was nothing that she could do that would prevent him from taking her again and again. She cried inwardly, loathing every minute of it, but she was determined not to let him see how much she suffered at his hands. He could use her body for his pleasure but he could not touch her heart or her soul. They belonged to Jared, and she prayed silently that he would understand and forgive her, if she ever saw him again. But even if he understood that she had been taken by force, she knew that she was now damaged goods. Jared had been so careful to protect her virginity, and it had been taken by his worst enemy. She was a fallen woman. History had repeated itself, and she was now like Ma. Tears of pain, shame and humiliation trickled down her cheeks as she wept silently, hardly daring to breathe for fear of waking Marceau who lay by her side, snoring loudly. If she had had a knife, she would have plunged it into his wicked heart. She stared up at the ornate canopy over the bed, until at last she too fell into a sleep of sheer exhaustion.

When she awakened, she found that he had already risen. She could hear the sound of water running in the bathroom. She raised herself on her elbow, uttering a cry of dismay as she saw Hardiman sitting in the chair by the fireplace. He turned his head to look at her, and he licked his lips at the sight of her naked breasts. 'I hope he done you over good and proper, you young harlot. Just wait until he gets tired of you. When it's my turn I'll show you what it's like to have a real man. You're even more tasty than Edie was years ago, and that's saying something.'

She pulled the sheet up to her chin. 'Get out of my room.'

'Don't give me none of your lip, girl. I'm here on the guv's instructions. I'm not to let you out of me sight all day. Where you goes – I goes.'

Clemency leapt out of the bed, wrapping the sheet around her. 'Well, you're not watching me take a bath. I'm telling you that now.' She ran into the bathroom and locked the door.

She was as closely guarded as any prisoner in the Tower of London. During the next few days Hardiman was constantly at her side, only going off duty when Marceau finished his daily business, and demanded Clemency's company. On the first day, he took her in his private carriage to the House of Worth in a fashionable quarter of Paris, where he ordered a complete new wardrobe, choosing each item himself. One thing that Clemency learned very quickly about him, apart from the fact that he was extremely wealthy, was that he had impeccable taste. He knew exactly what colours suited her and what style to pick. She tried desperately to think of a way to escape, but she was trapped as much by her inability to communicate as by Hardiman acting like a guard dog.

As soon as the first garments of her new wardrobe were delivered, Marceau selected the gown that he wished her to wear that evening. He sat and watched while the maid helped her to dress. He even instructed the girl as to how to style Clemency's hair, and which ornaments to place in her upswept curls. When her toilette was completed, he came to stand behind her, studying her reflection in the mirror. From his pocket, he took a jewel case. 'Tonight I am going to show you off at the opera, Clemency.' He thrust the case into her hands. 'Open it.'

She did as he instructed. An emerald and diamond necklace and matching earrings nestled in a bed of white satin, and she stared at the jewels in amazement. He leaned over, and his breath was hot on her shoulder as he took the necklace and fastened it around her throat. He allowed his fingers to trace the contour of her breasts, exposed above the décolletage of the silk gown. 'Perfect. Now the earrings.'

Clemency shook her head. 'My ears aren't pierced. I never had any jewellery before.'

Marceau clicked his tongue against his teeth. He reached over her shoulder and picked up a hatpin. With a swift jab he pierced one earlobe, and when she cried out with pain, he slapped her face. 'Silence, you fool.' He pushed the gold wire through the puncture wound. 'Don't let it bleed on your new gown. That cost me a fortune.' He signalled to the maid, who rushed over to staunch the bleeding with a lace hanky. He stuck the pin through Clemency's other earlobe, but this time she bit her lip and did not cry out. He smiled as he put the second earring in place. 'Now you look like what you are – a courtesan worthy of a man like myself. Tonight, at the Opéra Garnier, all heads will turn to admire the latest mistress of Gaston Marceau.'

Once again, they were in the carriage speeding through the streets of Paris. Clemency tried to find her bearings but she had no clear idea where Marceau's opulent mansion was situated, and by the time they reached the Opéra Garnier she was none the wiser. It was a grand and beautiful building and the interior took her breath away. She was aware that all eyes were upon them as Marceau escorted her up the splendid staircase. She almost forgot her perilous situation as he led her to a gilded box with an excellent view of the huge stage. Above them, an enormous crystal chandelier lit the auditorium as brightly as the midday sun: the emeralds and diamonds in her necklace blazed with reflected light. When the orchestra struck up the overture to *The Marriage of Figaro* she could have cried with delight, and when Dorabella Darling came on stage as Cherubino, the coincidence seemed almost too marvellous to bear. For a few hours she drank in the splendour of her surroundings, and lost herself in the operatic performance that made the production at the Strand Theatre seem quite amateur by comparison. She put aside everything, ignoring the pain from her sore earlobes, which was made worse by the weight of the jewels in their heavy gold setting.

During the interval, Marceau had champagne and orchids delivered to the box. He pinned the corsage on her gown. 'I was right, Clemency. All eyes have been upon you. I have taken the little cockney sparrow and turned her into a beautiful swan.'

She was tempted to spit in his eye, but this was neither the time, nor the place. She used all her acting skill to give him a coquettish smile, and sipped her champagne in silence. Her mind was busy formulating a plan as she saw a way of escape. If she could think of a way to get backstage, she was certain that Dorabella would be sympathetic if she heard her story. She might help her get away from Marceau, or at least to get word to Jared. He must be looking for her by now, although whether he would link Marceau's return to his native land with her disappearance, she did not know. When the final curtain came down on the stage, she felt quite bereft. It was as though a brick wall had cut off her one link with home and safety. In desperation she turned to Marceau. 'Could I ask you something, Gaston?' She had never used his first name before, and she saw by his expression that it pleased him. She leaned towards him with a provocative tilt of her shoulders.

His smile was wary. 'Perhaps.'

'I would dearly love to go backstage and meet the cast.'

His dark brows met over the bridge of his bulbous nose. 'Do you take me for a fool?'

'No. Of course not. I . . .'

He grabbed her by the arm, dragging her to her feet. 'We're leaving. And I warn you, Clemency. Try to escape and you will be very, very sorry.'

His mood had not lightened during their carriage ride home. He sent Clemency up to her room while he went to his study, and for a while she thought she might be free from him that night. Her maid, whose name she had discovered was Rochelle, was helping her to undress when Marceau strode in. The girl took one look at his face and scuttled out of the room, closing the door behind her. Clemency rose from the dressing table, clutching her robe up to her throat. She met his furious scowl with a defiant lift of her chin. He struck her across the cheek with a blow that almost knocked her off her feet.

'That is a warning to you. Don't think you can fool me with your simpering ways.'

Her hand flew to her face but she did not allow her gaze to waver. She shook her head. 'I don't know what you mean.'

'I know why you wanted to go backstage. That opera woman is English. You wanted to tell her how badly you have been treated.' He seized her by the shoulders and shook her. She did not answer and this seemed to infuriate him all the more. He ripped the emerald necklace from her throat and slipped it into his pocket. Then he tore the earrings from her earlobes, causing her to cry out with pain. 'Bitch.' He struck her again, and this time she collapsed onto the stool, gasping with shock. He had been drinking champagne all evening, but she caught a whiff of brandy on his breath, and she realised that he must have been drinking since their return. She had seen plenty of drunks, and she knew better than to antagonise him further. For a moment she thought he was going to strike her again, but he scooped her up in his arms and carried her to the bed. He threw her onto the satin quilt. 'Tonight you will make up for your ingratitude.' He began stripping off his clothes. 'I will have obedience, Clemency. And total loyalty. Do you understand me?'

She nodded silently and closed her eyes.

He was gone when she awakened, and it was

only then that she allowed herself to sob into the feather pillow. Her physical pain was nothing compared to the desperation in her soul. She was trapped, just like that fly in amber that she had seen so long ago. Home and family, and the man she loved more than life itself, seemed to be a world away. She was alone in a foreign land; she had been beaten, abused and used as a sexual plaything by a brute of a man. She sat up and wiped her eyes on the back of her hand. She would beat him, or die in the attempt. She rang the bell for Rochelle.

At breakfast, Marceau appeared to be in a good humour. He ate heartily and urged her to follow his example. 'I am going away for a few days,' he said, wiping his lips on a damask napkin. 'I will be visiting my vineyards in Bordeaux. You will stay here and Hardiman will be at your side by day. At night he will sleep outside your door, so don't even think about trying to make an escape. If you behave yourself, I will treat you well. If you misbehave, then you know what you will get. Do I make myself plain?'

Clemency bowed her head, nodding. She would not allow him to see the rebellious gleam in her eyes.

'Good. I see that I have taught you humility at least. Obedience will come next.' He rose from the table and came to stand beside her, lifting her chin with his forefinger. 'I am not a cruel man, my dear. None of my previous mistresses have had anything to complain about. When you have learned to obey me, you will not find me ungenerous. When I have tired of you, and if you have pleased me, I will send you back to England. If you displease me, I will give you to Hardiman.'

'You are a brute.' Shaking off his hand, Clemency leapt to her feet. He could kill her for all she cared; she was not going to be treated like a Billingsgate doxy. For a moment she thought he was going to strike her down, but he threw back his head and laughed.

'That is part of your charm, my little virago. You have a temper to match your flaming hair, and it amuses me.' He turned to leave her, but Clemency laid her hand on his arm.

'Wait. Am I to be kept to the house in your absence?'

He raised an eyebrow and then he shrugged his shoulders. 'You may go out, but only if Hardiman accompanies you and never lets you out of his sight. I will leave instructions to that effect.' He brushed her cheek with his lips. 'Au revoir, Clemency.'

She waited for a few minutes after he had left the room, then she went to the door and opened it just a crack. To her dismay she saw Hardiman leaning against the wall, picking his teeth with the point of a penknife. She closed the door and went back to the table. She would have to find a way to outwit him, but it was not going to be easy.

It was a message from the House of Worth that gave her the opportunity to get out of the house, if only for a couple of hours. The gowns that had been designed especially for her were ready for the final fitting. Later that morning she set off in the carriage, accompanied by Hardiman. She had written a brief note to Jared, telling him where to find her, and it was tucked away in her reticule. She knew that Monsieur Charles Worth was an Englishman, and she hoped that she could find someone in the fashion house who also spoke English. All she wanted them to do was to post the letter. It might take days, or even weeks, to reach London, but at least it would give her hope.

Hardiman sprawled on a spindly gilt chair in the salon, with his arms folded across his chest. The flustered assistant spoke to him in rapid French, emphasising her words with gestures, but he ignored her. Even though she did not understand the language, Clemency could see that she was trying to make him leave the salon, but he was sitting there like a great lump, refusing to budge.

'What's the silly cow saying?' Hardiman growled. 'Tell her to shut up.'

'She wants you to wait outside.' Clemency

pointed to the door. 'I have to try on the new gowns, and I can't do it with you sitting there.'

Hardiman grinned and licked his lips. 'I got no complaints. I'm only doing what the guv told me to do.'

The assistant cast her eyes upwards, gesticulating with her hands.

'Please, madame,' Clemency said in desperation. 'Is there no one here who speaks English?'

'I do.' A voice from one of the fitting rooms stopped the assistant in mid-flow. The curtain was drawn aside. Dorabella Darling stepped into the salon with a fitter still on her knees, attempting to pin the hem of her skirt.

'Miss Darling!' Clemency could have wept for joy. She rushed over to her and clasped her hand. 'Miss Darling, you don't know me, but I saw you last night at the opera. You were truly magnificent.'

Dorabella smiled. 'Thank you. It's always a pleasure to meet a fan. How may I help you?'

Clemency jerked her head in Hardiman's direction. 'It's a long story, but he will not leave my side and I cannot go into the fitting room with him in attendance. I don't speak French so I can't explain to the assistant.'

Dorabella stared at Hardiman and then she laughed. 'Your man has the look of a prison warder. I can see that you have a jealous lover who does not trust you, Miss er . . .'

'Clemency Skinner, ma'am. I am a singer too; at home in London they call me La Moineau. I took your part when you left the Strand Theatre to come to Paris.'

'Well, well. A fellow artiste. Leave this to me.' Dorabella swept across the floor with the fitter crawling on her hands and knees in her wake. She came to a halt in front of Hardiman. 'My good fellow, it would be better if you waited for the young lady outside.'

Hardiman scowled at her, but he did not move.

'Or I could summon a gendarme,' Dorabella said pleasantly. 'I don't suppose your employer would be too pleased if you were arrested.'

'I can't leave her on her own,' Hardiman mumbled, shooting an accusatory glance at Clemency.

'Miss Skinner will be with me. I will keep my eye on her. Now, be a good chap and wait in the vestibule.'

Reluctantly, Hardiman got to his feet and shambled out of the room, to the obvious delight of the assistant who clapped her hands and bustled into the adjacent fitting room, beckoning Clemency to follow her.

'Thank you so much.' Clemency swayed on her feet, overcome by a rush of dizziness.

'My dear, you'd better sit down. Are you unwell?' Dorabella said something in rapid

French and the assistant rushed forward to help Clemency to a seat. The fitter scrambled to her feet and disappeared through a door, returning moments later with a glass of water, which she held to Clemency's lip.

Dorabella sent the women away with a wave of her hand. 'Are you feeling better now?'

Clemency nodded. 'Yes, thank you.'

'Perhaps you would like to tell me what is wrong?'

'I'm in desperate trouble, Miss Darling.'

'That sounds intriguing. I was quite bored today, until now. Tell me more.'

In a hushed tone, explaining as briefly as possible, Clemency blurted out the whole story. When she had finished she was trembling violently. Her hands shook as she took the letter that she had written to Jared from her reticule. 'I am a prisoner in that house. If you could just send this to my – to Mr Jared Stone in London, I would be so grateful.'

Dorabella took the envelope and tucked it down the front of her gown. 'I will, of course. But you must get away from that place.'

'I'm guarded day and night, and I have no money. I can't speak French.'

'But you can sing?'

'Oh, yes. That I can do.'

Dorabella rose and began pacing the floor. 'I have it. You played the part of Cherubino?'

'I did.'

'And before that you dressed as a boy and sang in the streets?'

'Yes, but . . .'

'Do not interrupt. I will visit you at Maison Marceau tomorrow morning, and I will bring my understudy with me, dressed as a boy. You will exchange clothes, and she will stay behind while you walk out of the house with me. It is so simple.'

'But she will be left to face Hardiman. He might kill her.'

'He won't get a chance. She is French and he is English. Whose side do you think the servants in Maison Marceau will be on? They will protect her and see that she is not harmed.'

'What then? Hardiman will know for certain where to find me.'

'My dear girl, there are more than seven hundred people living in the Garnier. There are dormitories for the ballet dancers and the chorus girls. It would take a team of detectives at least a month to find you in that rabbit warren. Did you know that the theatre is built over a lake and a stream? A whole army could hide in the caverns and underground passages, let alone a slip of a girl like you. No, I will not have any arguments, Clemency. My plan is excellent and I am excited about the whole thing. My ennui has dissipated like morning mist.' Dorabella clapped her hands to summon the fitter and the assistant. She winked at Clemency. 'I will see you tomorrow morning. Be prepared.'

Chapter Twenty-one

It had all seemed too easy. Clemency alighted from Dorabella's private carriage outside the Opéra Garnier in broad daylight, and with no sign of their having been followed. Dorabella and her understudy had arrived just as Hardiman had gone down to the kitchens for his breakfast. The servants at the Maison Marceau had recognised the famous opera singer immediately, and had not thought to challenge her demand to see Miss Skinner in private. The exchange of costumes had taken place in the small salon adjacent to the dining room, and Clemency had left the house with Dorabella before Hardiman put in an appearance. She had worried a little about leaving Cécile to face his wrath when he discovered that he had been duped, but Dorabella had shrugged her shoulders and told her not to fret. Cécile, she said, had grown up in the dormitories of the Garnier and she was used to the backstage battles, catfights and displays of temperament. Besides which, she was a sly little thing, and was probably on her way home at this very moment, with a few valuables secreted about her person. Clemency was not to worry about Mademoiselle Cécile – she could take care of herself.

Clemency stood, gazing up at the imposing façade of the theatre. She breathed in the fresh air and felt the warm June sunshine caress her face. She was free at last and she wanted to dance and sing, but Dorabella had her by the arm and was propelling her up the steps into the foyer. 'We must find you something more suitable to wear,' she said, hurrying her past the women who were scrubbing the floors or dusting the gilded statues on either side of the grand staircase. 'When Cécile returns she will take you to the dormitory where you can hide until I have thought of a way to get you back to England.'

'Jared will come for me. I know he will.'

'Whatever happens, we must get you away from here before Monsieur Marceau returns to Paris. He is a powerful man, Clemency. We can fend off that fool Hardiman, but Gaston Marceau is another matter.'

Dorabella led her through a maze of passages to her dressing room close to the stage. She closed the door with a sigh of relief. 'I don't think we were seen by anyone other than the cleaning women, and they would not suspect anything. We will wait here until Cécile returns. In the meantime, see if you can find anything there that will fit you.' Dorabella pointed to a mound of clothes laid neatly over a chair. 'Cécile borrowed them from the girls in the corps de ballet. She spun them some sort of story about you being a runaway from an arranged marriage. Luckily none of them speak English, so you will not have to explain yourself.'

'I can't thank you enough for what you're doing for me. And I'll be gone as soon as I possibly can. I don't want you to get into any trouble on my account.'

Dorabella sat down at her make-up table and studied her reflection in the mirror as she took off her hat. 'You must not worry about me, my dear. But I am only here for a few weeks. When the Opéra Bastille opens for the bicentenary of the revolution, the opera will transfer to that theatre, and the Garnier will be devoted to the ballet. So you see, we must get you away from here as soon as possible.'

Clemency dressed herself in a plain white blouse and a black skirt. She tied her hair back in a severe chignon, in the fashion of the ballet dancers, and she attempted to keep her nerves at bay as she waited for Cécile's return. Dorabella had to leave the theatre for a luncheon engagement, and Clemency was left on her own in the dressing room with strict instructions not to stray outside the door. When Cécile had not returned by mid-afternoon, Clemency was almost beside herself with worry. She could hear the sounds of the opera house coming to life outside the walls of the dressing room. The orchestra was tuning up and singers were practising their scales; there were the soft thuds of blocked ballet shoes on bare boards as the corps de ballet rehearsed, and the constant patter of footsteps going past the door. When at last Cécile breezed into the room, Clemency could have cried with sheer relief. 'I thought something dreadful had happened to you.'

'Bah! It would take more than a pig like Hardiman to frighten me.' With a scornful toss of her head, Cécile took off her bonnet and shawl. 'But you will have to take a care, mademoiselle. He is nasty, that one. He threaten me with his fist.' She bunched up her fingers and waved them in front of Clemency's face, dancing about on her toes. 'But I spit in his face.'

'Crikey! What did he do then?'

'He chase me, but I run too quick for him. I am like the wind. I rush through the house and out into the street before he can catch me.' Cécile's triumphant smile faded and she clasped Clemency's hand. 'But he will come here. That one will not stop until he find you. We must hide you somewhere good. Yes?'

Clemency nodded in agreement, but she could not conquer a feeling of disappointment. She had thought herself to be free, but the reality was quite different. She was now in hiding; afraid to be seen outside the walls of the Opéra Garnier, and Hardiman was as great a threat as ever. She had no alternative but to follow Cécile, who took her up several flights of stairs to a huge, high-ceilinged room where the ballet dancers did their practice. The girls clustered around Clemency, eyeing her curiously as if she were an exhibit in a freak show. Cécile was obviously enjoying herself as she talked volubly, gesticulating with her hands to emphasise her words, none of which Clemency could understand. She could tell by their sympathetic looks that the dancers were on her side, but then a small woman, dressed severely in black, and with her hair knotted in a bun on top of her head, appeared as if from nowhere. She called for attention, striking the floor with an ebony cane. When she spotted Clemency, her winged eyebrows flew up into her hairline and she stalked across the floor, pointing the stick at her. The exchange of words between Madame and Cécile was fierce, but brief.

'What was that all about?' Clemency demanded as Cécile dragged her from the rehearsal room and up yet another flight of stairs.

'Madame will not have anyone in her class who is not a dancer. You are not a dancer?'

'No, I am a singer.'

Cécile stopped at the top of the stairs. 'The best disguise is to look just the same as everyone else.

Come.' She hurried along a dark passage and ushered Clemency into a large dormitory. 'This is where the girls of the chorus sleep. You stay here for now. I go and speak to Madame Darling.'

'Wait.' Clemency caught her by the sleeve. 'What am I supposed to do here?'

'You keep quiet like the little mouse. I speak to Madame and she speak to the director of music. Your pig of a man will come to the theatre – that is for certain. But if you are one of many in the chorus, he will not know you, and he will go away. Voila!' She rushed from the room, and the sudden silence echoed in Clemency's head. She sat down on the edge of the nearest iron bedstead, staring into nothingness.

That evening, wearing a thick layer of grease-paint, and the costume of a serving wench, Clemency went on stage with the rest of the singers in the chorus. She knew the opera inside out, although she had learned it in English. She mimed the French words, while attempting to memorise them, and it was not difficult to follow the actions of the others. None of the cast took much notice of her, and she could only assume that Cécile, who sang in the chorus as well as being Dorabella's understudy, had given them a plausible reason for her being amongst them. In fact, Cécile seemed to be thoroughly enjoying the drama of the situation and her new-found importance. She stuck to Clemency's side, off stage as well as on, and when the evening performance ended, she guided her up to the dormitory and found her an unoccupied bed. It was littered with articles of clothing belonging to some of the other girls. Ignoring their protests, Cécile swept everything onto the floor, and went off in search of clean bedding.

As Clemency lay down to sleep, she could not help comparing the crowded dormitory, smelling strongly of perspiration, garlic and cheap cologne, to the perfumed boudoir that she had occupied in Marceau's mansion. Uncomfortable it might be, but to her it seemed like heaven. Despite the lumpy palliasse and rough woollen blankets, she settled down to sleep, lulled by the sounds of gentle snoring and rhythmic breathing.

The next morning, after a breakfast of croissants and coffee, Cécile took her on a tour of the theatre, beginning at the top in the painted gallery, and working their way down the levels to the underground cavern and lake. The flickering light of the oil lamp was reflected in the dark green water as it lapped at the stone steps. The walls dripped with moisture and a cold breeze rippled the glassy surface. Clemency shivered. 'Where do the tunnels lead?'

Cécile shrugged her shoulders. 'Who knows? There is a stream, they say. Perhaps it goes to the Seine itself. This is not somewhere I like to come.'

'No.' Clemency stared down into the water. 'It looks bottomless. It makes my flesh creep.'

'Come. You have seen it all now. We will seek out Madame to see if she has thought of a way to get you back to your own country.'

Clemency needed no second bidding to leave the eerie subterranean cavern. She hurried after Cécile, who had broken into a run.

They found Dorabella in her dressing room, studying the libretto for her final performance at the Garnier. She looked up as they entered and a frown puckered her brow. 'Not now, Cécile. Can't you see that I am busy?'

'But, madame . . .'

'No. I cannot stop to think about Clemency's problems at this moment. I will give it some thought later, when I have more time.'

'You have been more than kind to me, madame,' Clemency said hastily. 'Perhaps if you could just lend me the fare I could get the train to Calais and the boat to Dover.'

'My dear girl, you don't speak a word of French, and you don't know your way around Paris. Besides which, your bloodhound has been seen wandering about outside the theatre. He even tried to get inside, but I had warned the doorman to be on the lookout.' Dorabella rustled the sheaf of papers in her hands. 'Now, please, leave me to get on with learning my part. We will think of something, or else you will have to wait for your man to come from England to rescue you. Now go.'

Outside in the corridor, Clemency caught hold of Cécile's hand as she was about to walk away. 'Could you lend me some money, Cécile? I would see that you were paid back.'

'Me? I haven't got a sou. What little is left after my board and lodging is taken out of my wages I send to my aged grandmother in Rheims. If you could borrow the fare from someone else, I could see you to the station, but after that you would be on your own, and that pig of a man is just waiting to get his hands on you.'

'But I cannot stay here forever.'

Cécile laid her hand on Clemency's shoulder. 'Perhaps the letter has arrived in London by now. Even as we speak, your Englishman could be on his way to rescue you. Come, we have the first rehearsal for the next opera. It looks as if you will be here for the Bastille Day celebrations after all.'

She had become one of the cast; attending rehearsals, eating and sleeping with the girls in the chorus, and they accepted her, some with better grace than others. She was quick to learn the words of the operas in both French and

Italian, and it was not long before the choirmaster singled her out for a small solo part. Clemency was aware that there were undercurrents of jealousy, but, in some ways, not understanding the language was an advantage, and it was only a small minority who seemed to resent her presence. Cécile told her that it was always that way, especially with a foreigner, and she must not take any notice of the spiteful bitches. The rest of the girls tolerated her, and some even donated articles of clothing to boost her meagre wardrobe. Oddly enough, it was Dorabella, her former saviour, who seemed to resent the fact that Clemency had been singled out and her talent acknowledged. Cécile shrugged her shoulders and said that Madame Darling did not like competition from a younger woman, particularly one with a splendid voice that was not adulterated by smoking cigarettes and drinking absinthe: both of which, she confided, were one day going to prove to be Madame's downfall. Clemency managed to keep out of Dorabella's way, but she had to acknowledge the fact that she could no longer look to her for help. Despite all this, the days passed quickly enough, and she had little time to brood.

She made several attempts to leave the theatre, but each time she found Hardiman either lounging on the steps or pacing the forecourt. He could not, she thought, be there day and night;

but on one occasion, late in the evening, she saw him giving coins to small boys who then scattered and took up positions where they could watch all the exits. Hardiman had always employed spies in London, and she could see that nothing had changed. She toyed with the idea of leaving in the middle of the night, but after a long day of rehearsals, fittings and the evening performance, she was only too glad to sink onto her hard bed and fall into an exhausted sleep.

Cécile told her to bide her time. Dorabella was now completely unapproachable, and Clemency had begun to think that Jared could not have received her letter or, worse still, that he had abandoned her to her fate. Even though she had been given a minor part in the latest opera bouffe, there was no guarantee that she could rise further. She could see herself being trapped in the chorus for months, even years, to come. Marceau would find another mistress, and Hardiman would eventually give up. She would end up like one of the shrivelled backstage women who had begun in the chorus, and, when their talent and looks faded, had been relegated to the sewing room, the kitchens or the wash-house. She tried not to dwell on thoughts of home. Ma and Jack must be frantic with worry, even if Jared could not be bothered to come looking for her. She had always known that men were unreliable and self-centred. He had probably forgotten all about her by now – at least she had her family and Augustus and Ronnie. Perhaps Augustus had found Lucilla and her child. If she could get home to London, they could start again, the Throop troupe, playing in the streets. She would get back to England, or die in the attempt.

It was early on Sunday morning, a week before Bastille Day, and there was a feverish air of excitement running all through the Garnier. Clemency had made up her mind that today she must make her bid for freedom. She had saved every last sou of her meagre wages to pay for her journey home. She would have to find her way to the Gare du Nord and board a train bound for Calais. Once there she would find a boat to take her to Dover, even if she had to work her passage.

A group from her dormitory were going out for a promenade in the sunshine, sporting their best hats and summery muslin dresses, intent on ogling the young men who were parading in their Sunday best after attending mass. Clemency decided that if she were to mingle with them, Hardiman and his young lookouts might not spot her. She pulled her straw hat down over her brow and kept her head bowed as they went down the steps and across the forecourt. She saw Hardiman, in his usual position at the foot of the steps, but he was leering at one of the more brazen girls, who was blowing kisses to him, laughing and swaying her hips suggestively. She held her breath, praying that he would not notice her amongst so many pretty young women. They had almost reached the relative safety of the Place Diaghilev when a hand clamped over her mouth and she was lifted off her feet and dragged to one side. A few heads turned, but the girls giggled, seeming to think that the man who held her was her beau, and they walked on.

She kicked and struggled but she was held by strong arms. 'Hush, Clemmie. It's me.'

For a moment, she thought she was dreaming. The hand loosened on her mouth just enough for her to turn her head and she found herself looking up into a familiar face. 'Ned!'

'It's me all right. I thought I'd never find you, and then I saw you and I couldn't believe my eyes.'

'Oh, Ned.' She laid her head on his shoulder, hardly able to believe her good fortune. 'It is you, isn't it? I'm not dreaming.'

'You've led us a fine old dance, my girl. We've been looking for you for weeks.'

'We? Do you mean Jared?'

'Who else?'

She glanced over her shoulder. 'Is he here?'

'He ain't – but I am.' Hardiman had come up

on them unnoticed. He seized Ned by the shoulders and spun him round. 'Get away from here, boy. I been stuck outside this bleeding theatre for weeks just waiting to get me hands on this little baggage.'

Ned brought his elbow back with a savage jerk, catching Hardiman in the ribs and winding him. 'Run, Clem.' He floored Hardiman with a punch to the jaw and stood looking down at him with a triumphant grin, rubbing his bruised knuckles. 'You had that coming, mate.'

Clemency grabbed him by the hand. 'Don't stand there you idiot. Come with me.' She broke into a run, dragging Ned behind her. She didn't stop until they were safely inside the foyer. In the distance she could see Hardiman. He had staggered to his feet, and was lumbering towards the main entrance. She could not see his expression at this distance, but it was obvious that this time he meant business.

'Come with me, Ned.' She led him through the corridors and down the narrow staircase to the underground cavern. She paused just long enough to pick up and light one of the oil lamps that were left specifically for the purpose of showing visitors round. 'He won't find us here.'

Ned ran his hand through his hair as he stared into the dark water. 'Well, I'll be damned. I've never seen anything like it in me life.'

'Never mind that now.' Clemency balanced the

lamp on a rocky ledge. 'Tell me how you found me. And where is Jared? Why didn't he come with you?'

'We thought the Ripper had got you,' Ned said, hooking his arm around her shoulders. 'That's what we thought at first, but then there was no murder reported, so we started scouring the streets, day and night.'

'But how did you know? I mean, we weren't on the best of terms when I last saw you.'

'Jared came to the pub. Out of his mind he was with worry, and so was I come to that.'

'But I wrote to him, Ned. I got Miss Dorabella to post the letter telling him that Marceau had taken me to Paris.'

'It took more than three weeks to reach London. By that time we'd almost given you up for dead. When Jared realised what that bloke had done, he was hopping mad.'

'But he didn't come for me himself. Where is he now?'

Ned took her hand and held it. 'He sent me to look after you while he took care of Marceau.'

Clemency's heart jolted against her ribs. She shivered and it was not just the cold blast of air from the lake that made her tremble. 'What do you mean?'

'He challenged Marceau to a duel.'

'No. He can't have. Nobody does that nowadays.'

'He said it was the only way to settle old scores. He didn't want me to tell you until it was all over, but they were meeting at dawn this morning, in the grounds of a château on the outskirts of Paris.'

'Oh, my God. He could be dead or injured. Take me to him, Ned.'

A shadow loomed over them. 'He'll be dead, all right. Monsieur Marceau is a crack shot.' Hardiman's bulk filled the entrance to the cavern and his harsh laughter echoed off the stone roof, coming back to them across the water in a mocking chorus.

Ned pushed Clemency behind him. 'You're lying. Don't take any notice of him, Clem.'

'Lying am I?' Hardiman advanced on Ned with his hands fisted. 'Come on, young 'un. You caught me off guard just now, but let's see what you're made of in a fair fight.'

'No, Ned. Don't,' Clemency cried, grabbing his arm. 'He'll kill you.'

'That's right. I'll kill him and then I'll take you back where you belongs, missy.'

Ned lunged at Hardiman with a roar, but was felled with a single blow to the back of his neck. Clemency stared in horror at his prostrate body. When he didn't move, she was certain that he must be dead. Hardiman turned on her, advancing slowly and with menace, cutting off her escape through the theatre. Behind her the lake was smooth as glass, inviting her to dive in and allow its cool green waters to soothe away her grief and terror. She took flight into one of the underground passages. She could barely see anything except the greenish-yellow phosphorescence of the lake's surface, but she could hear his footsteps coming closer and closer. She stumbled on the slimy rock path. Hardiman's hands were round her throat choking the life out of her. With strength born out of rage and desperation, she brought her arms upwards and outwards, breaking his grip. Wild with fury, she twisted round and butted him in the stomach, pitching him into the lake. She leaned back against the dripping stone wall, gasping for breath and trembling violently. In the faint beam of light emitted by the oil lamp, she saw his head break the surface as his arms flailed about, sending ripples across the surface. He uttered a cry for help as the water closed over his head again, but she could only stare in horror at the death throes of a drowning man. Even if she could have galvanised her frozen limbs into action, she could not swim, and there was nothing that she could do to save him. The water was oily calm now, and there was silence, except for the slow drip, drip, drip of moisture oozing from the rocky ceiling.

A low moan from the mouth of the cavern brought her back to life. 'Ned.' She felt her way towards him, hardly daring to believe that he could have survived Hardiman's vicious assault. She found him crouched down, with his head resting on his knees. She knelt on the ground, flinging her arms around him. 'Ned, I thought he'd killed you.'

'Where is he? Help me up and I'll give the bugger what for.'

'It's all right. He won't harm anyone ever again.'

'You mean . . .?'

Clemency nodded, shivering violently at the realisation that she had killed a man. 'I did it, Ned. I pushed him in, and he drowned. I'm a murderer.'

He wrapped his arms around her. 'He had it coming, ducks. Don't waste your sympathy on him.'

'I thought he'd done for you, Ned.'

'It wasn't for the want of trying. It's lucky I've got a thick skull.' His generous mouth twisted into a rueful grin. 'Are you all right, Clem?'

She nodded. 'I'm fine, or I will be when I know that Jared is safe.'

He scrambled to his feet. 'We arranged to meet at the Gare du Nord. If he is not there by midday, we have to leave without him.'

'Never!' Clemency stared at him aghast. 'He'll be there. He can't be dead. I won't let him be dead.'

He took her by the hand. 'I hope not, for your sake. I really do.'

As they climbed the stone steps, Clemency glanced back over her shoulder. 'Shouldn't we tell someone about him?' She jerked her head in the direction of the water.

'What? And have the French police holding us for questioning while they dredge the lake? I don't think so. Don't waste your time worrying about Hardiman – he got what he deserved.'

Outside in the brilliant July sunshine, the world seemed such a different place. Clemency breathed in the fresh air and put Todd Hardiman out of her mind. He had preyed on Ma, turning her into a prostitute and a drunk. He had almost ruined their lives and had probably committed murder amongst his many other crimes. There would be few to mourn his passing, if anyone even noticed that he was missing. Her one aim now was to find Jared and to get home. She would not allow herself to believe that Marceau had killed him in the duel. She would have known if he were dead – she would have felt it deep inside. She smiled up at Ned as they made their way to look for a cab that would take them to the Gare du Nord. The streets were already hung with bunting in readiness for Bastille Day: wrought-iron balconies groaned with the weight of terracotta pots overflowing with scarlet geraniums, and in the distance she could hear a band playing. The streets of Paris vibrated with anticipation of the festivities to come.

They reached the station a little before noon. Ned bought three tickets for Calais and Clemency craned her neck, searching for Jared's tall figure amongst the travellers who had just arrived or were waiting to depart. She was feverish with anticipation and suppressed anxiety – the train was already in the station, and people were boarding. She could not stand still. She paced up and down, struggling to remain calm, but without much success. The hands on the station clock moved inexorably towards midday, and porters bustled past them, pushing trolleys laden with trunks and suitcases. Guards waved flags and carriage doors were slamming as tardy travellers leapt on board.

'Clemmie, we've got to get on the train.' Ned caught her by the sleeve. 'Jared said we must leave with or without him.'

She shook off his restraining hand, anger welling up inside her as cold fingers of panic closed on her heart. 'No. I won't go without him. I won't leave him here in Paris.'

'If he doesn't come it's because he can't come. You've got to understand that.'

'Don't you dare talk that way. He's not dead. I'd know it in my bones if anything had happened to Jared.'

The guard nearest them was waving his flag at

the engine driver. He shouted something in French, but Clemency chose not to understand. She stood on tiptoe, staring into the crowd. 'I won't leave without him. He will come. I know he will come.'

Ned held the carriage door open. 'Get in, Clem. I won't tell you again.'

'No. You go without me if you must. If he doesn't come then I'm going to that place where he was to meet Marceau. I'll find him if it's the last thing I do.'

A loud blast on the whistle drowned her words. Ned caught her round the waist. 'You're getting on the train, even if I have to carry you.'

She kicked and fought, lashing out with her fists in desperation. 'I won't go. He might be wounded and lying there all alone, with no one to care for him.' Her voice broke on a sob. 'I can't leave without him, Ned.'

A cloud of steam belched from the engine and slowly, very slowly, the great iron wheels began to turn.

'He's not coming.' Ned shouted above the noise. 'He must be dead and Marceau will have the French police out looking for you. Jared made me promise to take you home, and I'm not going to let him down.' With one arm round her waist and the other holding the door, Ned struggled to get her into the compartment.

Her screams were drowned by the blasts of

steam from the engine. The train was leaving but she was desperate. Life without Jared was unthinkable, and she didn't care what happened to her now. All she knew was that she had to find him, alive or dead. She sank her teeth into Ned's hand and he let her go. The train was moving but the platform was not, and she lost her balance. She fell to the ground, cracking her head on the concrete. The world was spinning in concentric circles as she lay stunned and semi-conscious. Jared was dead – killed in a duel. She was going to join him in heaven or hell. She closed her eyes.

Chapter Twenty-two

'Clemency.'

She heard her name repeated again and again amidst a low buzz of chatter. Her head hurt, and the sounds were loud one moment and then faded to a whisper. The only constant was the achingly familiar voice that was calling her name. She opened her eyes and his face swam above her, now blurred and then more distinct. 'Jared?'

She felt a warm tear splash on her cheek, and she realised that it had spilled from his blue eyes. She looped her arms around his neck and he raised her gently to a sitting position. 'My darling, my darling.' He buried his face in her tumbled locks.

Dimly she realised that she had lost her hat. She had a sudden and overwhelming desire to laugh. She had lost her hat, but she had found the man she loved more than life itself. She leaned her head against his chest, clutching the lapel of his jacket with a trembling hand. 'Jared, I thought you were . . .'

'Hush, my love, it's all right.' He laid his finger

across her lips. 'I'm here now. No one is going to part us again.'

She gazed into his face and saw runnels of dirt where tears had flowed freely from his eyes. She reached up and touched his cheek with the tip of her finger. 'I thought he had killed you.'

'I'm very much alive, but I saw you fall, and I thought I had lost you.'

'We must get her onto the train, Jared.' Ned's voice held a note of anxiety. 'They won't hold it up any longer. At least, I think that's what the guard is saying.'

Clemency was suddenly aware that a crowd had gathered round them and the guard was speaking in rapid French, gesticulating and pointing his flag in the direction of the driver, who was leaning from his cab.

Jared winced as he shifted position. 'You'll have to lift her, Ned.'

As Ned helped her to her feet, Clemency saw a dark stain spreading from a jagged rent in Jared's coat sleeve. She stifled a cry of horror. 'You're hurt. We must get you to a doctor.'

He rose slowly, shaking his head. 'There's no time for that. We must get away from here before the French police come looking for me.'

'You did for him then?' Ned gave him a searching look as he helped Clemency onto the train.

Jared nodded. 'His seconds will inform the authorities.'

The guard blew a sharp blast on his whistle and slammed the carriage door. The train jerked forward, as if annoyed by the delay, and they were thrown down on the seats. Jared groaned with pain and fell back with his eyes closed. His face was ashen and beads of sweat stood out on his forehead. Clemency moved swiftly to his side. 'Let me take a look at your arm. Ned, help me get his jacket off.'

Between them they removed his outer garment, and Clemency stifled a gasp of dismay at the sight of the blood seeping from a wound in his upper arm.

Jared opened his eyes. 'I think the bullet went straight through. We both fired at the same time. I was lucky but Marceau was not.' He gripped Clemency's hand and his features contorted with pain and anger. 'He told me what he'd done to you. He boasted about it, and I wanted to shoot him like a mad dog, but I did it fair and square. I had my revenge for all the evil that man did to my family and to you, my love.'

'I'm glad,' Clemency said fiercely. 'I'm glad he's dead. Hardiman and he will meet up in hell.' She felt a wave of nausea as she peeled back the ripped material, revealing the extent of the injury. She knew nothing about gunshot wounds, but this one seemed clean enough. Jared had been right – the bullet appeared to have gone straight through the soft flesh just below his shoulder. 'The bleeding has almost stopped. I think we'd best leave it untouched until we can get some clean water and linen.'

Ned helped Jared on with his jacket. 'We'll find a doctor in Calais. Let's hope the gendarmes don't think to telegraph the port authorities.'

'I'll be all right. I'm just a little tired. I think I must have lost rather a lot of blood.' Jared's voice tailed off and he closed his eyes.

Clemency stroked a lock of hair back from his forehead. Her head ached miserably, but the pain in her heart hurt more. He looked deathly pale and helpless. She choked on a sob and covered her face with her hands.

'He'll be all right, Clem.' Ned patted her on the shoulder. 'Let him sleep.'

By the time they reached Calais it was quite obvious that Jared was far from all right. He had developed a fever and kept slipping in and out of consciousness. Ned had to heft him over his shoulder and carry him from the train. Clemency wanted to find a doctor, but Ned pointed out that to make enquiries would draw unwanted attention to them. The sight of a gendarme patrolling the streets was enough to send Ned straight to the quay in search of a boat bound for England. He was gone for what seemed like hours as Clemency waited, sitting on the ground in a quiet alleyway with Jared's head pillowed in her lap. She could feel the heat from his body as the fever raged within him, but there was nothing she could do until Ned returned. She was exhausted, hungry and terribly thirsty. It was shady in the alley, but the heat was intense and clouds of flies buzzed around them, attracted no doubt by the smell of blood. When at last Ned appeared, she could have cried with relief.

He squatted on the ground beside them. 'There are no ferryboat sailings until tomorrow morning, but I've found an English fishing boat that put in here to repair a fouled rudder. The skipper has agreed to take us back to Dover, but it won't be very comfortable.'

'I don't care, Ned. Just get us home.'

It was such a relief to hear English voices once again and to be heading home, that Clemency felt she could have suffered far worse than having to sit on the heaving deck of a small fishing boat. The crewmen gave them mugs of hot, sweet tea to drink, and hunks of bread and jam to eat, which tasted better than any of the elaborate meals Clemency had eaten in Marceau's Paris mansion. She could do little for Jared except wet his dry and cracked lips with tea. He was now delirious, and unable even to sip water. She cradled him in her arms during the crossing, and was thankful that the sea was calm and the weather mild.

It was early morning by the time they reached Calais and Ned carried Jared ashore with the help of the mate. They caught the first train bound for London.

As the cab drew up outside the house in Finsbury Circus, Clemency could have wept for joy. She was home at last. She paid the cabby and ran up the steps to ring the bell. It was Edith who opened the door, and her mouth dropped open with shock, followed by disbelief and then a screech of delight as she flung her arms around Clemency. 'Oh, you bad girl. You bad, bad girl. Frightening us all to death.' She held her at arm's length. 'We thought you was lost and gone forever.' She hugged her again, laughing and crying at the same time.

Clemency extricated herself gently. 'Let us in, Ma. Jared needs a doctor, double quick.'

Edith stood back, staring open-mouthed as Ned carried him into the house. 'Oh, poor boy. What happened? No, don't tell me now. Take him straight upstairs to his bed.'

Ned was halfway across the hall when the door to the morning parlour opened and Isobel rushed out, followed by Nick. 'Jared! Oh, my God! Is he dead?'

Clemency caught her by the hand. 'No, Izzie, he's alive, but he's in desperate need of a doctor.' She turned to Nick. 'It's a bullet wound. We couldn't do anything to help him.'

Isobel clasped her hands together, tears welling from her eyes as she watched Ned mount the stairs with Jared in his arms. 'He's been shot? Oh, my God.'

Nick kissed her on the cheek. 'I'll take care of him, sweetheart. My medical bag is in the parlour. Will you fetch it for me, please?' He turned to Clemency. 'What happened exactly?'

'He was in a duel.' Clemency gripped his hand. 'Don't let him die, Nick.'

'Don't worry. I'll take great care of him. After all, I need his permission to marry Izzie.' He smiled and squeezed her fingers. 'I'll need plenty of hot water and clean linen for bandages. Can you do that for me?'

'I can do anything if only you'll make him well again.'

Edith slipped her arm around Clemency's waist. 'Come on, ducks. We'll see to that. There's someone downstairs who's been as worried about you as I have.' She led her towards the baize door. 'You'll get the surprise of your life, Clemmie.' She pushed the door open and stood at the top of the stairs. 'Jack, look who's here.'

Clemency gripped the banister rail, overcome by emotion at the sight of their dear, familiar faces. Then, as though in a dream, she saw Jack walking towards her with the aid of leg irons and leaning heavily on crutches.

His face split in a huge grin. 'Blimey. Look at the sight of you, Clemmie. Where've you been, girl?'

Her hand flew to her hair. She was suddenly conscious that she must look a fright. Her hair was knotted and tangled into wild curls and was stiff with salt. Her dress, borrowed from Cécile, was torn, bloodstained and dirty. She knew she must smell of sweat and dead fish, but nothing mattered at this moment. Jared was in good hands and Jack was standing below her, on his own two feet. Fancy had hurried to his side, wiping her floury hands on her apron, and Nancy looked up from the range with a smile of welcome on her face. Augustus and Ronnie had been sitting at the table, but they rose to their feet with a cheer. 'Welcome home, Clem.' Augustus blew her a kiss and Ronnie clapped his hands.

Clemency walked slowly down the stairs and flung her arms around Jack. He dropped one of his crutches on the floor and gave her a one-armed hug. 'It's good to see you, girl.' He choked on a sob as he buried his face in her spiky hair. 'I thought you was gone forever.'

'Not me, Jack. You can't get rid of me that easily.' Clemency kissed his cheek and her tears mingled with his.

Fancy slapped her on the back. 'I never thought I'd say it, but I'm glad to see you too.'

'We all are, Clem,' Augustus said, striding over to her and ruffling her hair. 'Good grief, what have you done to yourself? And, if you don't mind me saying so, you smell like Murphy's fish cart.'

Edith bustled over to the range. 'Leave her be, Augustus. She'll tell us when she's good and ready. There are more important things to do at this precise moment. Jared's been injured and Nick is taking a look at him as we speak.'

'What's this?' Jack demanded. 'What's been going on, Clemmie?'

'Not now, Jack. We need hot water and bandages.' Clemency swayed on her feet as the kitchen swam before her eyes.

Ronnie rushed forward with a chair. 'Sit down before you fall down, Clem. You look done in.'

'Quite right, Ronnie,' Edith said, nodding her head with approval. 'You make her rest. Fancy, get a clean sheet from the linen cupboard and tear it up for bandages. I'll take a pan of hot water upstairs.'

Nancy grabbed the kettle. 'I'll make a pot of tea first. Young Clemency looks as though she needs some sustenance.'

'I suggest a drop of brandy,' Ronnie said, nodding his head. 'I think we could all do with a tot.'

'Good idea.' Augustus hurried to the dresser and fetched the bottle. 'You look after Jared, Edith. We'll take care of our girl.'

Despite everything, Clemency allowed them to fuss round her, accepting their ministrations of hot tea, brandy and a bowl of Nancy's beef broth. Fancy was moved to fill the tin tub with hot water, and she shooed the men out of the kitchen while she helped Clemency to bathe and wash her hair. Edith kept her informed of what was going on in the sickroom upstairs, and she was not allowed to see Jared until Nick had finished dressing the wound, and given him a dose of laudanum for the pain.

As she entered Jared's bedroom, dressed in her own clothes, with her hair still clinging in damp curls around her head, Clemency felt her stomach churn at the sight of him lying there so pale and helpless. Isobel was seated at his bedside, holding his hand. She looked up with tears sparkling on the tips of her long eyelashes.

Clemency's hand flew to her mouth. She turned to Nick, who was wiping his hands on a towel. His serious expression terrified her. 'Is – is he – going to die?'

'He has an infection of the blood, Clemency. I've done what I can. Now all we can do is hope and pray.'

Isobel uttered a low moan and buried her face in her hands. Clemency held herself upright with little more than willpower. She was trembling violently, but from somewhere deep inside her she summoned up all her inner strength. She was not going to let him die. Jared would survive. And they would live happily ever after, just as they did in fairy stories. She forced her legs to carry her across to the bed and she laid her hand on Isobel's quivering shoulders. 'I'll sit with him, Izzie. You go downstairs with Nick. I'll call you if there is any change.'

'If he dies I'll never forgive myself,' Isobel sobbed. 'I was hateful to him. I disobeyed him and went behind his back. I've been such a bad sister.'

'Nonsense. Don't say such things. I'm sure Jared loves you just as much as he ever did. All he wanted was the best for you, Izzie.'

Nick moved to Isobel's side and raised her gently to her feet. 'Clemency's right, my dear. You won't help Jared by making yourself ill.'

Clemency managed a smile. 'She's lucky to have you, Nick.'

He shook his head. 'I can't allow that. She is a splendid girl, and I love her dearly. When Jared recovers, and we must believe that he will, I'll ask him most humbly for Izzie's hand in marriage.' He took a handkerchief from his pocket and dried Isobel's tears as tenderly as a mother with a baby. 'Come with me, dear.'

Clemency squeezed her hand. 'Go with Nick. And what you should do is to send Ronnie to Half Moon Street with a message for Lady Skelton. She ought to know that Jared is ill.'

'Yes, I will. That's what I'll do. I'll send for Grandmama.'

When they had left the room, Clemency sat down beside the bed. The laudanum had made him sleep, but when the fever was at its height he thrashed about, mumbling incoherently. There was little that she could do except bathe his brow with cold water and talk to him softly. She found that the sound of her voice seemed to calm him, and she chattered incessantly, saying anything that came into her head. She lost all track of time, refusing to leave his side, until Lady Skelton arrived and insisted that she went downstairs to eat the meal that Nancy had prepared for her.

She ate without tasting the food, and she answered the questions fired at her by Jack and Ma, but did not elaborate on her stay in Paris. Although she longed to find out what had been happening in her absence, she could not concentrate on anything that was said. In the end, they lapsed into silence and she hurried back to Jared's room where she found Isobel pacing the floor and Lady Skelton sitting at his beside, looking pale and drawn: not at all her usual self. She seemed to have aged suddenly, and shrunk inside her skin like a wizened apple. Clemency shooed them gently from the room, insisting that they had some rest, and that they would do Jared no good at all by wearing themselves to a shadow. He would need them all to fuss over him when he was convalescent. She did not really believe what she was saying, but they appeared to, and, rather reluctantly, they left the sickroom.

Edith and Nick both tried to make her go to her own room and take a nap, but Clemency refused to leave Jared's side. She sat with him throughout the hours of darkness, willing herself to stay awake, and listening for any slight change in his breathing that might indicate he had reached the crisis. In the early hours of the morning she found herself nodding off to sleep, and sheer exhaustion forced her to lie down beside him. She held his hand, terrified that if she let him go he would slip away from her. Her eyelids were heavy and she closed her eyes.

'Clemency.'

She heard him calling her name. At first she thought she was still dreaming and they were back on the platform in the Gare du Nord. But as she opened her eyes she realised that she was in a bedroom – Jared's room. He was holding her hand and murmuring her name. She raised herself on her elbow, and saw to her overwhelming delight that he was looking at her, clear-eyed and smiling. 'Am I dreaming, or have we really slept together?' His voice was hoarse and little more than a whisper, but his eyes were alight with love.

'Oh, Jared. My own darling.' She felt his brow, and it was cool. The fever had broken, and she knew for certain that he was going to get well.

All her prayers had been answered. She had vowed to God that she would never do anything bad again, if only he would spare Jared, and he had. She leaned over, careful not to touch his injured arm, and brushed his lips with a kiss. 'I thought I was going to lose you. I was so scared.'

His eyes lit with a tender smile, and he laid his finger on her lips. 'You will never lose me, my love. And I will never let you far from my sight.' He closed his eyes and slept.

Although it was very early in the morning, Clemency ran through the house, rousing everyone with the news that Jared had come through the fever. Isobel and Lady Skelton left their beds to visit his room to see for themselves, on the promise that they would not wake him. Below stairs, no one grumbled at being woken at such an early hour, and Fancy urged the fire in the range back into life, setting the kettle on the hob and making tea for them all without a murmur.

Later that morning when Nick called to see the invalid, he confirmed their hopes that Jared was well on the way to recovery. At Lady Skelton's suggestion, he took Isobel out to choose an engagement ring. He would, of course, have to go through the formality of asking Jared for his sister's hand, but she was certain that he would not refuse. Isobel went off in a high state of excitement and Clemency could only be glad for her.

Lady Skelton then insisted on sitting with Jared, while Clemency spent time with her family below stairs. At first, she was going to refuse, but she had not properly congratulated Jack on his new-found ability to walk, and Ma seemed to have something on her mind that she was bursting to share. She went down to the kitchen and took a seat at the table. 'Well?' she said, looking Ma in the eye. 'I can see that you've got something to tell me. What have I been missing?'

Edith went to Ronnie and took him by the hand. 'We're getting hitched, Clemmie. Ronnie and me have decided to make a go of it.'

Ronnie twirled his moustache and beamed proudly at Edith. 'She's made me the proudest man in London, Clem.'

'And we're going to live with Hannah at the lodging house in Flower and Dean Street,' Edith continued breathlessly. 'She's getting too old to run the place on her own, and Jared has signed the lease over to us. He done it weeks ago, soon after you disappeared. He was in a terrible state, ducks. We all was, come to that. We thought at first that the Ripper had got you. Then, when he got the letter from Paris – well, I never seen a man so happy or so worried. That was when he give us the boarding house. He said he didn't want his mother-in-law breathing down his neck, but, of course, it weren't that at all. He done it for you.'

'For all of us,' Jack said, reaching out to hold Fancy's hand. 'Fancy and me are getting hitched too. Now I can walk on me own, after a fashion, I've got meself a place in the orchestra at the Gaiety Theatre in the Strand. Maybe I could put a word in for you, Clemmie.'

'Well, maybe you could, Jack.' Clemency beamed at them all. 'What a love nest this has become, to be sure.' She turned to Augustus, who was sitting at the head of the table, unusually silent. 'What about you? Did you find Lucilla?'

Augustus cracked a smile. 'I did. Or rather me and Ronnie did, on the day you disappeared. It rather spoilt my pleasure on finding my girl quite happy with a fine baby boy, and Tom Fall acting out the part of a good provider. They have rooms in Wimbledon and plan to follow the construction of the railways. I doubt if my little nightingale will ever sing again, but she seems content to be a wife and mother, so who am I to complain?'

Clemency patted him on the shoulder. 'You always were a good dad, Augustus. And Jack, yes I do plan to go back on the stage. I learnt a lot singing in the chorus at the Opéra Garnier. I was too young and inexperienced before, but now I think I could be a good performer.' She smiled at Augustus. 'If you've nothing better to do, maybe you'd consider being my manager again?'

He grasped her hand and his eyes welled up with tears. 'Really? Do you mean it?'

She nodded emphatically. 'I'd most likely have to start at the bottom, but that wouldn't matter.'

Nancy pulled a face. 'And what would Mr Stone have to say about you cavorting half naked on the stage with them other hussies?'

'Oh, Nancy,' Edith said, frowning. 'Don't be such an old stick.'

'Huh! You're all touched in the head if you ask me. All this soft talk about love and romance – it makes me want to puke.' She flounced off into the pantry.

'She's just jealous,' Edith said, cuddling up to Ronnie.

Clemency gazed round at their happy faces. Just a short time ago life had seemed intolerable. She had suffered so much at the hands of Marceau and Hardiman, and she had almost lost the man she adored, and who, amazingly, loved her in return. Now it felt as though the terrible times were at an end. Those whom she loved the most, and who had depended on her, were now settled with partners who would love and care for them, taking her place, and allowing her to live her own life. She left them happily discussing their future while she went upstairs to relieve Lady Skelton.

Within a week, Jared was well on the way to recovering his old strength. Isobel was sporting a minuscule diamond engagement ring as proudly as if it had been the Koh-i-noor, and she and Nick were planning to marry as soon as he had obtained his fellowship and found a permanent position. Jack and Fancy were looking for accommodation closer to the theatre, and planning a quiet wedding in Holborn Register Office, with Ronnie and Edith booking the same day. It would be cheaper, Edith had said, to have a double celebration in the pub afterwards: and, of course, it had to be the Crown and Anchor. After all, who would make a more fitting best man than Jack's brother, Ned? Edith confided in Clemency that, during the dreadful time when she was missing and they did not know her fate, she and Nell had made their peace, and renewed their friendship.

It seemed that Nancy was still sulking and pretending that she did not want anything to do with all the fuss, but Clemency smiled secretly when, one afternoon, she saw her poring over a rather old copy of *The Milliner and Dressmaker* with Edith, and chatting as excitedly as a young girl over the possibility of a new hat or perhaps a new dress for the coming nuptials.

She went upstairs to find Jared alone in his study. He was so absorbed in perusing some papers on his desk that he had not heard her enter, and she crept up behind him, covering his eyes with her hands.

'Clemency.'

'How did you know it was me?'

He twisted her round with his good arm so that she fell onto his lap with a squeal of protest. 'I would know you in a crowd of a million women.' He nuzzled her throat. 'You smell so good that I could eat you.'

'I'm not sure you should say such things to me.' She giggled as he nipped her throat gently with his teeth. 'You are a wicked man, Jared Stone. Taking advantage of a poor girl.'

His lips claimed her mouth in a kiss that made her senses soar and sent the blood pulsating through her veins. She wrapped her arms round his neck, responding to his embrace with mounting desire. She wanted him more than she would ever have believed possible, but the shadow of Marceau lingered in her memory, and she pulled away.

He stared at her with a dazed expression clouding his eyes. 'What's the matter?'

She turned her head away, unable to look him in the face. 'I'm not the same girl I was before he – before he forced himself on me. I'm tarnished by what he did to me.'

'It wasn't your fault.'

She shook her head. 'I wanted you to be the first man to make love to me. I was yours, body and soul, but he spoilt all that.'

'Look at me, Clemency.' Turning her head

slowly, she raised her eyes to his. She saw nothing in them except love and admiration. 'If there was any fault, apart from that brute who raped you mercilessly, it was mine for introducing him to you in the first place.' His eyes darkened but he held her gaze. 'My darling girl. I placed you in danger by playing my own selfish games with the Frenchman. You suffered for my desire for revenge and retribution.'

'But you didn't get your family home back.'

'Damn the family home! You are the only home I need, my love. You are my family, my love and my life. Without you I am nothing. All I want is to make you happy.' He ran his hand through her hair and drew her into a long and tender embrace, so that it seemed to Clemency that they lived and breathed as one. When at last he released her lips, he looked deeply into her eyes. 'All the game playing is over. I'm asking you, most humbly, to be my wife.'

She stared at him for a moment and an irrepressible giggle escaped from her lips. 'Humbly? You?'

His serious expression melted into a smile. 'Will you, Clemency? Will you marry me?'

'And make an honest man of you?'

'I'm not sure I could go that far. Not with a wife to support.'

She twined her arms around his neck, interlacing her fingers behind his head. 'Of course I'll marry you, Jared. But on one condition.'

His eyes widened and then crinkled into laugh lines at the corners. 'What condition is that, my love?'

'That we don't steal any more. I can go back on the stage. I can earn enough money to keep us, especially if we leave this big house and find something smaller. You could still do the charitable fundraising, but without keeping any of it for ourselves.'

He threw back his head and laughed. 'My God, Clemency. You'll have me in holy orders next.'

'Don't laugh at me. I'm serious.'

He kissed her on the tip of her nose. 'I'm not laughing at you. I'd already decided that we couldn't go on as we were. I don't want my wife to run the risk of arrest every time we go out in public. We'll be a respectable couple, darling. I'm not sure about you going back on the stage, though.'

'But I want to, Jared. I want to prove that I can be as good as Dorabella Darling. And anyway, I've promised Augustus that he can be my manager. I can't let him down.'

For a moment, she thought he was going to argue, but he kissed her again, slowly and sensuously, until she was melting with desire. 'All right, I agree that you can't let Augustus down. I won't stand in your way. As long as I have you, my darling, I don't care if you are La Moineau or plain Mrs Jared Stone. I will always love you.'

'And I you.' Clemency slithered off his lap. She moved towards the door, holding out her hand. 'I don't want to shock your grandmother, but I would really like you to make love to me properly – in your – I mean our bed. Even though it is broad daylight.'

Jared rose to his feet and took her hand in his. 'Grandmama is not easily shocked.'

She was about to open the door but she hesitated, casting a wary glance at his injured arm. 'Perhaps we ought to wait after all. I don't want to hurt your bad arm.'

He slipped his arm around her waist. 'I think I could bear the pain, my love. I could bear anything except the pain of separation from you for one moment longer than necessary.'

Clemency stood on tiptoe to kiss him on the lips. 'That sounds like a life sentence, Mr Stone.'

'In your hands, the future Mrs Stone, I'll take my punishment like a man.'